A PERFECT WOMAN

THIS edition, issued in 1956, is for members of The Companion Book Club, 8 Long Acre, London, W.C.2, from which address particulars of membership may be obtained. The book is published by arrangement with the original publishers, Hamish Hamilton Ltd.

Also by
L. P. HARTLEY

★

NIGHT FEARS AND OTHER STORIES
SIMONETTA PERKINS
THE KILLING BOTTLE AND OTHER STORIES
THE SHRIMP AND THE ANEMONE
THE SIXTH HEAVEN
EUSTACE AND HILDA
THE BOAT
THE TRAVELLING GRAVE AND OTHER STORIES
MY FELLOW DEVILS
THE GO-BETWEEN
THE WHITE WAND AND OTHER STORIES

"A blessed companion is a book"—JERROLD

A PERFECT WOMAN

WOMAN

*

L. P. HARTLEY

THE COMPANION BOOK CLUB
LONDON

To
MOLLY BERKELEY
with affection

*The author wishes to thank Miss Ursula Codrington
for her generous help*

"AND don't forget, my dear Harold, to find out about Irma for me, if you can. If I didn't live so far away, I would rout her out myself.

Yours ever,

Alec."

Harold sighed. After a moment's hesitation he took the letter to the file marked G, but before adding it to the others he lifted out the topmost two, and though he knew what he would see, he read them through again. Here was one operative sentence:

"Thank you for all your hospitality and for all the fun we had. I shan't quickly forget that girl behind the bar at the Green Dragon, either—Irma was her name, I think."

And here was the other:

"What a jolly girl Irma was. I wish I had had time to get to know her better. Could you do something about it?"

The two letters were dated respectively a fortnight and a week earlier than the latest arrival. Alec was a methodical man in some ways. Raising his eyebrows Harold put the letter with its fellows. There was quite a pile of them, but Irma only figured in the last three—the three Alec had written since he came to stay.

Harold's thoughts went back to their first meeting. They had met in a railway train. Harold had been to Bath on business and was travelling first-class at the firm's expense—the firm he was visiting, that is, for he worked on his own. There was only one other occupant of the carriage. It was not Harold's custom to talk to people in trains, he usually worked in them, and he opened his despatch-case intending to do so. But his day's work was done, satisfactorily done, and he felt disinclined to go on totting up figures. The lights in the roof of the compartment were none too bright or could it be that at thirty-five he was beginning to need glasses? He put aside his despatch-case and looked out of the window, but the November murk pressed so thick and close against it that he could see little but his own reflection—longish, sallow face, short nose, dark hair, dark, clipped moustache, dark straight eyebrows that, with his moustache, made the points of an inverted triangle: a tight face but conventionally good-looking. Harold, as conventional as his face, had been told in childhood that a man should never be caught studying his reflection in a glass, and he was just turning away when, with a shriek and a roar, the train entered the Box Tunnel. Immediately there descended on him that sense of suspended being that tunnels induce. He was sitting braced, taut and expressionless, as if expecting who knows what, when his glance fell on the man opposite, who was also sitting like a statue of himself. Harold was not much interested in people, but he was interested in their clothes. With the heightened perception that tunnels impart, and with more intentness than politeness warranted, he scrutinized his *vis-à-vis*, and was still scrutinizing him when, with a sudden softening of sounds and loosening of rhythms, as if it was running on to grass, the train emerged from the tunnel into the twilight which, in the brief interval, seemed to have turned to night.

Yet there was nothing so remarkable about the man. He was above the average size, loosely built and inclined to corpulence; he was wearing a good brown tweed suit, a brown and white check shirt, a knitted brown tie and a pair of heavy brown suède brogues. So far so good: all was in a rural symphony. But there was a discordant note, the socks. Dark blue and of cheapish material they were obviously meant for town. In his vacant mood the discrepancy worried Harold. Cautiously he lifted his eyes to the stranger's face. There, at a first glance, everything seemed to match. The general impression was sandy. The eyes, light brown with a greenish glint, exactly matched the hair which was brushed back from the forehead and wind-swept over the ears; the skin, deepening to red on the cheeks, had on the temples a brown pallor that might easily have been freckled but was not. A poster artist (Harold had had some experience of advertising) could have done the whole face in one tone,

6

thereby halving the outlay. But again there were discrepancies. Over the shaven upper lip the bold nose contradicted the weak jaw, and what was this about the eyes? Slightly protuberant, they were staring with tunnel-fixity and a hint of truculence into space; but the noticeable thing about them was that one was wider-open than the other. There was the suggestion of a cast about them, too.

Fascinated, Harold continued his scrutiny. The man was sitting with his knees crossed. One hand rested on his knee, the other loosely clasped his ankle. The hands were large and well-made, and had the same air of successfully resisting freckles; but here too there was an inconsistency, for whereas the first and third fingers of the upper hand had almond-shaped nails, the nails of the other fingers were blunt and might almost have been bitten. On the little finger was a large, round signet ring guarding a thin circlet of gold—his mother's wedding-ring, perhaps, thought Harold, who was devoted to his own mother.

Furtively, from an obscure desire to enter into the other man's mind, Harold copied his way of sitting, and at once realized that it was a physical device to reduce mental tension—whether simply tunnel tension, he could not tell.

One thing remained: to assess the stranger's income. This was, with Harold, an almost routine inquiry and he was seldom far out in his guess. Just as one wrestler is said to be able to gauge the strength of an opponent by merely touching his shoulder, so Harold could, by trifles light as air, take the measure of a man's material wealth. But again he was baffled. Fifteen hundred a year? Four thousand, five? To his mortification he could not narrow the bracket. When, afterwards, he learned the figure, it seemed to be inevitable —but was it? Meanwhile he looked about for further indications of the man's financial status. He was taking up a book that he had laid down during the tunnel crisis. *After the Storm* was the title on the jacket, and the author's name, Alexander Goodrich.

At this moment the door slid back and the ticket-collector came in. Harold held out his white ticket; the stranger fumbled and at last brought out a green one. Harold was

7

astonished. The last thing he had expected of the stranger was that he would be travelling first-class with a third-class ticket. At once he had recourse to his despatch-case, for the little parley between a ticket-collector and his possibly fraudulent fare was a thing that always embarrassed him.

Mentally he stopped his ears. He just heard the words "a very full train"—which were scarcely true of this train—the rest was a blur of voices, first rising and falling in argument, then meeting in the level tones of agreement and understanding. Harold saw the collector's hand raised in salute and the door slide back behind him.

"Decent fellows, some of these ticket-collectors," said the man, turning his eyes to Harold, unabashed. "But, God, the expense of travelling nowadays!"

Harold did not know whether to take this as evidence of a guilty intention, so made a non-committal sound, and his fellow-passenger went on:

"It's these taxes, you know, these bloody taxes."

"Yes," said Harold, feeling on firmer ground. Then, prompted by curiosity, he had an idea. "Perhaps you don't claim all the reliefs you might?"

"I claim precious few," the stranger said. "How can I? Being an author isn't like being in business."

"All the same there are things you could claim," Harold said. "I've never dealt with the returns of literary people, but I'm an accountant and I know the general form. Do you claim for the room you work in, for instance?"

"Good Lord, no. Could I?"

"Yes, and for lighting and heating it and paying someone to clean it."

"You surprise me."

"And for your stationery and typing and for a proportion of your telephone calls——"

"You don't say so!"

"And a proportion of your rail fares to London if you're going on business."

"Why, then, I needn't have——" the stranger broke off.

"——Well, no," said Harold, not sure what he was supposed to be agreeing with. "And a proportion of a good many other expenses," he concluded.

8

"I'm tired of all this proportion," said the stranger, moodily. "I should like *all*."

"I'm afraid that wouldn't be possible," said Harold, without a smile. He hesitated. "I could send you a list of items of expenditure for which you *could* claim."

"I don't suppose you'd do the whole thing for me?" asked the stranger, turning on Harold a curiously persuasive look, which was none the less persuasive for not quite hitting the middle of Harold's face. "I should be eternally grateful to you if you would."

"You mean on a business basis?" said Harold cautiously.

"A business basis?"

"Well, I usually charge a fee for my . . . professional services, you know," said Harold. "It varies according to the amount of the claim, and the work involved. In your case——"

"Ah yes, in my case," said the stranger gloomily, and as if his was a case indeed. He propped his chin up with his hand: the good nails and the bad nails touched each other. Suddenly his brow cleared.

"Well," he said, "where shall I send the dope? And to whom have I the pleasure of speaking?"

Harold gave him the address first. The stranger entered it in his diary. He wrote slowly, with a flourish. "And the name?"

"The name is Harold Eastwood."

"What a pleasant name. I shall enjoy writing it," the stranger said. Harold could see the letters curling across the page. "I'm Alexander Goodrich," he announced, looking up from his sandy eyebrows, as though to see if the name would register. For a moment it did not; then Harold asked:

"Are you the author of that book?"

Mr. Goodrich laughed.

"Well, yes, I am." He leaned forward, put his hand on his knee, and said with great intimacy, as to an old friend, "It's always been my ambition to find somebody in the train reading a book of mine. I never have, but sometimes I read one myself in the hope that someone will connect me with it. May I give it to you?" he asked suddenly.

"Delighted," said Harold, offering to take the book. But the author immediately withdrew it.

"Do you mind if I keep it till we reach Paddington?" he said. "I'm coming to a bit I rather like. The storm is over" —he sketched a rapid zigzag for the lightning—"and things are beginning . . . beginning to settle down."

"I'm afraid I'm not much of a reader," Harold confessed. "My wife's the reader in our family. Does it end happily?" he asked, making what seemed his first contribution to a literary conversation.

The author screwed his eyes up.

"Well, not exactly," he said. "No. definitely not. You might call it a tragi-comedy."

Isabel Eastwood was excited when she heard that her husband had met Alexander Goodrich. "Why, he's quite a well-known author!" she exclaimed. "And I'm a fan of his. I wish you hadn't told him that you hadn't heard of him."

"I didn't," said Harold. "I only——"

"Well, I'm afraid you must have given him that impression. Now if it had been me——!"

"Have you read this book, *After the Storm*?" asked Harold.

"No, but I'm dying to. It's said to be autobiographical. Not that that makes any difference," she added, with a sudden change into seriousness. "It's the quality that matters. Looking for an author's life in his books is vulgar anyhow, and can be most misleading." She broke off— talking to Harold often made her feel pretentious—and went on in a lighter tone: "Alexander Goodrich is what I call a chancy writer. He can be thoroughly bad. Some of the critics are terribly down on him."

"Bad in what way?" asked Harold.

"Oh, I don't mean morally, though old-fashioned people might say he was. I mean artistically bad, clap-trap, inflated stuff. I expect it depends on whether he's in love or not."

"Why, what difference does that make?" Harold asked.

"With some writers it makes all the difference," Isabel said. She was carried away, partly by her interest in the subject, partly by the thought that almost for the first time she was having a serious conversation with her husband about books. "Being in love—well, it does something to the imagination."

Harold felt that these words implied a criticism of himself. "Is Goodrich a married man, do you know?" he asked.

"I *don't* know," Isabel said. "I rather think not. Artists and writers often don't get married. There's a sort of mystery about him—he lives a long way off, somewhere in Wales. Did he look as if he was in love?"

"I couldn't say," said Harold disappointingly, and obviously disapproving of being asked such a question. "He seemed bothered about something—perhaps because he was travelling first with a third-class ticket."

"I shouldn't think that would worry him," said Isabel. "It must have been something else."

"Well, his income tax."

"Yes, it might have been that," Isabel agreed, and for a moment the animation faded from her face, leaving it heavy. She was a small woman with a high complexion, a well-shaped aquiline nose and dark eyes that could sparkle. Her hair, which was thick and dark, almost black, she parted in the middle and drew round her face in two dark crescents; she might have been a better-looking Charlotte Brontë. She read the Sunday papers and the weekly reviews and tried to keep abreast of culture. She had been in doubt about marrying Harold, but the quality in him that had first attracted her had worn well and strengthened its hold. She liked his seriousness, and some, though not all, of the forms it took. He was determined to be a good husband and father—it was the rôle in which he saw himself—and when disagreements arose between them she knew she would have this principle of his on her side. Even if it was only a principle, she was inextricably part of that principle; she was its inspiration and its guiding light. On the other hand, some of the manifestations of his seriousness irritated her, for he was also determined to arrange their lives according to a perfect bourgeois pattern. He was a sidesman at church and might soon be a churchwarden; he was a member of every society in the town which had a suggestion of the square or the circular about it, and which was at once

11

reasonably inclusive and reasonably exclusive; he was not unduly snobbish but he coveted the good opinion of his neighbours, and spoke of some who were in a slightly superior social position with so much awe that Isabel was inclined to smile. That was the safety-valve; she could smile at him and at the same time value his instinct—for it really was an instinct—to reach ever new heights and depths of domesticity, conjugality, paternity, and—to use a harsh word—respectability. Even that she was prepared to face. She had gone a good way to meet him in his ideals; he had not gone very far to meet her in hers. She did not altogether enjoy the cocktail parties and dinner parties they gave from time to time to his business friends. She did not dread them; the men were cleverer than she expected them to be, the women were nicer, and she had quite her fair share of a woman's natural interest in people. On such occasions Harold would take on a protective colouring from his guests, disguising, under a jocular manner, the fact that he took himself seriously as a breadwinner and a business man. Sometimes his older or more prosperous associates would notice this and gently rag him—a thing that Isabel resented for him, for if she sometimes laughed at him herself she did not like it if others did. Everything at these parties had to be just as they would be at other people's. Harold had almost a passion for the middle way.

Isabel knew the nemesis of the dream-fed, of Mme Bovary and Hedder Gabler; she knew what was likely to happen when a woman of slightly superior social standing, decidedly superior brains and greatly superior imaginative capacity married a dullish man and lived in the provinces, and she was on her guard against it. She believed she knew herself fairly well. She did not suspect herself of Bovarysme. She did not mean to shoot herself or take poison or break out in any way. But latent in her were feelings she had not quite subdued when she accepted Harold and his gospel of conformity; and sometimes when she walked along the tree-lined banks of the canal, now filled with the Ophelia tracery of floating leaves, or watched the soldiers setting off, rifle in hand, to their training ground beyond the brick-built barracks, she had to stifle a longing to be more to someone than she (or perhaps anybody) could ever be.

Once, not long ago, she had been walking on the promenade behind which the town nestled in its ancient security of church and trees and barracks and small, non-seaside houses: Marshport always seemed to her a town by the sea, not a seaside town. It was a blowy day and far out the waves were breaking; but in-shore for a hundred yards or more it was as flat as a lawn. Suddenly, from the midst of the flatness at her feet a long billow began to form. Fascinated she watched it mounting up, a hump of green water, marbled with foam, moving slowly towards her. Gradually it curved inwards, till it was as tall and hollow as a wave in a Japanese print. Then a crest began to form and the whole mass toppled forwards.

A sound like distant thunder, between a rattle and a rumble, assailed her ears. It was the noise of motor-traffic, crossing at its own risk (the notice said) the wooden-slatted bridge over the canal. Isabel was so used to it that as a rule she hardly noticed it: but to-night it seemed a warning.

"Jeremy and Janice in bed?" asked Harold.

"Good gracious, yes, it's nearly nine o'clock."

"Of course it is, I'd clean forgotten. It was talking to you about that fellow Goodrich. Did they remember to say their prayers?"

"I don't believe they did. Shall I run up and see if they're still awake?"

"It might not be a bad idea."

Harold said and thought that Alexander Goodrich would never remember his promise to send the details of his income: authors were like that, he declared. But he was mistaken. Within a few days a long envelope arrived, with his name inscribed in bold and loving characters, and within were the documents that disclosed the extent and sources of the author's income. But did they in fact disclose it? The vouchers were the oddest lot Harold had ever seen. Some of Goodrich's investments were in private companies unknown to Harold, unrecorded in the Stock Exchange List: some operated, or claimed to operate, in South America. Indeed, by far his largest single holding was in a company called The Cotopaxi Infiltration Trust. "Don't tell me to sell these shares," wrote Goodrich, referring to them in his letter; "they don't sound much and they're not doing very well now, but they have been my mainstay and I have a sentimental attachment for them." He went on: "I'm afraid some of the vouchers are lost but I expect that with your experience you will be able to make up the figures out of your head."

Never before had Harold had to exercise so much imagination on an income-tax return. There were times when he wished he had never taken it on and times when he even wanted to give it up. To experts income-tax figures have their elasticity, which even inspectors recognize; there is a considerable No-man's Land where the august precision of mathematics does not hold sway. Unconsciously Harold was quite alive to the poetry of figures. But in Goodrich's return there was really too much room for conjecture, too wide a margin of uncertainty. After all, a figure had to be arrived at, a definite sum in pounds, shillings and pence, a last chord in which all the conflicts and problems of the return would be resolved. But it would take time to find it.

"Where does he live?" was Isabel's first question when Harold told her he had received the letter.

"I can't remember—somewhere in Wales—oh yes, St. Milo's."

"St. Milo's?" repeated Isabel, breathing the words rather than saying them. "So that's where he lives." She knew little of St. Milo's except its name and its locality; yet these started in her mind a vision of strange, Wagnerian scenery, rock-pinnacles piercing the sky. Wild Wales!

"Yes, outlandish sort of place," said Harold. "Hasn't even got a railway. I wonder if he's able to keep any servants. I must ask him."

"Why?" asked Isabel.

"Because he could claim for their stamps."

"Oh," said Isabel. "Do we claim for Mrs. Porter's?" Mrs. Porter was their daily help.

"Of course we do."

"Is he rich?" asked Isabel.

"As well as Goodrich?" Harold laughed and Isabel joined in. "Yes, on paper he's very comfortably off." He hesitated: he didn't think it proper, or even decent, for women to know much about money matters. They were a ritual secret that men must keep to themselves. "Yes, on paper he's all right."

"Why do you say 'on paper'?"

"Well, I don't like the sound of some of his investments."

"Will you have to write to him again?"

"Yes, probably several times." Harold dropped the rather severe paterfamilias manner he kept for money matters, and added: "How are you getting on with his book?"

"Oh, I've finished it. It's one of his best, I think. It's a bit lifeless in parts, but it's got some wonderful things—where they all begin to settle down after the crisis, for instance."

"Funny," said Harold. "He said something rather like that himself."

"*Did* he?" Isabel experienced a curious thrill of pleasure at the idea that her thoughts and those of Alexander Goodrich were running on the same lines. It was almost as though she had entered into his mind.

At last, after a lot of correspondence, the final figure was arrived at—that precise figure, in the thousands, which seemed almost mystically to represent the living Goodrich—

his face, his eyes, his hands, his suit, his shoes, even his discordant socks—and make a synthesis of them. There, in that sum correct to a penny, were to be found, in embryo, the whole complex of his circumstances, personal and financial. Harold had nailed him down, robbed him of his mystery. His secret was out. Yet was it? Thinking of those investments and the element of fantasy, which slightly offended him, in those vouchers, which didn't seem to vouch for much, Harold wasn't so sure. One thing he was sure of: by claiming the relief to which Alexander Goodrich was entitled, he had saved the novelist at least two hundred pounds a year.

Then began the sequel. With old-fashioned courtesy, in his ornate, unhurried script, Goodrich expressed his gratitude for Harold's services, and added that if it was not presuming on his kindness, he would like to ask some of his friends to put their income-tax affairs into Harold's hands—thus converting them, he said with solemn playfulness, from poor men into millionaires. Harold didn't quite like this pleasantry; he didn't think that incomes were a joking matter—didn't everything, in the end, go back to them?—but he said he would be pleased to do what he could for Alec's friends, for by this time the two men were, at Goodrich's suggestion, on Christian name terms. Harold hadn't wanted this either, for he had known cases where a request for the more familiar form of address had been the prelude to the putting over of a fast one. Nor did he believe that any of Alec's friends would show up.

But again he was mistaken. Not many days elapsed before a stranger wrote to say that at the suggestion of his friend, Mr. Alexander Goodrich, he was asking Harold to take charge of his income-tax return. Another followed and another (one ended "P.S. Alec says you are a wizard!" which annoyed Harold but gratified him, too) until by Christmas time he had had several—including two from women. Some of the returns were mere chicken-feed, but the last was a real *bonne bouche*, a proper Christmas present. Coming home from his office Harold, who had hitherto made only the vaguest references to these windfalls from Alec, feeling that Alec was only a sideline, not covered by his terms of reference, felt constrained to mention this one to Isabel.

"That fellow Goodrich," he said, for so he still thought of Alec, "has been as good as his word, I might even say better. Quite a nice little packet of trouble arrived this morning, quite a nice one," and he rubbed his hands.

A glow diffused itself through the lounge, as Isabel tried not to call it, that warmed as well as brightened it.

"That makes the fifth, doesn't it?" she said.

"Yes, but how did you remember?"

"Well, I did," she said. "Now you will be able to buy me a fur coat."

"I didn't say it came to as much as that," said Harold cautiously.

"No, of course not, I was only joking. But we could get some things the children need, perhaps."

"We could."

The magic of unexpected affluence continued to enfold them.

"We really ought to do something for him," Isabel said.

"For whom?"

"For Alec—Mr. Goodrich."

"But we have done something for him—I have. He's got more out of me than I have out of him and his friends put together."

"Yes, but he went out of his way to. . . . Suppose we asked him down to stay?"

They argued about it and then discussed it and were still discussing it when, a few days later, a sixth client presented himself, not so glittering as his predecessor, but still, quite good.

"Now we must ask him," Isabel said.

"He'll never come," said Harold.

But again he was mistaken. Alec accepted with alacrity. "I have been wanting to ask you and Mrs. Eastwood to come here," he wrote. "The place looks lovely in the spring, and we have a mild, wild Atlantic climate which I think you would enjoy." (Harold frowned: he thought the weather should be taken more seriously.) "But it is so far to ask you

17

to come, and there is so little to do when you get here, and my *ménage* isn't all it should be, I am sorry to say. But I still have hope of stabilizing it. Thanks to you and my invaluable losses, I am better off than when I seemed to be making money. I telephone like mad, I lay in enormous stores of stationery, I subscribe to every periodical, I keep my room at boiling-point and have it vacuumed twice daily, and it all costs me nothing, less than nothing, in fact it saves me money. The week-end you suggest will suit me perfectly. It happens I shall be in London just before—but if I weren't, what matter? My journey, being on business, will cost me nothing, and they will never know it was on pleasure too. No more third-class tickets!

"Looking forward more than I can say", etc.

But when the day came Isabel was riddled with misgiving. All the secret excitement (for she did not betray it to Harold) that she had been feeling turned to nervousness. The word "suburban" haunted her; she felt she must apologize to Goodrich for "our suburban home". Everything they had, the house, the furniture, the garden, seemed to shout the word at her. Even the children were infected by it. Eight children would have been all right, or none, but two!— and the dreadfully bourgeois possibility of a third, if they could afford it! Perhaps he didn't like children at all; perhaps they ought to be kept out of the way. Like other young matrons of to-day, Isabel was used to having her children always with her; if she shut them up in their bedroom, which was also their nursery, they would never stay there. She felt that the whole of the Eastwood *train-de-vie* was wrong; (Isabel liked to recall French phrases from her cultured past). All the meals, except tea, should be at least an hour later than they were, and tea should be much earlier. Alec was probably a man of nocturnal habits: authors always kept odd hours. Ought she to make special provisions for him? Feed him on caviare and foie gras? Would he expect a lot to drink? Authors often did. Should she put whisky by his bed? Everything she knew or surmised about him, which had made him alluring and romantic afar off, were now the very things that made him formidable.

18

Yet she felt she was being unfair to herself. She was not really like this. When business acquaintances of Harold's who were in a better financial position than they were came to stay, Isabel never felt in awe of them. On the contrary, she had felt rather superior to them. How can they *bear*, she sometimes asked herself, to be as undistinguished as they are? So why worry about Mr. Goodrich? Worrying would do no good; indeed, it was just the thing she should avoid, it would stamp her as inexperienced and unworldly. If she couldn't appear experienced and worldly—and she wasn't sure he would like it if she did—she wanted to appear carefree and Bohemian, in sandals and with her hair tied up in a red duster, or in tight slacks and a high-necked yellow sweater. The last thing she wanted to appear was what she was doomed to appear, a fussy middle-class housewife with her hand on the door-knob and her eye on the clock.

But if her confidence waned at the prospect of the novelist's visit, Harold's mounted. With men of his own sort he was sometimes ill at ease, especially with the bigwigs. They made him deferential. But the idea of Goodrich didn't. To him the author was—if not exactly a figure of fun, as *Punch* in earlier days might have portrayed him—at any rate someone who was playing at life and therefore not to be taken quite seriously as a man. He was somehow incomplete. A man should marry and have children. Just as Dr. Johnson thought that every man was secretly ashamed of not being a soldier, so Harold felt that every bachelor was secretly ashamed of not being a husband and a father. And there was no evidence that Goodrich was either. No wife or children figured in *Who's Who*. *Who's Who* was rather reticent about him. It said he had been born in 1908, which made him forty-six (Harold had only been a year out in his guess). It said that he had been educated privately. It gave a list of his publications which was long, but not to Harold very impressive, as he knew what the latest book had earned, which was not much. It said his recreations were "mounting and dismounting", which suggested horsemanship and had a facetious ring, out of place in a book of reference. He belonged to a good club but Harold was man of the world

19

enough to know that obscurity was sometimes a safer passport to a club than fame. Altogether the entry contrived to suggest that Goodrich had something to conceal.

Harold might not be in *Who's Who* but he had nothing to conceal. Now that he knew how much Goodrich was worth (excluding the faery gold from Cotopaxi, that uncertain quantity which he tried not to think about), now that he had him taped, Goodrich had become much more manageable to his imagination: he was not the mystery man he had been.

A man, too, ought to earn his living. Goodrich did not do this and apparently could not. His money added no more to his essential stature than if he had won it on the football pools. To prevent it running through his fingers he had had to go to a real man who understood such things, to him, Harold. This made a bond between them—Harold didn't deny it. But comparing himself with Goodrich, he found an increasing number of things which he could do and which Goodrich couldn't. And arising out of them, like the aroma from the bowl of pot-pourri in the lounge, was the blend of protective qualities, hard to define, impossible to speak of, but easy to recognize, which a man owed to his wife, his children, and his home.

No such aroma arose from Goodrich, so why be afraid of him? He was just a man on his own, and they were a united body, the strongest and most resistant unit that history could show—a family.

★ 3 ★

EXCEPT for one episode, the visit was rather like what Isabel had pictured it. True, the cocktail party which was to precede the dinner party on Saturday night nearly came to grief, for Goodrich, who had promised to telegraph the time of his arrival, forgot to, and did not arrive until the party was well under way. This made Isabel miserably nervous, whereas Harold declared to all and sundry that it was exactly what he had expected; he would have been disappointed if their literary lion hadn't run true to form. He excelled himself in inventing traits of unreliability among literary men and made such a build-up for Goodrich that when the novelist did at last appear, wearing the same brown suit he had worn in the train, he seemed like a complete stranger even to Harold, a being from another planet, larger than life. But soon, without shedding these fictitious aids, he began to establish his own identity. He was far from shy—indeed he exhibited a self-confidence which would have irritated Harold had Harold not been on his own ground and backed up by the Tablers and Rotarians of his own town. As it was he kept his end up as host even when Goodrich was retailing the diverting and fantastic adventures which had made him miss his train. Hardened traingoer as Harold was, nothing of the sort had ever happened to him, indeed he would have taken care it shouldn't—and this he managed to convey by laughing a little at his guest as well as with him. The novelist talked with a great deal of gesture and verbal emphasis, and a complete absence of self-consciousness—unless, as Harold suspected, it was really an exaggeration of self-consciousness, a deliberate putting of himself across. Instinctively he cleared a space round him and took up more room than he needed. Yet Harold couldn't complain that it was a display of egotism, for Goodrich appealed for sympathy in his various embarrassments to each of the company in turn. Was it all true, what he was saying, Harold wondered; was any of it true? But it didn't seem to matter, so long as it amused people. At length only the three dinner guests remained and Isabel retired to perform those combined mysteries of cooking and of changing of which women nowadays have the secret. She forgot to say, and came back in some concern to say, that perhaps Mr. Goodrich would like to see his room—thankful that this was Harold's task, not hers, so ashamed was she of the room's inadequacy.

Dinner was what Isabel most dreaded. For cocktails people can talk any nonsense, but at dinner the conversation must be serious, she thought: she took Art seriously herself and believed its practitioners must want to talk seriously about it. She made a mental vow to introduce the names of Proust and Joyce, and if possible of Sartre and Camus as well. She prepared a sentence or two to slip in when the conversation flagged. One part of her knew that this was a mistake, but her anxiety to make a good impression on Goodrich stifled it. It would be throwing away something that was most precious to her; she owed it to herself; she would hate him to think that she was a Philistine like the others. She owed it also to him; she felt that like a champion in any field he must be given the chance to show his paces. But when the lull came and, turning to him, she said in a self-conscious voice unlike her own, "Do you think the stream-of-consciousness method has come to stay, or have Joyce and Virginia Woolf exhausted it?" she felt the cold air of affronted incomprehension blowing round her and knew that she had blundered. Goodrich's mobile features confessed embarrassment, then he said, "What an interesting question! I wouldn't know, you see; I've never used it. What does anybody else think?" Apparently nobody else thought anything; there was an awkward pause; faces were turned to Isabel mutely accusing her of highbrow pretentiousness. It was for her to take up her own challenge but she couldn't and felt her eyelids pricking. Gradually the conversation trickled down to its own lower level, the common ground of their least interesting thoughts: Goodrich had not snubbed her but neither had he encouraged her, perhaps he too took her for a blue-stocking. Throughout the evening she invented his responses to almost everything she said and did; it was exhausting, trying to live in his mind as well as in her own, she realized its folly yet she couldn't refrain—even when she saw the wary glances he turned in her direction.

Harold was well pleased with the evening; he told Isabel he hadn't thought Goodrich would be such a good mixer. Alone with Harold, she lost her feeling of apartness from him and reproached herself for having tried to be his foil. Henceforth, as heretofore, their lives should lie together.

In the morning Harold announced his intention of going to church. He invited Goodrich to go with him, but the novelist excused himself, saying he had writing to do and would Harold say a prayer for him. Harold lived by a code rather than creed; his private prayers in church were a routine that did not admit of novelties, but he promised he would. "Anything special you want?" he asked breezily. "Nothing that I ought to have," replied the novelist with a smile; "I desire but I do not deserve." Isabel usually went to church but to-day she felt her duty lay at home; she had extra cooking to do, and other household chores. The children had gone with Harold and she had promised Goodrich that no one should disturb him. Actually there was no one to disturb him but herself, but this she felt increasingly tempted to do. Just one word, she thought, if she could find it, would put things right between them. But what was wrong? Nothing, and yet everything. She had never been able to appear to him as she wanted to appear. How did she want to appear? she asked herself. Not as a priestess, she did not aim so high, but as a humble votary of culture, to whom he and his visit meant a great deal, in a perfectly natural and appropriate fashion that combined sense with sensibility. As someone who, with the staleness, the dull patina of housework and housekeeping still on her, could none the less breathe the same air as he did. As someone who, being a woman, could make good some of the deficiencies in *Who's Who*. As someone who . . . well, understood.

She had every right to enter the sitting-room—lounge, as

she must remember to call it. Twice she only approached the door but the third time she went in.

He was sitting at the writing table, looking much too big for it. Had her eye been as critical as Harold's was, she would have noticed that he was wearing a loud pullover with his sober Sunday suit. He raised his head.

"Am I disturbing you?" she asked.

"Of course not."

"About your book——" she said.

"Yes," he answered. "Which one were you thinking of?"

"The one you gave to Harold—*After the Storm*."

"Well," he said, "what about it?"

Instantly everything she had prepared to say fled from her. Only what should have been the climax to an ascending spiral of intoxicating talk remained.

"I wondered if you would put my—our—names in it. And yours."

"I shall be particularly pleased to do so," he told her, with the fullness of utterance and amplitude of expression that he often gave to trifles. "I have the pen; have you the book?"

As soon as she had put the book before him he began to write in it; she watched his pen-nib swooping in curves that were almost voluptuous. She did not notice the discrepancy between his fingernails. Without blotting the page he rose and handed her the open book.

"For my kind hosts and benefactors, Mrs. and Harold Eastwood," she read. "From their week-end guest and as he hopes, lifelong friend, Alexander Goodrich."

"How good of you!" exclaimed Isabel, overwhelmed by the dedication. Then she took thought, and at the risk of seeming to look the gift-horse in the mouth, she said:

"But how are we your benefactors?"

"Because your husband has saved me a great deal of money."

"Yes, I'm so glad he has been able to, but what have I——?"

"You have saved me from a dull morning with my book." She coloured and said with difficulty, half turning to go,

24

"Oh, but I didn't mean to interrupt you for more than a moment."

"But now you must stay," said he, "if you can spare the time from more important things, and tell me what you think of *After the Storm*. That is if you've read it, which I hardly dare to hope."

So Isabel had her book-talk after all, and established herself in her own mind as the kind of person she wanted Goodrich to think her. That was the important point, of course.

After luncheon (normally Isabel thought of their midday meal as lunch, but in connection with Goodrich she thought of it as luncheon) Harold offered to take their guest for a drive: he suggested alternative destinations. Goodrich voted for Dymport, "because there," he said, "is the home of the Master, and I should dearly like to see it." "The Master?" echoed Harold. "What Master?" Vaguely he thought of a schoolmaster, and then of a master of foxhounds. "But we don't have hunting round here." "He doesn't mean that kind of a master," said Isabel, after a moment's hesitation, for she didn't want to seem to be scoring off her husband; "he means Jacob Henry, whose house is at Dymport." She was rewarded by an approving look from Goodrich. But Harold said, with a shade of irritation, "And what kind of a master is he?" "A master to whom all we poor novelists bow the knee," said Goodrich, "in proportion as we have been able to profit by his lessons." Harold sniffed; since his return from church with the glow of duty done almost visible on him he had resumed his place as chairman of the board of hospitality. "What is he, when he's at home?" "He isn't at home," said Isabel quickly, "he's dead and his house belongs to the National Trust. They let you see over it." "But they won't let you see over it on a Sunday," objected Harold, glad to assert himself and be at last the Master's master. "Oh, I don't mind if you don't," Goodrich said; "all I want is to stand bareheaded outside the shrine." Harold thought this a rather foolish ambition, but a guest's preference had to be respected and to Dymport they went.

Isabel drove with Goodrich beside her and Harold in the back seat, for so Harold ordained it. Happy, but still feeling she was casting swine before pearls, Isabel was painfully conscious of the shortcomings of the scenery; above all its literal flatness. Flat the sea on the left behind its shingle bank, the flatness of which was emphasized by an occasional Martello tower; flat the illimitable marsh on the right; flat the prospect and flat, save for the disappearing outline of the hills, the retrospect. Isabel was glad that her duties as driver didn't let her look about too much. "I'm afraid this country must seem very dull after St. Milo's," she apologized; and was at once annoyed with herself, for after their talk she had no excuse for feeling ill at ease with Goodrich, and she knew the remark was even flatter than the landscape. "But it's fascinating!" he answered, contradicting her words but sympathetic with her mood; "and this wide sky's a basin full of sunshine!" At once her feeling about the landscape changed: she couldn't help seeing it through his eyes.

The house was closed as Harold said it would be. He was not unduly triumphant over this. But when Goodrich, standing hatless on the cobbles before the house's dignified but unassuming façade, said with a look at Harold, "I think we should all three salute the prince of fiction writers," Harold had to struggle with himself before he took off his hat. But take it off he did, and Isabel, with a strange sense of liberation, dropped a deep curtsy.

Harold was leading them away when Goodrich said, "It would be rather nice if we could see the inside of the house as well." "Oh, but that's quite impossible," declared Harold, shocked. For him a rule not only had its power of compulsion, legal or customary; it also had a halo of diffused acceptance which made it worshipful. "The caretaker must have his Sunday off like other people." "Of course he must," said Goodrich, "but all the same it would be rather nice." He broke away from them and went back to the house; they saw him studying its front as if to find a loophole for an entrance.

"We needn't bother," said Harold reassuringly to Isabel; "he'll never get in, the rules are much too strict." He had never before visited a house run by the National Trust and didn't know whether their rules were strict or not; he just assumed and hoped they would be. By now Goodrich had his finger on the bell.

"Good Lord!" said Harold, open-mouthed. The tall door opened and a man's face appeared. Harold turned away, as embarrassed as if Goodrich had been showing a third-class ticket. But Isabel couldn't help watching, though she, too, had no doubts as to the issue; she was fascinated by the by-play in the doorway—the garrison defending, with no weapon but a headshake, the besieger reinforcing his appeal with wide gesticulations. At last an understanding was arrived at, an armistice was concluded—on terms favourable, it seemed, to the invader; for the door remained open as Goodrich came towards them.

"It's all right," he said, his face radiant. "He didn't want to let us in at first, but when I told him we'd come all the way from St. Milo's on purpose to see the house, his flinty heart softened. It's extraordinary how decent some of these fellows are."

"You don't half like getting your own way, do you?" grumbled Harold, indignant at the broken rule and the caretaker's broken Sunday rest, but at the same time won to admiration.

Goodrich looked surprised. "Would you say that about me?" he asked, almost tragically, and his unequal eyes rested on Isabel.

"I think it was very clever of you," she said. "I never thought you'd bring it off."

On the way home Harold took the wheel, and Isabel sat with Goodrich on the back seat. Until he climbed in beside her she had not realized how much she had been looking forward to this rearrangement. As the red roofs and hilly, winding streets of Dymport dropped behind them, she said to Goodrich, "Why do you admire Jacob Henry so much? Your books aren't at all like his."

"Well," he said, "I am, I hope, under the influence, but you see I lead a very different kind of life."

"What kind of life?" she asked him, greatly daring. "After all, aren't you a celebrity, too? I mean, people ask you for

27

your autograph. Don't all celebrities lead the same kind of life in a way—I mean, their lives are more like each other's than like the lives of ordinary people."

He laughed and said, "You can't be a celebrity in your own house."

She was stung by curiosity but all she could think of to say was: "Mr. Goodrich, did you really come all this way to see Jacob Henry's house?"

"No," he said, "I came to see you and Harold. If you can bring yourself to call me Alec, I shan't be able to resist calling you Isabel. May I?"

Harold turned his head and said, "Excuse me butting in, but you'll have to get my permission as well."

"Of course," said Goodrich, "it must be a tripartite agreement. If you use your veto——"

"I'll consent," said Harold, "on condition that you both promise not to mention Jacob Henry again during the next half-hour." They both promised, but under the shadow of this prohibition their conversation did not thrive; perversely their tongues itched to utter the forbidden name. Alec speculated about the towns they passed. He made a piece out of each of them, half acting it, and suggesting the kind of lives led by their respective inhabitants, some of which were so scandalous that the back of Harold's neck turned red. Besides being shocked, not altogether disagreeably, by his guest's freedom of speech, he didn't like to hear respectable towns, which formed part of his background, being made fun of. But Isabel was enchanted.

At last Alec said, "The half-hour's up. May we at least refer to him as the Master, no levity intended?"

Harold didn't see the point of this, but was satisfied with having exercised authority, while the two behind him, now at liberty to discuss their favourite subject, found they no longer wanted to. In the slanting sunshine, which seemed to go ahead of them, every object they came to had its moment of glory; and some association of ideas made Isabel ask Alec:

"What is it like at St. Milo's?"

"Oh, St. Milo's," he said, as if St. Milo's was somewhere in the moon. "St. Milo's," he began, and she thought he was going to do a comic turn about it; "let me see." He looked around. "There's nothing like it here. The people say, 'Are you going up to England?' It's ancient and pagan —not Greek, I needn't say, but Celtic, and yet it's full of saints, local saints, that no one has ever heard of. Can you be pagan and holy at the same time? And there's the Cathedral, it's Norman; the arches are most richly carved and all different. The colour is wonderful everywhere. The land is quite bare; there are no trees of any size except an ash or two—but such wild flowers as you never saw."

"And hills?" asked Isabel.

"Oh yes, plenty of hills. And hills in the sea, too."

"Hills in the sea?"

"Islands. Islands behind islands, like a shoal of sleeping whales. It's difficult not to see them as forms of animals. St. Milo's Head is like a sphinx, a serene, sun-baked sphinx, watching the sea. But you can't always see them because of the soft warm mist that drifts about. St. Milo's is never cold."

"And are there rocks on land as well?"

"Yes, monoliths. There's one big rock, with buttresses like a church. But for the most part they don't suggest ruins, they suggest age—Nature's age, not man's. Man doesn't come into it very much at St. Milo's. Primitive man, yes, but not modern man."

Isabel looked about her at the busy road, the bungalows, the bathing huts, the island-less utilitarian sea, the tamed domesticated land; the sun still shone on them but the lustre was gone from them. Modern man was everywhere.

"How you must long to be back!" she exclaimed.

"Back?" he repeated sombrely. "I don't want to go back; I've had enough of it. Here I'm a celebrity, or so you say. I'm just a dogsbody there."

Isabel was startled, almost shocked. Hitherto her contact with Alec had been through many half transparent mediums, like the gauze curtains on the stage. She felt he was reporting himself to her through the *oratio obliqua* of his manner and mannerisms; she could almost see inverted commas when he spoke. He had, she noticed, different ways of speaking; one way with Harold, another way with her; one bluff and slangy, one roundabout and formal. Sometimes they got mixed up; he seldom seemed all of a piece. Which expressed him? Now he spoke to her directly and it was like an unexpected glimpse of naked flesh. She wondered if he had been acting up to her idea of him, the awe in which she held him. She wondered if Harold had heard. A comment, she felt, was called for; but they were running through the main street of Marshport, only a few minutes from home, and no comment suggested itself.

When Isabel had gone to see the children and the two men were alone, Alec said:

"Would it be in order if we went to the local? In the benighted place where I live they don't open on Sundays but here they do and I should like to buy you a drink."

Harold hesitated. He was always a slow starter and his instinct was to veto anything that was proposed; but now he had a stronger reason. It wasn't his habit, not did it agree with his idea of himself as a pillar of the place, to go to a public house, least of all on Sunday. It was the last thing that he wanted to do. People would wonder; it would get about. So he said:

"Thank you, I think I'd rather not. I'm a bit tired, and as a matter of fact I was just going to ask you to have a drink here."

"Delighted," said Alec promptly. "I know how good your drinks are. But couldn't we do both? I want to stretch my legs and I should like a glimpse of 'local' society" (his voice put inverted commas round the word). "It's the novelist in me. I'll go by myself if you'd rather not come. I can always find my way to a pub, but I should get more consideration, of course, if you were with me."

Alec smiled and Harold smiled back, doubtfully. Consideration, now he thought of it, was double-edged. Should a Rotarian or a Tabler be present, he might be impressed to learn who Harold's companion was. If he still hesitated, it was because he didn't want to yield to the other man's pressure, to Alec's gift for getting his own way. Renouncing his male pride, he called up to his wife:

"We're going out for a breath of fresh air."

"I never heard it called that before!" said Alec admiringly.

Thinking over the scene afterwards, in the light of Alec's letter, Harold couldn't remember its details very well. He remembered his embarrassment. The hot, heavy, heady smell of beer went straight to his moral sense: he felt it was not good for him to be there. He stood with Alec by the bar while Alec ordered the drinks, and vaguely registered the impression that the barmaid was different from his idea of a barmaid. She seemed to be a foreigner, for all she could say, or all she did say, was "Pardon" and "Please". Some of the men were teasing her and making jokes which she only half understood. She would say "Please" or "Pardon" and smile shyly at them. She had a lot of dark brown hair, in the shadow of which her face looked small and pale and pinched, and a slightly turned-up nose and blue-grey eyes. Without being pretty she gave an affect of prettiness, or perhaps of gentleness, which evidently appealed to the men. There was nothing brazen or barmaidenly about her.

Alec and Harold took their drinks to a table from which she was invisible, behind the heads and shoulders. Harold refused a second pint, but Alec got up to order himself one and it was then that he had his conversation with her— speaking a foreign language which Harold presently guessed to be German. Out of respect for this linguistic display the other drinkers edged away, leaving Alec plenty of elbow-room. In a minute or two he came back, with a quite different look on his face—it was only afterwards that Harold remembered how transforming it had been. Before they left he paid a third visit to the bar, to say some last words, not to get a drink. Harold, who was now standing up, thankful to have got it all safely over, saw how eagerly the girl responded to what Alec said, seeming to lose her shyness, and how the eyes of the other men turned from one face to the other, trying to understand.

When they were coming out of the stuffy room Alec said, "That was indeed a breath of fresh air," and Harold, who thought he was being ironical, duly laughed. Alec added, "She's called Irma, and she's an Austrian," but he didn't mention her again, and neither of them referred to their visit to the pub when they got back.

31

4

AND that, as far as Harold knew, was all. Alec left the next morning. At supper and after he was in high good humour, he seemed much more at his ease with them than he had been and talked more naturally. Harold attributed this to obvious causes: the impact of a happy home life on a man who had no home ties. Isabel, rather along the same lines, hoped that she had touched some spring in him, as he had in her—for she, too, was unusually vivacious. The next day, and for some days after, a sense of flatness possessed her: once she had a vivid dream of St. Milo's which she later tried in vain to recapture by evoking it before she went to sleep. Her thoughts of Alec were not uncritical but she liked what she believed to be his faults, they seemed to bring him nearer to her, and oddly enough his admission of being a "dogs-body" at home was like a secret balm.

Harold, for his part, was relieved that the visit had gone off so well. He had liked the novelist better than he expected to, and instead of being made to feel inferior was confirmed in his status of husband, father, churchman and useful citizen. The thought of Alec was on the whole a pleasant thought, confirming him in his masculine selfhood, making it more compact. Only when the letters with their references to Irma came did his thoughts, unwillingly, traverse unaccustomed paths.

At first he stalled. Stalling is no doubt an ancient practice but it has increased greatly of late years; Harold was only doing what everybody else did (his ideal in action) when in his replies he was silent about Irma. Once (again in conformity with contemporary usage) he promised to do something without having any intention of doing it. And this was his state of mind, fixed and unalterable, when he added the third Irma letter to Alec's file. He was under no temptation to change it, quite the contrary, for by ignoring

Alec's appeals he was building up his own picture of himself. But a few days later two letters came by the same post which made him think again.

He opened Alec's letter. It followed the usual pattern. First came business — some tax-saving, or tax-evading, project which a friend of Alec's had suggested to him and to which Harold had given his consent but not his blessing. Secondly a reference—which also followed the pattern, though in form it was different each time—to the delightful time Alec had had at Tilecotes. This included a warm message to Isabel. And lastly:

"If it isn't asking too much of you, do try to *get hold* of Irma for me. If you could find out her other name, that would be a help. I wouldn't bother you, but I'm so far away —at least a thousand miles—and you are on her doorstep, so to speak."

Harold restrained an impulse to push the letter away from him. Best answer it at once—the business side of it. But meanwhile he must read his other letters, and methodically he took the next one from the pile.

"Sir," it began,

"In deference to the repeatedly expressed wish of my old friend, Mr. Alexander Goodrich, I am writing to ask if you will be so obliging as to undertake the preparation of my Income Tax Return. I may say at once that I make this request unwillingly as I am perfectly well satisfied with my own accountant. But Mr. Goodrich has set his heart on my making the change, it would not be too much to say he has pestered me about it, and like a certain person in Scripture I feel I must yield to his importunity. Mr. Goodrich tells me that you can work wonders with the miserable pittance that a robber Government still allows us to call our own. If this be true I shall be compensated in pocket if not in pride for the distasteful step that Mr. Goodrich has persuaded me to take.

Yours faithfully,"

This time Harold did not restrain himself. Without bothering to read the signature he flung the letter across the room and remained for some moments staring at it with pinks cheeks and quickened breathing. Why had he let himself be involved with Alec, a man with no respect for the conventions, no sense of decency, even? Mutely he cursed the day when he had met him. Relieved by this, and at once ashamed and proud of his display of temper, he retrieved the letter. On a second reading it did not seem so insulting; the writer's natural exasperation was with Alec, not him. Who was he? The letter was typewritten, the signature in longhand. Haverfordwest it seemed to be. Haverfordwest was a town. How could a town be writing to him? Then it dawned on him: Haverfordwest was the title of a peer. . . .

Harold would have thought it silly and improper to be worked up, but worked up he was, and the various emotions which culminated in the realization of his correspondent's identity, as they subsided, left jangling nerves of his mind which were not in ordinary use.

Hitherto he had been inclined to take for granted the clients Alec had found for him. They had come to him in the way of business; they were windfalls. But now he asked himself, were they really windfalls? If so, it must have been a remarkably high wind. He remembered times when he had recommended to his friends various people whom he had hoped they would employ; his lawyer, his dentist, his plumber. Harold had a very strong sense of solidarity with the people he served and was served by; he felt possessive about them, they were extensions of himself, outposts of Harold in life's battlefield. His dentist in particular was a splendid man and he had often asked his friends to entrust their teeth to him. Had they ever done so? Never. To the best of his knowledge no one had ever, in this matter of choosing someone to "go to", taken his advice. Nor, when he came to think of it, had he ever, in similar circumstances, taken advice from any of his friends. It was, he suddenly realized, a point of pride with him, as it was with them, to stick to the people he knew.

But Alec had persuaded six—no, seven—of his friends to entrust their income-tax returns to him, Harold, a complete stranger to them. He had overcome their change-resistance, he had beaten down their pride. These jobs of his were not windfalls at all. The trees had taken a lot of shaking—how much shaking, Lord Haverfordwest's letter showed. Harold was aware of feeling quite differently towards Alec, and he so seldom changed his mind or his angle of vision (indeed, it was a point of honour with him not to) that the process was rather painful.

He took up Alec's letter again. "If it's not asking too much of you, do try to *get hold* of Irma for me."

It was asking too much, of course, much too much. And what exactly did "try to get hold of Irma for me" mean? What did Alec *want*?

He took out Alec's three previous letters and re-read the relevant extracts:

"I shan't quickly forget that girl behind the bar at the Green Dragon, either. Irma was her name, I think."

"What a jolly girl Irma was. I wish I had had time to get to know her better."

"Find out about Irma for me if you can."

After each there was a reference to the distance between Marshport and St. Milo's. "Five hundred miles between us, or I would get in touch with her myself." And now it was a thousand.

Just as Harold had stalled by ignoring Alec's requests, so Alec had stalled by ignoring Harold's silences.

That one good turn deserves another was an axiom with Harold: he would not have dreamed of doubting it. Indeed, he had applied it to this very matter of the Income Tax returns, he reckoned he had saved Alec as much money as Alec's "windfalls" had brought him—perhaps more. Such satisfaction as he got from his relationship with Alec depended largely on that—it was not personal: like many married men, Harold did not have men friends: he had acquaintances and boon companions. The advantages had been reciprocal, otherwise he would have been more uneasy with Alec than he was.

But though the advantages were reciprocal, the balance of obligation, Harold saw, was tilted heavily against him. What he had done for Alec had been done in the way of business, without any special effort on his part (except the

35

effort to reconcile his mind to the Cotopaxi Infiltration Trust). What Alec had done had demanded efforts which now seemed to Harold superhuman; he had, in the case of seven people, upset the habits of a lifetime.

Harold was (so he believed) nothing if not just; and in the light of justice, with the wish to square the account between him and Alec, he was prepared to reconsider the case of Irma.

"*Get hold* of Irma for me if you can. If you could find out her other name, that would be a help."

Well, he supposed it wouldn't be difficult to find out her other name. But wouldn't it? Wouldn't it be rather difficult to sidle up to the landlord of the Green Dragon and say, in a casual manner, "By the way, and as a matter of interest, what is the surname of your barmaid—rather nice-looking girl—Irma, I think they call her?" Would it be so easy, with possibly some Tablers and Soroptimists listening in?

But if lions in the path thought they would have an easy job with Harold, they were mistaken. Once his mind accepted its new orientation it would go on boldly. But how far would it go?

Unwillingly he had to consider Alec as a person, not as someone coming under a business heading, which was the way he thought of most men. Not even as a client, for his relations with his clients were also cut and dried: very little personal feeling could, in the nature of things, come into them. He had to think of Alec as a man and a benefactor.

As a benefactor was easiest. Alec, Harold now thought, had done what he did out of kindness to him, Harold. No use to say, "Oh, he wanted you to get hold of Irma for him, that is why he sent you clients—they were a bribe." The clients had started coming in long before Alec had spied Irma behind the bar. These clients were worth a good deal to him. Not only could he give the children things they needed but (with Lord Haverfordwest's help) he could replace his old car. As a benefactor, he owed Alec some return. And putting it on a lower level, supposing he went on disregarding Alec's request and Alec got tired of asking, might he not then withdraw his favours and persuade his friends to do the same? There seemed no limit to what he could persuade people to do. True, most men kept their private feeling out of business matters especially when it was to the advantage of their pockets; but spite was not unheard of. On both these counts he ought to do something to repay Alec the benefactor.

And Alec the man? Here Harold was much less sure of himself, for he was not used to considering men out of their context of business or social or civic or sporting life. He seldom asked himself whether he liked such and such a man: he esteemed him according as he fitted into the categories Harold knew. Alec didn't fit into a category, unless it was the category of dark horses, a mythical one to be dismissed with a shrug and a wink. About Alec, too, there clung something humorous and dubious, something slightly smelly. Harold couldn't put Alec into any category that he recognized except that of rather rich men.

All the same, if someone had asked him (no man ever did, but Isabel sometimes did, ask such a question), "What sort of a man is Alec Goodrich?" he could have given a more illuminating answer now than he could have given half-an-hour ago. When dark horse and Bohemian had been disposed of—"He's cranky, of course, but not a bad sort of fellow for a writer. A bit unreliable, you know, travels first-class with a third-class ticket, and very unbusinesslike, first altogether careless about his Income Tax, for instance, and then when he's been told of the possibilities, a bit too sharp, in my opinion. And impulsive, yes, that's it, impulsive, like a woman." Harold stops a moment to consider the quality of impulsiveness, and goes on: "He sent me some business without knowing me from Adam; I might have been a complete crook for all he knew. And made several of his friends do the same: think if I'd been a wrong 'un, where would he have been? But this is the odd thing (and here Harold frowns); though he's impulsive he's as obstinate as a mule. He can get round anyone (I'm not sure that he can get round me, though). He'll go a long way out of his way, a long way, to do you a good turn. And there's another thing he is (here Harold drops his voice) and that's emotional. I won't tell you how I know, but I do know. He takes sudden fancies to people—well, he did to me, but I don't mean that. And when he's emotional he's just as obstinate as he is when he's impulsive—I suppose they're rather the same, really (Harold dismisses this inquiry with an impatient shake of the head). He simply won't take no for an answer, but he may find he'll have to. He's emotional, and it doesn't do to be emotional if you're not married, it's a pity, if you see what I mean."

Harold paused in his (even to himself) unexpectedly sympathetic analysis of Alec's character to consider emotion in the abstract. In his view, emotion could not function properly except within the marriage-tie. Outside the marriage-tie, emotion was either funny, or a subject for smoking-room stories—or both—or if it went too far as it sometimes did, as it increasingly did, as it had done regrettably on the outer confines of Harold's and Isabel's own families, then it was something to be covered up, or passed over with a few short words uttered in a deeper, and slightly quelling, tone of voice. In any case, outside the marriage-tie emotion couldn't be taken seriously except in the way that disaster— a motor accident, a death, a bankruptcy—is taken seriously. Within the marriage-tie, of course, it can operate as much as it likes: and having that freedom, thank goodness, it need hardly operate at all. That is one of the things that marriage is for, decided Harold: to be a safety-valve for emotion and so to keep it at the lowest possible ebb. Were his relations with Isabel emotional? No, they were not. They were loving and decorous and dependable, but they were not emotional. Harold's ingrained prejudice against emotion began to reassert itself.

And emotion for a barmaid? At last Harold was brought face to face with Irma: Irma's pale, delicate little face and pointed chin beneath the shadow of her wild but not untidy hair—he had to admit it wasn't really untidy. Irma was not an ordinary barmaid, he recognized that, and she was a foreigner as well. Still, she belonged to the category of bar-maids, and though Harold knew little about them from personal experience—one might say nothing—the qualities with which the category endowed them were so clear to him, so well attested, that they put into the shade, and made unreal, the qualities Irma had which did not belong to the category. Thus: barmaids were brassy, blatant, loud-voiced, impudent, vulgar, venal and, above all, loose; they were any man's money. To a man of Harold's type, which meant the whole army of self-respecting citizens, rich and poor (for Harold was quite ready to grant respectability to the poor), they meant just one thing—he wouldn't say what, but they meant it. No one, not even an Austrian with a seemingly gentle face, could be a barmaid without meaning it. And therefore their emotions, if they had them, being purely mercenary, could not be taken seriously at all; even if they involved somebody one knew in disaster (as conceivably they might) they still couldn't be taken seriously. Not for them the tribute of the lowered voice, and the brief unwilling word, that was the epitaph for unfortunate happenings with people of one's own sort. Barmaids were fair game, so Irma was fair game.

"Do barmaids devour their young?" Suddenly Harold remembered this inquiry—perhaps a music-hall joke of long ago. It showed how little the average person (with whom Harold was proud to associate himself) knew about the species. They were as mythical as dark horses. Who had ever heard of a barmaid having a child? The idea was incongruous, indecent—so incongruous, so indecent, that it wasn't too far-fetched to suppose that if they had one, they might eat it—so little were their habits known. No maid could have a child, legitimately, least of all a barmaid. "Barmaids are barred"—one could make a joke of that. What else was the whole subject but a joke?

Needless to say the idea of himself as a "wide boy", so dear to many men, was foreign to Harold. Even at school—the small public school where he had spent four blameless years —he had always been law-abiding. But he believed himself to be a man of the world. A man of the world knows about barmaids, without knowing them and without having to be told about them: and he knows, in principle, what "get hold of" means. He has always known it from the time of Alec Goodrich's first letter. To a man of the world it is all quite plain and should be all quite easy.

But was it? When Harold had reached this point of admitting his indebtedness to Alec for seven clients, of varying value but totalling up to a considerable sum, neither his mind nor his imagination would take him a step further. Not being in the least neurotic or subject to indecision or (except when deliberately stalling) given to procrastination, his thoughts fretted at the *impasse*, trying to surmount it.

Women . . . women. It was all a question of a woman. Women understood women.

Except in household and domestic matters (where there was not much to confide) Harold had never confided much in Isabel. He kept his business affairs from her, his income, as far as he could, the times when he felt anxious about things, or didn't feel well. It was partly protective: anything that might worry her he kept from her—also anything which, by being known, might reduce his masculine authority in her eyes. It had been a deliberate policy and had become second-nature. He did not ask himself whether she treated him in the same way, and kept under cover her feminine secrets—though, taking her cue from him, she did. It was not that he didn't trust her or was unwilling to be open with her (though public-school training made that difficult) but he felt that convention had made a wall of partition between a husband's sphere of interests and his wife's—and, therefore, between his and hers. But reflecting on the quality of emotion, and its legitimacy within the marriage-tie, thinking also that she might—indeed ought to —have a slant on this matter other than his own, he suddenly thought to himself, Why not? Why else be married? What is a wife for? It was a revolutionary thought, which occupied him for several minutes; and then he remembered that people had sometimes said to him, "Damned intelligent woman, your wife—pretty of course, but intelligent, too," and he had grunted, gathering the compliment to himself without realizing that it belonged to Isabel. But he realized it now. Of course, she was intelligent, damned intelligent; she managed his household, she looked after his children, as few men's households and children were managed and looked after; and after lunch, when the children had gone back to school, he would consult her about Alec and the barmaid. It would all be perfectly plain-sailing, and he knew what her answer, in effect, would be: "Don't have anything to do with it, Harold; leave the poor girl alone. Let Mr. Goodrich do his own dirty work, if he wants to."

The conclusion was a surprise to him, for his thoughts seemed to have been leading him in the opposite direction. And the relief it brought was also a surprise, for he believed he had been looking forward to falling in with Alec's request.

5

ISABEL's father had been a clergyman and a man of saintly
life, but so unworldly that if his wife had not been naturally
a manager she would have had to make herself one. He
could not have got on without her; without her his saintliness would have degenerated into ineffectiveness. She was
determined that his light should shine—as it did, sometimes
putting hers into the shade; for in the comparisons that
were inevitably made between them she seldom came out
best. His parishioners sympathized with him for being hen-
pecked, and Isabel, though she knew how unjust the charge
was, also sympathized.

She benefited, too, from her mother's autocratic ways.
She went to a better school than it seemed they could afford
and it was thanks to this that, soon after the war began, she
got a civil service job in London which paid her keep and
a little more and brought her into touch with people she
would never have met in the country place of which her
father was the Rector.

Those London years! Even after her marriage Isabel
looked back on them as a Golden Age. At home she had
always been in rebellion against her mother. In principle
she accepted and even applauded her; she knew that her
mother was a wonderful woman and she was jealous of any
criticism of her. Had her mother been someone else's mother
she would perhaps have admired her unreservedly. As an
idea Mrs. Knighton was beyond reproach. But as a person,
exercising an influence that was perilously near to pressure,
and displaying an interest that was all too like interference,
she could not fail to irritate. What made it worse, Isabel
was annoyed with herself for being irritated. She asked
herself the question that so many people, even her mother's
critics, asked: Where would the Knightons be if it wasn't
for Mrs. Knighton? Up the spout, down the drain—anywhere but in the position of influence and honour that they

held. And she blamed herself because she couldn't bring her private feelings into line with her sense of justice.

But though she reacted against her mother when they were under the same roof she accepted her mother's principles and tried to think they could be separated from her mother's practice. If *she* had been her mother. . . .

At school she was among the law-abiding ones, her mother's daughter. She did not chafe at discipline or self-discipline; she felt that orderly behaviour in the playing-field, the classroom and the dormitory would help to win the war. She accepted the gospel of strenuousness. She thought that art was all right so long as it was a form of education: education kept it healthy. (Art was something to be learnt about, and the process of learning was anti-septic.) Many artists had led irregular lives, just as many kings had, but these biographical facts she did not translate into terms of everyday life: for her the important thing was to get the facts right. She played games with distinction, she won prizes, and she left school justifiably pleased with herself.

Her parents were equally pleased with her, and her mother, who never stinted them of feasts for ceremonial occasions, killed—as far their own diminishing means and war-time restrictions permitted such a sacrifice—the fatted calf. Never, even at school, had Isabel felt so much the heroine of the hour.

And yet within a day or two, insensibly but irresistibly, all the old feelings of rebellion and unease and grievance had come back. Why was it, she asked herself, that at school authority wasn't irksome whereas at home it was? It vexed her to feel as she did, and vexation turned to guilt, and guilt increased her unrest: it was a vicious circle. She longed to assert herself, and found herself being pert in small matters, almost answering back. Had her mother's domination been merely moral, Isabel might have found a way of circumventing it, but it was physical as well. Mrs. Knighton was a tall, fair woman, built on ample lines and of dynamic presence. She would come into a roomful of people like a great white galleon from whose prow (it was scarcely fanciful to think) a curving ripple streamed away

43

on both sides, and in whose wake a number of small craft lay madly tossing. Of these Isabel was one. Her mother made her feel small in every sense. In her mother's presence she felt several inches shorter and a tone or two darker, as if she had actually been put into the shade; and the darkness penetrated into her mind, and left a shadow there almost like wickedness. Always she tried to believe that she was taller than she was.

It was the second summer of the war. Isabel was nearly nineteen, and longing to be called up for service. But here her father unexpectedly put his foot down. The war had been for him an experience of unmitigated horror. His saintliness was founded on an unquestioning belief in the goodness of human nature. Without that belief it couldn't function, and he became, in fact, though not in name, a pacifist.

Isabel did not notice how withdrawn he had become, for he was always withdrawn, it was a mark of his saintliness; so she was utterly taken by surprise when her mother told her that he could not bear the thought of her putting on uniform.

"He thinks he will lose you if you do," she said.

Isabel couldn't help laughing. "Lose me!" she blurted out. "Why, he's never found me!"

"Don't talk like that," said her mother sharply, and Isabel at once apologized for a remark which would have seemed funnier at school than it did in the home circle. Then her mother told her of the effect the war had had on her father: how he could no longer take interest in his hobbies, bird-watching and stamp-collecting. Worst of all, from the professional point of view, he couldn't bring himself to preach about the war. The parish waited in vain for a lead from its Rector.

It was the first time that Mr. Knighton had interfered with anything that Isabel wanted to do, or with anything that her mother wanted her to do: but Mrs. Knighton was determined that his wishes should be respected. Unwillingly Isabel complied. Mrs. Knighton pulled strings; the school authorities, raising their eyebrows at the idea of a girl with Isabel's record seeking exemption from service (a bitter pill for her to swallow), also pulled them; and that was how Isabel came to find herself enrolled in one of the Ministries as a very junior civil servant.

At first she felt helplessly at sea. Not because of the work, the work was easy to her. Coming from school she had no difficulty in picking it up. But being still rigid with responsibility, and the wish to shoulder it, she took the work more seriously than her colleagues did. They teased her about this. "There goes Knighton winning the war," they said, when she brought a furrowed brow to the consideration of some minor matter. Like a self-appointed Sisyphus she was always looking for some stone to roll—whereas they were looking for a log. She couldn't get it into her head that what was done mattered very little—how could it matter?—compared with how it was done: the proper form, the appropriate language and the usual channels. Isabel chafed at this but she was adaptable and sensitive to the corporate spirit round her. So guided, her conscientiousness soon took on other forms—even the form of not being conscientious.

Outside the office, however, that warren of low-ceilinged passages and functional rooms with communicating doors, Isabel's colleagues were more direct in their approach. "Chastity is constipating!" was their cry—and not a bad one, for who would be chaste at the price of being costive? With one of them, an older girl called Julie Parsons, she shared a tiny flat. Neither, perhaps, would have chosen the other as a companion, but both were ready to make allowances — Isabel from a schoolgirl's excitement in adapting herself to wartime conditions, Julie because she was naturally easy-going. How easy-going, Isabel didn't realize. Julie explained her occasional absences from the flat by saying she was staying with an aunt, and Isabel accepted this just as she accepted the bottle parties that from time to time assembled in Julie's bed-sitting-room. Indeed, she enjoyed them and looked forward to the day when she would have enough friends to give such a party herself. She liked Julie's friends, she began to like their free and easy way, and she liked discussing books with them, for most of them had an interest in the arts.

What she couldn't at first get used to was the confidence with which, in aesthetic matters, they exercised the right of private judgment. They were not impressed by authorities, at least not by the authorities she had been taught to respect; they quoted authorities she had never heard of, and they each seemed to think that his or her opinion was as good as anyone else's. In all the arts they admired examples of the latest thing which she thought hideous. But through the medium of Van Gogh, whom everyone can appreciate, she began to change her views. She was a stranger to her own mental processes. When she went home, as she often did for week-ends, and on the one occasion when she revisited her old school, she felt out of touch, not painfully but rather pleasantly, with the affectionate amusement that one has in looking at an old book of fashion-plates.

But though she had changed her outlook on the arts and was ready to stand up for it, in other ways she lagged behind the times. Over such crimes as murder, arson, rape, etc., she shook her head. Somebody had just shot a policeman. "How wicked!" she was heard to say. Her friends smiled. "Well, perhaps it was rather naughty." In this sort of context naughty was the strongest word of disapproval they allowed themselves. The cat was naughty to kill the bird, the dog was naughty to kill the cat, the boy was naughty to kill the policeman. Naughty! Naughty! But in other departments of behaviour their judgments could be unexpectedly severe and from this arose an incident which, trivial as it was, profoundly affected Isabel.

A novel had just come out and they were discussing it, quite a crowd of them, in Julie's room. Isabel had read the book, for she now read eagerly all the books that interested her set, and it had rather shocked her, for though she liked some of the "descriptions" (as she thought of them to herself) the general tone jarred on her and the behaviour of the two chief characters seemed to her quite indefensible. She listened to what her friends were saying and was astonished to find that this aspect of the story hadn't struck them. So she waited for a lull and then said rather loudly—excited at the prospect of making what seemed to her an undeniable point:

46

"But she broke up his home life: he had been perfectly happy until she came along."

A pause followed this announcement, and then someone said—she could never afterwards remember who, or if it was a woman or a man:

"Knighton, I didn't know you were a prig."

For a moment no one spoke and Isabel realized that the word of greatest condemnation of which her circle was capable had been uttered, and applied to her. She had been called a prig. Emancipated in some ways, she had not been emancipated from the dread of popular disapproval. She was a prig, a social outcast. . . . The fumes of alcohol and tobacco rose up against her and she felt slightly sick. The blood rushed into her face, her knees quaked and her heart dissolved within her. Then came a dwindling and hardening of her personality such as might visit the doomed victim of a sacrificial rite.

Her misery had lasted only a moment, though it seemed endless, when another voice said, in a tone that was deliberately reasonable and kind:

"But you see he wasn't really happy. Emotionally he was quite unawakened and didn't know what love was. He was married and had children and all that, but he'd had no real experience. Experience is what matters. His love for Miriam was quite different in quality from his love—if you could call it love—for his moron of a wife and those tiresome children. With Miriam he found what he was capable of— he found himself, in fact. Surely you can see that?"

Isabel did see. In a flash she realized how superficial, and in a sense how vulgar, her reaction to the book had been. She had been brought up by her mother's precept and her father's example to have the utmost respect for love. During their courtship they had read Browning and Tennyson together and had made their own the poets' gospel of romantic love. Love was a word to conjure with, and she had defiled it by her cheap, ready-made judgment. She blushed still more deeply, blushed for herself, blushed for her thoughts, and this habit of blushing stuck to her, she was subject to it even in private when she remembered some moralistic dictum she had made.

She had done for herself, she knew. She was a prig and they would never again accept her as one of themselves.

But, in fact, and after a little teasing, Isabel was reinstated. Indeed, the episode gave her a kind of popularity. Her friends laid little conversational traps for her, and when she fell into them and delivered herself of some heavy-handed remark. they would laugh and say, "That's a perfect Knighton". Soon she began to take these baits even when she could see the hook, for the sake of raising a laugh: sometimes she even baited the hook herself. She became known as a wag and had the intoxicating experience, when she had started a laugh, of hearing latecomers ask: "What's Knighton been saying now?" Perhaps her moment of greatest triumph was when an appreciative listener said, "Knighton ought to write an essay on 'the necessity of being amusing'." And it was only sometimes, and at rarer and rarer intervals, that the shaft of remembered shame went through her body, reminding her of the slumbering Pharisee within. It struck again, a few weeks later, when Julie told her the true reason of her nocturnal absences; they were spent with a young man. Isabel's mind whirled; half a dozen stupid comments rose to her lips; then she said, "I'm so happy for you, Julie darling, I always hoped it might be that."

And it might soon have been that for Isabel, too, for neither the desire nor the opportunity was lacking, when her father's mental illness took a turn for the worse, and the Ministry released her on compassionate grounds.

Where had her eyes been, she asked herself, that she had not on previous visits seen the deterioration setting in?

What made it especially sad was that as his illness progressed Mr. Knighton began to develop tiresome and irritating traits that he had never had before. He had been a good man not only by nature but by design: he had deliberately weeded out his faults. Now with the weakening of his central controls he became petulant and peevish, complaining particularly of the food they gave him, demanding meat when meat was not to be had. Before his illness he hadn't noticed what he ate; it had been one of their jokes to ask him, and to enjoy his confusion when he couldn't remember. Now when he pushed away his plate with their best efforts on it, the joke was turned against them.

On Mrs. Knighton, too, her husband's illness had an unhappy effect; her unbounded energies could not be restricted in their operation to the care of one man in one room of one house. Like her husband, though for different reasons, she chafed and fretted. She felt that the new incumbent was mismanaging things. She did not like his innovations, she did not like his being High Church; she did not like anything that Mr. Newbold did.

Isabel was bewildered by this new challenge to her adaptability. She had been in London just over two years, and had acclimatized herself; now she had to exchange the *fais-ce-que-tu-voudras* attitude of her set for one in which her likes and dislikes hardly counted. Her nature was attuned to loving; but how could she love her father in his strange clouded state? She could only feel sorry for him and try to love him as he had been. And how could she love her mother, whom she had never easily loved, with the full current of her mother's will-power turned on her?

Harold Eastwood was a native of the place and Isabel had always known him, but not well, for he had never been a regular visitor at the Rectory. He had come once or twice to play tennis when he was a boy, but for Mrs. Knighton, who had social ambitions for her daughter, Harold, the son of a successful draper, did not make the grade. His image had not prospered in Isabel's mind. But the mere length of an acquaintanceship counts for much and when she met him again, his uniform setting off his neat good looks, she was surprised by how well she felt she knew him. She had escaped, almost for the first time, from the sad conditions at the Rectory to attend a cocktail party, and the sudden freedom, no less than the drinks, went to her head. In London she had lost her shyness with men; in the Army he had lost his shyness with women; before the party was over they were calling each other by their Christian names. Isabel returned to the Rectory refreshed by the feeling that life held something besides duty.

As her father grew worse something of the sweetness of his nature returned and with it, for Isabel, the inexpressible relief of not having to make allowances for him. Little of him as was left, it was the person she remembered. But to her mother, whose charge he had always been, his failing health was yet another drop in the bitter draught of defeat: for his sake she had imposed her will on life, but on death she could not impose it.

Not until after he was dead did Isabel tell her mother of her understanding with Harold; she had an instinct against doing so and it was justified, for her mother did not smile on the idea of her daughter's marrying a draper's son. Isabel pointed out that the tables were turned, and in the worldly sense it was Harold who was conferring a favour on her: the Knightons were now poor, the Eastwoods very comfortably off. Mrs. Knighton couldn't see it. "I confess I hoped you'd marry a different sort of man," she said. "Harold is all right, of course, but why must you rush into it? There's plenty of time, you're only twenty-three, and the war can't last much longer." "But I love him," Isabel protested. If nothing else, the literary associations of the word, its Tennysonian echoes, its meaning to the Brownings, should have impressed her mother. But all Mrs. Knighton said was, "Are you sure? You've seen no one to compare him with."

If Isabel could have gone back to London, Harold's image might have been effaced. But it was out of the question. Marriage was the only valid excuse for leaving her mother, and stay with her she could not. Already Mrs. Knighton's dominance was beginning to cast its shadow; beside her Isabel felt like a dwarf, a highly-coloured dwarf. If she gave Harold up. . . .

So they were married a few months later. The war was just over but Harold was still in khaki; he never looked so nearly a gentleman again when he had put it off. Not being able to find a house they lived at first with his mother, an easy-going, comfortable woman with a slight provincial accent. When Mrs. Knighton sailed into the room it was as if they were receiving royalty: for the first time Isabel knew what social inferiority felt like. She hoped that Harold had not guessed how lowly a position he held in Mrs. Knighton's esteem, but he had; in any case he was too conventional to like a mother-in-law. Isabel quite liked hers, but she missed certain things and minded others. She missed culture and the respect for culture; and she minded the mixture of shrewdness and placidity which, in one way, made her mother-in-law so easy to get on with. The quiet, bright eye whose vision was bounded by the main chance offended her innate idealism. Here, in her mother-in-law's house, she was up for the first time against people who had no ideals, as she understood them, and only one idea: to make more money. True, his parents had not wished Harold to go into the family business, but that was because his gift for figures destined him to be a chartered accountant—not because he would thereby pass into a higher sphere of usefulness, or cultivate in himself civilized emotions or romantic aspirations—still less help other people to. Help other people to: that was what her friends had done in London. Matchmakers one and all, though not in the accepted sense, they smoothed the way of experience for each other and found short cuts to seemingly distant beds.

She couldn't imagine Harold doing this. Had he inherited his mother's eye—her placid, watchful, calculating eye?

"I'll change him when we get away," she thought.

The opportunity soon came. Harold was offered a post in a firm in Downhaven. Downhaven was suffering from the housing shortage but they found a villa in the neighbouring town of Marshport and it was there, two months after their arrival, that Jeremy was born. Isabel did not take to Marshport. Its associations with the Eastwood outlook (Harold's mother had chosen the house for them and, indeed, paid for it) blinded her to its marked individuality: she thought of it in terms of the villadom in which they lived, the red-roofed housing estate perched above the town. But she decided not to mind about it, and by the time Janice was born she had accepted it and the kind of life— domestic, cultural and social—that went with it, just as she had accepted the names of Jeremy and Janice for the children. She would have liked other names better, and perhaps have liked the children better with other names. These were her mother-in-law's choice, and Harold had backed her up. He had a way of imposing himself: it was he who was changing Isabel, not she him.

6

THE Eastwoods' garden was divided from its neighbours by a split wood fence, high enough to suggest privacy but not so high as to seem unfriendly. It had a path down one side, bordering the lawn on which grew, up against the opposite fence, an aspen poplar and a silver birch. When she first came Isabel had taken a great interest in the garden; she had planted a pampas clump at the far end of the lawn and devised, beyond it, a small rock garden through which a grass path, edged with thrift, wound its way, suggesting a romantic destination but ending all too soon in the boundary fence. But with the coming of the children she had lost her interest in the garden and it had become for her, as a garden so easily does, a symbol of reproach and, when she looked at other people's gardens, a fertile source of envy. She had come to think of it as the children's playground; it was where they would almost certainly be, should she look for them—which was seldom necessary, for their voices carried.

Sometimes she caught Jeremy looking at Janice with what she thought was too intent a gaze. Eight years old, he was much taller than Janice who was six. Did he ever tweak her arm or pinch her? In some ways, in the most obvious ways, she was more advanced than Jeremy, though he was far better at his lessons. Janice did not seem to be afraid of him, far from it; she used him remorselessly as a mirror to show off in; she practised attitudes, gestures and facial expressions in front of him. Imperiously she would call him to come and look at her. The way she would preen herself in front of strangers, and ogle them with languishing looks, was a source of much mortification to Isabel. At this rate what would her daughter come to? Jeremy, on the other hand, was shy and reserved in company; he would look at visitors through the corners of his dark eyes, as if he was longing to escape—as in fact he was. Isabel did not regard her children as a social asset; she wanted other people to see them through her eyes, but she knew that they were at their worst in company—Jeremy at his most standoffish, Janice at her most oncoming. That was one reason why she had tried to keep them out of Alec's way—with Jeremy an easy task, but not with Janice, who, she was afterwards horrified to learn, had behaved in the most improper manner. She had kept opening the door of the lounge when Alec was trying to write, and peeping in; but when he spoke to her all she would say was, "Mummy says I'm not to bother you," and shut the door with a great parade of quietness, only to repeat the performance a few minutes later. This she learned not from Alec but from Janice herself, who seemed to think she had acted with exemplary restraint. She had not come in while Isabel was talking to Alec "because," she said, and her tone and her look made Isabel turn red—"I knew *you* were there."

Had she really wanted Alec to think that she was childless? If so, it was the first time she had ever wanted to give anyone that impression. But she had been slightly mad at the time, or, at any rate, very foolish in her feelings. Thank goodness, it hadn't gone any further; she felt sure that no one would have divined from her behaviour the fluttering in her heart.

"Janice, go back!"

The cry came through the open window of the lounge, where Isabel was laying the table for lunch. But it wasn't so much a cry as an order; an order delivered in a voice that was at once indulgent but firm, bored but implacable.

Isabel looked out of the window. The children were back from school, and were playing the game which was their latest craze—the ladder game, they called it, but it had other names, "Grandmother's Steps", and "Crossing the Farmer's Field". Harold was not a great golfer, but he played golf for exercise and because it was the thing to do; and for putting-practice he had marked out a ladder in white chalk which went nearly half the length of the little lawn. Harold's father had had such a ladder on his lawn, and Harold conscientiously tried to put in a quarter of an hour a day improving his putting, starting at the lowest rung and going back to the highest. He kept a record of his scores, and so far the best for the ten rungs was 22.

But the children did not use the ladder for putting. They had a game of their own. Isabel never knew exactly what its rules were: but it certainly had rules. It began with the ritual tossing of the penny which Jeremy was never without. The order of precedence thus established, each child would take up a position, one in front of the other. The one in front, the farmer, stood with closed eyes; the one behind, the trespasser, tiptoed forwards, to traverse the ladder which stood for the farmer's field. But if the farmer looked back, as he might at any moment, and saw the trespasser on the move, the latter had to go back to where he started. Jeremy and Janice had agreed upon a bye-law, suggested by the ladder, that once the trespasser had reached a rung, he need not go back beyond that rung. This made the game go quicker. The slow part was getting across the long strip of grass before the first rung, which sometimes took a quarter of an hour.

To-day Jeremy was the farmer; Janice the trespasser. though they often reversed their roles, at the dictates of the penny, they both really preferred it this way; Jeremy enjoyed keeping order, and Janice enjoyed evading it. She had not reached the first rung yet. She wanted to win quite as much as Jeremy did, but she wanted it in a different way. He played the game for its own sake; he measured himself against it, so to speak. She played it for the exercise it gave her will-power, her instinct to impose herself on life, and Jeremy—of which, thought Isabel, she has all too much.

If I had behaved as she did! It was a blessing that Alec lived so far away; her thoughts, as if they had a physical journey to perform, sometimes came back to her without reaching him. Childishly consulting Bradshaw, Jeremy's favourite book, she had looked up the stages along the route: Reading, Didcot, Swindon, Bath and Bristol: all these she had seen with the naked eye and they meant something to her. Beyond lay the Severn Tunnel, and Newport, Cardiff, Swansea, Haverfordwest: they were but names to her. Beyond the Severn she could not go, she must not go. There it was unsafe. Wales was unsafe. Reading

(36 miles) was quite safe. Didcot (50 miles) was nearly safe, and so on till you came to Bristol (117 miles), the halfway house. Bristol was not at all safe, but at any rate she could always take the next train back.

In her itineraries, she didn't reckon the distance between Marshport and London; wishful-thinkingly, she started from London: London was the first rung, so to speak.

London to Haverfordwest: 251 miles. Haverfordwest was sixteen miles from St. Milo's. That made 267 miles in all. The really fast trains went right through to Newport: they bypassed the intermediate towns, or didn't stop at them. But they were altogether too headlong for Isabel to take: she must have places where she could get off.

"Janice, go back!"

Isabel looked out of the window. Janice hadn't reached the first rung yet. She was back at the starting-place looking rather sulky. Jeremy stood with straddled legs, like the Colossus. He was really very tall for his age. Sometimes, instead of looking round, he would bend down and peep at Janice through his legs. Janice maintained this wasn't fair: she couldn't do it because her skirt got in the way: she couldn't see through it, she pointed out. Jeremy argued, in effect, that girls suffered from certain disadvantages and this was one: it was just too bad. In general, Isabel's sympathies were with Jeremy, but in this particular instance, she was wholeheartedly on the side of Janice.

What a long face, in more than one sense, Jeremy had, and what serious, impenetrable eyes! Isabel couldn't guess what went on behind them. Sometimes he looked like an idol waiting for a sacrifice. She knew much better what Janice was feeling, though she never knew what Janice was going to say.

Harold occasionally went to Bath on business: indeed, that was how he had first met Alec. Why shouldn't she go with him? Bath was a most interesting city, the most beautiful city in England, some people said, and she had never seen it. Bristol was interesting, too: Clifton, the Suspension Bridge, the Avon Gorge, St. Mary Redcliffe. Hitherto she had always pined to go abroad: now she felt that a town in the West of England would do just as well.

The next time Harold went to Bath she would ask if she could go with him——

"Janice, go back!"

But, of course, there were the children to consider. Children were a great tie. Perhaps her mother would come and look after them, or Harold's mother would. Both these arrangements had been tried, but each had its disadvantages. During her mother's visit Harold was apt to be restive: during his mother's visit Isabel herself, though theoretically she was forewarned against every peril of the mother-in-law dilemma—from its laughable aspect in the music-hall to its tragic *dénouement* in the divorce court—was also inclined to be on edge. Of course neither parent could be asked to stay just for the period of their absence; both before and after the visit the two generations must overlap. Besides, Isabel wanted to see her mother, and Harold wanted to see his. A better plan would be to take the children with them for a holiday—their summer holiday. Her thoughts jumped. Why not a holiday in Wales? A holiday at Tenby, for instance? She had always heard that Tenby (249½ miles) was a nice place. At Tenby there would be boating and bathing, and expedit⁷ons inland and along the coast, that beautiful coast; at Tenby they could feel they were abroad, for they would hear a foreign language spoken round them, at least she supposed they would. And in the evenings, the long evenings, there would be Celtic twilight, and Celtic mystery. Why not cancel the rooms they had taken and go to Tenby instead—not some August, but this very August?

"Janice, go back!"

Poor Janice, it was rather frustrating for her. Wondering whether she ought not to break up the game—for after all it was only a game—Isabel looked out of the window. Janice had returned to the back line: her little feet were conscientiously toeing it. They were also wriggling, as was her lower lip. Poor child—how good she was, how patient. She couldn't be enjoying herself. What did she get out of it. Why did she put up with so much vexation of spirit? Was it just to stand well with Jeremy, whom, though often defying, she really adored? Isabel suddenly felt critical of him, standing there so smugly with his long arms hanging down. Why couldn't he make it easier for Janice—pretend, just for once, that he hadn't seen her move?

Perhaps it would be best to give up Tenby, anyhow for this year. It would all need so much rearranging and perhaps they would have to pay for the rooms they had taken, a proportion of the cost, at any rate. A wave of self-conscious virtue swept over Isabel, as she made this renunciation; and, meeting it, a contrary wave of disappointment. So often her day-dreaming ended in this—the smacking, painful collision of two waves. From under their impact her thoughts crawled out, bruised. Wales was ruled out, Bath was ruled out, even Reading was suspect. She was chained to her place. But other people were not; other people could come and go as they pleased; people without home ties could take the longest journeys. A trip from Wales to London was nothing to them; and no one asked them the why and the wherefore—and if they did, business, the sacred word, business, covered it all. On business! Business was a perfect alibi.

If only business would bring Alec again to Marshport! But how could it? All his business with Harold could be done, no doubt, quite well by letter; and Harold would much rather it was done that way. Alec could plead business as a pretext for another visit, but why should he? Once would have been more than enough.

True, he had asked them both to stay with him in Wales, when he had "reorganized his household". A visit to a friend in Wales would be quite different from a holiday in Wales; it would only be a matter of accepting an invitation which everyone who knew them would agree should be accepted. In such circumstances a mother-in-law's visit would be heaven-sent; they would both jump at it. To stay with Alec in Wales! But, of course, he didn't mean it: that household of his would never be reorganized. No, the only hope was that something—business—would bring him to Marshport.

"Janice, go back!"

Suddenly, there was the most awful outcry; screaming, sobbing, stamping of feet. Isabel put down the last plate—

she had finished laying the table—and hurried into the garden.

Janice was as Isabel had expected to find her: a whirl of arms and legs and tossing hair, elbows and knees working like piston-rods, screwed-up eyes darting gleams of blue fire. Jeremy, motionless, was looking down at her, whether to comfort her, or threaten her, Isabel could not tell.

"Oh, children, children!" she cried, "do be quiet! Your father'll be home in a minute, and he won't be at all pleased with you."

No sooner had she said the words than she was sorry; she had made a vow never to use the children's father as an ogre to frighten them with. Goodness knew what might come of that. Besides it was unfair to Harold, who though not usually a frolicsome was by no means a heavy father.

"Now what is it all about?" she added persuasively. "Who has been doing what?"

Silence greeted this question. Then Janice's convulsive movements began to abate, and Jeremy said:

"She doesn't keep the rules." His voice was indulgent but his eyes were hard.

"What rules?" Isabel asked.

"Well, you see, I saw her move and told her to go back and she wouldn't."

"But you told her to go back so many times!" protested Isabel.

"But I saw her move so many times——" said Jeremy. "I couldn't pretend I hadn't, could I?"

"Well, perhaps you could have looked the other way just once," said Isabel. "After all, you're a boy and two years older than she is."

Jeremy looked horrified.

"But that wouldn't be *fair*!" he said. His mother's heart sank at the word "fair", for she knew no way of getting round it. "Besides," he added, "Janice wouldn't like me to, would you, Janice?"

"What?" hiccupped Janice, between subsiding sobs.

"Pretend I hadn't seen you move when I really had."

Janice gave several deep sniffs and to gain time she put her thumb in her mouth and looked archly from her mother to her brother. "It would be cheating, wouldn't it?" she said. "Janice doesn't want anyone to cheat, unless——"

"Unless what?" asked Isabel.

"Unless——" said Janice, and then changed her mind. "Unless, unless," she chanted, and began to dance. "I shan't tell you," she said, teasingly.

"It's no good talking to her when she's like that," said Jeremy. "She won't answer."

Through the open French windows of the lounge they heard the click of the front door.

"There's Daddy," said Isabel. "Now let's all put on our brightest faces."

But Janice did not hear. She was still dancing about, singing "Unless . . . unless . . . unless . . ." though she had quite forgotten, if she had ever known, the special conditions in which cheating was allowable.

7

THE meal followed its accustomed rhythm, except that Harold, who was never a great talker, was more silent than usual, and the children were more subdued. Occasionally Janice caught her breath, and looked round furtively, half hoping, half fearing, that her father had noticed it. Both children ate with conscientious attention to their table manners, though neither of them had conquered the habit of sticking out their elbows. Sometimes, between mouthfuls, their eyes would assume a dreamy, faraway expression. Janice, who was the most social of the four, and didn't like sitting in silence, suddenly observed:

"Is there a surprise to-day?"

"No, I'm afraid there isn't," Isabel said.

A surprise, in this context, meant something unexpected for the sweet course.

"We haven't had a surprise," said Janice, her upturned blue eyes sweeping the cornice in the effort of recollection, "since . . . since . . ." a sudden gasp, a backfire from the scene with Jeremy, interrupted her. "Since Mr. Goodrich was here," she concluded.

"No, I don't believe we have," said Isabel. She felt contrite. Why had she let weeks pass without giving the children a surprise? Because her thoughts were fixed on something else, she supposed.

"Shall we have to wait for a surprise until Mr. Goodrich comes again?" asked Janice.

"I'll make you a surprise to-morrow," said Isabel quickly. Janice's eyes lit up and a gleam appeared in Jeremy's; then Janice said:

"When is Mr. Goodrich coming again?"

Isabel felt herself reddening. That highly-coloured woman! Without looking at her husband, she said:

"I don't suppose he is coming again. We haven't asked him."

"Oh, but I asked him," Janice said.

"You asked him?"

"Yes, you see I was showing him my dolly."

"You showed him your dolly?" repeated Isabel, as if this was a most heinous thing to do. She added in a lighter tone: "Which dolly?"

"Pamelia," said Janice. "I don't love her the best but she's the prettiest. I said, 'Don't you think she's pretty?' And he said, 'Yes, I've fallen in love with her'."

"Oh, Janice, I told you not to bother him. And it's not Pamelia, it's Pamela."

"I know, but I like Pamelia better. And I wasn't bothering him, I was only keeping him from being lonely. And I said, 'If you've fallen in love with her, you must come back and see her again.' And he said he would like to."

Isabel was by now sufficiently recovered to exchange glances with her husband.

"That reminds me," he said, "there's something I want to say to you. *Mais pas devant les enfants*," he went on heavily.

"That means not in front of us, doesn't it, Jeremy?" said Janice. And when Jeremy refused to be drawn, she added accusingly, "You told me it did."

"Jeremy is coming on famously with his French," said Harold, spiking Janice's guns.

"Well, now you can go," said Isabel, and at the words both children jumped up as if there had been an explosive under them. "But don't start playing that silly game again."

Both their faces fell.

"Oh, but we like it," protested Janice. "Don't we, Jeremy?"

"She likes it and I quite like it," remarked Jeremy, with more than a hint of masculine patronage.

"Well, all I can say is," said Isabel, "that you didn't seem to be liking it before lunch."

"Oh, but we love it, don't we, Jeremy?" cried Janice, beginning to dance about. "It's our favourite, favourite, *favourite* game."

"Be quick, then, or you'll be late for school."

"Shall I give you a hand with the washing-up?" said Harold.

"Well, that would be kind," said Isabel, astonished, "but don't you want to get back to the office? I can manage quite well with this new steel sink." She felt she was contributing to a strip advertisement.

"I'm not in any special hurry, and there's something——"

"Oh yes, I remember."

Through the kitchen window she heard, far away, a faint cry:

"Jeremy, go back!"

But how different the order for retreat sounded when Janice gave it! Much more like an invitation to come on, thought Isabel.

"It's about this chap Goodrich," Harold said, taking a plate from Isabel and drying it.

"Oh yes, Alec," said Isabel, in a neutral voice. All the same, she enjoyed saying his Christian name.

"Well, Alec if you like. The fact is, he wants me to do something for him."

Isabel watched the white plates they used for everyday lying in the silvery grey steel sink, and swished the water round them. How dirty they were, how dirty the water was.

"But you're always doing something for him," she said.

"Yes, but this is different."

"Different in what way?" Isabel asked. And when Harold didn't answer she repeated the question.

"Oh, altogether different," said Harold shortly. He began to feel an overwhelming repugnance for the task of telling Isabel about Alec's proposition. An hour or two ago it had seemed so simple; now he couldn't imagine himself doing it. Casting about in his mind for a way out he said:

"Oh, it's about a market-garden. He wants to turn his kitchen-garden into a market-garden to get off income tax. Somebody put him up to it and he wants me to arrange it for him."

"And will you?" Isabel asked, surprised at being consulted by Harold in a business matter.

"Oh, I suppose I shall have to, but I don't really think it's a good thing. So many people nowadays are doing it, it's becoming a ramp. That's the worst of unbusinesslike fellows like Alec. First of all he doesn't know anything about the reliefs and so on he's entitled to, and then he rushes to the other extreme and tries to get what he's not entitled to. At least, he is entitled to it, but it's rather barefaced."

"It sounds so," said Isabel meditatively. "But, of course——"

"You mean he's entitled to anything he can get," said Harold. Applied to another context, the thought struck him unpleasantly. "I admit he's a difficult man to say 'no' to."

"Are you going to say no?" asked Isabel.

Harold hesitated. He had a curious feeling that in talking about this matter he was really thinking about the other, too.

"I don't see how I can get out of it," he said. "It's perfectly legal. Only, of course, I don't know the local set-up, or what sort of a chappie the Inspector is. It's an out-of-the-world place. Somebody on the spot would really handle it better."

"Only in that case you wouldn't——"

"Yes, that's it. I shouldn't get the rake-off. Besides, it's better that his affairs should be handled by one man. It makes confusion if someone else butts in. And also——" He stopped.

"Yes?" said Isabel.

"Well, he's been very decent to me, finding me work and so on."

"You like him, don't you?" Isabel asked.

Harold, who was drying a fork, stuck a prong that had worn thin into the fleshy part of his hand. "Damn!" he exclaimed. Isabel looked round in surprise. She had never heard him swear before.

"Sorry," he said. "What you were saying . . . We're all friends in business, you know, up to a point . . . Put each other in the way of a good thing, if we get the chance. Goodrich . . . Alec's certainly done that for me. He's a queer fish, but I suppose I like him. I hadn't really thought. But I wish he hadn't . . ."

"Have you been worrying about it?" Isabel asked.

"Well, yes, in a way. I——"

Isabel looked at him. His face was more preoccupied than

63

she had ever seen it. But business was his element; she had never known him anxious about it, except when they were short of money, which as far as she knew they were not, now. Could he have been *speculating*? The dread word smote her. Or did he suspect——?

With a flash of insight, she said:

"Or were you worrying about something else?"

Harold drew a breath and said:

"Well, as a matter of fact, my sweet, I was."

"My sweet"—an army officer of his acquaintance had used this term of endearment to his wife, and Harold, feeling its origin to be irreproachable, sometimes used it to Isabel.

"We've finished now," said Isabel. "What a wonderful washer-up you are, Harold! Everything's spotless." The strip cartoon again! "We'll go into the lounge," she added. "Just let me take this apron off."

"So that's the position," Harold said at length. "I didn't mean to bother you about it. . . ." He paused, and said rather heavily, "I thought you might have a slant on it. The woman's angle, and all that. And you seem to know more about chaps of Alec's sort than I do."

"I suppose all men are much the same," began Isabel, trying to control her thoughts, which were whirling about in ever-changing patterns. She had learned more about Harold in the last ten minutes than ten years of married life had taught her. She was learning a good deal about herself, too, but its nature was much less clear to her, nor did she want it to be clear.

"I suppose all men are much the same," she repeated, parrot-like, to gain time.

Harold frowned. All the way through the recital he had felt as uncomfortable as if it had been he, not Alec, who had made the infamous proposal. His wife's reception of it hadn't given him much clue to her feelings, except that she was not as shocked as he expected, and almost hoped, she would be. In a way he was thankful to be relieved of the momentary superficial embarrassment that comes of telling an improper story to the wrong person; but this,

Isabel's first comment, struck him as being too judicial.

"I don't know about that," he said. "It's not the kind of thing we're used to. It's a cad's trick, isn't it, to put it mildly."

"Oh, Harold," Isabel said, "aren't you being a little priggish?"

As she spoke she blushed once more for the *gaffe* she had made so many years ago.

"Priggish?" said Harold. "What on earth do you mean?"

"Well, isn't it rather priggish to . . . say that someone is a cad, because he happens to have fallen in love, and wants to. . . ." Her voice trailed away. Impossible to make Harold understand what she meant. She tried to substitute a moral for a human judgment. "He oughtn't to have done it, of course," she said.

"I should think not. I mean, whom does he take me for, wanting me to do his dirty work? For that matter, I don't really know what he does want me to do."

Isabel was silent, while her thoughts sought out his, trying to make out their shape and feeling. In a way she felt nearer to him than she had ever felt, and this was a bar to forming an objective, independent judgment. She must say what he wanted her to say; and yet——

"I suppose he wants you to make a . . . preliminary reconnaissance," she said at last.

"Yes, but what does that mean? Does he expect me to go round to old Hitchcock at the Green Dragon and ask him whether his barmaid is . . . well. . . . Or does he expect me to ask the girl herself?"

"There are other ways of finding out, I dare say," Isabel said.

"How?"

"Well, this is a small place. There aren't many Austrian or German girls in it, certainly not who are barmaids. You could say to someone, 'That's a nice-looking girl behind the bar at the Green Dragon'—and I suppose men do say that kind of thing to each other——"

"And then?"

"And he might say 'I hear she's this or that'. Things do get round, you know."

"You're not seriously proposing I should do this?" Harold said.

"Of course not, darling. You asked me, and I was thinking how it *might* be done. Or one could ask someone in another walk of life. One could ask Mrs. Perfect, for instance."

"Our daily woman?"

"Well, she might know."

Harold thought a minute.

"But she wouldn't say—no one would say—well, the kind of thing that Alec wants to know."

"My dear, it's the *first* thing people would say about a barmaid." Isabel spoke rather breathlessly; she had never made a remark of this nature in her life before, and it shocked and yet excited her to say it.

"You mean because all barmaids are——" began Harold.

"No, because they are not," said Isabel. "Think, Harold: how could they be, living the kind of life they do? Everyone would get to hear of it, and they wouldn't keep their jobs a moment. Besides, I've done some welfare work and I know that as a class they have a name for being chaste. That's why I said it would be the first thing people said about them —if they weren't, I mean. Everyone would be on the lookout. They have to be like Caesar's wife."

Harold didn't know about Caesar's wife, but he looked rather dubiously at his own. "It isn't what I was brought up to think," he said, as if his upbringing had had a special section dealing with the morals of barmaids; "but you may be right. But where does it get us? Shall I write to Alec, and tell him that he's barking up the wrong tree?"

Isabel thought for a moment and found she didn't want Harold to say that. But what *did* she want him to say?

"How did he put it in his letter?" she asked. "Can you remember the exact words?"

Harold did remember but he wasn't going to tell Isabel that Alec had asked him to "get hold of Irma". He said evasively: "It came at the end of his letter with something about having some more people to send me but not knowing if I wanted them."

"Do you want them?" Isabel asked.

"Well, I never want to turn work away," said Harold.

66

They looked at each other and then looked away.

"Shall I open the window?" said Harold suddenly. "It's getting a bit stuffy in here."

"Yes, please," said Isabel. "I ought to have done it this morning."

A breath of fresh, sun-laden air came into the room.

"He's a rich man, isn't he, Alec, I mean?" She knew, of course, that Alec was rich but for some reason she liked to hear the fact confirmed.

"Oh yes, very comfortably off." Harold remembered with irritation the fluctuating dividend from the Cotopaxi Infiltration Trust, and had a vision of the electric drills boring into that pure white cone. "I don't know the exact figures," he added carelessly. "Why do you ask?"

"Because," said Isabel, "he didn't strike me as a happy man. In fact, he told me he wasn't."

"How can he be unhappy when he isn't married?" Harold asked.

"Darling, you aren't very complimentary. Perhaps that's why he's unhappy."

"He oughtn't to be," said Harold. "He's got everything he wants."

"We don't know that," said Isabel. "We do know that he isn't married—at least we nearly know. Perhaps his home life——"

"But what has that to do with what I'm going to tell him?"

"Well, this," said Isabel. "A lot of literary people, and artists generally, lead what we should call irregular lives. It isn't their fault. It's the way they're made. Think of Dumas, think of Stendhal."

Not knowing about Dumas or Stendhal Harold shook his head.

"Well, they did. I don't know much about them, but I suppose they made some woman happy."

"Women, you mean."

"Women, then. What I mean is, it's possible that Alec might make this barmaid happy. He's got the means, and if he has the wish——"

"Well?"

67

"Perhaps we oughtn't to stand in the way. Many a woman would jump at it."

As she spoke she felt she was being the mouthpiece for words more important than herself. Were they just clap-trap? Were they a cry of rebellion against Harold's Philistine outlook, which she had acquiesced in for ten years? Or did they proceed from some deeper need of her being? She only knew that they seemed sincere.

"It's one thing not to stand in the way," Harold said. "It's another thing . . . to . . ." He stopped. "There's a word for it, but I can't remember it."

"Nor can I," said Isabel. "But why should we be afraid of a word? Think, Harold: she would go about with him, travel and so on, wear pretty clothes, meet interesting people, be protected and loved. He would open her eyes to new horizons, he would enrich her life. How do we know she wouldn't . . . choose that, rather than moulder away in this dull little place with nothing to look forward to, serving a lot of half-tipsy, red-faced men with drinks?"

"Are you suggesting I should do what Alec asks?" said Harold, looking fierce.

"Oh no, I was only putting the other side of the question."

"Let's be practical," said Harold. "I must be getting back to the office in a minute. Suppose I did find out something about her, though goodness knows how I am to——"

"Perhaps I could," Isabel said. "It might be easier for me."

Harold wrinkled his nose. "Well, suppose you did. And I told Goodrich that it was . . . well . . . O.K. What would be the next step?"

"He would want to see her, I imagine."

"And would she then be shipped off to St. Milo's, like a white slave?"

Isabel smiled.

"It wouldn't be done like that, of course. You're so un-civilized, Harold! Alec would come down here——"

"Come down here?"

"He'd have to, wouldn't he?"

"As long as he doesn't stop with us!"

Isabel ignored the interruption. "And then some arrange-ment would be made, very quietly, and discreetly, and then

68

she would go off and join him. There needn't be any scandal. She's free to travel about, I imagine, although she is a foreigner."

"But supposing he doesn't want her to join him, as you call it," argued Harold. "Supposing he wants to keep her here, in what I believe is called a love-nest, for occasional visits? It isn't likely he would want her for keeps."

"We don't know that," said Isabel. "A *coup de foudre* of that sort sometimes lasts. And if he did come down here a time or two——"

"It wouldn't be very convenient for us," said Harold.

"Oh, I don't know. He could stay at the Royal. Novelists don't have to explain what brings them to a place. He could have come here for copy."

"H'm," said Harold. "Do I understand, Isabel, that you're in favour of this . . . this arrangement?"

Isabel had to pluck her thoughts back from a day-dream in which Alec, bareheaded, was sauntering to and fro between their house and the Royal Hotel.

"I'm neither for it nor against it," she said. "I think that we could manage it, that's all."

"We?"

"Well, you or I."

Harold glanced at his watch. "Good Lord, I must be off," he said. "We can talk about this later. There's no desperate hurry, is there?"

As he shut the door the word Isabel had been searching for swam into her mind. "Procure," she said to herself. "Procure."

But Harold was mistaken in saying there was no hurry. A few days later another letter came from Alec asking him if he possibly could come down to St. Milo's. "I want to get this business of the market-garden settled," he wrote, "and everyone tells me that only you can get round the Inspector. It's the personal touch that counts. Do you think, by any chance, we could make the claim restrospective? I wish I could ask Mrs. Eastwood—Isabel, as you told me I might call her—to come too, but I can't until I have a proper staff. I don't so much mind asking you to pig it! Do try to come next week-end—all expenses paid, of course. Perhaps you'll have some news for me by then. Candidates for your financial wizard-work, your Midas touch, are queueing up and falling over each other, but I tell them, 'He's too busy! Besides, I like to have him to myself!' "

I shall have to do something about it, Harold thought.

★ 8 ★

By the time he boarded the train at Paddington Harold had done something. He had plenty of time before him—nearly six hours—to turn it over in his mind. But he never got further than a certain point; beyond, emotion waylaid his thoughts and would not let them proceed.

Without any definite plan in his head he had gone to the bar of the Green Dragon. He had gone without consulting Isabel, nor afterwards did he tell her he had gone. It was about half-past six on a cool summer evening, but the bar was thick with smoke; it took him a moment or two to see how the land lay.

The room was about half full. Some of the men, who were sitting at tables, looked up as Harold came in; one or two, who were perched on stools with their elbows spread out on the bar, turned round; when this small ripple of curiosity had subsided, no notice was taken of him. He recognized no one. He meant to ask for a pint of beer, but changed his mind and asked for half a pint: he could then repeat his order, and with it his inspection of the barmaid.

She had the softest face imaginable, so soft that he seemed to see it through a mist—the mist of her own diffidence, like a warm air that has clouded a window pane. She raised her eyes to his but dropped them without really looking at him: she tucked her chin in a little, it was her eyelids that he saw. It wasn't surprising that the other men took this for a challenge; the teasing that his order had interrupted began again. The young fellows were friends, apparently; they took up each other's jokes and nudged each other. They had good heads of hair which admirably set off the brilliantine. Harold had meant to take his drink to a table and consume it there; it was what he had always done, it was the thing to do: a rule. Not doing so, seating himself instead on the vacant stool, he felt that he was being rather daring.

The man sitting next to Harold said:

"Come now, don't you like any of us?"

The barmaid answered with difficulty, choosing her words:

"I like you all very much."

Spoken with her foreign accent, the words sounded very polite and rather funny.

The three men laughed and the first speaker said:

"She likes us very much but she won't come out with any of us. Won't you come out with Bert?" he asked her. "He's the best-looking of us."

She smiled her downward-pointing smile and shook her head.

"Or with Ernie here? He earns good money, he does, that's why his name's Ernie. He picks up a packet, Ernie does. You wouldn't go far wrong with him."

Still she shook her head.

"Well, what about me?" the man went on, turning to Harold and giving him a look. "What's the matter with me? I may not be an oil-painting, but I'm all right in my way. I'd give you a good time, wouldn't I, Bert? Wouldn't I, Ernie?"

But Ernie didn't agree.

"Don't listen to him, Irma," he said. "You couldn't trust him. Take my advice. You'd be safe with Bert or me."

The girl said nothing. She hadn't learned how to give a rebuff. Perhaps she could have done it in her own language, but Harold was doubtful; she seemed so intent on pleasing. Perhaps her job depended on it; perhaps she had been told she mustn't offend customers.

The third man said:

"Well, if you're too proud to go out with any of us, perhaps you'll go out with this gentleman here." He gave Harold a nudge and a wink, and Harold realized, for the first time, that he was more than a little tipsy. Too embarrassed to speak, and afraid of starting a scene, Harold buried his face in his glass.

"What do you say, Irma?" the man persisted. "He's a posh-looking chap: he'd do you well."

The girl seemed to shrink into her clothes: suddenly

they seemed too big for her. A strained look came into her eyes, and she said, her foreign accent more pronounced than ever:

"But he hasn't asked me."

Keeping at bay all other thoughts and feelings except that he must succour a lady in distress, Harold muttered, without looking at the girl:

"Well, will you?"

"Please, yes," she said.

Immediately there was a chorus of protest from the three young men. They had never heard of such a thing; they didn't know what girls were coming to; here they were, regular customers, who had always been as nice to her as they knew how, and she had turned them all down in favour of this—no offence intended—this comparative stranger. "What has he got that we haven't got?" demanded, plaintively, the drunkest of the three. "Perhaps he's a lord in disguise." Irma was a snob, that's what she was, we ordinary fellows weren't good enough for her. Well, there were other pubs besides this one where barmaids weren't so upstage and standoffish, and——

At this point, hearing the raised voices, the landlord appeared from the inner depths. "Gentlemen, gentlemen," he said, with a bland but quelling smile. He had a shiny red face and a hooked nose, with red-veined nostrils tightly tucked into his cheeks. He took in everything at once: the look he gave the naughty trio was quite different from the look he gave to Harold. The one implied a rebuke, the other an apology. A sheepish grin spread over the three faces, and the talkative one said, jauntily, but with a marked slurring of his consonants:

"Question of who'sh buying the drinks. We were arguing the tosh."

"Well, as long as one of you gentlemen pays," said the landlord, giving the word "gentlemen" the slightly ironic inflection he had given it before.

But there was no one to take the money. Availing herself of the diversion caused by the landlord's appearance, the barmaid had slipped away.

"You can pay me if you like," the landlord said.

Between them the three men settled their score, slid off their stools, and with a twinkling, a scissor-scape of narrow trousers, vanished almost as unobtrusively as the barmaid had. These last stages of the episode had had an hypnotic effect on Harold; perhaps the heavy stale smell of the bar and the wreaths of smoke, and people doing unexpected things before he had quite caught on, had something to do with it. He remained on his stool with his mouth open, gazing at the landlord whose countenance had now relaxed.

"Young lady's rather easily upset," the landlord said. "Emotional type—foreign, you know. When the chaps rib her she doesn't quite know how to act up. Far from home and all that. But she's a good girl."

"A good girl?" repeated Harold mechanically.

The landlord smiled.

"I don't mean her private life. She's got a boy, of course, a big lumbering German farm-hand: I wish her luck with him. No, I meant she's a good willing worker, which is more than you can say for most of them."

"How long has she been here?" Harold asked.

"Matter of a few months, no more. She isn't very quick at picking up the language. She keeps on saying 'please', or did, until some of the fellows teased her out of it. Now she sometimes says 'yes', instead. She doesn't know how to say 'no', or at any rate she won't, she finds a way round it."

"So she says 'yes' when she doesn't understand what's being said to her?"

"Well, sometimes. Rather a dangerous habit, I should say."

"And is she engaged to this German fellow?" Harold asked.

"I shouldn't know. I expect she has an understanding with him. She doesn't wear a ring. He'd lead her a dog's life, in my opinion. She's a good girl, we all like her. But she's too sensitive. She doesn't like to see a cat catching a mouse. She's gone out now to have a cry, but she'll soon get over it. Now what can I get you, sir?"

"Another half-pint of bitter, please," said Harold.

With an air of authority, as if every jug and bottle in the

place existed to do his bidding, the landlord gave Harold his drink; and at the same moment some newcomers began to dispose themselves on the vacant stools.

"Where's Irma?" one of them asked.

"Just gone out to powder her nose, I think," the landlord said, looking round as though surprised by the barmaid's absence. "She'll be back in a jiffy."

But she wasn't. Harold lingered on and on, and even treated himself to a third half-pint; and it wasn't till the hand of the large round serviceable clock had measured out ten thirsty minutes that she came back red-eyed and without a smile for him.

How much of this should he tell Alec?

He found he didn't want to tell him any of it, he wanted to keep it entirely to himself. He would tell Isabel, of course, when he got home: but until then——

But why? Why be so secretive about it? Why, when he had done what he had been asked to do, not cash in on it? The situation hadn't altered; he still owed Alec a good turn for favours past, and the same good turn might bring future favours. It would have been understandable not to go to the Green Dragon, but having gone——

What, after all, had he to tell Alec that mattered so much, one way or another? The evidence he had gathered was inconclusive; and in so far as the three men were concerned it was negative from Alec's point of view. The girl was a good girl: the landlord had been positive on that point. He hadn't extended the scope of the adjective to include her private life, but still—— She had a "boy" who might or might not be her fiancé. According to the landlord's account he wasn't up to much, but he was her young man, and she had turned down the offers of three other young men, who were all agog to take her out. She hadn't said "no", apparently she was incapable of saying "no", the word didn't exist for her in English: but she had shaken her head in no uncertain fashion, and when they persisted, and lost patience with her, she had taken refuge in flight. She had gone to have a good cry, or to powder her nose, or whatever women did in such circumstances, and she had not come back. Was that the behaviour of a girl who was easy money? "No, Alec, I'm afraid it's no go—the landlord, old Hitchcock, said she was too sensitive—she was so sensitive she couldn't bear to see a cat catching a mouse. I'm afraid we shall have to rule her out. I did my very best for you, but—— Now as for those people you wrote to me about——"

How easy it would be to say all that, and Harold could say it, perhaps would say it, without any awkwardness or false shame, without the feeling that he was going beyond his brief or letting anybody down, without the feeling that he was robbing himself of something.

But she had said she would go out with him, with Harold. When he had asked her she had quaintly said, "Please, yes." "Yes, please" would have been much more commonplace, and have suggested the greedy acceptance of a gold-digger; but "Please, yes" — well, there was something touching about it, touchingly eager, and Harold responded to this quality more strongly than some men might have whose hearts were more easily touched.

What had she meant by "Please, yes"? Perhaps nothing very much; perhaps she had just used the phrase to get herself out of a hole, as something to say to cover her confusion. Hitchcock had told him that she had a way of saying "yes" instead of "please" when she didn't want people to know that she hadn't understood what they said. But she had understood what he said, he was certain of it. If she didn't know how to say "no" she knew how to shake her head; she had shaken it quite vigorously at the other men, but not at him. To him she had said, "Please, yes", and whatever that meant it didn't mean "no" in any definite sense.

Supposing he sought her out again and conditions were favourable and he asked her what she really did mean? And supposing she repeated "Please, yes" in quite an unmistakable fashion? Well, of course, he wouldn't do anything about it, he wouldn't take her out for the evening, but it would be nice to hear her say it.

Sometimes when he went over the episode in his mind, as he did, every few minutes, he gave it a different ending.

He hit the third man, who then rolled on to the floor, and there was a scene, and everyone in the bar applauded him, and Irma didn't disappear, she came to his side and perhaps clutched his arm to stop him from laying anyone else out. At the time his interference had seemed too bold; now it seemed too faint-hearted. Sometimes he began to wonder what, in fact, had happened. But to whatever conclusion his thoughts led him they ended in emotion, in a warmth of feeling that was blissful but also very, very private. To tell it would be to lose it; to tell the occasion of it—Irma's absurd "Please, yes"—would be to lose it, too.

He could not tell Alec. And yet, another part of his mind warned him, he ought to tell him, for it was the only piece of evidence he had that pointed in Alec's favour. For if Irma had promised to spend an evening with him, Harold, an undistinguished super-ordinary man (and thankful to be), how much more readily would she accept the overtures of a well-known novelist who was rich, who was experienced, and who spoke her language? She would not have to say "Please, yes" to him; she could say whatever she wanted to say in German, as openly as she liked, for no one in the bar would understand a word. If Irma had favours to give, he could not hope to compete with Alec for them.

To do Harold justice he wasn't thinking in terms of concrete favours—for himself, that is; for himself he thought only of an evening in Irma's company, an evening together, in which his knight-errantry in the bar would form a background, soft-hued with tenderness and protectiveness. Yes, that evening together which, only a few minutes ago, seemed unattainable, now seemed within easy reach.

For Alec, of course, the favours would be of another kind; and if the idea of this didn't shock Harold as it should have, it was because he connected it with business, and business, as everyone knows, has its own standards. In business Harold worshipped at the shrine of Gain, and didn't allow his emotions to deflect his worship. If a client enlarged on the iniquities of the income tax, and grew hot under the collar, as some did, Harold's eyes would stray towards the door. Business was no forum for the emotions; they were irrelevant, they obscured the issue. And it was the same with moral standards. A lie in business, it has been said, is not a lie. Harold would not have subscribed to this, but as a business man he was prepared to depart much further from the truth than he would have dreamed of doing in his private life. Business had to keep a sharp eye on the law, but to ethics it could turn a duller eye. Moral indignation was as much out of place in business as the emotions were: it was all a question of what would bring in money. You could easily be too smart in business: Alec was too smart: Smart-alec, Harold had called him. But that was because he was an amateur who didn't understand what business was, didn't distinguish between the rules which were rigid and absolute, and those which could be stretched or squeezed. Imagination, too, was out of place—imagination in the sense of wondering what might happen when a deal had been completed. One reason why Harold was not at ease with Alec was because he distrusted the quality of imagination; it was a rogue quality that jumped the queue. Its gains were faery gold, not really worked for: and again he thought with distaste of the little men with drills, burrowing into the great white cone of Cotopaxi. But by doing business with a man, however unbusinesslike he was, you drew him, willy-nilly, into the fold of business: you endowed him with its restrictions and its latitudes. The bargain Alec wanted Harold to make about Irma was a business arrangement—wasn't it? If and when it was concluded, Harold would not be required—indeed from the business standpoint it would be most unseemly—to think any more about it. Unseemly to think of Irma in Alec's arms, for that would be a consequence outside the scope of his and Harold's transaction.

The two currents of Harold's nature, the professional and the private, flowed side by side like the Rhône and the Saône, almost without mixing, though each was acutely aware of the other's existence. Eventually, as the long journey drew to its close, they arrived at a kind of compromise, a plan of action in which each was to make a concession to the other. Harold would tell Alec about the scene in the bar, thus discharging the obligation of friendship — business friendship — which he felt was tipping

78

against him, and qualifying perhaps for further rewards. But he would withhold the vital piece of evidence, Irma's promise to spend an evening with him, and so turn the key on that private sanctum of delight which ravished his thoughts whenever they approached it.

★ 9 ★

On Saturday morning the mist was already thick, though not as thick as it afterwards became. Harold resented the mist, as being unfair to any holiday-maker; it was a legitimate, indeed a necessary grievance. "We always seem to have bad weather at the week-ends," he grumbled; and when Alec said he hadn't noticed this phenomenon, Harold said, "Ah, you're too busy thinking up your plots."

Driving at Alec's side to the market-town where the Tax Inspector had his office, Harold tried to make mental notes about the landscape. Not for himself; for himself he was not interested in scenery; but Isabel had begged him insistently to tell her what it was like. But what could he say, except that the road was undulating—steepest gradient about one in ten, visibility limited to about a hundred yards; and that the mist was none the less dense for being full of sunshine and always on the point, it seemed, of lifting; and that every now and then a big and ugly rock stuck up, often seemingly right in their path, and sometimes actually over-hanging it.

Of the house he could say little for he had had no time to explore it. It was a great rambling barn of a place (so he phrased it to himself) and possessed some very fine rooms—in one of which they had sat before dinner, in another they had dined, and in another they had sat after dinner—discussing, well, what had they discussed? It was a thing that Isabel would want to know, and one that he was very bad at satisfying her about. Deep down, Harold felt that conversation for its own sake was something to be got over and forgotten. Conversation should either be a means to an end, a business deal, or taking soundings for one; it should be of a semi-facetious character, with a good-natured dig at so and so's little weakness, to get a rise out of him and start a laugh. If the company was mixed, it should be spiced with gallantry. Always one must try to come out on top, though not in an unpleasant way, and one must leave the impression that one had untapped stores of wit and knowingness.

His conversation with Irma belonged to another category; he did not think of it as conversation. Indeed, with her, conversation was a one-sided and incomplete affair—that was perhaps the secret of its attraction; and it was also a means to an end—but what end? And whose? Driving from the station, Alec hadn't seemed much interested in Harold's adventure. "Oh, so you did go?" he said carelessly. "Good man. I thought that I'd just mention it, as I was writing. I didn't mean you to take it very seriously, of course. But we writers have to get our copy somehow." "Oh, it was copy that you wanted?" Harold said. "I somehow thought——" "That I might be interested?" said Alec with a laugh. "Oh well, as a writer so I was, I was. Such a queer juxtaposition, that pretty shy little Austrian behind the bar in an English pub. Surrealist, almost. I wasn't thinking so much of her, of course, as of her situation—that's the way we writers tend to think of things. She might fit into the corner of a picture. But tell me what happened, though I'm sure nothing did."

A little nettled, Harold told the story, he warmed in telling it, and told more than he meant to; he couldn't tell what effect it was having on Alec, for Alec was looking at the road ahead of him, and had a driver's rigid non-conductive profile. Besides, it was getting dark, though there was no sign of mist. When Harold came to the part where he had intervened on Irma's behalf (he didn't tell the sequel), Alec exclaimed, "Bravo, that was good—I must remember that!" just as if he was applauding an anecdote, not at all as if——

He felt at once relieved and let down, sold, you might say. Relieved that Irma appeared to be in no danger, if you could use such a term, from Alec, except possibly in the pages of a book; and let down because he had—well—worked himself up and put himself about unnecessarily. That was his first reaction; but after dinner, when they were discussing the question of the market-garden, and Harold's business self began to take control, he wondered whether Alec's apparent indifference might not be assumed.

After all, did one, in business, go straight to the point? Did one show one's hand? Did one betray one's anxiety that such and such a thing should happen? One did not; and if Alec had been a business man——

Harold couldn't think of Alec as a business man; he was a literary man, and the two were incompatible. Not that he wasn't quick to see his own advantage, when it was pointed out to him. Someone—not Harold—had told him of the financial possibilities of the market-garden—its value as a loss rather than as a profit—and he had got quite extravagant ideas of what might be done in this direction. "If I employed six full-time gardeners," he said excitedly, "I would reduce my income to almost nil—except for my little dole from Cotopaxi—and then I should get it all back from the Income Tax, and think what a saving that would be!" Inwardly Harold deplored this emotional approach; it would cut no ice with the Inspector; it would put him off. He ignored Alec's proposal about the six gardeners and his tone became dry and almost curt. "We may have difficulty, at this stage," he said repressively, "in persuading the Inspector that your market-garden is a market-garden at all. In my opinion, as I told you, it's premature to broach the subject now. It's premature," repeated Harold, as though to be premature was a grievous fault, almost a crime. "What have you done so far? You've sold a few delphiniums and some asparagus——" "Yes, and roses, lupins and larkspur and quantities of new potatoes—you forget them." "Well, roses, lupins and larkspur and new potatoes," repeated Harold, unimpressed. "How many new potatoes have you sold?" "Oh, I don't know, but several pounds." "Several pounds! But you ought to have sold several hundredweight, at least, or several tons if you want to persuade the Inspector that you're not in business for your health. And you'll have to organize some means of marketing your produce. You'll have to arrange to send it to Swansea or Cardiff, in bulk, it's no use relying, as you say you are, on people from the district dropping in to buy a few sticks of asparagus or a bunch of roses. I'll do my best with the Inspector, of course; and he's been very understanding, so far; remarkably understanding. His letters have been . . . well, they have been *friendly*. But

I don't mind telling you"—and now Harold's distaste for his mission and his simmering irritation with Alec's unbusiness-like methods began to boil up—"that I think it's decidedly premature to approach him now."

All at once an enormous rock loomed up. Involuntarily Harold closed his eyes. The car swerved and he looked up to see the rock receding into the fog.

"But in that case," Alec was saying, "I shouldn't have had the pleasure of your visit. I knew I could only lure you down here on business."

Harold was mollified—mollified by what had seemed like a hair's-breadth escape from death, mollified by Alec's pretty speech. He couldn't understand why his thoughts insisted on treating Alec as an enemy when he was really a friend, a benefactor who had substantially increased his income, and who might. . . . Ashamed of his outburst, and a little alarmed about its possible consequences, he said:

"Oh, I'm sure it will be all right. I shall get round him somehow. But I shan't even try to persuade him to make the claim for the market-garden retrospective—I mean, going back to the last financial year. It wouldn't wash—it couldn't. Why, everything you have sold" (Harold tried to make this sound as if it was an amount sufficient to supply Covent Garden) "has, on your own showing, been stuff that was scarcely out of the ground on April 5th. You'd have to produce accounts to prove the dates. All I can do is to establish the fact that the garden is a market-garden now, and next year we'll put in the claim."

Alec turned to him with a grin. "I'm sure you're right," he said. "We mustn't open our mouths too wide, must we? And now, though perhaps you wouldn't know it, we've reached our destination."

Low slate-coloured buildings with whitewashed gable ends were beginning to detach themselves from the fog. "It isn't a pretty place at the best of times," said Alec. "I'm really glad you can't see it. Don't be offended, but it's just the place for a murky business deal. No need to try to obscure the issue! Now I'll drop you at the field of battle and betake myself to the pub—it's called the Welsh Dragon, a more formidable beast than the Green Dragon. There

I'll wait, it's just on opening time. When you've beaten up the Inspector come and join me. It's only a few steps from his place, not that I've ever been to his place, Heaven forbid, but I've passed it scores of times. You'll have earned a drink even if you don't need one. But there won't be a pretty Austrian barmaid for you to rescue from a gang of toughs."

Getting out of Alec's battered old car that looked as if it had been in collision with many rocks, Harold had a feeling of relief, a more positive feeling than the relief one sometimes has on rejoining one's own company after a spell of other people's. Had he been nervous in the car, nervous of Alec's slapdash driving, nervous of the fog, nervous of the rocks? No, it was an obscure feeling that now he could think his own thoughts without having them interpreted and distorted for him by a stronger personality, somebody who—— The Inspector, ticklish as the case was that Harold had to argue, would be child's play compared with Alec.

And so it proved. Whatever the picture we build up of them, Tax Inspectors are but human, and this one—Harold guessed it in a moment—was flattered that Harold had come so far to see him. All the way from Marshport! True, they were on their guard with each other; each at once assumed the wary attitude of a chess-player. More important than the things they said were the things they didn't say—but in these suppressions there was little or no conscious deception, there was only the conventional caution that governed such encounters, and which was second nature to each of them. Arguing for themselves, they might have got heated, but each having someone else's hand to play, they didn't.

There was another factor, Harold soon discovered, that was telling in his favour. And it surprised him. He had come prepared to apologize for his client. In the first five minutes he found himself using such phrases as "a queer fish" and "with no head for business". The Inspector agreed that this was so, but added, in a sing-song upward-tilting voice, "He is an interesting man, however, and well-liked in the district. He is very open-handed, there is no doubt about it, and gives generously to any cause, especially religious bodies. Religious bodies have had a lot of help from him. He is a foreigner, of course, his ways are not our ways, perhaps that explains it. Some people shake their heads. You have seen his housekeeper?"

Harold said he hadn't.

"She is a foreigner, too. You would be surprised how many foreigners there are in this small corner of Wales. We do not always understand them or what brings them here. But I mustn't waste your time, Mr. Eastwood. You will be wanting to get back, I'm sure. Now, as to this market-garden, we mustn't be unduly rigorous with Mr. Goodrich, who, as you say, doesn't understand business. In Wales we think a great deal of our bards. If Mr. Goodrich is not a bard he is a writer, and his head is in the clouds, our Welsh clouds, Mr. Eastwood. You have explained that he will have to pay his gardeners agricultural wages?"

Harold said he had.

"And keep an account of his takings and expenses?"

"Yes."

The two men argued a little as to what sum, in a first year of market-gardening, could be considered a reasonable turn-over. The Inspector stipulated for seventy-five pounds; Harold maintained that with the difficulties of transport, etc., Alec would have to contend with, the minimum should be fixed at fifty. At last they agreed on sixty. "You will explain to him, Mr. Eastwood, that unless his takings amount to sixty pounds, we cannot admit that his garden is a market-garden or allow his claim."

Harold shrugged his shoulders.

"I doubt if he can do it this year. He's started rather late, you see."

"Yes," agreed the Inspector. "July is rather late. He must pray for fine weather."

There was a knock at the door and a clerk said, "Mr. Goodrich would like to see you, sir." Harold's heart gave a jump, and his face, could he have seen it, registered disapproval. But over the Inspector's face a smile spread like sunrise, and before Alec was fairly in the room he had risen to his feet.

85

"This is an unexpected pleasure, Mr. Goodrich."

"And a great pleasure for me too, Inspector."

Seated, and clutching his ankle with his hand, as he had when Harold met him in the train, Alec began:

"I'm sorry to butt in, Inspector, but there was one thing I forgot to tell Mr. Eastwood." He paused.

"Yes, Mr. Goodrich?"

"You remember Mothering Sunday?"

"Oh yes, Mr. Goodrich, a most beautiful festival." The Inspector's face softened.

"Well, it's been my custom, on that festival, to let the children from the villages round come and pick my daffodils to give as presents to their mothers. They come in shoals, on foot, on bicycles, in cars, even in coaches. It's become an established outing. There they all are in the field among the daffodils, picking for all they're worth."

Harold thought of Jeremy and Janice who had given Isabel daffodils on Mothering Sunday, the Inspector remembered the same ceremony in his family, and their hearts warmed to Alec.

"Well, times are hard, and I thought that on this Mothering Sunday I would charge the children something. So I charged them a shilling for a bunch of eight daffodils. Not much, was it? But do you know how much I got? Fifty-two pounds. Fifty-two pounds in daffodils!"

There was an astonished and respectful silence, then Alec said:

"I thought it might have some bearing on the market-garden question."

At that the atmosphere changed, it tightened; on the faces of the Inspector and the accountant was reflected not the warm glow of paternal pride and conjugal affection, but the cool stare of financial scepticism. The gold of the daffodils had turned into real gold.

"When was Mothering Sunday?" the Inspector asked.

"March 28th. The children came on Friday and Saturday and for most of Sunday. You should have seen how their little fingers twinkled. It was the prettiest sight imaginable. Would you believe it, they picked far more daffodils when they had to pay for them than when they were given them gratis. They left hardly a daffodil in the field; they stripped it. And the parents were much more appreciative. In other years, when I used to give the daffodils away, the parents took it as a right: this time they thanked me, and some wrote to me—such touching letters! I suppose that people only value what they pay for; what do you think, Inspector?"

"I think you are a sound psychologist, Mr. Goodrich."

"Well, that was how I got the idea of a market-garden, though I didn't get round to seeing about it until now."

"You said that 'Mothering Sunday' was on March 28th?" the Inspector said.

"Yes, but is the date important?"

"It is important," said the Inspector, "because it means you cannot count the sale of the daffodils in your takings for the current financial year."

Alec looked at Harold in consternation.

"I see," he said, "I see. But couldn't I count them as takings for the *past* financial year?"

ALEC had gained his point. As the two men stepped into the street he said, trembling with excitement:

"What a delightful fellow that Inspector is."

Harold grunted. He did not like to hear any man called delightful, least of all an Inspector of Taxes. A Tax Inspector should be civil, shrewd, hard-headed, and upon occasion, understanding; but not delightful.

"Seems fond of poetry," he said non-committally.

"Yes, doesn't he? He sees me as a bard. Well, perhaps I am. That was what did the trick, that and your support."

"I'm afraid I didn't support you very much," said Harold.

"That was just it. You were so objective. If you had pressed him, you would have put his back up. He wanted it to appear that the concession came from him. . . . Oh, how wonderful I feel! How are you feeling, Harold?"

"I feel pretty good," said Harold repressively.

"Not more than that? Oh, I could dance." Alec cut a caper on the pavement. "Don't I look twice my size?"

Oddly enough he did, and Harold, rather unwillingly, admitted this.

"Oh, I could sing." Alec carolled a little. "Should we have a drink now, or should we wait till we get home?"

"What time is it?" asked Harold, practically.

With a lavish gesture, as if he was administering a knockout, Alec bared his wrist.

"Good Lord, it's after one. . . . Still, it doesn't matter."

"But won't they mind if we're late?" Harold asked.

Alec poked him gently in the ribs.

"My dear fellow, there's nobody *to* mind. Nobody at all."

At last they were back on the road. The rising vapours inside him, no less than the golden mist outside, began to woo Harold from his ill-humour. But what a bad show it had been. Not business at all: that was just it. The Inspector had swallowed Alec's story whole; it appeared that he thought of Alec as a bard, and to a bard he could refuse nothing: a bard must have the benefit of every doubt. Harold didn't really mind that; he didn't mind his client getting away with something he had no right to get away with; he himself was always straining points in a client's favour. But it had been so *unprofessional*! Alec had appeared like a *deus ex machina* in an affair which did indeed concern him, but which he had delegated to Harold. By so doing he had won a triple victory—over the Inland Revenue, over the Inspector, and over Harold himself, who had declared that a retrospective claim for the market-garden wouldn't wash. At one stroke he had cut the knot, by-passing all the preliminaries—the manœuvring for position, the attacking at one point and giving way at another, the slowly-arrived-at compromise which was the essence of the matter, as it was the essence of marriage and, perhaps, of life itself. Procedure had been violated, and how could one get on without procedure? Procedure gives colour to transactions which without it would seem dubious and off-colour—as this one did.

Harold didn't dream of asking Alec if his story about the daffodils was true. It didn't occur to him, any more than it would occur to a solicitor to ask his client if he was telling the truth. In any case, it was beside the point; the Inspector had to decide on the evidence before him, and he had decided. There were a dozen questions he might have asked Alec but he hadn't asked them. There were a dozen ways in which he could verify the truth of Alec's story from outside sources, but apparently he didn't mean to use them. He had been hypnotized, impressed by Alec the bard and enchanted by Alec the man.

Alec certainly knew how to get his own way. This was the third instance of it that Harold had been present at. In the train with the ticket-collector; at the house of what's-his-name the novelist, when the curator wanted to refuse him admission; and now.

If he laid siege to Irma, could Harold doubt what the result would be?

He had as good as said he didn't mean to. He had said that he only wanted information about Irma for the sake of copy. Did he always take, and give, so much trouble in order to get copy? And what exactly was "copy"? Might not "copy" include much more than finding out something about someone?

Harold had been left at the end of the interview feeling very small. Not looking small; Alec had saved his face, had appealed to him several times during the discussion, had managed to give the Inspector the impression that Harold backed him up. Indeed, the Inspector would almost certainly think that Alec's irruption was premeditated, and that they were in collusion. But what matter, since apparently he didn't care if they were?

It really was most unprofessional, and intolerable, that Alec should have gone behind his back and forced his hand. Another sort of professional man, a doctor or a lawyer, for example, might well have decided to throw up the case and leave Alec to look after his own affairs since he seemed so eminently capable of looking after them. Supposing he, Harold, did so? He would only be forfeiting the £30 a year that he was charging Alec; his relations with the six other clients would not be affected. But wouldn't they? Supposing Alec, who seemed to have so much influence over his friends, persuaded them to withdraw their favours? Harold had his family to think of; could he afford to sacrifice £150 a year to gratify his pique? And not only £150; there might be another £150 in prospect from the other potential clients, who were lining up, tumbling over themselves, only waiting for a word from Alec. Would that word be given, if Harold started to cut up rough?

And Irma? What gain would she get out of Harold's loss?

Suddenly he said, "How did you collect the money for the daffodils?"

Alec turned to him and smiled.

"While the gardeners were there one of them collected it. As soon as they went off, I took on. It was quite fun, you know. I don't belong here, but I have the same sort of relationship with the people as if I did. Some of the little devils tried to get away with extra bunches tucked away somewhere in their meagre little persons. When I saw an ominous bulge, or a stalk sticking out, I used to poke at it and say 'What's this?' And the children were so innocent about it. I don't know what the world's coming to. . . . Aren't you getting hungry?"

Harold admitted that he was.

"Let's put on the pace a bit."

Alec was driving much too fast already. And smelling slightly of drink. Another rock loomed up and they only missed it by a fraction. If they survived the accident that seemed inevitable, Alec would certainly get his licence endorsed. Or would he?

It was long past two when they sat down to luncheon.

Hendre Hall,
St. Milo's.

Dearest Isabel [wrote Harold],

I said I'd try to tell you something about this place, but I can't tell you much, because the whole place is wrapped in fog. You wouldn't know that you were near the sea, except for some old foghorn that keeps moaning and wailing. It's always the way at week-ends, isn't it? We never seem to get a good one. When I woke up this morning visibility was about 200 yards. When we drove out it was 150 to 100, and now it's about 50, I should think. I can't see the garden wall, which I could see quite clearly this morning.

The house isn't what we mean by a hall, it's really an old farmhouse, with a wing added on to make an L. (Alec says there aren't any really big houses in this part of Wales.) There was an older wing, but it was knocked down by a bomb in the war, and Alec got it rebuilt when licences were almost unprocurable—trust him for that! So he's got a library, a great big room with two fireplaces, and rooms for the staff over it. My room is in the old part of the house. The door opens by itself if you don't latch it. There are six doors opening out of the corridor, and they all move by themselves—so Alec told me—and I tried them, to make sure. He won't say if the house is haunted or not. When I asked him he said, "Not at this moment." I don't know what he meant, but I think he often doesn't know himself.

He's in wonderfully good spirits—a good deal because of something that happened this morning; I can't tell you what it was, it was to do with business, but Alec did very well out of it. I was rather annoyed at the time, but I'm not now, it's no concern of mine what he chooses to say or do. He's a good host though, I will say that, and I can't imagine what he meant when he said he wasn't on a good wicket here. He has everything he wants and servants who wait on him hand and foot—no washing up or anything of that sort—and if he isn't happy then he ought to be. But he is. It's quite childish the way he goes on.

I wish I could tell you what we talked about—but it was mostly business and wouldn't interest you. He did mention the Austrian girl at the Green Dragon, but he seems to have cooled off her altogether—he says he only wanted to know about her in order to put her into a book! We needn't have got so het up about it! But he did say he would like to come and stay with us again.

Now he's having a siesta, and says he won't be up till teatime. He wanted me to have one, but I said I was afraid I was too English for Continental habits, so here I am writing to you. I wish you were here, and I can't think why he didn't ask you. It's such nonsense about his household not being up to scratch. He's got too much money, that's his trouble. But it's silly not to enjoy yourself when you're on holiday, and I mean to. Besides, he's done a good deal for us, I keep remembering that, and Monday will soon be here.

To-morrow we're going to do a motor-trip and see some places on the coast, if the fog clears. Alec says it seldom lasts more than two days. You don't think much of Marshport, I know, but at any rate you can see where you are, which is more than you can here.

Now I'm going out to get a breath of air, or fog, or whatever the local mixture is, and then I'll come in and finish this.

At the end of the passage a staircase led down to the library. This way Harold went, remembering that the library had a door that opened into the garden. He let himself out with the caution, the irrational sense of being watched, that as a visitor one sometimes has, finding one's way about a strange house, alone; and the fog with its finger on the lips of the house seemed to have a special message of secrecy and silence.

Should he leave the door into the garden open or shut? If he shut it, it might lock itself, or somebody might lock it; if open, some alien creature, a cow or hen or other denizen of the countryside, might get in. Like many town dwellers, Harold regarded domestic animals with fear and suspicion. Finally he compromised by leaving the door on the latch, just not closed.

Conscientiously—for he always tried to do what he had promised to do, even when there was no witness but himself —Harold sniffed up the sweet, warm, moist air, laden with golden motes. Above, the thinning mist still disclosed glimpses of blue sky; around, it was thicker than before. He could just discern the hedge which, like a shadow, enclosed this part of the garden on three sides—framing, with the house, an oblong of grass, of which a patch the size of a tennis court was mown, and the rest left rough and tussocky. The contrast between the shaven lawn and the wild field from which it had been reclaimed pleased Harold; but he couldn't help wishing that the whole tract had been mown as far as the hedges; Nature, he felt, ought always to be tamed.

A feeling of expectancy possessed him, a slight tingling of recovered self-hood; after the strain of adapting himself to Alec's alien mind and presence, it was refreshing to be alone. He was savouring this sensation when he noticed on his left a thickening, like a shadow in the mist. It wasn't stationary, it was moving about, just on the further side of visibility. Then, breasting waves of mist, the shadow advanced, took shape, and was a woman.

The intruder stopped and then came slowly towards Harold. Under her white piqué hat her sun-glasses gave her face a bluish look. When she didn't speak, Harold said:

"Were you looking for anyone?"

She laughed musically.

"Well yes," she said, in rather a deep voice. "I was. I was looking for Mr. Goodrich."

"He's in the house," said Harold doubtfully, "asleep."

"Oh, he's asleep?"

"Yes," said Harold. He hesitated. "Can I take a message for you?"

"If you would be so kind," the lady—for such she obviously was—replied.

"What shall I say?"

"Tell him that Elspeth is here."

"Nothing more?"

"No."

Harold went off towards the library door. It seemed rather rude to shut it in her face, so he left it open. Looking back through the library window he got the impression that she was following him into the house.

94

BUT while in faraway St. Milo's the scene was so deep in mist that Harold, as an observer, might just as well not have been there, to Isabel, at Tilecotes, it was brilliantly, even dazzlingly clear. She had heard about it from Alec's own lips; she had read about it in novels and in guidebooks until its forms and colours were printed on her mind; and not only its forms and colours, but the feeling of it. Indeed, the feeling had come first; and what she heard and read had only confirmed and intensified it.

So there was no mist in her mind nor was it getting dark when they took the long drive from the station farther and farther into the west until they saw the islands, sunlit, faraway and beckoning, and the sun itself going down into the sea.

It was pagan, Alec had told her, and added, "You'd like that, wouldn't you?" When she assented rather doubtfully, he said, "It's not a classical paganism, it's something to do with Tir n'an Og—Celtic, I suppose. And yet there is a terrifically strong feeling of the age of the saints, with ruined chapels by the sea-shore, and holy wells, and the huge roofless Bishop's Palace, with its beautiful arcades and perfect rose-window and grass-grown floors. And all that," he had told her, "is not like 'religion' kept for Sundays, but seems just part of the background, slipping in and out of the people's lives—like the Cathedral, which is so clear and uncluttered, and empty except for tombs of crusaders and bishops and Welsh princes. Heaps of people who would never dream of going to church 'up in England' on weekday find it the natural thing at St. Milo's; they hear the single melancholy bell, and drop in and sit peacefully in some richly carved old stall. I'm not a churchgoer, but I've done it myself! Everything at St. Milo's seems to change colour with the light, but the Cathedral most of all; sometimes it is grey and slaty-looking, sometimes it is amethyst, sometimes deep violet. Nothing ever looks the same twice over; and that is one of the drawbacks—you can't really trust things to be themselves: there's an element of deception somewhere."

* II *

"Mummy, what do you think Daddy's doing now?"

It was Janice who asked the question. Jeremy gave her a disapproving look, but she paid no attention. Isabel looked at the clock—the kitchen clock. It said half-past ten, half-past ten on Sunday morning. She was preparing some vegetables for their midday meal.

"Well, darling, he might be getting ready for church."

"Mr. Goodrich didn't go to church when he was staying with us."

"No, but he sometimes goes when he's at home."

"Is Mr. Goodrich a good man, Mummy?"

"Yes, darling, of course he is. That's why he's called Goodrich."

Janice laughed heartily at this and even Jeremy deigned to smile.

"Oh Mummy, how silly you are! You know names haven't anything to do with people. Daddy's Mr. Eastwood, but he isn't east and he isn't wood, and I'm sure he's much gooder than Mr. Goodrich!"

"She means better, not gooder," observed Jeremy.

"Well, better then. Daddy's better than Mr. Goodrich, isn't he, Mummy?"

"Why do you think so?" Isabel asked.

"Oh because he is!" cried Janice, beginning to dance about. "Daddy's very, very, *very* good."

"Yes, he is," Isabel agreed. "But why do you think Mr. Goodrich isn't?"

Janice frowned, pouted, and laid her finger on her lip.

"She doesn't know," said Jeremy flatly.

"Oh yes, I do know. It's because, because, because . . . he isn't married!"

"But lots of good people aren't married," said Isabel. "Think of Auntie Ethel, for instance."

"She's mad about marrying," remarked Jeremy. "Sometimes she says she's married herself."

96

"Oh, Jeremy, I never! Only, only, only sometimes."

"Whom are you married to?" asked Isabel.

"Well," said Janice, rolling her eyes, "it's a great secret, but I *have* been married to Mr. Goodrich. That's how I know he isn't a good man."

"She said a moment ago that Mr. Goodrich wasn't married," Jeremy remarked.

Janice saw she had been caught out. Her face began to crinkle; then it brightened again.

"It was a very *private* marriage," she said hurriedly. "Not like in church. Very, very, *very* private. Only us two. Of course, it was only a pretence marriage. That's why we have only one baby."

"What is it called?" asked Isabel, unguardedly.

"It isn't it, it's she. How many times have I told you that? Pamelia, of course."

"I told you she was mad about marrying," said Jeremy. "Mummy, isn't it time to go to church?"

"Oh, Jeremy, of course it is. What have I been thinking about? Hurry, hurry, we must run."

"What do you think Daddy's doing now, Mummy?"

Involuntarily Isabel looked up at the clock. It was the sitting-room clock, the lounge clock, a French clock, of ormolu and imitation tortoiseshell, almost their nicest wedding present. It didn't look right on the brick chimney-piece over their ancient Roman fireplace; perhaps, when their ship came in, they would be able to change the fireplace for a plain Regency one, which goes in any house. Meanwhile, however incongruous its setting, the clock still told the time. It was just four o'clock, and they were sitting down to tea.

But they wouldn't be sitting down to tea at Hendre Hall. In larger houses tea was a movable feast and seldom happened before five o'clock. Sunshine was pouring into the room. Isabel said:

"He might be having a bathe."

"Did he take his bathing suit?"

"Yes, darling."

"The big one or the little one?"

"The big one, I think."

Janice looked disappointed.

"I like the little one better. . . . Will Mr. Goodrich have a bathing suit?"

"Of course he will, darling."

"I wonder what it will be like."

Isabel felt the colour mounting to her face.

"She always wants to know what clothes people wear: she's potty about it," said Jeremy.

"Yes, but I do want to know. Do you think it will be dark red, with a swallow on its side? That's my favourite, favourite, *favourite* kind."

"It's a treacherous coast, though the sea is such wonderful colours. But there are terrible currents and quicksands and rocks, and I think treachery is probably at the bottom of it, really. There is violence, too . . . It's a very seal-y place. We often used to bathe in the autumn with two or three bobbing in the slow waves quite near, and gravely looking at us."

At "us"? Yes, he had said "us".

"But you don't think Daddy will get drowned?" asked Janice, when Isabel had told them something of this.

"Of course he won't, you silly. Daddy's a very good swimmer," Jeremy said.

"He might get drowned trying to save Mr. Goodrich. People do, then he might get a medal."

"It wouldn't be much use to him after he was dead," said Jeremy.

"But Mummy could have it. Then perhaps she could marry Mr. Goodrich."

"You horrid child, you mustn't say things like that!" cried Isabel.

"She sometimes says what she would do if any of us died," said Jeremy.

"Oh Janice! What would you do?"

"Well, first I should get a very nice black dress."

"And then?"

"Then I should cry terribly, and then people would feel sorry for me and perhaps want to marry me——"

"No, they wouldn't, Janice!" cried Jeremy, tried beyond

98

endurance. "I've told you over and over again, and I keep on telling you, they wouldn't want to marry you, you aren't old enough to marry, is she, Mummy? And she'd have to have all sorts of things that grown-up people have."

"What do grown-up people have, that I haven't?" demanded Janice.

"Oh, I don't know."

"But you would want to get married again, Mummy, wouldn't you, if Daddy was drowned? I'm only saying 'if'," persisted Janice.

"Certainly not, no, I won't listen to you, you heartless little monster! Now finish your tea and run out and play a game with Jeremy."

"But we don't know what to play, do we, Jeremy?"

"Play the ladder game."

"We stopped playing that long ago—it's stale."

"Well, you must think of another game."

"She can't think—it's bad for her," said Jeremy.

"Yes, I can, let's play a game about getting m——"

"No," shouted Jeremy. "I won't play that game. I'll go and play by myself!"

"Well, let's play a game about getting di—di—di—di—di—" Janice couldn't finish the word, and there was a pregnant pause.

"She means divorced," said Jeremy, in a neutral voice.

For a moment Isabel was horrified and shocked, and wondered what she had done to merit such a daughter. Then she laughed and said:

"Well, go away and play *something*."

Washing-up the tea-things, out of reach of Janice's graceless tongue, Isabel suddenly felt lonely. Harold had been gone for nearly three days and would not be back until Monday night at earliest. It would be one of the longest separations they had had since their marriage. At first she hadn't missed him; she had rather welcomed the opportunity to think her own thoughts and, in her spare moments, to read the books she wanted to read, unworried by the feeling that she was making a life for herself apart from him. She knew that she was in danger of doing that, in danger of

99

letting their lines of communication get blocked up and disused, in danger of taking him too much for granted. Of course it was essential to a successful marriage that you did take many things for granted—things that you couldn't take for granted even in the closest friendship. It would be unbearable if you couldn't—if you had to make conversation when you didn't feel like it, if you had to explain your reasons for doing some trifling action, if you had always to be on your guard against touchiness, if you had to keep propping up the edifice you had built together in case it should fall down. You must never feel that his presence called for a special effort on your part—unless, for some unusual reason, it obviously did. Nor must he; Isabel was fair enough to see that, and she knew that women were prone to set more store on small attentions—conscious efforts to please —than men were. At first she had felt a pang when Harold gradually dropped his newly-wed habit of opening the door for her; afterwards she felt relieved that her exits could be effected without this reminder of the marriage-tie. There must be familiarity in marriage, that was certain, and familiarity meant taking many things for granted.

But too much familiarity was a danger, too, it bred if not contempt an apathy of the feelings; that was one reason why, after the first shock, she had welcomed with excitement the conversation about Irma; and the opportunity it gave to get in touch with Harold's mind and feelings once again, almost as if they had been a stranger's. Yes, the strangeness she felt then was a measure of the extent to which their feelings for each other—or was it just their capacity to express their feelings?—had been blunted.

Of course, in itself it was a strange conversation, a joint glimpse into a world which was quite alien to theirs, with other rules, other standards—or perhaps no rules, no standards?—but which one had to accept because one mustn't be priggish; it couldn't be dismissed with a snigger or a sneer, or even with raised eyebrows—for who were we to pass by on the other side? And her sense of her own happiness and security with Harold would be strengthened by contact with a way of life so different from theirs, and with such different problems. And to be of any use to him, to

Alec, one, they, she (the pronouns were so difficult to choose) must see those problems through the eyes of the people concerned: it was no good to look at them through the blessed but perhaps blinkered eyes of unswerving conjugal fidelity and domestic bliss. That was why she had chosen the realistic way, and tried to persuade Harold that (given Alec's nature) it would be a *good* thing if he saw something of Irma, and a *good* thing, too, for Irma, whose experience would be immeasurably broadened and deepened and enriched by it. One has a duty towards experience. Barmaids were, as she had told Harold, notoriously chaste. That meant they were not promiscuous; it didn't mean that they never took a lover, or that they wouldn't be faithful to him —touchingly faithful through thick and thin—and if she, Isabel, was a barmaid——

Irma had rejected the crude advances of the three young men. She was evidently fastidious; but that didn't mean she would necessarily be indifferent to one man, who had it in his power to give her so many things that she wanted—that she must want, that she ought to want.

Isabel was sure that Alec was unhappy; he had as good as told her that his home life was unhappy. Isabel was not a feminist, but she knew that bachelors couldn't make a home for themselves as single women could; men's minds were draughty and uncomfortable and if tidy, then tidy in the wrong way—the barrack-room style, spit and polish, everything numbered, present and correct—tidiness as an end in itself, one of the life-denying idealisms that they were so prone to. Tidiness was only a means to an end—a graciousness of living, a balanced, creative, flowering amenity of which women had the secret. Men were either grossly untidy or soullessly tidy. Harold belonged to the second category; if he was left to himself——

But at the moment it was she who was left to herself; and what could this sudden sense of emptiness and loss mean except that she was missing him, missing him dreadfully?

"What do you think Daddy's doing now, Mummy?"

Once more Isabel looked up at the clock. It was the clock in the children's bedroom, their night-nursery, as it would have been called in larger houses. But it didn't help her; it pointed permanently—a rigid right-angle—to the hour of three, for it was a toy clock, dating from the days when the children were learning to tell the time but couldn't be trusted with a timepiece of their own. You could move the hands round: but they hadn't been moved for a year or more. Was it a sense of frustration from this small circumstance, or because the question fell on what was becoming a tender spot, that made her answer almost irritably: "Oh, Janice, darling, I can't tell you"?

"Then what do you think Mr. Goodrich is doing?" Janice promptly asked.

Isabel found to her surprise that she was neither unable nor unwilling to answer this question.

"Perhaps he's going for a motor-drive," she said.

"But wouldn't he be taking Daddy with him?"

"Yes, I expect he would."

"Would his car be bigger than ours?" asked Jeremy.

"That I'm afraid I can't tell you."

"Ours has an over-all length of twelve feet seven inches," Jeremy said wistfully. "His might be bigger, to climb the mountains with. Our book says Wales is very mountainous."

There are the Prescelli Hills, which always have a far-off look and are changing colour the whole time and are where the stones for Stonehenge came from. Then there's a line of rocky hills, a beautiful clear outline lifting up from the sky as you come near, and running down to the Head, which ends in barren rock, but farther back is heather and gorse and turf, and it has never been built on since whoever built the hut circles! The name of the highest hill means the Hill of the Black Host—no one knows who they were.

"Do they have flowers like we have here?" asked Jeremy. "Or is it a jungle?" He evidently hoped it would be a jungle. "Do the inhabitants live in houses, or just in huts? Are they very fierce? Is it safe to go out alone?"

It's a bare country, mostly small fields, and white-washed or colour-washed cottages and farm-houses. No big houses. The gentry mostly live in converted farm-houses, gaunt

102

and bare, with a few ash trees clustered round them, all bent one way by the wind, and immense derelict kitchen-gardens with crumbling walls and fading, painted doors, and hydrangeas and fuchsias and tangled rhododendrons. There is Roch Castle, eight miles away, just one tooth of a tower sticking up out of the landscape. There are castles all over Pembrokeshire, some ruined and some still lived in. That is another layer, but all the layers blend in . . . He had a feudal relationship with the country people, he said, although he didn't really "belong". Anyone they look on as gentry they treat as such. Before the war, they did, at any rate. Everyone seemed in their right place and not spilling into someone else's, and that made for ease in any relationship. You could talk as a friend to anyone.

"It sounds a nice place," said Janice, "nicer than Marshport. Would you like us to go and live there, Mummy?"

"Oh no, darling, we couldn't. Daddy has his work here."

"Couldn't we live with Mr. Goodrich?"

"He hasn't asked us, and besides——"

"Besides what, Mummy?" Janice asked. "Besides what?"

"Oh well, we couldn't. Now say your prayers."

They said them, kneeling down beside their beds, their fists pressed hard into their eyes, their toes and shoulders wriggling with the effort of adjusting themselves to prayer, looking very small and sweet. As they neared the end they began to gabble, having, so Isabel suspected, a secret understanding between them that the one who finished last should pay the other a forfeit.

"Not so fast, please, not so fast!"

At once the pace became much more decorous. "For Jesus . . . Christ's . . . sake . . ." they intoned together, and then, their rivalry getting the better of them, "Amen!" like the crack of a whip.

Rubbing his eyes, Jeremy struggled to his feet but Janice remained on her knees.

"Can I pray for Mr. Goodrich?" she asked.

"Yes, if you like," said Isabel.

"God bless Mr. Goodrich and make him a good man and make him happy for ever and ever. Amen."

Janice looked up slyly.

"Now you say 'Amen', Mummy."

"Amen, then," said Isabel.

When they had promised faithfully to go to sleep at once Isabel left them, feling soothed and strengthened. But soon her restlessness returned, with the vision of St. Milo's that Alec's remembered words evoked. She went out of the house and climbed the hill to a viewpoint above the housetops. Below her were the red roofs of the clustered villas, each in its bower of greenery; below them the town straggled aimlessly and the church tower stuck up; beyond the public gardens and the barracks was the sea-front, a level line of concrete broken by the hideous silhouette of the Royal Hotel. And beyond the promenade was the sea; but what a sea! The putty-coloured sea, the useful English Channel; and the waves came slowly in, with machine-made regularity that seemed the expression of a vast fatigue, as if the ocean itself was yawning in her face. "How can anyone call Marshport a pretty place?" she thought.

At intervals she heard a rattle and rumble of cars crossing, at their owners' risk, the hump-backed wooden bridge.

12

HAROLD knew which Alec's bedroom was: it was the last room in the passage, next door but one to his. Easy to knock and go in, but somehow he didn't want to. He had a vague puritanical feeling that Alec ought not to be asleep in the afternoon, but also he felt the reluctance that anyone not a sadist feels to wake somebody up—to make him exchange the pains of consciousness for the bliss of sleep. "It's a shame to wake him!" Harold thought. He would certainly be startled and perhaps be angry; some people were angry when they were suddenly woken up. Also it would be taking him at a disadvantage, unprepared, without the front that everyone, however artless, puts on to face the world. And the room itself, tenanted yet untenanted: how would it receive an unauthorized visitor?

Harold was not given to hesitating, but he hesitated now.

Who was this Elspeth, and why had she given him a message, instead of ringing the front-door bell? And why had he offered to take it?

Well, he had taken it and must now deliver it.

No answer came to his knock, so he knocked again, hammering away until at last a sleepy voice said, "Come in!"

The room was in darkness: that was the first surprise. Harold paused on the threshold.

"Who is it?" said Alec, suspiciously.

"It's me, Harold."

"Half a tick, and I'll put on the light." As the switch clicked a huge four-poster bed sprang into view, with Alec on the far side of it, propped up on his elbows. He was wearing a shirt; the rest of him was hidden by the bed-cover. His hair was tousled and his face looked odd.

"What time is it?" he asked.

His voice was as peculiar as his face; the words came out slurred and throaty. Harold thought he must be drunk. Consulting his watch, he said:

"It's about half-past four."

"Good Lord, is it really? How right you were to come and wake me up! I might have slept till midnight. Oh, but I do feel better! I never felt so well. Do you know, you've had a wonderful effect on me! If you can give me half a minute——" There was a convulsion and his trousered legs appeared from under the counterpane.

"Of course," said Harold. "Only let me give you my message first."

"Your message? What message, old boy?"

"It's from somebody called Elspeth," Harold said.

He never forgot the effect of this anouncement. Not that Alec cried out or anything; he did nothing positive, he slumped back on the bed and his face was almost hidden between the wings of the pillow.

"A telephone message?" he asked, and his cramped, crippled utterance was more marked than ever.

"No . . . I met her coming across the lawn, and she asked me to say to you, 'Elspeth is here'."

"Here?" Alec's voice sounded incredulous. "But she's away, spending the week-end in Shropshire somewhere. Are you sure you haven't made a mistake?"

"Quite sure."

"Oh, it's too bad, too bad," said Alec, as much to himself as to Harold. "She might have stayed away this once. She said she would . . . she promised she would. Well . . . where is she now?"

"I don't know," Harold said. "I thought she was coming after me."

"Coming after you?"

"Yes, she seemed to be following me into the house. If I see her," said Harold, backing towards the door, "shall I give her a message?"

"Yes," said Alec, "tell her . . . tell her to go to the Devil; no, that would be too unkind to him, he doesn't deserve it. Tell her . . . tell her I'm dead."

He lay so still on the bed that for a moment Harold almost thought he might be. It also flashed through his mind that Elspeth might not be a living woman. She might not be *real*. Alec had said something about the house not being haunted *now*. But the now had become *then*. The plain man in Harold protested against this fantastic interpretation of the appearance in the garden, just as it protested against all his dealings with Alec; but he had nerves like anyone else, he had no rational person to consult, he was not on his own ground and the room seemed charged with calamity and *night*; for since he had been in it, behind those thick curtains, he could scarcely believe that outside it was daylight.

"I didn't mean to let her in," he said.

"My dear fellow, you couldn't have kept her out."

The implication in this made Harold uneasy.

"But why has she come back?" he asked.

"To take a look at you, I should imagine."

At this, Harold's uneasiness increased. For though he knew how well Alec could take care of himself—he had had many object lessons in it—yet subconsciously he still thought of him as a child at sea in the world, and had a protective feeling for him.

"What would you like me to do?" he asked, his hand on the doorknob, longing to escape.

"My dear fellow, there's nothing we can do, short of . . . short of . . ."

"Short of what?" asked Harold.

"Well, short of some kind of exorcism, and you aren't qualified for that, nor am I. We must just make the best of it."

"But who is she?" asked Harold.

"You'll find out soon enough. My *âme damnée* . . . my big mistake."

His voice sounded utterly dispirited, and the mumbling was more marked than ever. But it didn't come from drink; as Harold was shutting the door, something on the washstand flashed a lipless grin at him—it was Alec's false teeth in a tumbler.

Far from being disgusted, Harold was touched by this evidence of imperfection, this chink in Alec's armour. He was rather proud of his own teeth, and almost for the first time he was able to see Alec from a standpoint of superiority, almost to look down on him, and feel sorry for him.

Now Harold really had something to tell Isabel, and his first thought, when he had shaken off the unnerving atmosphere of Alec's bedroom, was to return to his unfinished letter. The door of his own room stood open: surely he had left it shut? He went in, closing the door after him, and made straight for his writing-table. But the envelope was not there, nor did search reveal it. It had gone; somebody must have taken it. The tinkling of a bell disturbed his speculations. It must be a summons to tea. He went into the passage, looked about for Alec, and then slowly descended the staircase into the library.

The stranger, Elspeth, was standing by the tea-table. When Harold came near she said:

"Did you give Alec my message?"

Harold said he had.

"And what did he say?"

"He said," Harold began, "he said . . ."

"That he was glad I had come back?"

But Harold was spared the trouble of answering, for at that moment Alec came into the room. Swiftly and without the least show of hesitation she walked towards him, her intention so evident that it was no surprise when Harold saw them in each other's arms. He turned and looked out of the window, automatically noticing that the fog was clearing. Then he heard Elspeth's voice saying, with a suspicion of a chuckle in its deep-throated modulations:

"But you haven't introduced me to your guest, Alec. I don't even know his name."

"Harold," said Alec, "come and be introduced. On my left, Mr. Harold Eastwood, on my right, Elspeth. That's how they do it in the boxing-ring."

"Are you suggesting that Mr. Eastwood should try to knock me down?" asked Elspeth, taking Harold's hand.

"He's a lion-tamer by profession," Alec said. "He tames the British Lion, the Inland Revenue."

"Oh, then I've heard of you," said Elspeth. "Alec doesn't always tell me about his friends. I sometimes have to find out for myself. Does your wife have to find out about your friends, Mr. Eastwood?"

Wondering how she knew that he was married, or whether

it was just a shot, Harold replied, "I haven't many friends. My wife knows most of them, I think." In conversation, as in most things, Harold always played for safety.

"Does she know Alec?"

She put the question with so much intensity that Harold tried to catch Alec's eye before he answered. Getting no cue from him he said, "Yes, Alec's been to stay with us."

"He's been to stay with you? He never told me. Well, how amusing!"

"Come along, Elspeth, let's have tea," said Alec.

"Of course, Mr. Eastwood must be dying for it."

She sat down as of right behind the teapot. Harold sat down too, but Alec remained standing.

"Aren't you going to sit down, Alec?"

"Yes, I might as well."

He sat down on the edge of the chair like a child whose one wish is to get up again. Elspeth took a quick look at him and then said to Harold:

"How do you like your tea, Mr. Eastwood?"

"Just as it comes."

"No peculiarities of any kind?"

"No, just milk and sugar."

"How accommodating of you. I like my tea weak, Alec likes his strong—don't you, Alec?"

"I used to," Alec said.

"What, have you changed? You never told me. How does your wife like her tea, Mr. Eastwood?"

"Much as I do," Harold said.

"And in general you share the same tastes?"

Harold thought for a moment.

"Well, no, my wife's rather bookish. I don't go in for that sort of thing, but Isabel's a great reader."

"Has she read Alec's books?"

Feeling that the subject of Alec's books was thin ice, Harold answered cautiously:

"Yes, some of them."

"Does she like them?"

"Oh, yes," said Harold mechanically.

"She might not, you know. Not everyone does. Did she discuss them with him?"

"Oh, yes," said Harold again. "But I'm afraid that sort of talk's rather above my head."

"You don't discuss books with her?"

"No, I'm afraid not."

"You should, you know. I always talk over Alec's books with him. He often asks my advice and sometimes takes it, don't you, Alec? I have an intuitive understanding of his mind, you know; I can see right into it. He must have enjoyed talking to your wife about his work. But I expect you have other interests?"

"Other interests?" said Harold.

"Interests outside the family circle—golf, billiards, a club, perhaps? I don't suppose you spent all your time in the house?"

Harold told her about their trip to Dymport.

"Oh, yes, I might have guessed you would go there. A pious pilgrimage, wasn't it? Alec is so keen about Jacob Henry, but I'm glad to say he doesn't write like him. He's much too cerebral for me. But perhaps your wife likes him?"

Harold again took refuge in saying what a great reader Isabel was.

"Ah yes, you told me that before. I'm sure they had some very good cracks together. But tell me—you see, I have to ask you, Alec hasn't told me anything—didn't he want to take you pub-crawling?"

"No, Elspeth, on this occasion I didn't," Alec put in.

"Were you going to say that, Mr. Eastwood?" asked Elspeth innocently.

"We had some drinks at home," said Harold, thinking to himself: "And that's no lie."

"Well, I'm disappointed," Elspeth said. "I'm really disappointed. He didn't run true to form. The first thing he usually does, when he goes to a new place, is to pay a visit to the local. He nearly always finds copy there, he says. But sometimes I think there must be other attractions. Your wife must be a very charming woman, Mr. Eastwood, to keep him from his favourite haunts. Why didn't you bring her with you?"

Again Harold glanced interrogatively at Alec, but he was still keeping himself moodily aloof.

"I couldn't," Harold said. "She can't get away. She has the children to look after."

"Oh, children," said Elspeth. "So you have children. What a tie they must be." She stifled a yawn. "But I'm sorry she couldn't come. I'm sure we should have found a lot to talk about."

"What I don't understand," broke in Alec, "is why you came back, Elspeth—delighted as I am to see you. And how you got here. Was there a taxi at the station?"

"No, but I got a lift. Oh yes, Alec; there are always ways and means. I didn't ring you up because I thought you would be working. He told me he would be working, Mr. Eastwood, *all* this week-end."

"And your luggage?"

"My kind benefactor left it at the door. I didn't come in, because——" She stopped.

"Because?"

"Because I didn't want to interrupt you at your work. I have to keep him at it, Mr. Eastwood; he wouldn't have written a line if I hadn't. You see, I make him *feel*, and a novelist can't write unless he feels. Do you know how many of his books he dedicated to me?"

Harold shook his head.

"Five . . . He said it brought him luck, to have my name on the first page. The last one was inscribed to someone else . . . I forget who. It didn't do so well. Your work is dedicated to a woman, Mr. Eastwood, isn't it, although it doesn't bear her name?"

Rather surprised at seeing his career in this light, Harold agreed that it was.

"So you see, I mustn't leave him too much to himself. I can be with him in thought, of course, prompting him, encouraging him. I daresay your wife's thoughts are with you now, Mr. Eastwood. One's thoughts carry a long way. And they aren't invisible, they bring the thinker with them, by a sort of television. But this time——"

"This time you thought you'd come yourself?" said Alec.

"Yes, I had a hunch . . . that you might be needing me. And it was so uncomfortable there. Such short wavelengths, such poor reception. I love Alice, of course, but not her

111

friends. Her friends are pure asbestos, fire-proof, sound-proof, thought-proof. Everything one sent out came back like a ball from a wall, or just dropped dead. Not an eye lit up. I felt like rain running off a mackintosh. Now here——"

"Here you can penetrate," said Alec.

"Yes, but why put it like that? Why does he put it like that, Mr. Eastwood?"

When Harold couldn't answer, Alec said:

"What I don't understand is why you stayed outside pattering on the roof instead of coming in. Couldn't you find a hole, a tile loose, somewhere?"

"Oh, yes," said Elspeth. "But I like circling, I like a gradual approach, I like to feel myself getting nearer and nearer . . . and then I just slipped in. I didn't want to disturb anyone. Then I had a letter to write, to catch the post. It was lucky for you I did, Mr. Eastwood, for you, too, had a letter."

"Yes," said Harold. "I wondered——"

"I'll explain. The housemaid found it in your room and asked me should she post it and I said yes, seal it up. I couldn't ask you but I felt sure that's what you'd wish. So now it's gone and you have gained a day. There's no post out on Sundays."

"Oh, but there is," said Alec. "It's just a question of taking them to——"

"I know, but so often we forget, and letters take days to reach this place, and days to get away. Now Mrs. Eastwood may get hers on Monday."

"Oh, so you knew it was for her?" said Alec.

"I may have seen the name. But why are we staying indoors this lovely afternoon? Look, Alec, I've brought the sunshine with me. The mist is clearing, and the dear old place is coming into view. Mr. Eastwood, don't you want to go out?"

"I'm all for going out," said Harold. "What does Alec say?"

"I'm not especially keen," said Alec.

Elspeth's full face clouded over, and suddenly her eyes looked tired. She had taken off her dark glasses, but it was as though they had left their imprint, a blue shadow, round her eyes. Her eye sockets were caverns which revealed the skull. Behind the pillared bone, her slightly concave temples lay in shadow. Her make-up was not intended to make her look younger, in some way it emphasized her age, which must be, Harold thought, about forty-five; there was much femininity, but not a trace of youth about her. Her old-fashioned type of beauty gave her a dowagerish look. Harold could not place her at all.

"Then shall I take Mr. Eastwood round the garden?" she suggested.

"He's seen it," Alec said.

"Yes, but only in a fog."

"It looks its best in a fog."

"Then what do you want to do?"

Harold glanced at Alec. All the glow and bounce and boyishness had gone out of him and he looked shrunken and peevish.

"I don't know that I want to do anything," he said. "We're in your hands, Elspeth."

Elspeth pushed her chair back and stood up. It was like a gesture of dismissal but Alec didn't rise and Harold, after a moment's hesitation, also remained seated. He caught sight of his wristwatch; it was six o'clock. Imprisoned in the conflict of wills, which was so complete as to resemble apathy, Time seemed to stand still. Harold had a moment of boredom so intense as to be almost panic; Monday morning seemed immeasurably far away, a point in another life which he would never reach. How could he reach it, counting the heavy minutes one by one? And this was succeeded by an access of acute nostalgia; he was back in the little lounge at Tilecotes, and could hear the voices of the children, asking for this and that, pressing forward into the future, eagerly claiming their share of life, and Isabel directing and controlling them and making plans for them, while he himself looked on, putting his word in now and then, subconsciously busy with his work for the next day. Everything forward-looking, the hum of bees—creating, in the present, the life they were going to have; while here, in this large sunlit room, crowded with objects which Harold supposed to be valuable, all was static, because the emotional relationship on which these two people depended had lost its balance and they had nothing to put instead of it. The very air seemed stagnant and oppressive, as if it was an indoor product.

"Then you'll look after Mr. Eastwood, Alec," Elspeth said. "I'll go to my room, I think, and rest till dinner-time."

Carrying her head high and walking very straight she left them.

13

ALEC did not speak immediately. He stirred his teacup and fixed his eyes on the table. Then he said:

"I'm sorry about this, Harold. I thought we were going to be alone. But Elspeth always springs a surprise or two. We'll have to make the best of it. She's a very interesting woman really, only she's a bit . . . a bit . . ." He didn't finish, and went on. "Don't feel offended, but what she really came back for was to see your wife. Rather a sell for her, wasn't it?"

"I wish Isabel could have come," said Harold, forgetting that Alec had not asked her.

"Spoken like a good husband," Alec said. "But do you really? I mean, in the circumstances . . . as it turned out . . . Blast her, she *said* she was going to be away. I'm very fond of her, you know, but there are times . . . and this is one. I had all sorts of plans. . . . Well, they don't seem so much fun now, even if she lets us carry them out. But there's one thing we can do."

"What is that?" asked Harold.

"Go out and get drunk."

Harold said he had already drunk enough for one day.

"Yes, but this is rather special. You don't meet Elspeth every day. I'm not married to her, you know; I sometimes wish I was."

"Why aren't you?" Harold asked. Since Elspeth had left them he suddenly felt more intimate with Alec.

"Oh, for several reasons. She has a husband living, for one. But she isn't very marriageable, is she?"

"They why do you wish you were married to her?" asked Harold.

"Because then I could get rid of her more easily," said Alec. "Now let's get the car and I'll tell you all about her— no, not all, but something. And then perhaps you can tell me something."

"What?" asked Harold, as they got up to go.

"Well, you're so good at getting one off Income Tax, perhaps you could. . . . You see, I want somebody, but somebody quite different."

Harold was on his guard, but not against Alec's next remark.

"Your wife would understand. She struck me as being very perceptive."

"Isabel's a clever woman," Harold said. "Everyone says so."

"Yes, but she's more than clever. Damn the car, it won't start."

It started so suddenly that they were both jerked forward.

"Good Lord, I must have left the thing in gear. You see, I'm tired of her and yet I depend on her. I'm afraid of her, too."

Harold saw that Alec's hands on the driving wheel were not quite steady.

"I can't imagine being afraid of a woman," he said, trying not to sound unsympathetic, and unaware that he was afraid of Isabel.

"Oh, can't you? Well, you don't know Elspeth. She holds me down like a conquered country. She's a terrific cat-and-mouser, too."

"Cat-and-mouser? I'm afraid I don't quite understand," said Harold.

"Why should you understand my private language? I mean, she lets me go, and then catches me again. It's a game, as they say. She plays it to perfection. She knows instinctively how much scratching and fondling I can take before I long for freedom, and how much freedom I can take before I long for the next pounce. I suppose I enjoy it, but how sick I am of it. She has an awful temper, too."

They turned out of the drive into the road. The mist had lifted, the evening sun was shining, and Harold could see the landscape that Isabel was seeing, though how much less clearly than she saw it. For one thing his attention was distracted by the wobbling of the front wheels. Was Alec in a fit state to drive? And would he be, on the return journey? No man likes to question another's competence

116

in a matter so nearly touching his pride as the driving of a car; but Harold decided that of the two risks it might be the lesser.

"You've been driving all day," he said. "Why not give yourself a break and let me take your place?"

Alec grinned at him rather wanly.

"You wouldn't know the way," he said. "I shall be all right when I've stoked up a bit. It was the shock, you know —well, the surprise—of Elspeth coming back. I thought we were going to have the week-end to ourselves. Now——"

As so often, he didn't finish the sentence, but took his hand off the wheel to make a gesture of disappointment or resignation. The car plunged, and he clutched the wheel again.

"We shall get through it somehow," he said. "You must draw her fire, Harold. Play up to her, won't you? Be the husband who's taking a holiday—playing while the cat's away. I wasn't ripe for another pounce, I must admit."

Harold persuaded Alec to let him drive them home. The drinks hadn't cheered him up; they had depressed and fuddled him. Harold, who wasn't used to men with moods, thought that the best and kindest policy was to ignore Alec's. If he himself was out of spirits, he hated anyone to comment on it. It was a measure of self-protection dating from his schooldays, when a long face was a sign of weakness and the pack would turn on him if they saw him looking sad. A cheerful countenance was the first line of defence. Most of Harold's men friends felt the same, and if they had seen one of their number looking quite suicidal, would never have dreamed of asking him the reason.

During the visit Harold's own outlook had undergone a good many changes. It was natural to him to feel critical of another environment than his own; he suspected hostility at once; the herd instinct was very strong in him. In so far as he was a snob his snobbery only operated within his own social group; he didn't envy those above it, though he tended to look down on those below it. Both seemed to him a little unreal, and as if they didn't know what life was about; and this was especially the case with Alec and his outfit, for Alec belonged to no group or social stratum, he appeared to have the freedom of several but to be indigenous to none. Harold disapproved of this, he was suspicious of any man who couldn't produce a dozen men who wore the same uniform as he did. Alec had friends, of course, didn't Harold know it? And these friends were prepared to do a good deal for him. But the ties which bound him to them were emotional and personal, not social. The emotional and personal sides of Alec's nature were, in Harold's view, much too highly developed. Nearly everything that Alec said to him during their expedition to the pub embarrassed him; he felt he was overhearing things he was not meant to hear, and that later Alec would be sorry he had said them. Besides being indecent it was risky. How did Alec know that Harold wouldn't take advantage of these confidences? To lay all his cards on the table like that! To expose his whole being to another person's view! With one ear Harold listened; with the other he tried not to listen. It all came, Harold told himself, from Alec's being educated privately; at a public school he would have learnt reticence; he would have learnt to conceal his feelings until, under the salutary influence of self-discipline, he would have ceased to have any—any, that is, outside the married state, where it was still permissible to indulge them.

And really it was all such a storm in a teacup, to make this fuss about somebody (no need to say exactly what she was or stood for) coming back unexpectedly to spend a Sunday! Forgetting his own moment of acute boredom at the prospect, Harold, making an unwonted imaginative effort, tried to think how he would feel if the woman who bored him most—his mother-in-law—were suddenly to descend on him for the week-end. He wouldn't have been pleased, of course, but he would have shrugged his shoulders and for Isabel's sake put a good face on it. And in the nature of things mothers-in-law were a headache to husbands. But Elspeth, Mrs. Elworthy, wasn't Alec's mother-in-law, she was his—— And anyhow she didn't seem *such* an awful woman. As far as Harold could tell she was much like other women; they were a world apart. Alec's dread of her seemed

118

ridiculously exaggerated. Now if she had been a disease-carrier or a blackmailer——!

And yet in spite of himself Harold was flattered by Alec's confidences and every now and then felt himself being unwillingly drawn into the vortex of his feelings. Thankful as he would be to get away from the place and all it represented (this is what happens when you step outside your proper sphere in life) he couldn't help feeling a little excited at being present where such scenes went on, and a little sorry for Alec, who seemed so sorry for himself. Again he tried to put himself in Alec's place and wondered what he would have done (an exercise full of self-congratulation) if he had been silly enough to fall into it. For however unreal the Alec-Elspeth relationship might be, his own relationship with Alec did impinge at points on reality. There was £150 already on its way to him; there was the promise of another £150 if—Harold's thoughts sheered off, and at that moment Alec said:

"Turn right here, old man, you've overshot the mark."

Apologizing, Harold backed the car.

"As I was saying," Alec said, when they were once more on the right road, "she always tries to keep me guessing. I get rather tired of that. Does Isabel try to keep you guessing?"

"No," said Harold, stiffening as he always did when Alec mentioned Isabel's name. "But of course she's——"

"She's your wife," Alec finished for him. "But wives sometimes do, you know; it's a habit women have. And I don't like it. My guessing days are over. If there's to be any guessing, I want it to be done by someone else, someone *I* could be a surprise to—like the little Austrian in the Green Dragon down at your place."

"I thought you were only interested in her for the sake of copy," Harold said.

"So I was, so I was, but I can't help feeling a *bit* sentimental about her. You didn't, I gather."

"Me?" said Harold. "I'm——"

"A married man, you were going to say. Yes, but even so you have a heart. Didn't you detect a sort of tenderness in her, innocence, trustfulness—I don't know what to call it—a

119

guarantee of feeling? That's what I should like. Somebody like that shows up the rest of us, don't you think?—one nice person. Pity you didn't make any headway with her. Couldn't you try again?"

"I suppose I might," said Harold carelessly. "But I don't think it would be any good."

"You never can tell. Have a go, as they say." Alec looked round. "Good Lord, we're nearly there. Well, this time Elspeth hasn't kept us guessing. We're for it all right, and Sunday is another day. Don't think I'm not fond of her—I am, devilish fond of her, but am I bored with her at this moment? Not so bored as you must be with me though."

They put the car away and in silence walked towards the house. Even to Harold it had a curiously expectant air, as if Elspeth's eyes were behind every window. They tiptoed up the stairs. As they stopped outside Harold's bedroom door, Alec said in a lowered voice, "Dinner's supposed to be at half-past eight. Don't change unless you'd rather. We mustn't be late, though, or she'll skin us."

When Harold came into the library Alec was already there. Wearing a green velvet smoking jacket he was walking up and down the hearthrug.

"You told me you weren't going to change," said Harold.

"I thought I'd better put on this thing. She likes it, you know. It doesn't matter about you; you have an alibi. Would you like a drink? There's just time if we're quick."

Infected by his host's uneasiness, Harold said he would.

"Elspeth doesn't drink herself," said Alec, moving to the tray. "She doesn't need a stimulant; her alcoholic content is so high already. Here you are, Harold; I'll abstain for once."

"Oh, but you said. . . ."

"No, I really think I'd better not."

Harold, who had taken less at the pub than Alec had, sat down with his drink while Alec resumed his sentry-go.

The bell rang for dinner.

"She should be here any minute now," said Alec. "You know, in spite of what I said, I hope you'll like her. She can be great fun. You see, she's always pleased or not pleased, never in a neutral state of mind, like most people. She'll want to know all about you—that's her technique. She'll probably want you to do something for her."

"What sort of thing?"

"Oh, find something for her in some shop in London."

"And supposing I can't."

"She'll think of something else. She likes to feel one is doing something for her."

"And what does she do in return?"

Alec looked at him.

"She injects you with the vitamins of her interest . . . quite a strong dose. In one way it makes life easier . . . in another way not. I hope you'll like her. I didn't want you to meet her, but now——"

The parlourmaid came in.

"Dinner is served, sir," she said.

"Thank you, Mary. We'll wait till Mrs. Elworthy comes down."

Again he paced the hearthrug.

"If she wasn't so damned jealous! She'll be jealous of you, you know, jealous of the good turns you've done me. She'll set her cap at you, I dare say. She doesn't like things to go on as they are. She doesn't like a stable situation. She comes into most of my books, you know, some aspect of her. I'm glad you're going to see her, really."

He went to the staircase, and called up it, "Elspeth!" Getting no answer, he came back again. "She's late sometimes," he said. "Just so that one shan't count on her being punctual. She won't say she's sorry, in case you might believe her. She's dressing up for you, perhaps. If she's in good form, you can't beat her. She may be a bit tired from her journey. I think I'll have a drink after all. Between drinks I don't feel too good. You'll have another?"

Harold refused.

"It would have been a pity if you'd missed her," Alec said, mixing himself a drink. "I shall enjoy seeing you together. You'll take what she says in good part, won't you? She likes people to stand up to her."

The parlourmaid reappeared.

"Please, sir," she said, "I knocked at Mrs. Elworthy's door and got no answer."

"Got no answer?"

"And she isn't in her room."

"Not in her room?"

"No, sir. Would you still like dinner kept back?"

Alec looked round irresolutely.

"Oh well. Yes, please, she may be in the garden."

It was nearly nine o'clock, and twilight was falling. Alec went to the garden door and Harold joined him.

"Elspeth! Elspeth!"

They waited nearly half an hour, Alec in growing agitation. He tried to tell Harold what Elspeth meant to him; his tone about her changed completely, but everything he said in her favour made Harold like her less. "She must be somewhere about," he kept repeating. Finally, in the darkness, they made a complete circuit of the outside of the house, Alec peering into the shadows and calling softly. His voice got rather husky. "She didn't think she was welcome," he said, "she didn't think she was welcome."

They sat down at the dinner-table and ate the ruined meal, almost in silence, trying not to look at Elspeth's empty place, and at the chair which Alec would not have removed. "Forgive me for being so dull," he said more than once, "but this has been a disappointment to me, a very great disappointment. I did want you to meet her."

"I did meet her," said Harold. "Perhaps she didn't like me."

"Oh no, it wasn't that. I'm sure she would have liked you. She thought I wasn't glad to see her. I deserve to be shot, really."

There's no pleasing him, thought Harold. First he's in despair because she comes back, and now he's miserable because she's gone away—if she has gone. By rights he should be tickled to death and yet he isn't, he's kicking himself. It doesn't make sense.

Before they went to bed, they stumbled round the garden once again, and Alec left the front door open, in case she should come back.

14

MONDAY morning brought Harold's unfinished letter. Isabel
was puzzled by it; it left her in the air. Lacking the last
words the whole letter seemed inconclusive. And it was so
unlike Harold to have sent it incomplete. He must have
been interrupted; yes, but how?

Piqued by the mystery, suddenly made restless, her
imagination began to work on the letter in a way it never
would have if Harold had finished it. She persuaded herself
that he had been going to tell her something very important,
something he had left till last. About what? About Irma,
perhaps. Harold had said, in effect, that Alec was no longer
interested in Irma. But Isabel didn't believe it. She didn't
believe that a man who had taken as much interest in a
woman as Alec's letters showed he had, could give her up
so quickly.

She found that she herself was taking an interest in the
girl, and wishing that she could get to know her. Down
the two avenues of her bifocal vision she saw Irma approaching. In one she was the girl whom Alec had fallen in love
with, and for whom it was in his power to do so much.
Had she believed herself to be in love with Alec, she might
have hated Irma as a rival, but she did not; the thought of
him was a thought that warmed her heart, and that was
all. And Irma had it in her power to do a great deal for
Alec. Alec was lonely, Isabel was sure of it. Irma could fill
that gap, and by helping her to fill it Isabel would herself
be filling it, vicariously. The idea that unknown to Alec she
might be solving the problem of his emotional life was
blissful.

Down this avenue Irma appeared as Alec's mistress. Isabel
blushed. "Knighton, we didn't know you were a prig." She
saw the accusing faces round her. She felt her spirit shrinking
spirally, dwindling into a hard dry core: and blushed again,
for blushing. To be a mistress was as justifiable an aim for

123

a woman as to be a wife; it was equally an experience, and experience was the touchstone.

Down the other avenue Irma appeared as somebody quite different—a hapless foreigner, a displaced person, exposed to who knew what dangers and temptations, someone in urgent need of help. The instinct for good works, implanted in Isabel by early training, was as strong as ever. She was on two or three committees for the relief of the unfortunate —committees that did their work unobtrusively, without fuss, and without taking themselves so seriously as men did. None of these committees exactly covered Irma's case; she was not blind, she was not (Isabel supposed) an unmarried mother, she was not related to a soldier or a sailor or an airman—at least not in England. But she was, she must be, lonely: she must need interests and companionship. The ideal was to find the two together, and they could be found—in the local branch of the Women's Institute.

It was twelve o'clock; Jeremy and Janice would not be back from school for another half-hour yet. But the public houses would be open, the public houses which Isabel had sometimes visited in her London days but which she now regarded, along with other dubious but inevitable forms of popular entertainment, as a social phenomenon which might be improved or controlled by means of a committee. She had nothing against public houses as such.

She did not stop to ask herself whether Harold would approve. Just as he had his work, in which she had no part, so she had hers. She seldom talked to him about it, for she did not think that it would interest him; she knew he liked her to do welfare work, because it consolidated their social position, increased their weight as units of the community. Defence in depth, that was Harold's idea. His instinct was to occupy, not to spread, to put on social weight, to be more solid. How he adored the status quo! And Isabel would be doing nothing to jeopardize it by going on this errand: rather the contrary.

So it was as a welfare-worker that she stepped out of the house on that rather ambiguous July morning, feeling the need to act, and glad to be in action.

Yes, the landlord of the Green Dragon said, receiving Isabel in his sitting-room; he certainly did employ a girl called Irma. Her other name he never could pronounce but he could spell it. If Mrs. Eastwood would kindly take a chair he would write it on a bit of paper.

Did he think Irma was lonely? Well, he couldn't answer that one; she had no time to be lonely in the bar. Loneliness was a matter of feeling time hanging heavy on your hands, wasn't it?

Isabel agreed, but said she was thinking of the Austrian girl's time off.

"Well, she has a young man, you know."

"Oh, she has?"

"Yes, a German farm-worker, a steady-going young chap, but not much up here"—he touched his forehead.

"Is she engaged to him?"

"That I don't know, but they are walking out."

Isabel received this news in silence, then she said:

"All the same, I think she might like to join our Women's Institute. It would give her—well, certain advantages. Companionship and interest, and make a background for her. The women like it, you know; the single ones, the married ones, and, well . . . the others. We have talks and classes, but it's all very free and easy. You wouldn't have any objection to her going, would you?"

"Me? No," the landlord said. "It's up to her. As long as you don't teach her that there's anything amiss in serving drinks. Would you like to speak to her herself? She's in the bar."

"Well, if I might," said Isabel.

"I'll go and fetch her. But she's sure to say yes. She doesn't like saying no, she thinks it's rude. But can't I bring you something, Mrs. Eastwood? A glass of sherry? On the house, of course."

Rather to her own surprise, Isabel accepted, and the landlord went away. The opening door let in the sound of voices. Awaiting his return, she felt her heart beginning to beat uncomfortably and the red flooding her face.

The landlord came in first; he held the door open, so that Irma seemed to make a little entry; with her meek looks and downcast eyes and the gentle radiance stealing off her, she might have been a young saint in a picture, modestly offering herself for martyrdom. Touched and pleased and suddenly happier Isabel rose to greet her; the hand she took was soft and warm, the eyes that met hers gleamed with a misty sweetness before they dropped again.

"And here's your sherry," the landlord reminded Isabel, who hadn't noticed it.

"Oh, thank you. Well. . . . Shall I tell Irma what it is we do?"

"Yes, give her the low-down on it, and meanwhile I'll do her trick inside."

Shutting on him, the door shut out the hum of voices, giving the room the thrill of privacy. Isabel leant forward.

"So that's what it is," she concluded. "We get an opportunity to meet each other, in an informal atmosphere, which some of us mightn't get otherwise. Sometimes we have someone to talk to us, sometimes we work, sometimes we play games. . . . You'll find us all wanting to make friends with you. Do you like the idea?"

"Please yes," said Irma. "When should I come?"

"Well, actually, the next meeting is on Thursday, and as it happens, at my house, a red house with a white gate in Lytham Road. They're all alike, but ours has Tilecotes on the gate. Shall I write it down for you?"

"Please."

Isabel did so. Tilecotes: what a name, she thought. "We have tea at four o'clock. If you were to come a little early we could have a talk. I mustn't keep you now." Isabel rose.

"Oh, but it is so nice to talk," cried Irma, evidently wanting Isabel to stay. "I shall look forward to it very much, Mrs. . . . Mrs. . . ."

"Eastwood."

"Thank you, Mrs. Eastwood, for being so kind to me. I do not have many friends. It is not quite amusing for them when I have to ask and ask . . . and then I sometimes the bad answers make! You do not speak German, Mrs. Eastwood?"

"Only a few words," said Isabel. "But," she added, "I might be able to find someone who does."

"I must not in German too much talk," said Irma, "because you see I want to learn speak English. But here in this hotel I do not learn very quickly, because the people who come say always the same things."

"What sort of things?" asked Isabel.

"Oh," said the girl, as though she might have given a wrong impression, "not unkind things but—what do you say?—things to make me laugh. Sometimes I do not understand, and still I laugh. But I do not learn much that way, because we must sometimes be serious."

"You like being serious?" said Isabel.

"Oh yes, I like. And to learn interesting things about the public monuments. I should like someone to teach me interesting things."

"We'll see what we can do," said Isabel. "Good-bye, my dear. Don't forget Thursday."

Isabel walked home in a state of some elation. Why? What had she done to congratulate herself on? She had roped in a recruit to the Women's Institute. Well, that was something. She allowed her mind to dwell on this good deed. And she had also brought herself nearer to Alec; she felt a little as she had felt in his presence. But this sensation she did not translate into thought; she let its warmth enfold her, and was still basking in it when she heard Janice's voice, dipping on its minor third, its cuckoo-call:

"Mummy! What is Daddy doing now?"

Harold. Harold. She had forgotten him. He had gone clean out of her mind, and stayed out, for an hour. Now he came back, not by himself, but obscured by a dancing cloud of question marks, like midges.

"Daddy's in the train, I expect," she said.

"Would it be the Fishguard Boat Express?" asked Jeremy innocently.

"It might be," Isabel hazarded.

"Oh no, it couldn't be," said Jeremy. "That was a catch. The Fishguard Boat Express doesn't run on Mondays."

"You are too clever for me," Isabel said.

"Besides, there's no connection."

"Oh dear, oh dear."

"Besides, he would have had to get up in the middle of the night."

"You don't say so!"

"When will he get here?" asked Janice, practically. Jeremy didn't answer; a theorist, he was only interested in what couldn't be done.

"Perhaps he'll send a telegram," said Isabel.

"Will you let us stay up till he comes?" asked Janice.

"Yes, if it's not too late."

By now Isabel could see Harold as clearly as if he was on the doorstep.

"Will he bring Mr. Goodrich with him?" Janice asked.

Isabel started. For the moment, Harold's image had eclipsed Alec's.

"Oh no. Why, would you like him to?"

"Yes . . . I want to show him . . . I want to show him . . ." Janice's voice took on its teasing sing-song—"my other dollies."

"Not Pamela?"

"It isn't Pamela, it's Pamelia, Mummy. No, because she hasn't been good."

"What has she done?"

Janice thought a moment. She was improvising a sin for Pamelia.

"I *think* she told a lie."

"Oh, what about?"

"She said. . . . She said. . . ." Janice suddenly became aware of Jeremy's inquisitorial eye fixed on her. She wanted to provoke him, but it flustered her.

"She doesn't know," said Jeremy.

"Oh yes, I do. She said . . . something untrue about Mr. Goodrich."

"What did she say?"

"She said . . . he wasn't a gentleman."

"Did she say why?"

The strain on Janice's powers of invention was obviously becoming terrific.

"Well, because he . . . because he . . . because he hadn't got a real wife."

"How do you mean, a real wife?"

"Well, not like Daddy has. And I said, 'That has nothing to do with being a gentleman.' And she said, 'Oh yes it has, gentlemen always have wives.' And I said, 'No they don't, you only say so because you want to m——' "

"Oh, shut up!" said Jeremy.

"I won't shut up. 'Because you want to marry him yourself.' And so I smacked her, and she's still crying."

"I think you were rather unkind," said Isabel.

"No, because I can't let her grow up into a liar, can I?"

"She doesn't always tell the truth herself," said Jeremy, and Isabel, to avert a scene, quickly changed the subject.

The children were in bed and, Isabel hoped, asleep when Harold arrived. She expected to find him somehow changed, and the fact that he looked so much himself at once reassured and disappointed her. She hoped that he would open up at once about his visit, but he didn't; he talked about his journey back, and the punctuality or lateness of the trains, almost as if he had been Jeremy. Really he was wondering how much he should tell Isabel of his adventures; he didn't see how he could edit them; if he told her anything he must tell her all, and that was against his code. He still thought of her, and preferred to think of her, as not quite grown-up. It was a defence against her cleverness. But when the second course of his supper appeared, and the whisky he allowed himself after long tiring days had mellowed him, he felt the need to communicate. So that when Isabel, who wisely had not tried to force his confidence, said carelessly, "I didn't quite understand about your letter," he began to unburden himself, and told her the story, not selectively, as he had meant to, but chronologically, each revelation leading to the next, so that by the end Isabel had heard pretty well everything. While she listened, her London self was uppermost; she was not shocked, and hardly at all surprised by what she heard: in an odd way she felt that Harold was merely confirming what she had known before: indeed, both visually and emotionally, she could fill in many details that he didn't give her. It didn't change her opinion of Alec that he had been so weak with Elspeth: she liked him the better for it. She had suspected all along that there was someone in Alec's life she ought to hate.

So this was what Elspeth meant, or a small part of what she meant, when she said that she made Alec "feel". Did she suffer herself while she was making him suffer, or was she absolutely cold-blooded about it?

"And did she come back?" she asked, when Harold had reached that point in his story.

"No, she didn't. We waited in for her most of Sunday morning, and her place was laid for lunch and again for dinner. But she didn't show up. She telephoned, though, late on Sunday night."

"What to say?"

"To apologize to me for not saying good-bye. She didn't say where she was, or when she was coming back. Alec got quite worked up about it. I should have let her rip."

"I'm not so sure you would have."

"I've no use for that kind of woman," Harold said. "But, of course, it was his fault, really. If he had to have her around, he should have taken a strong line with her from the first. Thank goodness, darling, you don't go on like that."

"And thank goodness you don't," Isabel said, a remark so obvious that she reddened at it. "So nothing happened after that?"

"No, we just mooched about all Sunday, killing time, and next morning Alec took me to the station. There was just one thing, though."

Isabel became all ears.

"It wasn't anything, really. Only the telephone call came from our part of the world."

"How do you know?"

"The operator said, 'Downhaven on the line.' "

"But could she have got there in the time?"

"We must ask Jeremy."

For a moment Isabel and Harold both sat guessing, as possibly Elspeth would have liked them to, and in that moment Isabel's London self receded, and was replaced by the clergyman's daughter, wife to Harold and mother to Jeremy and Janice. No longer did St. Milo's seem desirable, the target of her thoughts, the lodestar of her hopes and dreams; her place was here, in the lounge at Tilecotes, where Harold's taste and hers, contending not too violently, had achieved a sort of harmony, a compromise, bourgeois no doubt to look at, but to feel, how safe and cosy! It was seldom that Isabel's imagination could work on it, to transform it, but now it seemed a fortress. She drew the curtains which she had forgotten to draw and sat down by Harold's side, and took his hand: and when he said, "There's no place like home, is there?" her thoughts did not wince at this too obvious remark.

After a while he said, "And what have you been doing while I was away?"

Isabel was startled from her drowsiness. "I? Oh, nothing. The daily round, you know. Looking after the children. Missing you."

Harold gave her a loving look which sat rather self-consciously, but none the less dearly, on his neat, tight-skinned, self-disciplined face. Her conscience pricked her, and she said:

"Oh well, I did do one thing. I asked that girl at the Green Dragon—Irma something—to join the Women's Institute."

"Oh!" said Harold, jumping to his feet and turning his back on Isabel. "And what made you do that?"

Isabel was too much occupied with her own emotions to notice the effect that her announcement had had on Harold.

"I thought it might be a kind thing to do. You told me she was lonely and that some of the customers teased her. She seemed very glad to join. She's coming to the meeting here on Thursday. She seemed anxious to improve her English."

Harold turned round and said:

"Will she understand anything?"

"Oh yes, she understood everything I said to her, and she can read English quite easily, she said. Why don't you come, Harold? There's going to be a talk on modern novelists."

"Well, Thursday is my afternoon off," said Harold, "but should I be allowed in?"

"Oh yes, women's clubs and societies aren't exclusive like men's. They don't have such sticky rules. Men sometimes give us talks, though this time it's a woman. Besides, it's your house: you have a right to be there."

"I expect I shall be terribly bored," said Harold ungraciously, "and it'll all be above my head."

"Then you will come? Splendid."

"I'll think about it," Harold said. He thought about it, and about Irma's pretty, gentle face framed in a throng of middle-aged, faceless, or hard-featured women, and the radiance it cast over his own thoughts, even now when they were tender for another reason—perhaps more than ever now.

A cry came faintly through the closed door of the lounge. "Listen, Harold, it's Janice! The children are still awake! They have been talking about you ever since you left! Come and say good-night to them!"

15

"I'M not finding my bread-and-butter letter to Alec very easy to write," said Harold, when he came home to luncheon the next day. "Would you like to hear what I've said? I don't want it to sound too businesslike."

Isabel almost gasped.

Harold pulled an envelope out of his pocket and cleared his throat. Then he began to read in a discouraged voice, strangely unlike his own, and rather as if he had been reading a lesson in church.

"'Dear Alec, I had quite a good journey home. The train was five minutes late at Swansea and a quarter of an hour late at Cardiff, but had made up five minutes by the time we reached Newport. I had an excellent lunch, nothing fanciful, you know, but good plain food well cooked. I sometimes think that people who complain of train food would be quite glad to have it in their own homes.'"

Harold broke off.

"Do you think that's all right?" he asked.

"Perfectly," said Isabel. "Was Alec's food fanciful?"

"Well, it was a bit frilly. Does it sound as if I was having a crack at him?"

"No—more as if you were having a crack at me."

Harold stared. "Oh well, yes, I see. But I'm not; you know that."

"Of course not, darling."

"Well, that turns the page. Now:

"'I have to thank you for a thoroughly enjoyable week-end. The countryside, after the fog had cleared on Saturday, was a delight to the eye.'" (Harold seemed better pleased with himself at this point.) "'And I thought your well-appointed house with its beautiful surroundings most attractive. Your hospitality was lavish and I have never fared better or had better fare.'"

Harold stopped. "What about that?" he said.

"Yes," said Isabel. "It ought to make him smile."

"I didn't want to be too heavy. Well:

" 'If there was any unpleasantness I would rather not refer to it, for your sake, as it had nothing to do with you and you did your best to minimize the inconvenience.' "

"I'm not so sure about that bit," said Isabel. "Would you say anything about her?"

"How can I help it? She spoilt the whole thing. It was bad enough when she was there and worse still when she wasn't. I haven't called her a bitch or anything, which was what she was. No, I'll keep that bit."

"Very well."

" 'I also very much enjoyed our drive on Saturday, our visits to the two locals, and found Sunday quite restful to me personally in spite of the anxiety which in the circumstances you naturally felt.' "

"H'm," said Isabel.

"Well, I have to show myself a bit sympathetic, don't I? There was the wretched fellow nearly mad with worry. I couldn't pretend I didn't notice it. No, I think I'll keep that bit."

Isabel began to suspect that Harold was better pleased with the letter than he professed to be, and wanted approval and even admiration rather than suggestions.

" 'Now, turning to business,' " said Harold in a different voice. " 'I confess that the Inspector took a more broad-minded view of the market-garden than I thought he would. He z-z-z-z-z' (this wouldn't interest you, Isabel) 'Of course, if we—z-z-z-z-z' "—Harold buzzed like a wasp—" 'from your point of view, and of course from mine, too, an extremely satisfactory result ...

" 'In conclusion, may I again say how much I enjoyed my time under your hospitable roof. It is an experience which I shall long remember when the clouds, both literal and metaphorical, which marred the scene have passed away. I came back to find my wife and children in the best of health and apparently none the worse for my absence. My wife wishes to be remembered to you'—is that all right, Isabel?"

"Yes," said Isabel.

" 'And my daughter Janice (aged six) asks me to send you

her love—rather forward of her, I think, but you made a big hit with her.' Do you think that's too colloquial? I could say 'worships the ground you tread on'."

"I think that would be going a bit too far," said Isabel. "She's only a little girl."

"Yes, but I think I like it better. If she was older, or was going to see him again, I shouldn't say it. I shouldn't write in this strain at all to anyone else, they might think I'd gone potty, but it's the sort of way he talks, and I think he needs cheering up. Now, then: 'It's something to have a family after all, nuisances though they can be at times.' (You don't mind me saying that, do you, Isabel? He'll see it's not meant seriously.) 'And so with renewed thanks for a most unique visit, Yours very sincerely, Harold Eastwood.

"'P.S. I forgot to say that there are some interesting returns among those you sent me, and I am doing my best to sort them out. August will soon be here, and we shall be off on holiday, but I usually take some homework with me, and could fit in a few more returns, if any came along. I think you said you knew of one or two people to whom I might be useful.' "

Harold hurried a little over this bit, and then said, rather self-consciously, "Well, do you think it's all right? I'm not sure I could alter it, even if you didn't."

"It's excellent," said Isabel, adding unguardedly, "It isn't very much like you."

"Well, I explained that."

"Yes, but even so. . . . Do you think the visit's changed you, Harold?"

"Changed me? Good Heavens, no. Why should it?"

"Well, somehow I thought you'd take a different line about it all."

"About Elspeth, you mean? Oh well, one can't be too straitlaced in these days. I can't see what he saw in her, of course, either one way or the other. But I suppose it's his business. . . . Had you anything else to say?"

Isabel thought.

"Nothing about the letter. Only—what you were saying about Janice—she'd be rather sad, poor child, if she thought she wasn't going to see him again. Couldn't you put in, after 'worships the ground you tread on' something about 'hopes, as we do, that you will soon pay us another visit'?"

"But do *we* hope so? I think once is enough."

"We could leave the door open. It must be a relief for him to get away from that horrible woman."

"We don't want to leave the door open for her."

Isabel laughed. "No, but I think it would be only civil, to leave him a loophole, especially when he may be sending you more work."

"H'm," said Harold. "I don't think we really *want* him here."

"Perhaps not, but if it's good for business——"

"All right, I'll put in something. I did feel rather sorry for the fellow. Hullo, there's the children." Through the open window came the cry, so usual that Isabel didn't always notice it:

"Janice, go back!"

136

16

ISABEL hired the extra chairs and tea-things and arranged
for the meeting to be held on the lawn. On the lawn there
was plenty of room for the score or so of women whom she
expected to turn up, and if the neighbours on each side
didn't want to listen to a talk on "Modern Fiction," well,
they needn't. If it rained—that terrible if—she could just
squeeze the party into the lounge. Isabel was a good
organizer; although, for the meetings, very little organizing
was necessary: the women did most of it themselves, including the washing-up, so her duties as hostess were not onerous,
and her thoughts were not unduly preoccupied with ways
and means, or with wondering whether the meeting would
be a success, for within certain limits they always were successful; the women came to enjoy themselves.

Tea came first, then the talk. By a quarter to four Isabel
was more than ready; she had reached the stage of inspecting
all the arrangements for the second time and moving flower-
vases and chairs a few inches this way and then back again.
The party feeling, the community spirit, the coming loss of
personality in the crowd was beginning to steal over her, but
one thing held it back—the thought of Irma.

Irma had promised to come early for a little initiating talk
—a talk before the talk. What should it be about? The
minutes passed and Isabel was still debating this problem.

Harold was not coming on duty until four o'clock; he
hadn't actually promised that he would come at all. He had
been unusually cagey about his intentions, had assumed airs
of masculine secrecy and unpredictability. This attitude was
in part a hangover from his visit to Alec; he had realized
how humiliating it was to be in thrall to a woman. Irma was
a woman—a girl—to whom one could never be in thrall;
whenever he thought of Elspeth he thought of Irma as her
antidote. Towards Irma one could only feel protective: and
protectiveness was an emotion which every man had a right,

even a duty to feel. Isabel did not need protection: she was too clever. All the same, Harold's instinct of self-preservation advised him strongly to avoid the meeting. It even took him to the golf club, his usual resort on Thursday afternoons, where he hung about casting furtive glances at his locker, and half-heartedly refusing more than one offer of a game.

Ignorant of what was passing in his mind, and so preoccupied by her own plan that she would not have taken it in if she had known it, Isabel awaited Irma. But what was her plan? She had none, except the vaguest: to get in touch with the Austrian girl, to get in closer touch with her, to get to know her well enough to—well, what? She no more knew what her next move was to be than, if she had been taking a country walk in a strange place, she would have known what lay round the next corner. It did not occur to her that this life of dream could ever impinge upon her real life; they were entirely separate, as separate as her London and her Marshport self, as separate as the moods in which she saw Harold in so many contradictory guises—as tiresome, as pathetic, as lovable, as unlovable—as almost everything except unreliable. His reliability she took so much for granted that she gave him no credit for it—indeed, it sometimes irritated her, it was such a dull quality.

But one thing had taken firm hold of her mind, as it had of Harold's: the thought of Alec's humiliating dependence upon Elspeth. Though she would have said, if asked, that love had its own laws, that it could not be legislated for, and that it was not only priggish but futile to think otherwise, she suspended this reasoning when she thought of Elspeth. Elspeth was outside the pale, a bloodsucker, a monster. Alec must be saved from her, and Irma was his road to freedom.

The first arrivals were nodding and smiling their way in, making appreciative remarks, but Irma was not among them. Of course she wasn't—how could Isabel have ever thought she would come, plunge into a crowd of women who were strangers to her, and who didn't speak her language—timid as she was? She had said yes—hadn't the landlord said she couldn't say no?—all the time meaning not to come. And while Isabel was thinking this, she suddenly saw Irma standing on the threshold of the lounge—for Isabel had left the front door open—looking shyly round her from under the shadow of her bushy hair, a gentler face among the gentle faces, almost like an angel in a picture, and like an angel softly glowing, as if she had brought light in with her. Isabel went up to her at once and took her hand—but no private conversation was possible; so she bethought her of her duties as a hostess, and began introducing Irma to the women who were nearest.

"This is Irma, our new member. I can't remember her other name. She is an Austrian, so we must be specially kind to her." The women responded at once, putting on their best smiles, piloting her through the French window, out on to the lawn, where in the sunshine the tea-tables with their gaily-coloured cloths gleamed the welcome that only a tea-table can give.

Suddenly they all stood up.

> *Bring me my bow of burning gold!*
> *Bring me my arrows of desire!*
> *Bring me my spear! Oh, clouds, unfold!*
> *Bring me my chariot of fire!*
>
> *I will not cease from mental fight,*
> *Nor shall my sword sleep in my hand,*
> *Till we have built Jerusalem*
> *In England's green and pleasant land.*

It was the song that traditionally opened the proceedings. Isabel loved it: it epitomized and called forth all her faculties of aspiration. And never had she thrilled to its challenge as she did to-day. Though she did not name the enemy to herself, she knew who the enemy was against whom this angelic armoury was arrayed.

She didn't get much tea herself, she drifted about carrying cups and saucers, moving plates of cakes and sandwiches into strategic positions, making and answering remarks, planting smiles where smiles seemed needed, absorbing the collective gaiety and giving it out again; and never did her feeling of being a fairy godmother among fairy godmothers seem stronger than when she passed the chair where, between two rather ample, red-cheeked women, Irma sat, trying with speaking looks and broken sentences to make them understand, though there was no need, how much she was enjoying herself. All these nice women round her, radiating good-will, were like a protection, a bodyguard, ensuring happy days, and Isabel was their chief.

She had other helpers, Jeremy and Janice. As usual she had been in two minds about the children and would have preferred them out of the way; Jeremy didn't like company while Janice liked it only too well. Jeremy would gladly have absented himself but not so Janice; the suggestion that she should stay indoors and have her tea with Jeremy in the kitchen at once provoked a scene: "But I want to show them my new dress!" So here they were, treated as attendant spirits, ministering angels, by the kind ladies on whom they waited—though Jeremy's expression when he handed a cup of tea might well have turned the milk sour. But gradually the women thawed him, and as for Janice, it made Isabel quite hot to see her ballerina airs.

She did not notice Harold come in and it was not until Janice called out "There's Daddy!" that she saw him hovering on the edge of the company like an unsuccessful competitor at Musical Chairs. Which table would he sit at? Isabel hoped it would be Irma's, but no, room was being made for him at another. It took the company a minute or two to absorb this masculine element in their midst. Harold became self-consciously male when women were about: pride of sex oozed out of him, making Isabel want to scold him for being late. Instead she brought him a cup of tea and thanked him for coming. "Oh, I thought I might as well," he said.

Now the tea-things were being cleared away and the tables pushed into the background, all save one, behind which the speaker and the chairman took their places. The chairman announced that Mrs. Rattray, a novelist of repute herself, would speak on "Modern Fiction": they had every reason to be grateful to her, for she was a busy woman who had come a long way to give them this treat.

Mrs. Rattray was a woman with rather frizzy fair hair, a

long face, and earrings: her expression was sardonic. Isabel didn't know her books. She spoke with authority but without making any concession to her less well-read listeners. Perhaps she was giving a talk which she had prepared for a more highbrow audience.

As she listened Isabel wondered how many of the women would have read the authors Mrs. Rattray was discussing, and how much Irma, for instance, was taking in of what she said. Irma was listening intently, her lips a little open, and soon Isabel was listening intently, too, for now her subject was Alexander Goodrich.

He was an unequal novelist, the speaker said, whose sensibility (she made a great deal of sensibility) did not always fertilize his subject matter. When this happened he wrote, she considered, from the wrong part of his mind, and his work, though accomplished, was contrived and rather lifeless. He was at his best in describing an unhappy love-affair. He was, apparently, a misogynist: nice women cut no ice in his novels. "As a writer, I don't say as a man," said Mrs. Rattray, "he wouldn't be interested in any of us here." She paused, and got the laugh she was waiting for. One situation repeated itself in several of his novels: the situation of a man attached to a woman who did not really care about him but who would not let him go even if he wanted to be let go— which usually he didn't. It was infatuation on one side and power-complex on the other. This, or some variation of it, had been the theme of many novelists besides Mr. Goodrich, and in *After the Storm*, for instance, he had made good use of it. Any woman with a heart, the speaker said, who read that book, must long to rescue the hero from his entanglement. She added with a grim smile that a band of women, a sort of rescue squad, ought to be let loose over the field of fiction pledged to save such heroes as Mr. Goodrich's from themselves and their attendant harpies. This brought a laugh from the audience, but Irma looked puzzled.

But it was not an inexhaustible theme, and had, moreover, the disadvantage of being false to most people's experience. Every woman—she shrugged—was not a harpy; most people, certainly most women, wanted their love to be returned and would not go on with a one-sided love-affair. There were signs that Mr. Goodrich had got all he could out of this theme. The last novel in which he exploited it was shrill in tone and weakened by self-pity. One could hardly feel sorry for the hero, he felt so sorry for himself. Moreover, the book did not draw its juices from life as a whole but from this single specialized situation. It would be interesting, the speaker added, to see what Mr. Goodrich could make of the theme of requited love; he was still a comparatively young man and there was no reason to suppose that he had written himself out.

Alec came last on the speaker's list. Afterwards the audience were invited to ask questions. There was a long pause; the speaker's eye travelled invitingly from face to face but nobody seemed inclined to start the ball rolling. At last Isabel, who had been very busy with her thoughts, asked whether, in the speaker's opinion, a novelist always drew on his or her experience for the subject-matter of a novel. Mrs. Rattray replied that it would be rash to make such an assumption. Most novelists wrote about themselves and made use of their own experience, some indeed transcribed it so faithfully that the people who had contributed to it in life could recognize themselves. But the purely autobiographical novel was rare. The average novelist transposed his experience—sometimes in obedience to the dictates of his wishful thinking. He might have been in love with a plain woman; but in his book she would be beautiful. He might have behaved timidly in life: in the book he would be bold as a lion. Such transpositions were necessary to the creative spirit, which could not thrive on literal transcription: it must add something of its own. But in spite of these transpositions, the general pattern of the experience was preserved, because only that experience was fertile to the author's mind. Where would Mr. Goodrich be without his chip on the shoulder, his grievance against women? It was that that made him tick, to use a vulgarism.

Then did she, Isabel asked, think that a new experience, in fact or in imagination, could change the current of an author's work?

Mrs. Rattray replied, cautiously, that she thought it

might, if the experience gave him a new view of himself.

Isabel then dried up, and the rest of the questions were mainly about routine matters of the novelist's craft—at what times of the day did he find it easiest to write, did he work regular hours or did he wait for inspiration, etc. "Any more questions?" asked the chairman in a tone that though encouraging had the ring of finality in it; and when none was forthcoming the audience began to shift on their seats and reach down for their bags.

Suddenly Irma piped up and said:

"Please, what is a harpy?"

Spoken with Irma's foreign accent the question raised a kindly laugh.

"A harpy?" said the speaker, returning to her rostrum. "A harpy?" she repeated. "Well, can any of you define a harpy for me? I'm sure there isn't a harpy here, but I'm equally sure that you all know what it is."

All the women looked rather self-conscious and some giggled. One bolder spirit ventured: "A harpy, Mrs. Rattray, is the sort of woman who gets her claws into a man and won't let go."

"Excellent," said Mrs. Rattray. "I couldn't have done so well. A harpy," she said, turning to Irma, "is a woman who gets her claws into a man and won't let go."

"Oh, how horrible!" cried Irma, shocked.

"Yes, isn't it? But, you know, I think most men deserve the harpies they get, and not all harpies are women, either."

Pleased with this thrust, one of the few manifestations of feminist sentiment that had occurred during the proceedings, Mrs. Rattray withdrew. A little lane was made for her between the members of the Institute, down which she strode with an air of duty done. The bands that held the community together began to loosen and it was as individuals that they drifted towards the French window of the lounge. It had been a good meeting; they had all enjoyed it; everything had gone off well, the conviction of having made the world a better place (though they would not have phrased it so), kindlier, sounder, safer, more capable of innocent but deep-seated pleasures, was present in all of them. This meeting was over; well, they looked forward to the next.

Isabel said to Irma, "Can you wait a moment?" She went to the door to make her farewells and receive murmurs of thanks for her hospitality, but seeing that Harold had been entrapped into performing this office she returned to where Irma was standing alone on the lawn; the children had been banished to the dining-room when the talk began: she could see their small faces flattened against the window.

17

"I HOPE you enjoyed it?" she said.

"Oh yes." said Irma, lifting a radiant face. "I very much enjoy it."

"Did you understand what the speaker, Mrs. Rattray, said?"

"Oh yes, I understand some of it quite well."

"You understood what she said about Mr. Goodrich's novels, about his not being very happy and so on?"

"Please?" said Irma.

As Isabel repeated it, the red mounted to her cheeks, and a note of urgency crept into her voice.

"Yes," said Irma, adding unexpectedly, "But I think she mean that the man in his books is not happy, not he himself who writes"—she made a little gesture with her hands and sighed. "I do not very well explain."

"Oh yes, you do," said Isabel. "But you see, he, Mr. Goodrich, isn't happy either, because, you see" (in spite of herself she couldn't help half smiling), "there is a woman, a harpy, who has got her claws into him."

"Oh, but how dreadful!" Irma cried. "How very sad for him!"

"Yes, isn't it?" said Isabel, speaking more rapidly though she meant to speak more slowly. "But what I wanted to say is this: I know Mr. Goodrich, he is a friend of mine, and you, too, know him, Irma."

"I know him?" said Irma, wonderingly. "I do not think——"

"Yes," said Isabel. "He spoke to you one day at the Green Dragon—one Sunday it was. He spoke to you in German. Surely you remember; try to remember, Irma."

She felt that by repeating Irma's name she was riveting her to Alec with it.

Recollection began to dawn in Irma's face and her wide pretty mouth dropped open. "Oh yes, I do remember—a tall gentleman, how shall I say—with hair that was not quite fair, and eyes that did not the same way look. He speak German very well and I like him."

"Yes," said Isabel, breathless and almost panting. "And he liked you, too. He liked you very much, Irma. He wrote to us about you, he spoke of you several times in his letters. He would like to see you again. Would you like to see him?"

"Oh, please yes," said Irma, kindling to the prospect as Isabel hoped she would. "He very kind—he ask me all about my family. Please can I see him?"

"Yes, you shall. Not now, he isn't here—he lives a long way off, in Wales—but soon, I don't know how soon—but perhaps very soon, he'll be coming here to stay. He'd like to see you, Irma, I know he would."

Isabel stopped and looked up. Harold was standing at the door of the lounge, watching them.

"Would you like to read one of his books?" she hastily said. "I have one here—his best book—*After the Storm*. He put his name in it, his autograph. Do you think you could read it?"

"Please?"

In an agony of embarrassment Isabel had to say it all over again.

"Oh yes," cried Irma enthusiastically. "I read English much better than I speak—much, much better."

"Then I'll get it for you."

In the doorway she said, as casually as she could, to Harold: "That's the Austrian girl, you know, the one that you and Alec spoke to . . . I'm going to lend her a book. Be an angel and talk to her for a moment."

"All right," said Harold, "if you want me to."

Isabel disappeared into the house, and rather slowly and unwillingly Harold went out to Irma. "Hullo," he said. "You here?"

"Oh yes," said Irma, scared by the tone which suggested she had no right to be there, and might be ordered off. "Do you mind? I——"

"Of course not," said Harold gruffly. "I'm glad to see you again. What have you been doing with yourself all this time? Happy and all that?"

"Please?" said Irma.

146

"I mean, have you been enjoying yourself? Have they been nice to you at the Green Dragon?"

"Oh yes. The landlord, Mr. Hitchcock, he is very kind to me."

Harold was not altogether pleased to hear this. "Fellows who come in been teasing you at all?"

"Oh yes," said Irma automatically, adding, "They would not like me if they did not tease me."

"H'm," said Harold. "Do they still ask you to go out with them in the evening?"

"Sometimes, yes."

"And do you go?"

Irma looked down.

"I do not go," she said, "because if I go with one I should have to go with another, and afterwards they quarrel. Besides, I do not like them that much well. But I do go out sometimes with——" She stopped. "With a friend," she said. There was a slight reserve in her voice.

Harold's heart sank.

"Who is he? May I know?"

"Oh yes, his name is Otto. He is a German. He works on a farm. He was a prisoner of the war and now he want to stay in England. There are many such."

"Are you engaged to him?" asked Harold.

"No," said Irma, and it was the first time Harold had heard her use the word. It seemed at once to make a person of her. "He want me to engaged be but I do not want."

"You don't like him enough?" said Harold.

"I like him," Irma said, "but he is too—how shall I say?— too much in a hurry—he want me to say yes, yes, and when I cannot say yes, but 'wait', then he gets angry with me, and so we quarrel sometimes, and he says, 'Oh well, I find some other girl'. But always he comes back to me."

"So you don't want to marry him?" said Harold, anxious to have this point cleared up.

"I say to him, 'I no want to marry you, I no want to marry anyone just now, I am only twenty-one, there is still time.' How do I know that I shan't go back to Austria, to my parents and my family?—only there is more money here. But Otto, he wants me to stay in England. He wants me to

147

do just what he wants and he always will. Sometimes he frighten me, he is so violent, but then, it is strange, I am not angry with him. Only he is so rough, and eats so badly, and thinks that nothing matters but that I marry him."

"But still you don't want to?" Harold asked, determined to wring another negative out of her.

"Yes, in a way I do, because you see he is like a beeg warm stove which sometimes is so hot one wants to keep away but it is nice to know that it is always there. And he is not like those others that ask me to go out but only want to play with me."

Harold looked round; there was no sign of Isabel. What could be keeping her?

"You said you would go out with me one evening," he remarked.

"Oh yes, you were so good to me, you saved me from having to say no which would them have angry made. Always, always, Mr. Hitchcock tell me, I must humour them —humour, you see, means to not say no. There is always the bar between you, he says, and I am not far away. But it is not always easy when they have four or five pints drunk, and then it amuses them that I speak English so badly."

"Well, humour me," said Harold. "Don't say no."

"To going out with you? But what would Mrs. Eastwood say?"

That was just it; what would Isabel say?

"Oh, I can arrange it with her," said Harold airily. "She takes an interest in you, too, you know."

"Oh, but I think—ah, here she is," cried Irma, obviously relieved.

Isabel came towards them, walking slowly down the golf ladder which, with the removal of the tea-tables, had become visible again. "She looks like a stranger," Harold thought; and she had the same feeling about him. She felt she was acting in a play. The stage direction, "Enter Isabel. She and Harold converge upon the barmaid," ran through her mind.

"Here you are," she said, holding out the book to Irma; "it took me longer than I thought to find it."

Irma gazed rapturously at the jacket, which depicted a

man sitting alone on a heathery hillside, while purple clouds shot with lightning rolled away in the distance.

"Oh, but the storm is over!" she exclaimed. "I am so glad of that!"

"Wait till you read it," Isabel said, on whose cheeks the tell-tale red still lingered. "Wait till you read it, Irma. That storm need never have happened if—but I mustn't spoil the story for you."

"Oh yes, don't tell me! don't tell me!" Irma cried. "Oh, how I shall enjoy reading this book, and thinking I have the author met. I have actually known and spoken with him!"

"I told Irma," Isabel said, "how much Mr. Goodrich had enjoyed his conversation with her at the Green Dragon."

"I too, I too, enjoy it very much," said Irma, and suddenly a cloud swept down on her face. "But I forget the time, think, I have not once looked at my watch since I came here, I have enjoyed myself so much, and it is half-past five. I shall be late, I shall be late!"

She was on the point of breaking into a run.

"Before you go," said Isabel, "give us your home address. We shall need it to send you the notices of future meetings. You'll come again, Irma, won't you? You'll come again?"

"Oh yes, oh yes!" said Irma, her agitation calmed by Isabel's tranquil manner. "What I most wanted was to meet a nice kind English family."

"Harold, you have a pen, I'm sure," said Isabel.

He took it with his note-case from his pocket, and at Irma's dictation wrote down the address.

"Now we can always keep in touch with you," said Isabel, and Irma, murmuring incoherent thanks, made for the door.

"I'll see you out," said Harold, and on the doorstep said: "Remember, you're coming out with me one evening."

"Please yes, please yes," cried Irma, over her thin shoulder, her slim bare legs already twinkling on the pavement.

"Leave the front door open, would you?" Isabel called out. "They're such nice, cosy women, but they seem to have made the house rather stuffy."

"Close, you mean," said Harold.

"Or close, if you like it better."

But was she humouring him? thought Harold, turning back into the house. Whether she was or not, he felt extraordinarily calm, and as if he had fulfilled some deep need of his being. The sensation didn't seem to arise from the particular thing that he had done, or from any circumstance; least of all did he wonder whether he ought to have done it. And even when he saw Isabel, still standing where he had left her half-way up the golf ladder, he hardly connected it with her.

"You were a long time looking for that book!" he told her, smiling.

She did not return his smile, but said seriously:

"I stayed away on purpose, because I wanted you to have a talk with her."

At that his own smile faded.

"Why?" he asked.

"Well, oughtn't we to try to get to know her better?"

He took her meaning and it deeply shocked him. He did not look at her but when the weight of the shock had rolled away, it let in to another part of his mind a ray of piercing brightness.

"Well, what can I do to help?" he said. "Take her out one evening to dinner?" He made his voice sound incredulous and sarcastic, and was quite unprepared for Isabel's answer.

"I think that would be a very good plan," she said. "Not here, of course. Perhaps in Downhaven."

"I'll remember that," said Harold. "But what on earth shall I talk to her about?"

"Why not about Alec?"

The sense of shock returned, but muffled this time. Whatever he talked to Irma about, it would not be about Alec.

"Let's go and find the children," he suggested. "We don't know what mischief they may have been getting into."

That night Isabel wrote Alec a long letter. Though she did not know it, it was a love-letter. She had never written to him before, and she had only been with him once, for a week-end; but her thoughts had been so constantly with him—and never more than when they were forbidden access to him—that she felt she knew him through and through. She also felt that the process of getting to know him must have been reciprocal, and that just as she knew him, so he must know her. They had been poured into one another like water into wine, and the fusion had been complete. So she was able to write without self-consciousness.

It was not a declared love-letter, of course; Isabel made no profession of her feeling for Alec. But she instinctively made the assumptions and used the tone of someone who has been a long time in love, whose nature has soaked up the experience, so that every word reflected the mood it sprang from. It was not, as far as Harold's visit to Alec went, an indiscreet letter; she hoped it was not a letter in bad taste; she did not hint at knowing things about Alec's private life that only Harold could have told her. But the quality of sympathy and intimacy that her letter expressed flowed naturally from a knowledge of those facts; she might have been writing to someone who had suffered a misfortune or a bereavement of which she knew the circumstances so well that they need not, indeed could not be referred to, for they had become irrelevant; their importance consisted solely in the legacy of suffering they had left. For all this she consoled him, nor did she have to grope for the right words or wonder if he would take it in the sense she meant it; her mind and heart were perfectly in tune with his, the same vibrations, the same wavelength, served them both. He would never ask himself, "Who is this woman who is writing all this stuff to me?" because she would have established her position with him from the first word, just as a picture establishes itself with the beholder and does not have to be introduced or learnt or talked about or doubted. She went on:

"We have found a new fan for you, and a new friend for ourselves. Can you guess who it is? An Austrian girl who serves behind the bar at a little public house called the Green Dragon—I won't call her a barmaid because she isn't like one, at least not like my idea of one. Harold seems to be quite *épris*, and talks of asking her out to dinner! I ought to be jealous of her, I suppose, for I have seen her—indeed, she has been to this house—and she is very pretty and attractive and somehow rather touching; but how could one be jealous with dear Harold? Anyhow he hopes, we both hope, to see more of her (she opened out a good deal while she was with us), for we are getting rather set in our ways, rather middle-aged and stodgy, altogether too domestic, I'm afraid, and this infiltration of young blood (what a dreadful phrase) will brighten us up. I think you would like her, too. I have lent her *After the Storm* to read, and you are already a great hero to her.

"Do come down and see us again if you could bear to, we did so enjoy your visit. I wish we could make Marshport more alluring for you, but perhaps business will bring you. Or could we persuade you to come and address our Women's Institute?

"Harold enjoyed his visit to St. Milo's wildly. You know how devoted I am to Jeremy and Janice; the only time I've ever felt they weren't an unmixed blessing was when they would *behead* the conversation!

"Janice (of whom you made a conquest) could tell you better than I how much we want to see you. I can only hope that some good wind will blow you to us.

Yours very sincerely,

Isabel Eastwood."

Posting the letter Isabel felt as Harold had when he asked Irma out to dinner. She had embraced experience; she had grasped her destiny. But when day followed day and no reply came she began to feel uneasy; first individual phrases began to haunt her, then the whole letter seemed a ghastly mistake and the mere thought of it sent the blood rushing to her cheeks. So that it was a tiny relief, as well as a great shock and sorrow, when, some ten days later, she received a type-written note from a secretary to say that Mr. Goodrich thanked her for her letter, but he had had a nervous break-down and might not be able to answer it personally for some time.

18

THE second half of September was wet and stormy; with October the leaves began to fall. The blue of summer had gone out of the Channel, the sparkle from the wave-tips. No longer did the ships ride buoyantly on the surface, or seem to float above it in the vapour, trailing a long pennon of smoke as flat and motionless as the horizon, suggesting that their distant destination held them on a string; they laboured and plunged, and the smoke was whirled away from them in thick angry coils or sometimes blown ahead of them, like hair streaming from a forehead. One did not connect them with their future in some far-off port; only with their immediate present, their hand-to-hand encounter with the grey, monotonous sea.

The earth has seasons with which man can co-operate and see the results of his handiwork; the sea has moods, changes of temper which man may wait upon but cannot affect.

Below the hanging suburbs with their bright, too bright red roofs lay the town, built by man, the canal, dug by man, and the long belt of trees, planted by man, that marked its course even when they hid it from view. The rich sadness of autumn, a sentiment to which the heart so readily responds, lay upon the scene, civilizing it, giving it human, almost moral values. There was surely no sympathetic fallacy in the idea that the earth reflected one's own moods and that one could project oneself into it; not to have felt akin to it would have argued insensitiveness, lack of imagination. But with the sea, beyond and seemingly above it, the heart felt no such kinship; it negatived one's thoughts and feelings, presenting them with an ultimatum as indifferent as death. Only in moods of almost mystical awareness, when the self, consenting to its lot, no longer strives for expression, could one feel in harmony with the sea. At other times it seemed irresponsive, or alien, or even hostile, like someone who has heard a question and will not answer it.

Each of these prospects answered to a need of Isabel's spirit—the need to attach herself to what was going on around and in her, and the need to detach herself from it. She didn't know which need was the greater or which she should indulge.

Her severance from Alec had been a crushing disappointment: she couldn't understand why, for she had only seen him once, and he hadn't paid her any special attention: but it was as though the sun had been withdrawn from the heavens. All her thoughts that had been stretching out towards him were nipped. She couldn't picture him any more: she couldn't even remember what he looked like. The breakdown was like a sentence of banishment: she couldn't write to him, she couldn't even write to find out how he was. At first her strongest feeling was a personal smart, as if he had used the breakdown as an excuse for rebuffing her; she couldn't quite believe in it, it partook of the fabulous, like so much that was connected with him. If truth was a great conspiracy, as some people thought, then Alec was not a party to it. People don't have breakdowns as suddenly and as conveniently as that. And yet he might have had: what more likely, indeed, after the strain of living with Elspeth? That nightmare week-end might have been the last straw. Sometimes she thought of him as in his own house, sometimes as in a nursing home. On the latter her imagination could work but little, but she could always ask Harold for new light on Hendre Hall. He had penetrated into Alec's bedroom. . . . She had to make out what she could out of his replies, which were not very illuminating, and always touched by mockery, as if everything to do with Alec rather amused him. "The whole set-up is just a survival," he would say; "it's an anachronism, pure and simple." She would not betray that she was wounded; after all, Harold was bound to see it that way.

Their holiday with the children followed almost at once upon the news of Alec's illness. It was a seaside holiday in the south-west, with a sea that was milder than theirs, and a coast that was wilder. Isabel would have liked to go somewhere inland, but to Harold, as to the children, a holiday implied the sea. She knew the danger to happiness of a dream-life, and how it drained one's own of colour; against what risks was she not forewarned?—and tried to throw herself with a will into life among the deck-chairs, spades, buckets, baskets, books, newspapers and Thermos flasks. She was not naturally a deck-chair addict, she could not, as Harold did, assume that what everyone else was doing was the right thing to do. He had an instinct for being indistinguishable from the rest; on the beach she could hardly tell him from the other fathers, he seemed the archetype of a beach father, while she had self-consciously to assume the rôle of a beach mother. Harold quickly made friends with neighbouring parents and nearly every day they occupied contiguous deck-chairs; by some sixth sense he contacted people with just the same outlook as his own, the same interests and almost the same appearance. He was not too old to wear shorts or a bathing suit becomingly; indeed, like everything he wore they suited him. The other wives looked at him with approval, as at a husband who had made the grade; with their eyes and sometimes with their tongues they complimented Isabel on him. He was soon Harold to them, and she, not quite so soon, was Isabel.

All this pleased the part of her that was attached to Harold; and if its impact was not very great at any single point, as Alec's had been, it touched in a hundred ways the nerves and fibres of her being, confirming her in her sense of security, of being loved and cherished and admired, for in public Harold was a more demonstrative husband than he was in private. And a more demonstrative father, too. At home he didn't play with the children much; that task fell to her; but on the beach he emulated the other fathers, and indeed surpassed them, in devising games for Jeremy and Janice. And this was all to the good, for in new surroundings they rather lost the power of entertaining themselves; they threw off such maturity as they had attained, and even Jeremy became quite babyish. Harold encouraged them; the beach seemed to go to his head as it did to theirs, he crawled about on all fours or lay, prone or supine, while mounds of sand were heaped upon his body, and Janice and Jeremy shrieked and giggled uncontrollably. Left to themselves, or to her, they fretted, asking plaintively what game they should play next. Once she suggested "Crossing the Farmer's Field". "You can mark out the ladder on the sand," she said. But Janice answered promptly, "Oh no, we couldn't play that here. That's a game we play at home. *You* come and play with us, like Daddy does. Daddy *likes* playing with us."

Why was Harold in such high spirits? Isabel wondered. For the same reason that her spirits were low? Was Alec's illness, which was a weight on her mind, a weight off his? Did the way he talked about Alec, his amused, slightly contemptuous references to him, imply that he was jealous of him? Did he imagine that Isabel had fallen in love with him?

What an absurd idea! For if Isabel had fallen in love with Alec, if she had been the least bit attracted by him in that way, would she have fallen in with his scheme for getting hold of Irma? Surely it was the last thing she would have done. When she had doubts about her feelings for Alec, such as any fairly intelligent woman might have entertained, she could always set them at rest by recalling, with a wry smile, her behaviour in the Irma business. No woman who was in love with a man deliberately threw another woman in his path.

One day Harold said, "Pity about old Alec cracking up, though I never thought he had his head screwed on very tight. He told me he had some more friends who wanted their income tax straightened out. Expect he's forgotten all about it now—too busy seeing snakes or whatever literary men do see when they have nervous breakdowns."

Trying to ignore his tone, Isabel answered:

"Still, we owe him something, don't we? We are in a better position than we were, you told me that. We can afford things that we couldn't afford before."

She coloured, for one of the things they thought they could afford had been another child. Yet now she felt she didn't want it, or not so much. Was her family becoming a problem to her, something static, instead of a growing organism? She had hoped that Harold would take her in his arms and kiss her, encouraging her, banishing her doubts. But as if he, too, had cooled off that idea, he said:

"Yes, we'll order the television set as soon as we get back. The kids will love it."

"I'm not sure it will be altogether good for them," said Isabel.

"Why ever not? It will keep t..em quiet. Jeremy will soon be old enough to go to boarding school. We must be looking out for one. Nothing too grand, we don't want that, but still a good school. Now if Alec hadn't. . . . He's left things in rather a tangle."

Again Isabel's thoughts turned to Irma, but not as to a woman, not even as to a living problem, to nothing that was active in her consciousness; but as to a symbol of anti-climax, like a milestone on a disused road. Into anti-climax her feelings were already moving, before the time came for the Eastwoods to pack up for home. Those last days with the shadow of departure on them, a shadow which, with its practical implications, fell heavier on Isabel than on the others, were like a purge to the spirits: only the strongest preoccupation could have survived the avalanche of petty cares that overwhelmed her. Their new car would have taken all the luggage, but the new car hadn't been delivered yet: their increased prosperity was a fact, but the proofs of it still tarried. On Saturday, at a certain hour, at a certain minute they must catch a train. Until they caught it life was like an ever-darkening tunnel, clamorous with cries, for the children, in their different ways, resented the inevitable departure as if it had been a super-bedtime. Happily Harold, who, on these occasions, was usually as restless and irritable as they were, and for the same reason that he, too, was going back to work, was now much more cheerful; he had enjoyed his holiday but he looked forward to getting home, he said. But even so, Isabel, with a mother's obligation to conceal her own moods while appeasing other people's, underwent a partial rebirth at this time and arrived at Tilecotes a different woman from the one who had set out possessed by Alec's image.

There had been no meeting of the Women's Institute in August, but shortly after Isabel's return another was due. Not at her house, of course; her turn to be hostess would not come for several months. Something of her mother came out in Isabel at these meetings; she looked forward to them and felt the better for them. Much of her routine work, she felt, was unprogressive; it was merely a way of keeping things from slipping back. But sometimes at these meetings she was conscious of a forward movement, of gaining ground and holding it: a spiritual advance. Assembled, the women were far more forthcoming than when by themselves; and so was she. In the interval between their occupations they chattered cosily. It was a wet day, the meeting was being held in the Parish Hall.

"Bring me my bow of burning gold!" She sat down next to a woman she knew and felt the relaxing warmth of fellowship, and so absorbed was she in the conversation that she didn't notice that a late-comer had occupied the chair on her other side. Nor had the late-comer noticed who her neighbour was, for when their eyes met she exclaimed, "Oh, I didn't know it was you!" and half rose from her chair.

"Oh, please don't go!" said Isabel. "Irma, please don't go!"

But she said it, she knew, half-heartedly, for in a flash she realized that the Austrian girl had ceased to be of any interest to her, was, indeed, of less interest than the other women, a minus quantity. But had she shown this in her face, that she had startled the poor creature so? She blushed for herself and her bad manners, and said as gently as she could:

"I am so glad to see you."

"Oh yes, of course," said Irma, getting muddled. Recovering, she added: "I mean that I am very pleased to see you." But she still looked startled.

"Now let us talk," said Isabel energetically. It was a phrase her mother used. "We have been away, you know, for a holiday in Devonshire, such a pretty place." The carefully-spaced-out words sounded stilted and formal. "We only got back, when was it? Oh, last Saturday week."

"Oh yes, I know!" said Irma.

"You knew?" said Isabel, surprised.

"Oh no, I did not know!" cried Irma, confused and

agitated. "I just had an idea you might be back."

Her English is improving, Isabel thought, and she congratulated Irma on it.

"Oh yes, I do speak better," Irma said, radiant at the compliment. "And I read better, too. I have read all through the book you lent me, Mrs. Eastwood."

"Oh, have you?" Isabel said. How extraordinary: she had quite forgotten lending Irma Alec's novel. That transaction had withered in her mind like a posy laid long ago on some alien, pagan altar. She said with an effort:

"Mr. Goodrich has been ill, you know, very ill, I'm afraid. He had a nervous breakdown." She spoke of Alec as she thought of him, in the past tense.

"Oh, but he will get better!" Irma said, lifting her face and opening her eyes. "He will get better, I am sure of it!"

"What makes you think he will get better?" Isabel asked.

Haltingly, Irma told her of cases she had known who had got well. "Like the man in the story, he got well, too."

"Yes, he did," said Isabel thoughtfully. Why was it that she dreaded the whisperings of hope that Irma had started in her? Because in her heart she wanted to have them silenced? "But she didn't," she said.

"Oh no, poor thing!"

"You say poor thing," said Isabel. "But hadn't she treated him very badly? She deserved all she got, I thought."

Irma shook her head. "Oh yes, she was cruel to him. But she was so unhappy, too! She suffered, that was why she made him suffer. I think that Mr. Goodrich only could have known unhappy, cruel women, to write about us as he does. I should like to comfort him. I am sure he is unhappy."

"He didn't seem so when he was here," said Isabel.

"Ah no, because with you it was different. You were so kind to him! You are kind to everyone! You were kind to me, too."

Isabel felt acutely uncomfortable.

"If he ever comes again," said Isabel slowly, "you must come too and meet him."

"Oh, but how I should like that!" There was no mistaking the delight in Irma's voice.

All at once the other part of Isabel's mind, which told

her that Alec wouldn't come again and that it was better
that he shouldn't, spoke up. At the same moment, and
almost for the first time, she was aware of the Austrian girl
not as a pawn in a game she was playing, or as a milestone
on a disused road, but as a person in her own right whose
presence was fortifying and consoling.

"But whether he comes or not," she added briskly, "you
must come. I should like to see you and so would the
children and so" (she knew she was inventing this) "would
Harold, my husband."

To her surprise, embarrassment returned to Irma's face.

"Oh," she said, "I should so much like to but——"

"But what?"

"But you have been too kind to me already."

And yet, thought Isabel, she wanted to come when it was
to meet Alec. Is she a snob? Or has she fallen in love with
the idea of Alec? Or is it just diffidence—the displaced
person's fear of being in the way? Or doesn't she like
Harold?

Deciding to ignore Irma's protest, she said, "Anyhow
please come if you feel like it. And if you can't make anybody hear, open the door and walk in. Sometimes we leave
it open, for the children."

The lights went down and on the square board at the
end of the hall a thrilling rectangle of light appeared. The
magic lantern!

Conversation was hushed and Irma spared the trouble
of answering.

160

★ 19 ★

In his office at Downhaven, Harold was opening a letter. He knew whom it was from, partly, and paradoxically, because the sloping handwriting was unknown to him, partly because the envelope was marked "personal", and few of his letters came thus inscribed. The others were opened by his secretary. As he put his thumb under the flap of the envelope it trembled and his heart began to beat uncomfortably. Yet why? Even if his wife discovered that he had asked Irma out to dinner she couldn't take it amiss, for she had as good as asked him to. If she hadn't put the idea into his head, she had given it her blessing. Supposing Irma said yes, he needn't even bother to conceal it from her. He might even boast of it. "I've done what you wanted me to, Isabel. I've asked what's her name—the Austrian girl, out to dinner. I'm going—well, I'm going to *sound* her, you know what about." "Splendid, Harold, I'm so glad." "But, of course, I'm not expecting her to rise. She's not that kind of girl, by all accounts." "You can only find out by trying." "But do you want me to try?" "Of course I do." "But how?" "That's not for me to say. How do men do such things?" "You mean you would like me to kiss her?" "Don't be disgusting, Harold, I don't want to hear any of the details. What do you take me for?"

Logically, the dialogue would go along such lines. Logically, Isabel should egg him on. Logically. . . .

But how unreal it all was, how untrue to his feelings. To his feelings, the mere idea of Isabel in connection with Irma was distasteful. Once they were together, he and she, he would put the thought of Isabel away. He would be just a man, and she would be just a woman: no other context, no other set of circumstances, must come into it at all. And least of all must Isabel get to hear of it: it would spoil all his pleasure if she did.

He took his thumb out of the envelope and thought

again. Again Isabel was speaking, but not to him, this time.

"Yes, darlings, Daddy has a friend, a new friend, and I'm very glad about it and I hope you will be too. You've seen her—she's the Austrian young lady who came here with the Women's Institute. Daddy is very fond of her and so must we all be. We shan't see a great deal of her, because Daddy doesn't want that; but we must all be very, very nice to her when we do. She'll be a kind of godmother. You don't see your godmother very often, Jeremy, do you, and you don't, Janice: well, she'll be like that: someone who's very fond of you and gives you presents, but doesn't worry you at all, like some grown-ups. She'll never say 'no' to you, for instance, for that's something she doesn't know how to say. She doesn't belong to Daddy, you know, darlings, not as you and I do, she isn't one of the family, so to speak: she's just someone we're all very fond of. She really belongs to another gentleman; well, you know him, too, he's Mr. Goodrich, the novelist, who once paid us a visit. You remember him, Janice, you showed him your dolly, Pamela, or Pamelia, as you call her. Well, she belongs to him, just as Pamelia does to you. Daddy's just keeping her warm for Mr. Goodrich; no, I don't quite mean that— it's like this. Daddy bought Pamelia, but Pamelia doesn't belong to Daddy, she belongs to you. Well, Daddy bought the Austrian young lady but really she belongs to Mr. Goodrich: Mr. Goodrich gave Daddy the money to buy her with. She's Mr. Goodrich's dolly, really, his Pamelia, but he keeps her here and sometimes he lets Daddy play with her."

Perish the thought!

If there was one thing that Harold would save Irma from, one fate that should never, never be hers, it was the fate envisaged in this picture. Not a single word of it should come true. Just as he had saved her from the embarrassing attentions of the rowdy youths at the Green Dragon by asking her to come out with him, pitting himself against her handicaps and disadvantages—her youth, her poverty, her ignorance of the language, her defencelessness in a strange land, all the minus quantities which together made up her appeal to pity—so now, by taking her out to dinner, he

162

would save her from the whole sum of humiliations that the picture conjured up. In a word, he would save her from Alexander Goodrich.

But—his thoughts took another turn—she was already saved. The danger no longer threatened. Alec had been put away: he was gibbering in a madhouse: he had passed completely out of their lives, leaving them £150 per annum to the good. The way was clear then; the door was open.

And ah, the sweetness of that downcast look! That hovering smile, which every man who saw it must feel was meant for him! But it hadn't been meant for any of those flashy, overdressed young men, it had been meant for Harold. There, in that hovering smile, one found something that one didn't find here in the office; that one didn't find in the streets or on the roads; that one didn't find at Tilecotes. At the office one kind of self-discipline prevailed, on the roads another, at Tilecotes yet a third, perhaps the most cramping of them all: the discipline of being a father and a husband. Routine happenings and routine emotions: enforced adaptability: compromises: being nice to the children, but not so nice that they took advantage of you: being nice to Isabel, but not so nice that you lost the authority of a husband. Always a part to play, a part that involved keeping one's end up, being in the right: thus far and no farther. For with Isabel he had to be on the defensive: he realized it now though he had never realized it before. It hadn't been so when he was courting her: then she had been glad to take him on any terms to get away from the life she was leading with her mother. But since then, with the security he had brought her, her habit of despising him had taken root. Now she remembered her different upbringing, her superior social status, her links with the world where people tried to stick out from the mass, instead of being content to be like their fellows, and this had raised a barrier between them, the barrier of contempt. Yes, Isabel despised him but he hadn't realized it till he met Irma, to whom, for one blessed minute, he had been all in all.

He glanced up from the half-open envelope, frowning. The room looked strange: he hardly recognized it. There was a knock on the door and his secretary came in.

"A Mr. Anderson to see you, Mr. Eastwood."

He gave her the look, friendly but distant, that office discipline demanded. "Ask him to wait a minute, Miss Malone. I've got one or two things I want to do."

"Very well, Mr. Eastwood."

The secretary nodded and withdrew: she didn't know if the delay was genuine, for sometimes her employer deliberately kept his clients waiting: he didn't want them to think him too easy of access.

Harold picked the letter up again.

"But she won't come," he said to himself. "She may not say no, but she'll refuse all the same. She won't come, she won't come."

Trying to fortify himself against disappointment he tore the letter open. It was very short.

"Dear Mr. Eastwood,
    I have had the pleasure to receive your kind letter, in which you have given yourself the trouble to kindly ask me to dine with you and Mrs. Eastwood one evening when I free shall be. How happy I am to say I free shall be on Thursday night to meet you at the Hotel Bouverie in Downhaven, at eight o'clock."

Harold took up the house telephone and said in an uneven voice, "I'm ready now, Miss Malone."

As Miss Malone ushered the client in she caught Harold's eye and received from him the smile, naked, undisciplined, and lover-like, that he meant for Irma. "Good heavens," she thought, "what can have come over Mr. Eastwood?" and as soon as she got back to her room she started making up her face.

Harold, of course, had no intention of asking Isabel to make a third with Irma, but he reasoned: Will she come if I don't include Isabel in the invitation? I don't believe she will. And he had thought, Supposing I were to ask her to meet me alone, mightn't she show the letter to someone, try to use it against me? The suspicion offended his idea

164

of Irma, it came from another layer of his mind, but he was too practical not to entertain it. With his wife's name in the letter he was safe: and when Isabel didn't turn up he would only have to explain and apologize—she had been kept away by a headache or by one of the children being unwell.

It was odd how Harold, who had never since his marriage taken a step along the primrose path, never gone off the rails in any way or wished to, proved himself a past-master of intrigue. Yet intrigue was only his instrument: he didn't think of it as such, he thought of it as the means whereby he could realize, in action, the obsessive sweetness of his thoughts of Irma, and the protective feelings she aroused in him. From whom and what was he protecting her? Sometimes from the young men at the Green Dragon; sometimes from imaginary persons who might call out at her, "Yah, you're a German!"; sometimes from the whole English nation; but, above all from one particular person who had the basest designs on her innocence and virtue: Alexander Goodrich. But the fact that Alec was three hundred miles and more away, not dangerous at all, not, in fact, at large, but an object of ridicule or pity, trussed in a strait jacket or watched over by a keeper, did not alter Harold's feelings about him in the least.

By habit, training and preference Harold was a tidy man. Just as, in his office, he had a file for every client, so his mind was furnished with compartments: labelled "church", "golf", "bridge", "Rotary", etc.; and for each a personality to match: he never thought or acted with his whole nature. But the two main compartments were his business life and his home life. These he regarded as antithetical, and took pains to keep them separate: the others functioned automatically. The system had always worked, because Harold was as used to living in a honeycomb as a bee is.

The thought of Irma was an intensely private thought that he would share with no one, least of all with Isabel. Now at a moment's notice he had to improvise a third compartment, and a secret one, a cupboard for a skeleton. Was there room for it?

Harold assumed there was, and that it could be accommodated without disturbing the others. But there he was wrong, for the moment he crossed the threshold of his home and sought for his Daddy-come-back-from-the-office personality—joviality stiffened by a steel thread for the children, affection with a touch of badinage for Isabel—he couldn't find it, and paused in the doorway of the lounge, uncertain how to look or feel.

"Doesn't Daddy look *funny?*" Janice giggled. "He doesn't know whether he's coming or going."

This was all too true.

"Come in, dear," invited Isabel, smiling at him. "Your tea's all ready for you."

Thus encouraged Harold came in, but he didn't sit down at once at the tea-table, as his habit was, he went to the fireplace and stood with his back to it. "Daddy isn't hungry," observed Janice. "He's lost his appetite." She made it sound a serious accusation.

Jeremy, who was lying on the floor playing a game of patience, looked up.

"She says that because she lost hers yesterday," he said. "She's lost it eleven times since we came back from Yarncombe."

"Oh, what an untruth!" sighed Janice.

"Now, now, children," said Isabel pacifically. "Come along, Harold, or your egg'll get cold." The Eastwoods usually had high tea, and supper when the children were safely in bed and asleep. "You aren't really feeling poorly, are you?" she added, noticing for the first time how bright his eyes were, and the flush of colour on his still sunburnt cheeks. "Would you like me to take your temperature?"

"Oh no, I'm quite all right," said Harold. "I just thought I'd like to warm myself a bit."

"Oh, Daddy, but it isn't cold," said Janice.

"That's what *you* think," retorted Harold.

"She doesn't really *think*," observed Jeremy from the carpet, "she just *says*."

"Oh——" Janice's eyes travelled round the room, as though to gather from the atmosphere a withering reply.

Failing, she put on a look of haughty unconcern and moved towards the tea-table.

"Please may I sit down?" she asked, with icy politeness.

"Yes, let's all sit down," said Isabel, "if Daddy's thoroughly thawed out."

Janice, however, remained standing, to register affront.

"Oh, I'm as warm as toast," said Harold, adding, as though he had been too expansive, "With the evenings drawing in as they are, I have to keep my calories in trim."

He left the fireplace and sat down abruptly in the first chair that came to hand.

"Oh Daddy!" exclaimed Janice, outraged. "You've sat down in my chair!"

"Good gracious, so I have," said Harold. "But"—remembering he must not allow too much liberty of speech—"you needn't shout."

When the exchange of seats had been effected, Janice said, mysteriously:

"I know what's wrong with Daddy."

"What is wrong with me?" asked Harold rashly.

"Don't ask her," Jeremy said, "she's sure to say something silly."

"What is the matter with me?" repeated Harold, ignoring Jeremy.

"You must have fallen in love."

"Fallen in love, why?"

"Because you're forgetting everything—you forgot to kiss Mummy when you came in, you forgot to say 'Hullo, how's tricks?' to us, you forgot to have your tea, and then you sat down in my chair."

"Thank you, Janice, that's quite enough," said Harold repressively.

He did not smile but Isabel did, and her eyes sought his, trying to draw him into her amusement. How often had she tried and failed! How often, since the early days of their marriage, had she tried out some joke on him, only to find it fall flat! But at last he did smile, rather sheepishly. Could it be the dawning of a sense of humour?

She mourned her lost cleverness and her gift to amuse. "The necessity of being amusing"—she remembered that ancient tribute to her talent. But you couldn't be clever or amusing in a vacuum. Harold had killed her cleverness, she thought, by harping on it to their friends. "Of course, Isabel's so clever!" Really, it was a dig. And as for being amusing, how could you be, if every time you tried you had to hoist a flag, for fear of being taken *au pied de la lettre*? And perhaps a failed sense of humour, such as hers, was worse than none. Often she had something to say to Harold that she very much wanted to say. It should be quite easy to say and there was no reason she shouldn't, she went over it in her mind beforehand: yet when she was with him she found she couldn't say it, it had all dried up.

Well, to-night she would try again.

"ISABEL," said Harold, later in the evening, "I shan't be in for supper on Thursday night, I've got to dine with a man in Downhaven."

"Nasty wretch, why didn't he ask me?" said Isabel.

"We shall only be talking business. You wouldn't be interested."

"You never know, I might be, and anyhow it would have made a break, as you say. Where are you going to dine?"

"He hasn't told me yet."

"I hope he'll do you well."

"H'm."

"Harold," said Isabel suddenly.

"Yes?"

"Have you thought any more about Irma?" Then as he looked blank, she added, "The Austrian girl, I mean."

"Can't say I have," said Harold, in his curtest way.

"You said you might take her out one evening."

"I know I did," said Harold. "But what would be the point, when Alec isn't here, or likely to be? He's gone completely out of our lives. Mad as a hatter, most probably, poor chap, and shut up somewhere."

"We don't know that. And didn't he say he was going to send you some more clients?"

"Yes, but how can he, when he's in the loony-bin?"

Isabel had to make an effort not to hate Harold for talking about Alec so callously. A small dog snapping at a big one, that's what he was.

"Still, we already owe him something. The new car, to some extent."

"Yes, and he owes me something, too."

"I know, but that was in the way of business. What he did for us was done out of pure kindness."

"The other clients, you mean? Well, perhaps they paid him a commission. He's an artful fellow, Alec is, a real smart-alec, when he has his wits about him."

"I wish you wouldn't talk about him in that unfeeling way," Isabel burst out. "One might think he had done you an injury instead of . . . instead of . . . well, a benefit. Don't you see how unhappy he must be with this . . . this woman of his making his life a hell? That's why he had his breakdown—I'm certain of it—because she played him up so! What he needs is somebody quite different, somebody sweet, and gentle, and considerate, like . . . like this Austrian girl. Somebody who would understand him and make things easy for him—not an irritant, like she is. It couldn't do any harm just to find out what she's like. She might be no good at all, of course—I mean, from his point of view."

"How do you expect me to find out?" said Harold, sombrely.

"Oh, darling, we've been into all that—how *do* men find out? You've been in the Army, you must have had experience. . . . I've never asked you, of course. Besides, there are so many things you could tell, simply by talking to her."

"She hasn't much to say for herself," said Harold, "from the little I saw of her."

"No, but it isn't so much what a person *says*, it's the way they look, and react, and feel. I'm sure you could tell in five minutes whether she is the sort of woman to make a man of Alec's type happy. I *have* talked to her, and I think she is."

"Why are you so keen on making Alec happy?" Harold asked.

"Why, don't you see, because he's a very exceptional man, really exceptional and outstanding. He isn't like us—forgive me, Harold—I mean, we're quite all right in our way, but nobody's going to *mind* what happens to us."

"I like that!" Harold exclaimed. "Jeremy and Janice would mind, I hope, if anything happened to us."

"Of course they would, if we fell ill or died or got divorced, but we aren't the sort of people who do. What I mean is, we don't matter to posterity; our work doesn't matter, whereas his work does, he might become a classic! That's why it's so terribly important that he should find someone to share his emotional life and put him first always, and be a sort of feather pillow to him, not a nutmeg grater."

"That Elspeth woman said she helped him to write because she made him feel," said Harold. "She said a novelist couldn't write without feeling. It's one of the things she said that I remember."

"Yes, but don't you see she made him feel in the wrong way. She lacerated him, she tortured and embittered him; that's why there isn't a single nice woman in any of his books. They are all harpies, they play on his feelings out of sheer cruelty—they are power-maniacs. Now this Austrian girl——"

"Yes," said Harold.

"Well, she would put him first, she would heal the sore places, she would build up his nature. She wouldn't argue with him, or oppose him, or make scenes for the fun of seeing him crawl afterwards. You've no idea, Harold, what a really loving woman can do for a man."

"Yes, I have. What about you?"

"Oh, *me*!" With a shrug Isabel dismissed herself, and with herself the emotional problems of the Eastwoods. "I don't count—at least, not in that way. You, Harold, thank goodness, you don't need bolstering up. You wouldn't like it. You've got your business, and your clubs, and your societies, and your golf, and us to come home to in the evenings—you've got a splendid, firm, strong nature that knows what it wants and gets it, you're popular and respected, you're *rangé*, as the French say, your emotional life is self-supporting, you don't need a woman butting in. But he—Alec's—quite different. He isn't sure of himself, like you are. His nature is full of needs and gaps that he can't fill. Oh, I know he seems to be getting his own way in life, but he isn't really. He grasps at things greedily, like a child, just because he hasn't any inner certainty to fall back on, and then he tires of them."

"You seem to know a lot about him," Harold said.

"Yes, from what you told me, and from things that he said, but mostly from his books. It's all in his books—the way he's always been a slave to women—one woman, really—who take away with one hand while they give with the other, or just hold it out and snatch it back. A sort of emotional strip-tease. Now another kind of woman——"

"Yes?" said Harold.

"Like this Irma, she would put a stop to all that. She would heal the soreness out of his mind, and alter his whole outlook on life." "You said all that before," said Harold. "Yes, but I'll say it again. He wouldn't be unfulfilled and restless any more—he's only forty-something—and he'd be able to strike a new view in his novels. If human nature was really like he pictures it the race would have died out. He can only see the destructive element because Elspeth is a destroyer, but she's a parasite, too—she doesn't destroy him utterly because then she would have nothing left to feed on! But she poisons him all the same. She's like one of those hormone weed-killers, she makes his emotions outgrow their strength and in the end she'll kill them. That's why he repeats himself with every book and his tone gets shriller, as the reviewers say. If he could learn by experience that an emotional relationship between two people isn't necessarily a sort of jockeying for position, before a fight in which one wins and the other loses, but a sort of partnership—well, he could write all that he has it in him to write. It's true that a raw surface is more sensitive, in a way, but it only feels one thing, and that is pain. What would the sense of touch be worth, if every contact made you flinch? A curse, and not a blessing. Alec wants comforting, not hurting, both as a writer and a man."

Confronted by Harold's silence, the conviction had faded out of Isabel's voice. She waited for him to speak.

"What do you want me to do then?" he asked in a neutral tone.

"What you yourself suggested—ask her out to dinner."

"I don't believe she'd come."

"Then let's both invite her to meet us—in Downhaven. Tell her it's easier for me there than here, because of the cooking. Then when the time comes I could make some excuse for not coming, and fade out."

Harold sat quite still, his eyes fixed on the carpet. His thick eyebrows and his dark moustache ruled stern transverse lines across his face. He's good-looking in his way, Isabel thought. It's a way that doesn't appeal to me now, but it did once and still might to some women.

"I'm afraid I couldn't, Isabel," he said. "It wouldn't be ... it wouldn't be. ... Well, I couldn't, that's all."

Isabel stared at Harold unbelievingly, so sure had she been of her power over him in an important issue. Then, as the tide of disappointment rolled over her, she realized that she had drained herself of personal force. Abruptly she rose and left the room, so that Harold should not see that she was crying.

HAROLD made sure that a table had been reserved and then went to wait for Irma in the lounge.

His stern, set face expressed his state of mind. Since the evening of his struggle with Isabel he had had many struggles with himself. To be his own battlefield was quite a new experience for Harold, hitherto he had felt only pity or good-natured contempt for undecided people. And probably he would still have felt it for he did not connect, much less compare, his own emotions with other people's.

He glanced up at the clock. There were still five minutes to go. Would she be late? Women, he knew, had a habit of being late. He knew it from hearsay more than from experience, for Isabel was not unpunctual and he had few women among his clients. Since his marriage he had never asked a woman to dine with him alone. Soon after they were married he and Isabel occasionally dined out for the fun of it; but when the children came they gave it up. Really he knew less about women than he had before his marriage. His relationship with Isabel had become so stereotyped and regularized that he scarcely thought of her as a woman at all: she was the chief circumstance that made him a married man, as necessary and as taken for granted as the air he breathed. For this state of things Isabel was herself a great deal responsible. Not for nothing had she studied the art of marriage and made it for her husband, and almost for herself, a pre-digested meal. Adaptability, the great ability, had become second-nature to her. Until just lately they had lost the power and even the wish to spring surprises on each other.

Remembering the occasional romantic encounters he had had before his marriage, Harold realized that surprise, or at any rate a plunge into the unknown, was the essence of them.

Should he show irritation if Irma was late? With drawn

brows he was considering this when all at once his heart began to thump and sensations he hadn't known for years rushed over him.

Irma wasn't late. As the clock's hand touched eight she was in the doorway, peering round her in her diffident, short-sighted way; and before he had time to rise the thought shot through Harold—what a blessing it was that the poorer classes now dressed as well as those better off, you couldn't tell the difference: Irma in her soft red dress looked every inch (though that suggested an upstanding figure, which she wasn't) a lady.

When she espied him she almost ran towards him, such was her eagerness, which made him feel relatively self-possessed; but when, after their greeting, she looked shyly round and said, "But where is Mrs. Eastwood?" the embarrassment was all on his side. Haltingly, he explained that Isabel had had a sick headache all day; she had hoped to the end to be well enough to come, but had finally decided against it. She sent many apologies.

Bewilderment and woe spread over Irma's face.

"I hope you don't mind?" he said awkwardly. "I——"

At once she took his meaning and her face partially cleared: it was extraordinary how quickly her expression followed her moods. "Oh no, but I am so sad for Mrs. Eastwood! I, too, I, too, have headaches and they make me feel quite dreadful. I am—how do you say—beside myself."

"Hers are not as bad as that," said Harold, who, even at this juncture, could not repress his dislike of over-statement. "To-morrow she'll be as right as rain."

"As right as rain?" said Irma doubtfully.

"It's a thing we say in England," said Harold in a rather lofty manner. "We have such a lot of rain, you see, we think it's the right thing."

Irma laughed delightedly at this; her head swayed a little and her soft bushy hair lightly touched her shoulders. The success of his sally put Harold on better terms with himself. He asked her to have a drink. But did barmaids drink? Did they devour their young? He was handicapped by his ignorance of their habits.

"Please yes," said Irma, and asked for a tomato-juice.

Harold was disappointed by her choice. A desire to take the upper hand came over him. "I think you should have something stronger," he said firmly.

"Oh, please not," she cried. "You would not like to see me dronk."

Perversely, Harold wasn't sure he would have minded. But, of course, she was quite right. She wasn't right, though, to say "please" so often. He would take her to task about it.

"In English," he said, sipping his dry Martini, and watching Irma's lips, which looked pale against the tomato-juice, for she wore but little make-up, "we don't say 'please' as often as you do."

"Oh, please," began Irma, and stopped, confused. "But isn't it polite?"

"It may be polite," said Harold heavily, "but it isn't good English." Seeing Irma look troubled, almost despairing, he felt a twinge of self-reproach and added, "But say it if you like. It doesn't really *matter*."

"I was hoping my English improved had," said Irma wistfully.

"And so it has," said Harold heartily. "Now let's go in to dinner."

At dinner he prevailed on her to take some wine. It wasn't easy; he had to fight his way through a fluttering undergrowth of "nots" and "pleases" (she still had an inhibition against saying no). He got an intimate pleasure from filling up her glass, and still more pleasure from watching her drink and seeing the colour come into her cheeks.

"Don't you ever drink when you're . . ." "in the bar," he was going to say, but substituted "on duty". "On duty" sounded better: nurses, policemen, Members of Parliament, perhaps, were "on duty".

"Well, only sometimes," she said, "when someone wants me to very, very much."

"Well, I want you to very much," said Harold. "And you're not on duty now."

"Oh yes, I am," she answered unexpectedly.

"Why?" growled Harold, hurt.

"Because isn't it my duty to do what you want me to, Mr. Eastwood?" she said gaily.

"Well, if you call *that* duty!" Harold's mind stumbled forward, as though several obstacles that he had been counting on his power of persuasion to remove, had suddenly given way. "If you call *that* duty," he repeated, feeling his way. Could she be a flirt? His heart was thumping. "I wish you'd call me Harold," he muttered in a thickish voice, "instead of Mr. Eastwood."

"All right then, Harrold," she said, doubling the "r". "Harrold is a nice name, I like it very much."

In Harold's plans for the evening, this stage was to have come later in the conversation, if at all. The wind was taken out of his sails, but he collected himself enough to ask:

"And may I call you Irma?" He pronounced it in the English fashion.

"Please, yes," she said. "But Eerma, it is not a pretty name like yours, it is a name that anybody have."

"I think it's a very nice name," said Harold, masterfully.

After this second unlooked-for advance, Harold was again at a loss. Like an unadaptable commander who has gone further forward than he meant to, he didn't try to consolidate or improve his gains but fell back, and the conversation became as formal as it had been before Irma's *démarche*. He couldn't think of a single sentence into which her Christian name seemed to fit naturally. For the first time he furtively looked round him to see if anyone he knew was in the room. The other diners seemed as engrossed as he was, or had been, but supposing one of them had spotted him? The explanation that Isabel had dropped out through illness now sounded woefully thin, and what of Isabel herself, if she should hear of it? Well, he was only doing what she had pestered him to do. It was far more her idea than his, and he would tell her so. Oh to be at home with his feet up instead of trying to make mis-fire conversation with a foreigner who only understood half what he said! A sudden realization of how false his position was swept over him; a sulky look came into his face and Irma said:

"Oh Harrold, you look tired, I am thinking that you work too hard."

"I do work pretty hard," admitted Harold, quite pleased to have this noticed. It was a long time since Isabel had told him that he looked tired or that he worked too hard.

"But you look well all the same," said Irma, brightening. "Not like that gentleman who did come into the bar with you one day. Mr. . . . Mr. . . . Good——"

"Goodrich," said Harold shortly.

"Oh, yes, he did not look well at all, and now Mrs. Eastwood she tell me he has been very ill. I am so sorry."

"I don't think you need feel very sorry for him," Harold said. "He had only himself to thank, he didn't take care of himself."

"Oh, but he must be so lonely! He has no one to look after him!"

"How do you know?" retorted Harold, and was tempted to tell Irma the true facts about Alec. "He had plenty of money, he didn't have to work for his living."

"But isn't a man happier when he has someone to go home to? Now you, Harrold, you are quite happy, I see it from the first moment."

"Oh well, I jog along," said Harold. "My life isn't exactly a bed of roses."

"A bed of roses?"

"Well, sort of soft, you know, and downy," said Harold with some distaste.

"But Mrs. Eastwood is so kind and good I think you must be happy really," Irma said. "And then you have two children, they are darlings."

"Jeremy and Janice are all right," said Harold grudgingly. "But, of course, they're rather a handful."

"Please," said Irma, "what does a 'handful' mean?"

"It means—" said Harold, and realized, to his surprise, that instead of being put off by Irma's lack of English he rather enjoyed teaching her—"it means that they take up a lot of one's time and attention. At least Janice does. And then they're always falling ill. Children aren't an unmixed blessing, by any means."

"Poor Harrold," Irma said.

Harold rather liked the sound of this. In fact he liked

it very much. Isabel never said "Poor Harold" to him; for her his rôle was simply that of breadwinner.

"Oh well," he said, "I haven't much to complain of, really. Life's a bit dull at times, that's all. I expect it is for you, too."

"Oh yes," said Irma, "sometimes it is very dull." She said this delightedly, as if dullness could be the greatest joke; and the awareness of her power to banish care, which he had recognized when he first saw her, came over Harold afresh.

"You see," she went on, "it is very different here to what it was at home. At home I have friends, I know so many people, we are in and out of each other's houses every day. Here I am just a face among the other faces. A face, an arm, a glass, and that is Irma! But I have come to England, because we are so poor. And I am very happy now!" She glowed at him across the table.

"Go on," said Harold. "Say some more."

"Oh, but what can I say? I am not at all an interesting person, not good family, nothing—just a poor Austrian girl who come here. And now I am much less lonely, because you see I have the Institute of Women, who are all kind, nice people—oh yes, in the street to me they nod, and sometimes they shake hands. They are not too proud to shake hands with a barmaid. And Mrs. Eastwood—she do all this for me—I owe it all to her, and you too, you are—how shall I say?—a present from her."

Harold did not altogether like this.

"I saw you before she did," he said possessively.

Irma's face, which had become quite solemn with the thought of her debt to Isabel, brightened suddenly.

"Oh yes, that is true, and you were so good to me when the men teased me. But she, she likes me too, she wanted to come out to dinner with me. In Austria a lady would not."

"Why not?" Harold asked.

"Oh, because in Austria we have different customs. A lady would be more proud, and might be jealous. In Austria we are quite, quite jealous."

"Are you jealous?" Harold asked.

"I? I have no one to be jealous of. Now Otto he is jealous."

"The farm-worker chap you were telling me about?" said Harold.

"Yes, he is like a bear, he hug me till it hurts, and if he was here, where you are, he would not even let me lift my eyes from the table, to see who else is in the room, he would pretend I was being untrue to him. Oh, he is very jealous!" An indulgent smile flitted across Irma's face. "I tell him, 'I am not yours, so do not treat me as if I was. I do not like it. I am not to you engaged,' I say. Oh yes, I tease him, I tease him a great deal, but sometimes I am frightened of him, he is so rough and clumsy. I do not like to be taken in that way."

"Taken in that way?" repeated Harold, and all at once everyone in the room seemed to stop talking. "What do you mean, Irma?"

"Oh, I express myself so badly," Irma said, her face puckered in self-disapproval. "They say to me, 'You never will English learn.' What I mean is, you must not take by force what is not yours—all in good time, all in good time. Then he say he will leave me and marry another girl."

"Should you mind if he did?" Harold asked.

Irma considered.

"Oh well, not if she make him happy. That is a great thing, isn't it, to make some people happy?"

She raised her eyes to Harold's.

"Yes, I suppose so," Harold said.

"Yes, I am sure it is. But whether I could make Otto happy, that I do not know. He speak my language, that is how we did come to be friends. But I am not the only German-speaking girl, and——"

"What were you going to say?" asked Harold when Irma hesitated.

"Oh well, in the early morning we do not yet know how the day will turn out. And you, Harrold, you are happy, you are not disappointed because Mrs. Eastwood cannot come?"

"Well, it was bad luck on her, of course," said Harold.

"Oh yes, but she must come another time, if you are so kind."

"Should you mind if she didn't come?" asked Harold.

Irma's eyelids contracted.

"You mean she not want to come?"

"I don't say that," said Harold. He began to breathe more quickly. "But supposing she didn't come, supposing I didn't ask her, would you still come?"

Unlike Harold's, Irma's breath came more slowly; it seemed to escape from her in sighs. Her face looked older.

"So I shouldn't be one of the family!" she said.

The picture she had formed of their relationship made Harold wince, for it had once been his. But now he couldn't fit her into it, and he had gone too far to draw back if he wanted to.

"Of course you'd always be welcomed there," he said, "only they mustn't know——"

"You mean that Mrs. Eastwood mustn't know——?"

"Yes. That we—well, that we dine together."

After a pause, Irma said, her eyelids fluttering:

"But she not know that we dine here to-night?"

"Yes," said Harold, "she knows." He couldn't bring himself to say that Isabel didn't know. "But, in future, when we dine together, don't say anything about it to anyone, that's all."

Irma sat a long time silent, looking into her glass.

"And you, you will not anyone tell, either?" she said at last.

"Of course not, Irma."

"Very well then, Harrold. Please yes."

Immediately they began to talk of other things, things personal to each but not to both of them; they spoke excitedly, laughing a good deal, strangers to themselves, but growing the less strange to each other. It was not until Harold stopped his car in an unfrequented lane not far from Irma's lodgings that he brought out the question the urgency of which, during the five-mile drive, had kept him almost silent.

"When can we meet again? To-day fortnight?"

"Please?"

He explained how long it was.

"Oh, but that is so far away!" she said.

"Yes, but it's safer so," said Harold firmly. "But not at that hotel, at the——" and he named another. This he had rehearsed; he had rehearsed their parting kiss, too, but not the feeling that it gave him.

All the way to Tilecotes he could have kicked himself for not having made the engagement for next week.

He thought that Isabel would be in bed, and perhaps asleep, but she was not; she jumped up when he came into the lounge, her cheeks flushed, her eyes shining.

"Oh Harold, guess what's happened!"

"I couldn't," he said shortly. His mind was so full of Irma that it wouldn't harbour another thought. "Is it something pleasant? By the way," he added, with husbandly authority, "you ought to be in bed, you know."

Isabel disregarded this.

"Do try to guess."

Harold couldn't, and the idea that there could be, anywhere in the world, an event comparable in excitement and importance to the one that had just befallen him, in fact one that could matter to him in any way at all, irritated him.

"Alec is here! He rang up soon after you went out. He's staying at the Royal. He's quite well, he says. Isn't it wonderful?"

"It is certainly extraordinary," said Harold. His mind felt like a record that was being played over to him backwards, each revolution scraping out what had been written before.

"It is extraordinary," he repeated, to gain time. "Do you mean he's really at large?"

"Oh yes," said Isabel, too happy to be hurt by Harold's tone. "He sounded perfectly all right. Nearly all artists are highly-strung, Harold; it's the price they pay for their gifts. You and I wouldn't know. . . . Oh yes, and he said he was longing to see you: he had some business he wanted to talk over with you."

"Oh, did he?" said Harold more amiably, for the word "business" was a clarion that would have roused him on his deathbed. "Well, that won't take long. . . . What's brought him here, anyway? Did he tell you?"

"He said he wanted to see us again . . . and something about getting local colour for a novel."

"I thought these writing fellows got that sort of thing out of their heads," said Harold. The threat to his thoughts of Irma made him feel prickly all over. "Did he say how long he meant to stay?"

"No," said Isabel. The tone and drift of Harold's remarks had begun to discourage and offend her; they seemed to epitomize everything in him that had made their marriage disappointing. She couldn't go on discussing Alec with him, he was too unsympathetic. Making an effort, she wrenched her mind away and said, rather coldly:

"How did you get on this evening? Did it go off all right?"

"Oh yes," said Harold carelessly. "It followed the normal pattern, you know. Nothing out of the way."

22

Soon after half-past eleven the next day Isabel heard a taxi drive up to the door. It was a sound she had been waiting for all the morning, ever since ten o'clock, in fact, when Alec had told her he would come; yet it took her by surprise, for she had almost given him up. How should she present herself to him? It was a problem she had been unable to solve. Just as she was, in her apron, the busy housewife, straight from the kitchen, cooking the midday meal? Or as the lady of leisure, reading a book? Three minutes could bring about this transformation; but when she decided on it, it was too late. There he was, standing in the hall, which all at once seemed very small; and so luminous was he to her imagination, so radiant with the brightness that her thoughts had given him, that she could scarcely see him.

"The door was open," he said, "so in I came."

Stretching out her hand, she saw how encumbered he was; a high, peaked, purple parcel gleamed in his left hand, while in the crotch of his arm he hugged another. And he was not alone; behind him on the doorstep stood a taxi-driver, even more laden than he was.

"You see, I don't come empty-handed," he remarked. "Not as the hymn says, 'Nothing in my hand I bring'. Now could we put them down somewhere?"

"Of course," said Isabel, recovering herself, and led the way into the lounge, which soon took on the air of Christmas. The taxi-driver, cap in hand, withdrew, and Alec who, as usual, was bareheaded, asked if he might take off his overcoat. "But first," he said, "I must give you these," holding the purple parcel out to her.

"These" proved to be a bunch of dark red roses, far too numerous to count, wrapped in purple Cellophane. They had the indescribable air of smartness that some picked flowers have, and the room, with its medley of decorations, at once looked very shabby. "I had them sent from France," he explained, "to greet you with."

Isabel could find no words to thank him, she felt utterly unreal, adrift, as if there was nothing in her that would speak for her, no mouthpiece for her essential self. He didn't seem to notice her embarrassment and said, with a wave of his hand, "These others are for the children. Or for you, if you like," he added.

Isabel looked doubtfully at the parcels. "Shall we undo them now?" she asked. "Or wait till the children come back from school? They'll be here"—she glanced at the clock—"in about twenty minutes." She realized that, as a measure of time, twenty minutes meant nothing to her at all.

"Oh, let's wait," he said. "It's fun undoing things, more fun, often, than what you find inside."

Isabel thought this over.

"You could make it the title for a novel," she said. "'Untying the parcel', or something of that sort."

"The undoing and the undone," he suggested. "If you could put it in French, which I couldn't, it would make a sub-title for *Les Liaisons Dangereuses*. Have you ever read that book?"

Isabel admitted that she hadn't.

"You should," he said. "It's about two people, a man and a woman, who set out to seduce a young girl. She eggs him on. It isn't a pretty story, I suppose that's why it's not as well known as it ought to be."

"What happens to them in the end?" asked Isabel.

"Oh, they get what's coming to them. Rather a mistake, I think: it doesn't happen in real life, but I suppose Laclos was bound by the moral conventions of the eighteenth century. Personally, I felt rather sorry for them."

"Why?" asked Isabel.

"Well, because they are so amusing, gay about it all, you know, the others are just victims."

That teasing phrase, "the necessity of being amusing", flashed into Isabel's mind. And she herself had been amusing once!

"Do you think that—bad people . . ." she reddened—

"well, let's say naughty people, tend to be more amusing than good ones?"

He smiled. "I'm afraid they do."

Isabel smiled back at him.

"What does the title mean exactly?" she asked.

He shrugged. "There isn't a translation for it. 'Dangerous connections, dangerous relationships', something on those lines."

"How much do you think a title matters?"

Alec laughed. "Now you're asking. Personally I think the book makes the title, not the other way round. Would *Jane Eyre* have seemed a good title, or *Adam Bede*, if they hadn't been good books?"

"Of your own titles, which do you prefer?"

"Well, perhaps *After the Storm*."

"And I think it's your best book."

"Well, there you are, you see."

"I told you you had a fan in Marshport," Isabel said. "A young Austrian girl. Actually, she's the barmaid at an inn."

Alec glanced at Isabel.

"Yes, I know," he said contritely. "You wrote me an enchanting letter, and I never answered it. That's the worst of being a novelist—we never answer letters—but it isn't our fault, really. After a day at the desk, one really can't. It's like asking a postman to take a walk for pleasure—well, most of them have cars now, but when they hadn't. It wasn't that I didn't appreciate your letter. But you can guess what it's like when one is writing—one's most cherished friendships, even one's own life, seem like an intrusion—they break the spell one is trying to weave. I loved your letter, which makes it all the worse."

"But you were ill," Isabel reminded him.

"Yes, so I was—really quite ill. These damned neuroses! And they often get hold of one when one is writing best. It's something to do with the subconscious. You have to have, well . . . a liaison with it, to be able to write at all. But it's a *liaison dangereuse*, for the wretched thing gets almost literally above itself—ceases to be a sub, you know, and becomes super. Most awkward. But I fancy—touch wood—I've put my subconscious in its proper place. I've got it under."

"You have? I *am* glad!" Isabel exclaimed.

His prominent, amber-coloured eyes searched hers and held her with a half-smile. Suddenly he hooked one ankle round the other, almost with the suppleness of a contortionist.

"Did Harold tell you anything about our *ménage* at St. Milo's?" he asked.

Isabel drew a cautious breath. Could she refuse this offer of intimacy? No.

"He told me something," she said.

"About Elspeth?"

Isabel nodded.

"Well, she's cleared out."

"*Has* she?" Isabel was careful not to put into her voice anything but surprise.

"Yes, she has. She's cleared out before, of course, but this time I think it's final. That's why I'm so much better."

Given her cue, which chimed in perfectly with her own immediate reaction, Isabel exclaimed:

"Well, I *am* glad!'

"She made me feel guilty, somehow."

"What a shame!" said Isabel.

"Well, I don't know about that. I've plenty to feel guilty about, but not her, really. I always treated her pretty well. She saw to that. Anyhow, she's gone, walked out, slung her hook."

"I *am* glad," Isabel repeated.

"Yes, it is a cause for rejoicing, isn't it?" he answered rather drily. "This freedom! So now I've come down to pay you all a visit—quite heart-free, for the first time for years. You remember the parable about the seven devils? Well, that's my state—though why I should bore you with all this, I *don't* know."

Isabel was not uncritical, and if Alec had been a lesser man, or lesser in her esteem, she might have thought him too egotistic as well as too unreserved. As it was she felt immensely sorry for him and much flattered that he had made her his confidante. What could she do to keep him near her? "We must try to find some way of entertaining you," she said, "though not with devils, of course." She felt as though someone else was speaking; in Marshport she never talked that way. "You saw some of our local lights last time; they weren't literary lights, I'm afraid. Would you like to meet your Austrian fan? She's quite an intelligent girl. I came across her at the Women's Institute."

"I should very much like to meet her," Alec said.

"Well then, we'll arrange it. How long will you be here?" Alec grinned.

"That's the kind of thing I never know."

"I wish we could persuade you to stay with us, but I expect you are more comfortable at the hotel."

"Not more comfortable, certainly, " said he, "but you see I keep rather odd hours—I'm not properly house-trained yet."

"If I could trust Janice to leave you in peace——" Isabel began, and at that moment there was a scampering of feet; the door, after one or two furtive pushes, was flung open, and in came Janice—Jeremy, like a shadow, following her. At the sight of Alec she stopped.

"We didn't know you had company," she said reproachfully to her mother.

"Darling, it's Mr. Goodrich," Isabel said, a little put out by Janice's unwelcoming speech. "You remember him, don't you?"

"Yes, of course I do," said Janice, rather as one might say "I remember having the influenza". More than ever mortified, Isabel thought what a blessing it was that Jeremy's manners, distant as they were, could always be relied on, "though I hope Mr. Goodrich doesn't think him a dull boy," she thought illogically, her anxieties shooting out in all directions.

But now Janice's manner had completely changed. She went up to Alec with a winning smile, at the same time hunching one shoulder, to give an effect of shyness that she was far from feeling. As he rose and ceremoniously shook hands with her, she said:

"Of course I remember you, Mr. Goodrich. You were lonely sitting here all by yourself, because Mummy wouldn't let anyone come to see you, so I brought you my dolly and you fell in love with her."

"Yes, so I did," said Alec. "She was an ash-blonde with blue eyes called Pamela."

"It's Pamelia, really," Janice patiently corrected him. "And she wasn't ashy at all—that's an untruth—because I make her wash herself every day, all over, and if she won't I do it for her. Pamelia's very, very, *very* clean because, you see, she hardly ever goes where she could get dirty. Would you like to see her now, Mr. Goodrich? Shall I bring her? Unless she's still washing: she does get up rather late sometimes."

"I should love——" Alec began, but Isabel interrupted.

"Of course he doesn't want to see Pamelia, Janice. Now you go off and have a wash yourself, your fingers are all inky, and then perhaps Mr. Goodrich will be kind enough to look at Pamelia. He isn't really interested in dollies."

Janice's face began to crinkle.

"Oh yes he is," she sobbed. "He told me that he loved Pamelia! He said he wished she was his! He said he would like to m-m-m-marry——"

"I'm sure he didn't," burst out Jeremy, in whom his sister's references to marriage always seemed to touch a sensitive nerve. "You didn't say that, Mr. Goodrich, did you?" Jeremy spoke as if all masculine common sense and independence were at stake. "She made it up. All you wanted was to nurse her for a moment, to see if her eyes would shut, and then get rid of her!"

"How do you know when you weren't there?" stormed Janice. "You weren't sorry like I was for Mr. Goodrich, because Mummy had left him alone with nobody to talk to!"

Stung by this reflection on her hostess-ship Isabel said, "Mr. Goodrich has to be alone sometimes, Janice, to write his books. I'm sure he was glad to see you although I told you not to bother him"—here she gave Alec a rueful look—"and glad to see Pamelia too, but when he's busy he likes to be alone."

"But *you* saw him," Janice objected. "*You* saw him whenever you wanted to. *You* saw him at breakfast, dinner, tea and supper, and after we had gone to bed. It wasn't fair! He couldn't say he didn't want to see you, because he's too polite!"

"Now, now," said Isabel, "do as I say and go and get yourselves tidy for . . . for luncheon," she added, for Alec's benefit.

"What's luncheon?" Janice demanded. "We always say lunch, when we don't say dinner."

Caught out, Isabel coloured deeply.

"Now, Daddy'll soon be here, and he won't be pleased if he finds you looking so schooly."

Jeremy took the still heaving Janice by the arm and gently piloted her from the room—they looked rather like Adam and Eve, thought Isabel, being ejected from the Garden.

She turned apologetically to Alec—how his Bohemian fastidiousness must have been outraged by this grossly domestic scene—and said, with a social air:

"What were we talking about when they burst in?"

"They're darlings," Alec said, perhaps a shade perfunctorily. "Absolutely super children. Now let me think—weren't we talking about that Austrian girl?"

"Oh yes," said Isabel, "and I was wishing you could meet her. I could ask her to tea—Harold has met her, too—but it depends on how long you mean to stay."

"Oh, I expect I could stay as long as that," said Alec, without specifying how long "that" was. "My time's my own, you see. Though I ought to get back to St. Milo's to see that the bulbs aren't put in head-downwards—we're going to make rather a feature of daffodils, next year. Harold could tell you why."

Isabel remembered and smiled collusively.

> *"And then my heart with pleasure fills*
> *And dances with the daffodils,"*

she quoted. "All that yellow gold——"

His answering smile delighted her; no one in Marshport would have seen the point.

"Well, should we say next Thursday?" she said, glad that the date was distant. "That's Irma's day off, and Harold's day off, too."

"Thursday would be perfect. How kind you are! You know," he said with sudden seriousness, "kindness has been missing from my life for years. All sorts of other things I've had—tempers, scenes, reconciliations, giving in sometimes, sometimes holding out, saying cross things, saying nice things, flattering, cajoling, being a flame, being an icicle, surprises, shocks, revenges, emotions with hard edges, or sharp edges, or rough edges—all useful to write about, perhaps, but kindness, no! Kindness is a way of living, isn't it, perhaps the only way! The only way of making literary experience—which isn't based on kindness, or hasn't been in my case—compatible with life! And I've had to come all this way to find out!"

As in a trance Isabel looked and listened, while his words, so unlike anything she had expected him to say, so like everything she had hoped to hear, wound their way into recesses of her heart which had long been sealed, or never opened. To have done this, to have been this, for anyone, would have been much; but to have done it, and been it, for Alec!

She lowered her eyes, as if they had been blinds to shield her inward vision from contact with the world of sense; she raised them at a sound and there stood Harold, his mouth half open with astonishment.

23

"Why, Alec!" he said. "Fancy finding you here—though Isabel did tell me you were in these parts. How are you? Quite fit again?"

His dark eyes probed Alec's light ones searchingly, as though to find in them some sign of mental instability; simultaneously he was aware of his own neat dark office suit and of Alec's oatmeal-coloured tweeds, which sagged in places.

"Bit thinner, aren't you?" he said, ignoring Alec's assurance that he was very well. "You look a bit pulled down, you know."

"Oh, I'm quite all right," protested Alec.

"Must go carefully all the same. Not too much . . . well, not too much excitement. You must build yourself up for the winter. Hope you won't go away, of course, but I shouldn't stay too long, it's rather bleak."

His short, clipped sentences might have been intended to illustrate the blustery nature of the weather.

"Oh, Alec's staying for some time, we hope," said Isabel. "He's looking for local colour."

"Oh well," said Harold, "as long as he doesn't overdo it. Must take things quietly, you know, old boy. No pub-crawling, for one thing."

Alec raised his sandy eyebrows.

"I was rather hoping you'd join me for a drink at the Green Dragon."

"I don't know about that," said Harold, "but I can give you a drink now." He looked round and saw the pile of parcels, topped by Isabel's roses, spilling out of their shiny purple sheath. "What the——?" he began.

"Oh dear," cried Isabel, aghast. "I'd forgotten all about them, we were so busy talking. They're Alec's presents for the children, Harold; isn't it good of him? And these roses came all the way from France and I haven't even put them in water! Excuse me, I'll go and do it now." She hurried out

"It's really kind of you, old chap," said Harold awkwardly, and inwardly wishing Alec's presents, and Alec, at the bottom of the sea. "You—well, you spoil us." He was rather pleased with this phrase and repeated it. "And I'm afraid," he added firmly, "that there's nothing we can do for you in return, except give you a drink." He suited the action to the word.

"Cheers," said Alec, taking up his glass with a hand that trembled slightly. "I may have got something for you, too, old man, but I wouldn't dream of calling it a present, it's too boring."

"Oh yes?" said Harold, sipping his Martini.

"I know you're much too busy for one thing," Alec said.

"Well, I'm not all that busy," said Harold cautiously. "Could squeeze in a bit more."

"If I could be sure of that! You see, old fellow——"

"'M," said Harold.

"Well, there are two or three more people, as I think I told you, fellow-victims of the Inland Revenue——"

"And you'd like me to take on their Income-Tax returns?" said Harold, going to the point.

"Well, something like that was actually in my mind. But now I don't feel I ought to ask you."

"Why not?" Harold asked, replenishing their glasses.

"Well—thanks, old fellow—there are some things one can't ask a man to do."

"You must let me be a judge of that," said Harold.

"I don't want to be a bore, old chap. I know how busy you are."

"My dear fellow, don't mention it. As I said, I can always find time——"

"Yes, you say that, old man, but——"

"I'm being quite honest with you, my dear chap."

This went on for some time, then Alec said:

"Well, you must let me think it over. One of these would-be tax-dodgers, Sir Jabez Wilkinson—something to do with the Alloy Exchange—must have got his affairs pretty well mixed up, I should think: it should be quite a headache sorting them out. I shall ask Isabel if she thinks you ought to add to . . . your other commitments. We can't have *you* getting a breakdown from overwork!"

"Me a breakdown?" said Harold, as if a breakdown was a thing that only happened to writers with too much time on their hands, and too much money. "Hard work never did anyone any harm."

"I'll think about it, I'll think about it," said Alec. "When I've asked Isabel, I'll ask Irma her opinion."

"Irma?" repeated Harold, taken completely off his guard.

"Yes, Irma: you've seen her, haven't you?"

Harold had no means of telling whether this was a shot in the dark. Having hesitated, he saw that he was lost.

"Well, I have seen her," he admitted in a low voice.

"Good man! But don't worry; I didn't expect you to proclaim it on the house-tops, and I shan't either. Well, and what conclusion did you come to?"

"What conclusion?" repeated Harold.

"Well, whether she was disposed to make a fellow happy."

"I didn't come to any conclusion," said Harold, trying to keep the agitation out of his voice. "I——"

"Don't bother to tell me now. Tell me later, when we've had time to sort everything out." His voice lightly underlined the word "everything", and the implication of this was not lost on Harold: it meant—no Irma, no Sir Jabez Wilkinson. Before he had time to answer, before he had time to realize anything except his dilemma, the door opened and Isabel came in. She was carrying the roses in front of her, in a china basket; it had been a wedding present to her mother, which her mother had made over to her, and she had never dared use it until now. She had also seized the opportunity to make a complete change that banished every reminder of the kitchen.

"Enter Lavinia," said Alec, "with a basket of flowers."

In Isabel's London days she had looked at pictures, and studied books of reproductions, and she remembered Titian's portrait of the daughter. The fact of the compliment, added to the fact that she recognized the allusion, gave her such a thrill of pleasure that she almost dropped the basket.

"Oh, but Lavinia was fair!" she said, and coloured deeply.

She saw that Alec was impressed. "Yes," he agreed, "she was. But I'm sure that Titian wished she had been dark!"

Harold scarcely heard this piece of gallantry, so busy was he with his own thoughts, and he wouldn't have understood it if he had, though he was dimly aware that Isabel had scored a point. What he did hear, what indeed none of them could help hearing, was the altercation outside the door.

"No, Janice, you mustn't!"

"But I will, I want to!"

"But I tell you he doesn't *want* to see her! He knows how her eyes open and shut—it's the weight inside her head! The weight is attached to the back of the eyeballs, and the eyes work on a pivot——"

"I don't care how they work, and nor does he. He wants to hold her in his arms because he loves her!"

"How can he love her, silly? He's only seen her once!"

"That's why he wants to see her again, so that he can go on loving her! Why do you want to see the same old motor-car so many times? Because you love it!"

"No, because it's real and a doll isn't! It's only pretending to be real! Grown-up people never pretend, except when they are talking to us."

"I don't care, I don't care, and you don't care, Pamelia darling, do you? There, she says she doesn't."

"I didn't hear her," Jeremy said.

"No, because she said it to me. Sometimes she only speaks to me. She quite likes you, because you're my brother, but she hardly ever speaks to you."

"Will she speak to Mr. Goodrich?"

"She might do, I don't know."

There was a moment's pause. The eavesdropping grown-ups exchanged glances.

"Look here," said Jeremy, changing his ground, "if Mr. Goodrich loves Pamelia as much as you say he does, he might want to take her away."

"Oh no, he'd never! I shouldn't let him. And you wouldn't go, would you, Pamelia darling, dearest, sweetest, prettiest?"

"Ooh!" cried Jeremy, as if each endearment had been a pin stuck into him.

"She says she wouldn't," said Janice triumphantly.

"But," said Jeremy, evidently making a last effort to stave off a scene which for him would be unbearable, "supposing Mr. Goodrich *asks* you to let him keep Pamelia? You couldn't say no because no one ever says no to a grown-up person when they ask for something like that."

"Well," said Janice dreamily, "perhaps I'd let him keep her a little, little, *little* while if he promised faithfully to be kind to her and bring her back unbroken."

Apparently this silenced Jeremy, for after one or two false starts the door opened and the couple entered. Janice looked neither to right nor left; her downcast eyes were bent in an ecstasy of maternal devotion on the doll, whom she was gently rocking in her arms; Jeremy looked as if he was being taken to an execution.

Janice went straight up to Alec and said in a sugared voice, "Mr. Goodrich, here is Pamelia. She is my Pamelia but I'll share her with you."

With that she deposited her burden in Alec's lap while Jeremy turned away as if he was going to be sick.

Suddenly Isabel lost her temper with Janice. Usually her surface sympathy was with her daughter, who was getting all she could out of life, while Jeremy, with his insistence on rules and regulations, his instinct for decorum in all things, seemed to her a spoil-sport and a life-denier. But now she felt that Janice had gone too far. What would Alec think of her? That she was hideously spoilt, no doubt. The way she monopolized the limelight, and assumed that she must always be the centre of attention! This Madonna-act was really too much. She was reducing that almost unbelievable miracle, Alec's return, to a farce, and not a very funny farce, either. It wasn't really funny, about the doll; it was rather disgusting that Janice, at her tender age, should be forcing upon Alec this symbol of her maternity. And beneath all these feelings, and unknown to her, something like sex-jealousy stirred in Isabel, resentment that her daughter should be free to express her feelings in a way that she, Isabel, was not.

"Janice!" she said sharply. "Mr. Goodrich doesn't want to be bothered with Pamelia. Take her away at once."

Ignoring her mother, Janice said with outraged dignity to Alec:

"But you wanted to see Pamelia, didn't you, Mr. Goodrich?"

For once at a loss, not wanting to offend either, for Janice had enough personal force for two ordinary grown-ups, Alec looked down at Pamelia, nestling against his pullover, stroked her once or twice half-heartedly, and said:

"I don't mind if you don't, Mrs. Eastwood. I'm perfectly happy with Pamelia."

The "Mrs. Eastwood" was a slip, an unlucky slip, and it exasperated Isabel still further.

"Janice, did you hear me? Please, Harold, make her take the doll away from Mr. Goodrich." It cost her something to forgo his Christian name.

Together they all converged—Harold irresolutely, Isabel threateningly, Jeremy unwillingly—on Alec and on Janice who was standing by his chair, her eyes darting from one face to another.

"If you dare to touch Pamelia," she screamed, "I'll, I'll, I'll——" Such was the fury in her voice, and the tension generated by her tiny, taut, defiant figure, all its curves turned to angles, that when she finished up, "I'll kill you," it seemed an anti-climax.

"Janice, don't be so silly," Isabel said sternly, and was stretching out her hand to take the doll from Alec when Jeremy cried:

"Oh, please don't, Mummy! You see she's quite potty about Pamelia, Janice is! It's all because she loves her so much. It's a great pity to love anyone as much as Janice loves Pamelia—I've told her so again and again, but she won't listen! I've said to her, 'Why don't you try to love more quietly, like Mummy and Daddy do? Why you'd hardly know they loved each other, they never say they do for one thing, nor do I, because boys don't, they aren't supposed to!' But of course she's only a girl and she doesn't know any better. I say to her, 'Try to be more like me', but she doesn't want to—she wants to be like herself! She would be much worse if it wasn't for me, really she would! You only have it sometimes, but I have it all the time! And then she says that I don't love her, because I want to stop her doing silly things! But I do love her, or I shouldn't want to stop her, should I? It isn't what she means by love —she means by love doing a whole lot of silly things that no grown-up person would dream of doing! I tried to stop her just now, but she wouldn't listen! But you mustn't be angry with her, because she'd be quite all right, except for love!"

At the conclusion of this speech, the longest any of those present had ever heard him make, Jeremy's tears began to flow, and simultaneously the tension in the room relaxed and broke. When he admitted that he loved her, Janice's face, which had been screwed up into a mask of fury, suddenly cleared, a beatific smile spread over it; she went to Jeremy and took his hand and looked up into his face; and the faster his tears fell, the more seraphic did her smile become. Alec, hugging Pamelia with a lover's fervour, raised her to his lips and kissed her.

The tableau lasted for a second or two, with only Jeremy not enjoying it. Then Isabel kissed his unresisting face; his father gave him an approving look, Alec a nod charged with deep masculine sympathy, and Janice remarked:

"Pamelia says that she's *quite* happy now."

In the magical calm that succeeded the squall Isabel said:

"But, children, you haven't seen the lovely presents that Mr. Goodrich has brought for you!"

A blissful twenty minutes followed, in the course of which Janice said more than once, without incurring reproof or even a reproachful look from Jeremy, "Oh, Mr. Goodrich, we do love you so."

Alec was the hero of the hour. Before he went away he promised Isabel that he would ring her up and make a plan. Blissfully thinking about this she didn't notice how the meal passed, or how silent Harold was. For a few minutes afterwards the children lingered among their presents, solemnly appraising them, getting to know them, feeling the strangeness wear off and the thrill of ownership begin. At last they were packed off but Janice, before she left, whispered to Isabel:

"Mummy! Mr. Goodrich has done something to Pamelia."

"Darling, what has he done?"

"I don't quite know, but she's different."

"Different, how?"

Janice rolled her eyes.

"I don't really like to tell you."

"Oh, come on."

"Well, I think she's dead."

"Dead?"

"Yes, I think Mr. Goodrich *killed* her."

"What makes you think so?"

"She doesn't answer when I speak to her."

Rather ashamed of herself for doing so, Isabel later carried out an inspection of Pamelia. She could see no difference in her after her supposed ordeal with Alec; true, she didn't test her orally. She didn't speak to her: that would have been going too far. What could have put such an idea into Janice's head?

Alec didn't ring up, and when, after some days of bewildered waiting, Isabel rang him up, she learned that he had left the Royal and would not be back till Thursday.

Bitterly disappointed as she was, Isabel consoled herself with thinking that that was how a man of talent should behave, and that it was another proof, if proof were needed, of the emotional strain from which Alec was suffering, and from which he would go on suffering unless someone rescued him.

24

WHEN Isabel told Harold of the coming tea-party he did not, as she expected he would, demur; he raised a few objections that showed he thought the idea was a futile one, and that was all. For one thing he did not dare betray the strength of his feelings in the matter, and for another his own wish to see Irma was at least as strong as his wish that Alec should not see her.

When he thought of her it was her gaiety that he remembered chiefly. In repose her face had a sad look that came partly from her habit of hanging her head. It was this that provoked her clients at the bar to tease her, for when she lifted her head she nearly always smiled. It was like the sun coming through the clouds, a thing for which everyone everywhere is grateful. Having its origin in sadness her smile always seemed a gift, and was never automatic like the smiles of other barmaids, a grimace imposed on circumstances. If she did sometimes look up without smiling, it was because she didn't understand what was being said to her; the mere fact of understanding made her smile. Frown she could not, except in self-reproach, any more than she could say no.

With Harold, to understand was often to look glum, or at any rate serious, and Isabel had caught this habit from him. Gaiety was a thing he kept for special occasions, usually for convivial or gregarious occasions, organized for mirth. He could join in it but he couldn't originate it, except by way of telling a funny story when several people might be made to laugh. Gaiety was for him essentially a social experience and not meant for private use. When they were first married he and Isabel often enjoyed a joke together; courting they had laughed a great deal, almost insanely; but as they grew to take each other for granted they lost the wish to entertain each other with private jokes.

If Irma's gaiety had implied a lack of fundamental

seriousness Harold would have found it tiresome and unreal, but he knew that it did not. She was gay in spite of things that would have soured many people. And because it implied an attitude to life her gaiety was infectious: he could be sure of sharing it when he was with her.

Could he share it with someone else, with Alec, that was the question. From his parents—from his mother especially —Harold had imbibed the idea that business was all-important; it was more important than what it led to, advancement in life: it was not a means to an end but an end in itself: a first priority, as strong as death and much stronger than love. Marriage, children, a home and all the rest were but a partial fulfilment of the business instinct. When Alec alluded to Sir Jabez Wilkinson, the glitter of the Alloy Exchange touched Harold's most sensitive spot.

Harold didn't really dislike Alec, but Alec made him feel inferior because of his private means and his success in a world which Harold regarded as unreal and a little crazy: no wonder that Alec had gone off his rocker. He laughed, if he remembered to, whenever Alec's name was mentioned, and sometimes to Alec's face, and called him "poor old Alec", just to keep up his end with him, and drown his sense of inferiority—which was strengthened by the benefits Alec had conferred on him. It was a defence-mechanism, like the irony he used against Isabel's cleverness.

Could he share Irma with Alec?

Away from home, away from her, in the privacy of his office, it didn't seem impossible. A barmaid is for everyone, and no one. In the bar, half surrounded by a crescent of grinning faces, she seemed to have no favourites. She herself was a general favourite: then why not the favourite of two men?

Well, he would find out.

On his way back from the office he dropped in at the Green Dragon, carrying his evening paper. The bar had only just opened and was nearly empty: if he had come a minute or two sooner he might have found Irma by herself. She seemed a little confused when she saw him, but he felt very calm. When he had ordered half a pint of bitter he said, "Would you like to look at my evening paper?" and handed it to her, folded, across the bar, at the same time giving her a look. With a quickness he hadn't expected of her she disappeared within to reappear a minute later with a flush that told him she had read the note he had put inside the paper. Raising her head, she said, "Please, yes", then her eyes dropped again.

The note pre-dated his dinner engagement with Irma by a week: they were to meet next Thursday, after the tea-party.

Very soon the bar filled up and Harold noticed that she was much more expert at her business than she had been; she hadn't lost her shyness but she had found a way of dealing with the men, and they with her, which preserved her status of foreigner, which they evidently found intriguing, and yet admitted of familiarity. He paid his score, then lingered, watching her.

"What, another dinner in Downhaven?" Isabel said. "You are going the pace, my dear."

"Can't very well get out of it," said Harold. "It's another business engagement."

"How is business?" Isabel asked. She looked excited and happy.

"Oh, not too bad. Just ticking over. Nothing special, you know."

Harold wasn't usually as expansive as this about his affairs.

"Did Alec bring you any new clients?"

Harold took out his pipe, raised his chin and blew a smoke ring.

"He said something about it. Nothing definite. You can't depend on him, you know."

"He produced the others all right.'

"That's true."

"We owe him something, Harold."

"Yes, I suppose we do."

They owed him Irma; but would the debt be paid?

The next morning, the morning after the second dinner

in Downhaven, Harold went betimes to his office, because he wanted to be there before his cleaning woman or his secretary. Stealthily he let himself in. He looked about the room, all was in order; he needn't have troubled to take these precautions.

Business was rather slack that morning, and Time behaved in a most curious way, sometimes racing, sometimes standing still, never proceeding at its normal pace. At ten o'clock he felt as if it was eleven; at eleven he thought it must be ten. Usually his consciousness ticked as regularly as a clock; his whole organism was time-conscious. To-day he couldn't keep pace with himself at all, his thoughts continually travelled backwards, and when they became contemporary again he couldn't tell how long the interval had been.

At his first sight of her, sitting with her back to him in the lounge of the hotel, her rebellious hair restrained by a coloured handkerchief, his business instinct had been uppermost. He was ready, so he felt, to do a deal with Alec about her. Isabel had almost convinced him that it would be for the benefit of all concerned. His goodwill towards her found an outlet, an escape, in this. As Alec's mistress she would enjoy every material benefit; as Alec's benefactor he would enjoy substantial material benefits. Isabel, Jeremy and Janice would enjoy them too, and Isabel, whose heart was set on bringing this about, he couldn't think why, would be appeased. As for Alec—well, he didn't feel responsible for Alec, as Isabel seemed to, but Alec would have got his share of the bargain, and presumably he would be satisfied.

At the tea-party Alec certainly had made the running with Irma. Apologizing to his hosts who didn't know the language he had chattered away to her in German; he had drawn her out, he had made her laugh; they had leaned towards each other, animation lighting up their faces. Isabel had looked on benignantly, and when conversation between the two had shown signs of flagging, which it seldom did, had skilfully revived it. Harold himself had been an onlooker. He didn't like the rôle he was playing, but then he hadn't expected to like it. He had been brought up to think that in business matters, and in most other matters, his likes and dislikes didn't count—just as he had been taught to eat what food was put before him. Some of the conversation, being about Alec's books (Irma, it appeared, had now read three of them), was over his head, so he couldn't be expected to take part in it: he had never pretended that he was a novel-reader. The furthest he would go in this connection, the utmost concession he would make, was to suggest that such and such a person, or such and such an incident, was odd enough to go into one of Alec's books. He would say this for a joke, and as if the whole subject of novel-writing was a joke; and in the same spirit Alec received it. What an amazingly elastic personality Alec had, thought Harold with some distaste. He believed that a man should be himself, solid enough to be an obstacle: indeed, he thought of himself as an obstacle, something to be reckoned with, something in people's way. The Alec who conversed with Irma was a different Alec from any he had seen—a grimacing, flaunting creature who might at any moment make love in public. Well, he knew his own business best, if business it could be called: certainly he knew how to captivate Irma: she seemed to hang upon his lips. Harold rather wished that Jeremy and Janice hadn't been present; but there was nowhere else for them to go, and they had been so successfully schooled by Isabel not to interrupt that even Janice sat round-eyed and silent; in fact, the first and only contribution that they made was Jeremy's "Please may we get down?"

The conversation went on for some time after that, and it seemed to Harold, whose training and experience had given him a sixth sense in such matters, that with every word an agreement was being reached. How often had he been present at conferences where the parties had at first seemed to be at loggerheads, all their interests conflicting, yet in the end, almost miraculously, a solution had been found that satisfied them all. And in this case the interests hadn't even been conflicting: it was just a question of acquainting each party with what the other wanted for full agreement to be reached.

So Harold felt on firm ground; nor did he stop to ask

himself why he hadn't told Isabel the object of either of these dinners—these business engagements, when to know would have given her so much pleasure; and if he had, he might plausibly have answered: "Because I don't want my wife or anyone else to know about my affairs."

When the preliminary politenesses were over, which were more perfunctory on Harold's part than at their earlier dinner together, when they had settled what they were going to eat and were nearing the end of the soup course, Harold said:

"Well, what did you think of Mr. Alexander Goodrich?"

He couldn't help saying the name with a slightly ironical inflection, though he realized that this was not the best way of selling Alec to Irma.

"Oh," she said, "he is a very nice gentleman, isn't he? I find him most amusing."

She looked a little sad when she said this, but then she always looked sad.

"We thought you would," said Harold, pleased to have started off so well. "He's a really good chap, Alec is, a very decent fellow."

Irma agreed. A waiter came and took away their soup-plates, then poured a teaspoonful of wine into Harold's glass. Harold tasted it and nodded sagely, after which ritual both their glasses were filled. Harold raised his and said, "Cheers, Irma."

"Cheers, Harrold," Irma said, not very gaily. There was another pause while the waiter brought them their main dish. When he was out of earshot Harold said, resolutely:

"But to go back to Alec. I think he is rather taken with you, you know."

Any woman should have looked pleased at this, but Irma didn't.

"Please?" she said.

Harold had been told that in talking to deaf people one mustn't repeat a thing in exactly the same words, so he thought for a new phrase.

"He's taken a fancy to you," he said, very slowly and distinctly.

"Please?" said Irma again.

Had she really not understood, or was she pretending not to understand?

Harold tried a third time, and to do him justice he was a little embarrassed.

"I mean, he seems to like you," he said flatly.

"Ah yes," said Irma.

Harold sighed with relief. So far, so good. She didn't seem as excited as he hoped she would be, but this was a business deal, and he couldn't expect her to put all her cards down on the table.

"He's rather lonely," Harold said, with all the warmth he could command; "he isn't married, you know, I don't know why, but writers often don't settle down like other people. It isn't because he hasn't money, because he has, plenty of it. He's just . . . well, he's just lonely."

"I see," said Irma. "Poor Mr. Goodrich."

Harold wished she would look up from her plate: this downcast business with her eyes was rather baffling. But, of course, it was her habit.

"Well, that's how it is," said Harold briskly. "He's lonely, and he's taken a fancy to you, and he'd like to see more of you. How do you feel about it?"

Irma's sallow face slowly turned a dull red. The colour went right up to her eyes and down her neck. She put down a forkful of food untasted, and said in a choking voice:

"Do you want me to be his mistress, Harrold?"

Harold was genuinely horrified at this plain speaking.

"Of course not," he exclaimed, almost huffily. "I was only telling you what he felt about you. He would have told you himself but . . . but . . . he's off to-morrow to Wales. Of course, if you don't like him, Irma, then there's no more to be said. The . . . the deal's off. There was no question of your being his mistress, as you call it: he's lonely and he wants a friend, that's all. If you don't want him as a friend, don't have him. But I thought you liked him. You seemed to at tea to-day."

Harold knew that attack was the best form of defence, and made quite a good show of seeming the injured party. He knit his brows, straightened his lips and looked his sternest. But he was quite unprepared for Irma's next remark.

"Oh Harrold, you are so sweet!"

As she said this she laughed, for the first time that evening, and couldn't stop laughing because (though Harold didn't guess this) she was also on the verge of tears.

Harold had never been called sweet before. It was not in the language of the conference room, and not a thing he wanted to be or to be thought. He knew that in cinemas and on the wireless women sometimes called men sweet, but that made it seem all the more unreal to him. On the other hand he couldn't take it as an insult for it obviously wasn't meant as one, and an unused nerve in his male make-up answered to it favourably. Drawing in his chin, he said:

"I'm sorry. I thought I was doing you a good turn, as well as him, by . . . well . . . by bringing you together. I didn't realize you didn't like him."

"But I do like him!" Irma surprisingly exclaimed.

Recovering from the shock, Harold said:

"Then if you like him——"

"But I do not love him, Harrold."

Each of Irma's remarks had been like a blow in a new spot: Harold was no longer the Harold of the conference room, dapper and self-assured. He tried to make a come-back, however.

"I didn't say anything about love."

Again Irma laughed: it was a delicious sound.

"You did not, but I do. In Austria——" She stopped. "What I have been trying to say is, that to be friends with Mr. Goodrich without love, it is not possible."

Harold saw the truth of this, and for the moment he had no answer to it. Instead, he changed his ground.

"But why couldn't you love him?" he demanded. He was so ashamed and suspicious of the word "love" that he had to put it in inverted commas. "There's no harm in being in love," he added, daringly and insincerely. "You might love him when you got to know him."

At that Irma's sadness seemed to come back. Her eyes were still gay, but her lips were trembling. She made a movement to get up, and then sat down again.

"Do you want to know why I could not love him?" she said, speaking very carefully and pronouncing the word "love" with the broad O, as if loaf, that foreigners, and music-hall artists, sometimes use.

Conscious now of the pitfalls spread around him, Harold said warily:

"If you think there is anything to be gained by telling me, by all means do."

"It is because——" Irma began and suddenly stopped. She raised her face and looked everywhere but at Harold. Many expressions chased each other across her features; tender looks they were for the most part, but with a hint of impatience in them that Harold didn't fail to note. At last she said:

"I do not think it would be right to tell you."

Reassured by her confusion, and really curious to know, Harold leaned back and said:

"Well, out with it."

"It is because," said Irma, "it is because—but you will not understand, Harrold—it is because I love *you*."

She looked at him with something near to terror in her eyes and then dropped them, and it seemed as if she would never lift them up again.

Harold sat quite still. He was dumbfounded. Dimly he realized, in a flashing compendious vision of their relationship, that this was the outcome of it, and that he had no one but himself to blame. To blame, that was his first reaction—the guilt and embarrassment that someone feels who has been given an expensive and unwanted present. Astonishment succeeded. Since his courting days, since the days of his honeymoon, since the days of his first settling down with Isabel, since the time when all those emotions had been stabilized in matrimony, he had never once thought of himself as a man with whom a woman other than his wife could fall in love. It was utterly outside his calculations: as soon might he have thought of himself as a deep-sea diver or a racing motorist. He had inherited his mother's realism: day-dreaming had been an almost unknown pastime to him and sex a canalized enjoyment. Extra-marital love affairs were things that other people had. Love, in that sense, had been absorbed in matrimony. Isabel didn't need it; apart from being his wife, with whom he would have thought it hardly decent to be in love, she had other interests —interests outside his range, interests which, added up, distanced her from him, set her on a plane of cleverness. He thought of her as someone to be proud of, someone to be stood up to on occasion, someone to be secretly afraid of as a partner with a larger number of shares in the concern than he had—but not as someone loving him, still less someone in love with him. His masculine pride, that asked for tenderness and surrender, had been starved for many years before he had met Irma. Now, in spite of the many sublimations he had found for it, it reasserted itself.

"Do you mean that?" he asked.

He had been so long without speaking that she started; her colour came and went.

"Yes, I mean it, Harrold," she said.

He was pale, too; his eyebrows and his dark moustache might have been drawn on paper.

"Oh, I ought never to have said it!" she exclaimed. "It is not a thing a woman should say. Please, Mr. Eastwood, do not let us think about it! Let us talk of something else! Let us be happy, as we were the last time!"

She smiled through unshed tears; and at the sight Harold's heart melted.

"My dear," he said, "my darling."

Saying those words liberated something in him. He stretched across the table and touched her hand: it was delicate and fragile like the rest of her. She did not draw it away, and he held it in his palm, feeling the thrill of possession run through him.

"Oh," she sighed, "I am so happy, Harrold—but——"

"But what?" he said, not tentatively, not shyly, but as one who has the right to demand an answer.

"But I am afraid," she said. "Does not to be very happy make you feel afraid?"

"I can't say that it does," said Harold, who was now bursting with self-confidence. He felt as though his personality could over-run the world. He felt he could easily

209

have talked to Irma in German. But with eyes newly opened to the feelings of another person, he saw the shadow of fear in her eyes, and said almost tenderly:

"What are you afraid of? The German fellow?"

She raised her eyebrows a little and smiled.

"Oh no, not of him. I tell him ever so often"—she shook her head—"that I am not for him. A ring in pledge he gave me, but I have given it back to him. We do not see each other so often now. He will soon find another girl—at least I hope. No"—she seemed to take pleasure in using the word when it did not imply disagreement or refusal—"it is only married that he wants to be."

"Then what are you afraid of?" Harold persisted.

"Of everything," she said, withdrawing her hand from his, "and nothing. It is everything for me here with you to be, but it must be nothing, because——" She couldn't find words, but Harold holding her to it said inexorably:

"Because?"

"Because"—she tried to summon laughter to her aid, and partially succeeded—"because, you see, you are so sweet."

"You said that before," said Harold, not feeling at all sweet, and resenting Irma's laughter yet unable to take umbrage. "And if I am I don't see what it had to do with being afraid."

"Oh, but it has." said Irma, "and I do not want anyone to say, 'Because he has met this blinking Austrian girl he is no longer what he used to be'."

"But who's to know?" said Harold, in whom this sudden revelation of his feelings had destroyed his native caution, "and if they knew, what would it matter?"

"Oh, but it would matter," said Irma, laughing again her brittle, nervous laugh which jarred on Harold and yet inflamed his passion, "because I should feel so sad. Then they would say of me, 'This bloody barmaid'" (Harold laughed involuntarily at the word and then looked fierce), "'this bloody barmaid has . . . has . . . helped herself to Mr. Eastwood, and now we do not know where to look because we are so ashamed'."

Her laughter was an invitation to Harold to join in, to dissipate their feelings in a bright cascade of mirth, drown them, lose them, forget about them—but it had the opposite effect on him.

"Who would say that?" he demanded, wilfully obtuse.

Irma tried once more.

"Oh, anyone might say it, I don't mean nasty people, but anyone who liked me and had been kind to me. They would say, 'It is thus that this goddamned barmaid has our kindness repaid, so that we cannot look each other in the face, and yet we cannot say the reason, because some of us we are too young to be told.' Then I should be very sorry, and so perhaps would you, Harrold." She laughed again experimentally, as if the picture she had been evoking was the greatest joke.

But humour had never been Harold's strong suit, and he did not feel like laughing.

"Look here, Irma," he said, at last alive to the meaning of her parable, "if it's my family you're thinking of, they're my concern. They don't come into it. You said just now you loved me. Well! What else matters?"

"To me, nothing," she said sadly.

"Well, then."

Irma became extremely agitated.

"I think I must go home," she said. "I am not well. It is the wine, I think. Here in England I am not used to it."

Even as she spoke she drank some and it seemed to steady her.

"You'll be all right in a moment," Harold said. "You'll be all right if you think about it in the right way, Irma."

He spoke with intense conviction and she gave him a wide-eyed look as if she too would like to be convinced.

All at once he felt master of the situation.

"Now eat your dinner," he commanded her, "and then we'll talk about it."

Meekly she obeyed him, and with that act of obedience her appetite returned. But she ate in a subdued way and as if eating wasn't natural to her. Harold was touched by this.

"Good girl," he commented.

Somehow or other they managed to keep up a fairly continuous conversation, from which the chief topic of their thoughts was absent. They couldn't have done this—

certainly Harold couldn't—but for the lover's irresistible impulse to explore the mind of the beloved. Antennae long disused send out and receive all kinds of messages. And if Harold had one aim in view, and Irma another, and if they both knew this and knew that the aims were contradictory, in a deeper sense they were agreed, for love unites. Cleverer than Harold, and more adroit despite linguistic handicaps, Irma kept steering the conversation towards a lighter mood —the mood, perhaps, of a Viennese waltz, a *ländler* mood, looking back on love, not forward to it. She told him comic incidents about herself and made deliberate mistakes in English, mistakes within mistakes; consciously and unconsciously she tried to give him the impression that she was a creature who existed only at the comic level, not to be taken seriously, least of all by an intending lover. And Harold, though a part of him saw through this ruse, did not object to it, rather he welcomed it as an opportunity to woo her: and while the core within him glowed more fiercely he kept its light from shining out of his eyes, until quite suddenly, when they had drunk their coffee, he took the hand which she had allowed to rest defenceless and unsuspecting on the table, and said:

"Shall we go now?"

"Oh yes, Harrold," said Irma, and closed her eyes in secret thankfulness. "What a lovely evening it has been." She left her hand in his, and who can blame her if together with her relief she felt a pang of disappointment that her diplomacy had succeeded?

Harold examined the bill in his careful way, checking the items. A glance up the column of figures and a glance down —they tallied. The waiter bowed his thanks.

"Irma," said Harold, when they were in the car and he had tucked the rug round her, "I want to show you something."

"Yes, Harrold," said Irma, "what is it?" Released from strain, the sudden contact with the cold had made her sleepy: the sentinels were off their guard.

"My office," Harold said.

"Your office, Harrold?"

"Yes, it's quite near here.

"But shall we be able to see it in the dark?"

He didn't answer, but drove on through the streets. Presently the car stopped.

"Here we are."

Irma slewed herself round and tried to look out of the window.

"What a great beeg building," she commented as enthusiastically as she could.

"Yes, my office is on the second floor."

Irma tried to identify it.

"Would you like to see it, Irma?"

"I think I can see it now," she said. Then, with the air of one discovering a jewel, she added, "*There* it is!"

"Yes, but I meant the inside. Would you like to see the inside, Irma?"

"Oh, is it pretty?" asked Irma, idiotically.

"It's quite comfortable. Would you like to see it?"

Gently he drew her head away from the window and took her in his arms. "Would you like to see it?" he murmured, between kisses.

"Please yes," she whispered back.

He didn't switch the light on in the hall; his arm directed her. But as they were waiting for the lift to come, she looked round and said:

"Oh, Harrold, you have left the street door open."

"Why, so I have," he said. "How careless of me. Stay here, I'll go and shut it."

In the basket beside him on the writing table his morning post lay still unopened. A knock disturbed his meditation and he glanced at the letters with distaste.

"Yes, Miss Malone?"

"Mr. Goodrich to see you, sir."

Harold stiffened.

"Please show him in."

Bucolic and expansive in his oatmeal-coloured tweeds, but wearing an incongruous pair of black town shoes, Alec came in, displacing a large quantity of air.

Harold got up to shake hands.

"Hullo, old fellow, I thought you were off to Wales."

"So I am, old chap, I'm actually on my way to the station, but I thought I'd just blow in to see how you were bearing up."

"Not too badly, Alec, all things considered."

"I'm glad to hear it. So am I, and all the better for our tea-party. You missed the first part of it, such a pity. Isabel was wonderful, wasn't she? So gracious and benevolent, just as if she had been presiding at a meeting of the Women's Institute. We didn't quite sing 'Bring me my bow of burning gold,' but we might have. Not that I needed my arrows of desire brought, for I had them by me. I fell for Irma in a big way, Harold. 'This is one of the latest and most enthusiastic of your fans,' said Isabel, introducing us. I didn't like to say, so soon, that I was her fan, too. The girl's intelligent, you know; she'd really read my stuff and she made some quite perceptive comments on it." He glanced at his watch. "We can speak frankly, can't we?"

"Of course," said Harold mechanically.

"Well, what do you think of my chances?"

Harold didn't reply at once, he could not. A dozen answers pressed into the breach, the narrow breach, all hopelessly inadequate. His love for Irma was no part of his normal make-up, he hadn't had time to relate it to his everyday consciousness, still less to assimilate it. Even to himself he was inarticulate about it; and how much more to Alec.

"Your chances?" he repeated. "I'm afraid I don't quite get you."

"Oh yes you do, my dear fellow," said Alec, tolerantly, but giving Harold a keen look from his prominent, tawny eyes. "But to put it more plainly, how, in your opinion, would she respond to my advances?"

The question was agony to Harold. He could see no way round it. He felt as though Irma was in the room listening to them. His temper flared up and he almost shouted:

"I know how I should!"

Horrified by the outburst, he looked across at Alec, sitting in the client's chair, for which he looked too big. Alec said, reasonably:

"Well, don't get angry with me till I make them."

Harold didn't understand this quip and merely glared.

"But seriously, Harold," Alec went on, "I'm sorry if I've trodden on your toes."

"My toes?" said Harold, looking down at them, and suddenly his sense of his own safety, put out of action by the thought, came to his aid. Was it too late? Had he betrayed himself?

"From what I can make out, she's not that kind of girl," he said as civilly as he could.

Alec looked at and through him, and a smile widened his lips.

"My dear fellow," he began, "if I'd known that you were interested in her yourself——"

"I'm not," said Harold. "I've only seen her two or three times."

"Once was enough for me."

"I tell you I'm not interested in her," repeated Harold.

"Well then, you're not," said Alec, in the tone of one accepting without question a friend's statement. "I only thought you might have been. I shouldn't blame you."

Love is its own torturer; and, like cruder tortures, it makes its victim want to tell the truth—the truth about itself. It is by nature self-betraying; if nothing else, the eyes give it away. Denying Irma, Harold had denied the thing that meant most to him; now, instead of the sweet thought of her, he had only this monstrous lie, which came between him and his image of her, threatening it with extinction. In a panic, feeling she would be lost to him unless he testified, he said: "You were right, Alec. I am . . . well, I am interested in Irma."

Relief came instantly. So might the victim feel when the thumbscrew is loosened.

"Well, my boy, I congratulate you," said Alec, untwisting his ankles and leaning back in his chair. "I won't ask you any questions—no names, no pack-drill—but go ahead, I wish you luck. And by the way, I must be off." He glanced at his watch. "Yes, I must fly."

"Shall I ring you up a taxi?" Harold said solicitously.

"No, I've got one at the door." Alec rose and shook hands. "You'll be seeing me again one of these days." He waved and went.

25

"I WONDER if anything will come of our tea-party," said Isabel, when the children had been put to bed.

"Come of it? Oh, I see what you mean. No, I don't think so."

"Why don't you think so?"

"Well, actually Alec told me. He said there was nothing doing."

"Then he must have seen her again."

"Yes, I suppose so."

Isabel thought a moment.

"I wonder where. . . . And you, you saw him, too?"

Harold explained that Alec had called in at his office.

"I think it's a pity," Isabel said. "I do think it's a pity. And I'm surprised, too, because she seemed to like him. It would have been such a wonderful chance for her, and have made all the difference to him. She seemed *such* a nice girl."

"Perhaps that's why," said Harold acidly.

"Oh, Harold, you really are too old-fashioned. We went over all this before, but what harm could it have done to anyone? Surely the question in these matters is, whom does it hurt? So long as it's done in a civilized way, and we're all civilized, I hope, it hurts no one. If it breaks up a home, or separates people who are really fond of each other, of course it matters terribly and I should be the last to say it didn't. But in this case it wouldn't have hurt anyone. Alec wasn't going to seduce Irma; except in the narrowest sense it wasn't even a dishonourable proposal. He might even have married her. She would have had all that to look forward to, and he would have been saved from that frightful harpy who clings to him." Isabel's voice always roughened when she spoke of Elspeth.

"You forget," said Harold, "he's got rid of her."

"Well, yes, he has. But that makes it so terribly important for him to find someone quickly in her place who's kind and sweet, and who won't lead him the dance Elspeth did. Irma would have been the perfect person. She would have given him back his confidence in life——"

"You've said all this before," said Harold.

Isabel coloured. She couldn't keep her tongue away from the sore place.

"I should have thought he had plenty of confidence in life," Harold went on.

"No, Harold, he hasn't. He seems to have, and perhaps he thinks he has, but you can tell from his books he hasn't really. In his books people always treat him badly, especially women. At some time somebody has mauled him—well, we know who it was, Elspeth."

"He may have asked for it," said Harold.

"He may have, Harold, you're quite right, he may be the sort of man who brings out the worst in people. There's bad in people, goodness knows, but at heart humanity is sound, I'm sure of that, and if only he could have found someone he could rely on, someone who didn't play him up, as Elspeth did, someone who would take care of him—oh, well, he hasn't, that's all."

Isabel looked absurdly dejected.

"I think he can take care of himself all right," said Harold.

"But he can't, Harold, that's just it: he's had this breakdown—she caused it, of course."

"She said she made him feel," Harold reminded his wife. "She said she made him feel, and unless he felt, he wouldn't write."

"Maybe she did, at one time. But don't you see, he has outgrown her. She was an irritant. Well, an irritant is all right when one is young, and still has plenty of resilience, but not when one is getting older and less adaptable; one doesn't want it then. The trouble with Alec's work is that he's not quite grown-up——"

"Not quite grown-up?" said Harold, astonished.

"Oh, he's grown-up, but his work isn't. It's stuck at the point—I feel—where he met Elspeth: it's stuck at Elspeth, it can't get beyond her. That's why he singles out in human nature the ugly elements—the elements that hurt him. I won't call them bad. They're not really bad, of course, they're the effects of maladjustment and unhappiness—there's no real badness, the world over, there's only unhappiness."

"Perhaps Elspeth was unhappy," put in Harold slyly.

"Oh no, she couldn't have been, a woman of that kind—it was her happiness to make him unhappy. But I wasn't thinking of his art so much as of his heart—I mean, the other way round."

"Now which were you thinking of?" said Harold teasingly. "Art or heart?"

"His art, of course. Every great artist has come to terms with life—think of Beethoven—how tortured he was, in middle-age, and how serene at the end. Reconciliation, the power to feel the good in human nature, that's what Alec needs, and what Irma could have given him. Tiresome girl, I feel that I could shake her. Looking at it from the most selfish point of view, what duty can a girl like Irma have except towards experience—the experience of making some man happy. *Her* experience doesn't matter much, I grant that. But his! She might have given posterity a great writer, instead of a fascinating but incomplete one."

"Oh, Alec'll bob up again," said Harold.

"He won't come here again," said Isabel.

Isabel's unhappiness endured for two more days, and then came Alec's letter. It had been posted from St. Milo's.

"My dear Isabel,

"This is just a word to thank you for all your kindness to me. Even with your insight you may not have guessed that it was a sort of resurrection for me, a return to life. I myself didn't realize how ill I had been, how *not* myself, till I came to myself in that pretty, sunny sitting-room of yours. I know you sometimes make fun of it, calling it the lounge and so on, but dear Isabel, you're wrong, it's an enchanted place and should be called the Hall of Healing, or some such name. I rack my memory in vain for its counterpart in literature; perhaps you can think of one. I daren't say Venusberg, for fear of shocking you! We must hold on to *health*—and the *hygienic* aspect! But be that as it may, you will never know what being

218

with you and, indeed, all the Eastwoods has meant to me.
I was still a wreck when I arrived—every nerve a-twitter—
and then the transformation! It was almost worth-while
having the breakdown, to feel what it was like, coming
out of it. And the effect was so immediate. How did you
do it? No medicine, no treatment. I just opened the door
—I don't think that I had to open it—I just walked in,
and then the miracle took place!

"Well, I only wish I could repay you. But how can I?
You have everything you want—happiness, health, husband, children—such blessings can't be added to, or
taken away from you. You mightn't think they could be
communicated, but they can, and without robbing you, I
hope, for I only had to feel them round me to become,
well—a new man. It was partly the contrast, I admit—the
contrast with what things had been like here—and it *was*
a contrast, I can tell you! Such scenes, you wouldn't
believe it! and then the crash. But even without that I
should have felt the enchantment operating just as I felt
it the first time I came.

"I mustn't ramble on but what I was leading up to was
—since I can't do anything for you, would you, again,
do something—everything—for me? Such a fair exchange!
But would it really be a great bore if I came down again,
before so very long? You said something about my giving
a talk to the Women's Institute—well, that would give
you an excuse for further well-doing, and I don't need
one. You can make me part of your good works. I needn't
say that I should come for *love*—no fee, no expenses,
nothing of that sort. Any time you like, and that suits
the 'Women', but for *me*, the earlier the better.

"I don't expect an answer to this shameless proposal,
but if there is one, and it's favourable, I shall, I shall——

"Words fail me, but not my gratitude, nor (may I say?)
my love to you all.

Yours,

Alec.

"I've begun to write again—in quite a cheerful vein,
for me."

The children had gone to school; Harold had gone to the office. Except for the daily woman, Isabel was alone in the house. It was her usual practice to help the daily woman to wash up the breakfast things, but on this occasion she sat down at once to answer Alec's letter. It did not seem to her overstated or overwritten—or if it did, she welcomed the departure from the ordinary Englishman's cramped, inhibited style. Everything in the letter delighted her, not least the postscript. He was writing again, and in a happier mood.

She was handicapped because she wanted to use the language of love, but knew she mustn't. Every sentence, every phrase, had to be denied its proper feeling. As each word sprang into her mind it underwent a process of purgation. How could she suppose he cared for her? Her deepest instincts warned her not to betray herself. How different, when she had written to him before, when she didn't suspect her feeling for him, still less his for her! Then it had been so easy; the words poured from her pen. Now she must dissemble everything. It went to her heart to say that if he would feel freer at the hotel she mustn't press him to stay in their hugger-mugger household, much as she would like to. But something could be implied, perhaps all could be implied; and if she spent an hour over the letter, it was to get into it the maximum of implication; it must not, it must not, seem like a rebuff.

There was to be a meeting of the Women's Institute in a week's time, she told him; it would be on a Monday—could he come for the week-end and stay on for it? She felt sure she could arrange for an exchange between the speaker for that day and himself.

She debated long over how she should sign herself: "Your most sincere friend" was the compromise she arrived at, and she didn't like it much.

With her tongue against the envelope to seal it, she suddenly had misgivings. Would the exchange of speakers be so easy to arrange for after all? The letter in her bag, she hurried round to the Secretary; from the Secretary to the President; she was shocked and bewildered to find that they didn't regard Alec as a first priority. Was she sure that he could come? they asked her. She had to admit she wasn't. On a sudden inspiration she said she would telephone and find out.

Returning home, frustrated and ill at ease with herself, she remembered that Harold always examined the telephone account most carefully. Any extra large item he would be sure to query. Arming herself with the household money, which later she would repay, she went off to a public callbox. She had with her coins of every denomination, but it turned out she was still short of shillings. All the shillings in the world, it seemed, were in the gas meters and electric meters. Somewhat grudgingly the Bank gave her some: at last she was properly equipped. But new misgivings assailed her. Would all this hysterical extravagance be for nothing? Would Alec be at home? All the feeling she had started out with—the immense afflatus of spirit—had perished in the search for ways and means to express it.

With trembling fingers she dropped the coins into the slot. A woman's voice answered: Yes, Mr. Goodrich was there and she would go and get him.

But if he was annoyed at being disturbed? If he answered her coldly? If, after all, he couldn't come?

His voice reassured her on the first two points: it had all the warmth of his letter. She was in ecstasy—too ecstatic to remember her mission. At last she got round to it, but too late: another seven-and-fivepence, said the operator.

She hadn't got it. How could she explain? "They're cutting us off, they're cutting us off!" she wailed. "All right," he answered gaily. "Tell them to reverse the charge, I'll gladly pay!"

How clever of him to have thought of it! In a moment they were reconnected; their voices flashed along the wires, falling, rising, mingling. Yes, he would come, nothing would keep him away. "As a matter of fact," he said, "I'm with you now!" "A letter, my letter, I'm just going to post it!" She wanted to explain the cool tone of her letter. "What, a letter? Really? You've actually *written* to me? What did you say?"

"Another three minutes?" asked the operator's voice, professionally.

"Oh no, oh no!" from Isabel.

"Yes please, yes please," from his end. "We haven't half finished!"

At last, after yet another three minutes, they had finished as far as temporal, verbal communication went; and Isabel opened the door of the telephone-box into another world.

As soberly, as detachedly as she could she announced to the Secretary that Mr. Goodrich had consented to come. She was trapped into adding: "Isn't it kind of him?" "Well, I suppose so," said the Secretary, without enthusiasm; "it will mean some extra work, you know."

Work!

Isabel couldn't go home; four walls, the walls of home, would have stifled her. She went down through the town, crossed the canal, with its sad burden of Ophelia leaves, skirted the gardens and the tennis courts, abandoned now till the next season, took the path between the stunted oak-trees which wound its way like a green artery into the heart of the town, and found herself on the front, the concrete esplanade, that defends Marshport from the English Channel.

She felt morally certain now that Alec loved her. One grain of doubt she kept—or thought she kept—in reserve, as insurance against the possibility of deception: but this misgiving was like the blob of dark that brings out the colours in a picture. "He loves me!" The three words kept repeating themselves as she was blown along the causeway. A warm, stiff south-westerly breeze followed her, making her almost run: it whipped the blue waves into white horses. He loved her, and the ocean loved her too: it urged her on her course. The ocean! There it was, coming right up to her; she needn't go in search of it, it was reaching out to her with every hungry, white-capped billow. What freshness, what a tang, what force it had! Even here, on the cement-protected earth, it showed its power: the power that lay hidden in its illimitable, vast extent, and seldom came to the surface. And on the other side, the landward side, what a difference! Low hills rose behind the town, green hills already fledged with autumn yellow, and pimpled over by a rash of villas. One of those red roofs, nestling so snugly and smugly in the foliage, was hers: one of them sheltered all her earthly obligations, Harold, Jeremy, Janice, the pledges she had given to the future, villadom incarnate. At the thought of them she shook her head, and turned her eyes to the sea, the undutiful, irresponsible sea, where not a funnel, not a sail, was in sight: flurries of wind kept erasing whatever was written on the water.

The sense of spiritual expansion, which she once used to have, came back to her; the hard core, the feeling of a centrifugal force at work in her, contracting her—her will, she thought it was, her will, forcing her nature against its grain—began to loosen and dissolve, to be replaced by a soft pliancy of being, receptive not rebellious. The shadow stalking at her side made her feel taller than she was. Ah, here was something she liked better than the villas: the long plain Georgian façade of the convent, a white oblong against the parti-coloured hillside. Why did she like it better than the villas? Because it spoke of an unmixed resolve, a single-minded wish to serve—she didn't trouble to ask whom; the wish to serve, the self lost in serving, was sufficient. And further on, behind a dip in the hillside, and so like a puff of smoke that strangers seldom could distinguish it, rose the grey tower of Attenbury Castle. This, too, fostered her mood, for it was from here that the four Knights rode out to Canterbury. No matter on what errand; for her the main thing was that riding out they didn't count the cost: they had one end in view—to serve their King. Not for them to court worldly success by nibbling at the royal bounty as if it were a cheese; theirs was a nobler appetite than that; at one swallow they gulped the whole of fame. Let posterity blame them if it liked: she, Isabel, would not.

But the Castle had another, practical meaning for her, as old as this was new. The sight of it was, by private rule, her *but de promenade*, and meant she must turn back. Yes, she must hurry home. But how could she hurry with the wind against her, and such a wind! Worse than the wind, the grit from the sea-shore kept getting in her eyes. They ran, they smarted. She had to blow her nose. Yet all this struggle with the elements exhilarated her; she felt she was making headway, literally making headway, not only against the elements but against—against what? Against her false self, and the conditions she had imposed on it.

An intermittent thunder began to assail her ears: it was the sound of traffic crossing the humped wooden bridge. Persons using the bridge do so at their own risk, the notice said. Superstitiously she had always avoided crossing it, as if it was a sort of Rubicon. But now! Hardly had she set foot on it than she began to tremble with its vibration: across the slatted boards the other side seemed very far away.

Then came the hill, and the wearisome climb between the hanging gardens of this suburban Babylon. When she reached Tilecotes she was out of breath, and hardly had she crossed the threshold than the burden of domestic cares began to subdue her spirit. The lounge was stuffy, and smelt of stale tobacco like a bar. Between them, she and the daily woman had forgotten to ventilate it and let out last night's fug. As she opened the French window she saw the children standing on the golf ladder, immobilized, stiff as statues. She turned away, from some impulse not to reveal herself to them: and a moment afterwards she heard Jeremy's inexorable voice:

"Janice, go back!"

26

As Harold became more and more an acquaintance, almost a stranger, Isabel also took to noticing him more: hitherto she had taken him for granted; and if she loved him less she liked him better: he was a man, he represented Alec's sex. And Harold, too, was unusually considerate to her: she was a woman, and she represented Irma's. Husband and wife were kinder to each other, and more aware of each other as human beings, than they had been for many years.

One evening, after supper, when they usually exchanged such reflections on the day's events as they thought might be of interest to each other, Isabel saw that Harold had something on his mind: he looked slightly portentous. She couldn't help noticing it, though her thoughts were busy with Alec's second letter.

Harold did not always spill the beans at once; he would bide his time and adopt a sphinx-like air. Sometimes he went to bed with whatever ace he had still up his sleeve; and Isabel, from pure lack of curiosity, didn't always call his bluff. But with an acquaintance, and still more with a stranger, one has a duty towards conversation, and to-night she said:

"Has anything interesting happened at the office, Harold?"

Puffing at his pipe he said:

"Well, one day's rather like another."

"Yes," she agreed, "but sometimes something happens."

Harold took out his pipe and gave her his level-browed look.

"Well, there was a thing—I don't know if you would call it something."

"Tell me," she said.

Harold relit his pipe.

"Well, it's to do with Alec."

"Oh?"

"Yes, he's sent me two or three more clients. Not the one he spoke about—chap on the Alloy Exchange. He said something about not being able to 'dislodge him from his primordial slime'—what a way of putting it."

"Oh, so you've heard from Alec?"

"Yes. I must say it's the first time he's failed to get his own way."

"Is it?"

Harold considered. "Well, perhaps not quite the first time. But I'm a bit disappointed."

"Still, he sent you the others."

"Yes, nothing sensational, you know, but still, quite useful. Isabel?"

It was the call to attention.

"Yes, Harold?" she said.

"We've —well—we've got a bit more money than we used to have—nothing to boast about, mind—but we could do something with it."

"What sort of thing?"

"I thought I'd ask you that."

He means another child, thought Isabel. Her heart turned over, and she felt as affronted as if a stranger had made an infamous proposal to her. But Harold was her husband: he had every right——

"I know we *used* to say——" she began.

Harold was busy with his own thoughts, and they were not hers.

"Yes, we did," he said.

To Isabel the situation suddenly became pregnant with doom: it loomed up like a wave: green caverns yawned upon her, there was no escape.

"Of course, if you wanted it," she temporized. "I had begun to think——"

"You don't want us to launch out at all?"

"Well"—she was terribly embarrassed—"not perhaps in that way." The hated red began to stain her cheeks.

"In what way?" asked Harold, and then he took her meaning, and her colour. It was a long time since she had seen him blush. It suits him better than it suits me, she thought confusedly: Nature's make-up is the thing for men. Her whirling thoughts would not settle into a pattern, or yield a single sentence. She waited for Harold to speak.

He was as much confused as she was, and for the same reason. With his mind full of another woman he could not contemplate the act of love with Isabel; it almost shocked him. Equally, he could not bear to let her know this: it would be an intolerable insult to which he could never expose her. His narrow nature was sharply aware of insults, given or received; in the earlier days he might have fought a duel. His eyes grew sterner as he said, with a painful effort at tenderness:

"My dear, that is for you to decide."

She gulped.

"Well, perhaps sometime. Not now, I think, not *just* now."

"It is entirely up to you," he said. The flush had faded from his cheeks, by speaking he had overcome his shame. But hers still flamed.

"Well, then. . . ." She could not meet his eyes, which the boldness required by business deals had hardened. "We have Jeremy and Janice to think of," she said suddenly.

"Their education, you mean?"

She nodded.

Jeremy and Janice, she had snatched at them like a lifeline, but, truth to tell, they were far away from her, almost as far away as the thought of another child. They would be close to his thoughts, she imagined. But she was wrong: to him as well as her, Jeremy and Janice were an alien notion, flotsam that the current of his life, finding another channel, had left behind on the bank. Their names did not evoke an image to him; neither before his mind's eye nor Isabel's did they appear, lying in their beds upstairs, asleep.

"About their education?" he said slowly. "Well, we've more or less decided on that, haven't we? Jeremy will go to Penthouse, that's where I went, it was good enough for me. They say it's come on now, a long waiting list—besides, it's an advantage to have your father an Old Penthousian. You get more consideration. And Janice will go to the Henhurst School: she won't be far away. We settled all that, didn't we?"

Isabel agreed. At that moment, her imagination wouldn't work on Jeremy and Janice. She couldn't see them, in the present, or as she used to see them, at different ages and different stages in the future, with a face and appearance suitable to the age and stage they had reached, each with a creditable past and a glorious future, achieving what she and Harold had never been able to achieve. They might have been someone else's children, about whom their parents had asked her for advice, but who, in the nature of things, could not mean much to her. All the same, Harold had asked her something and the conversation must be kept up.

"We want to give them the best chance we can, don't we?" she said, but without much conviction.

"Yes, but you know my views on that," said Harold. "We don't want to educate them above their station. We want them to be like us. As you know, I hope that Jeremy will come into my business—it'll be a pretty good start for him—and as for Janice, Janice will take care of herself. I wouldn't mind betting that Janice gets married early."

"I think so too," said Isabel, "but——"

She had no idea of what she was going to say, but Harold had.

"But we want them to do better for themselves, you were going to say. I'm all for them getting on in the world, as you know, but I haven't got extravagant ideas for them. I want them to develop on the lines that we have—and be safe, reliable sort of people with a stake in the place and in the country. People you can look up to, but no frills, no snob-stuff—solid, you know, and just above the average. I should like Jeremy to be better at games than I was—he's better at his work already—but that's about all. The trend of the time is against making yourself conspicuous—people don't want that now. They want the type that can keep their place in the queue without trying to jump it. I don't want Jeremy to be Prime Minister or anything of that sort. He'd only fall down on it. And if Janice takes after you, Isabel, I shall be satisfied, I promise you."

She smiled at him for this; and it seemed to her then, that Harold's ambitions for their children's future were quite adequate. So long as they prospered and were happy, why want them to fly high? Hand in hand, but faceless, voiceless and almost formless, they drifted past their mother into an unheeded future.

Having thus disposed of her children, born and unborn, Isabel was sensible of a great relief. Released, her thoughts raced in another direction. Her husband's voice recalled her to the present.

"No, I don't want to spend more on their education. They'll only get ideas into their heads. We've seen it happen time and time again. Parents scrape and save and sacrifice themselves, and then their children look down on them. I don't mean my children to look down on me. No, it wasn't of them I was thinking, Isabel, it was of you."

His softening voice gave Isabel a new twinge. I can't bear at this moment, she thought, to receive a kindness from him.

"It's like this," he said. "You're at it all the time, you never get a moment to yourself."

"Oh well," said Isabel, smiling at his serious tone, "that's the lot of every housewife nowadays."

"I know," he said, "but I don't mean it should be yours. You want time to read, don't you, and . . . and get away sometimes. I don't want you to go away, goodness knows, but with the children on top of you all day, and then the housework——"

"Yes?" said Isabel.

"Well, you don't get a break. What's against us having a servant to live in? There's room for one."

There was. Tilecotes had four bedrooms—theirs, the children's, the spare room, and another room used vaguely as a boxroom. If it was filled the household couldn't expand any further. It couldn't expand. . . .

"But do we really need a resident servant?" Isabel asked.

"For you, dear, not for me. I'm quite all right. But you do need someone to take the children off your hands occasionally. They can be an awful bore, I know. You might want to run up to London sometimes, or go to see your mother. You've often said you want to stay with her. I don't want you to go, heaven knows, but all the same——"

"We might try it," Isabel said. "It's very good of you, Harold," she added humbly, swallowing the gilded pill. "We used to have servants in the old days—I don't know if I could manage one now—if we could find one. And some are more trouble than they're worth."

"I think I've heard of one," said Harold, "who might do. She's said to be very fond of children."

"Well, that's a recommendation," Isabel said. "I wonder how Jeremy and Janice would like a stranger about the house."

"Oh, children are more adaptable than people think. They like new faces—think how quickly Janice took to Alec. She made up to him quite disgracefully."

Isabel turned away.

"And if she was a bit of a disciplinarian it wouldn't do any harm. It would do Janice good, she's such a handful. I don't mean her to grow up spoilt. Well, shall we try it?"

"Yes, let's," said Isabel.

27

JANICE and Jeremy were out playing. It was a warm, squally day; the windows on the garden side were shut against the blast. Every now and then the pennons of the pampas clump bowed almost to the ground. Janice caught one on its downward sweep and held it.

"Mind you don't break it, Janice."

"Who's to know? Daddy won't notice."

"Mummy will, when she comes back."

"I don't believe she's coming back."

"Why not?"

"Well, Susan said so."

"When?"

"Yesterday, to Mrs. Hidcup. She said it through the kitchen door." Mrs. Hidcup was the last in a long line of daily women.

"You shouldn't have been listening," said Jeremy.

"I wasn't, they were talking so loud I couldn't help hearing. I did try not to hear. It was just after we got back from school."

"Mrs. Hidcup's always gone by then," said Jeremy.

"Yes, Mr. Know-all," Janice said. "Mr. Know-all" was a nickname Jeremy had got at school. It was originally a tribute to his learning, but had come to be used as a gibe, and Janice used it as such. "But she was staying on to say good-bye to Susan. 'Susan, my dear, good-bye,' she said. 'I shan't be seeing you again.' "

"Oh, but she will," said Jeremy. "She's coming once a week to help with cleaning. Susan said she couldn't do it all herself, it was too much, so Mummy said, 'Well, come back once a week.' "

"Mrs. Hidcup didn't say that," said Janice. "She said, 'Good-bye, darling, and look after those poor mites while I'm not here.' What does 'mites' mean, Jeremy?"

"They're things that grow in cheese," said Jeremy.

"There, I knew you'd know."

"But you needn't mind eating them because they're made of cheese. But most people put them on the side of their plates."

"Ugh, how nasty of her to call us mites, then. She's a horrid old so-and-so."

"Yes. What else did she say?"

"Oh, where was I? She said, 'Good-bye, dearest, look after those poor mites while I'm away. Their Mummy won't come back to them, you mark my words.'"

"She didn't!" Jeremy exclaimed.

"Yes, Jeremy, she did. And she said, 'Their Mummy has found someone she likes better than the master, and she won't come back in a hurry.' Who do you think it is, Jeremy, Mr. Goodrich? Oh, I do hope it is."

"You don't know what you're talking about," said Jeremy.

"Oh yes, I do, and I do hope it's Mr. Goodrich, because he's my favourite, favourite, *favourite* man."

After a pause, Jeremy said:

"Why do you think it's Mr. Goodrich?"

"Because he's been here such a lot," said Janice. "All that time when he came to make a speech to the Institute's Women."

"Women's Institute," said Jeremy.

"Well, Women's Institute, it's just the same. And Mummy said, 'We must have some nice flowers because Mr. Goodrich is coming.' And she put the flowers everywhere— she used up all the vases—and she put some in his bedroom, too."

"That doesn't prove anything," said Jeremy. "He only stayed one night with us and then he went to the hotel."

"Yes, that's what I was saying," said Janice unblushingly. "And then she took the flowers from his room and put them into hers and Daddy's, on the table by their bed. Oh, I'm sure it's Mr. Goodrich!"

Janice did a little dance: the wind caught her skirts: she pirouetted gaily. Jeremy stood lost in thought.

"She hasn't been away very long," he said.

Janice pranced up to him and tried to drop a curtsy.

"Oh, but it's years and years and *years*," she said. "It's I don't know how long."

"I know how long exactly," Jeremy said. "It was last Thursday—a week ago to-day. She caught the 5.45 train from Downhaven—the best train of the day—it averages fifty-four miles an hour, start to stop. Daddy came back from the office to take her, they started at 5.20, which didn't give very much time and I was afraid they might miss the train. And Mummy kissed us both and said to Susan, 'Look after them carefully, Susan, won't you, I shan't be away long.'" His lips trembled as he looked at Janice for confirmation.

"Yes, and Daddy went to Downhaven for the evening on business, and he's going to-night—he's always going to Downhaven—and Susan put us to bed. I didn't like Susan to begin with, but I do now. It's nice to have a maid, isn't it? We're the only people we know who have one. Clementine's mother said to me the other day, 'I hear your Daddy has a maid,' and I said, 'Yes, Mrs. Richards, and she's very pretty.' Supposing Daddy fell in love with her?"

"People don't fall in love like that," said Jeremy. "It takes them a long time, years and years, and after that they have to decide about getting married."

"If Mummy married Mr. Goodrich," Janice asked, "she would still be our Mummy, wouldn't she?"

Jeremy didn't answer for a moment, then he said:

"She couldn't marry Mr. Goodrich, because she's married to Daddy."

"Pooh!" said Janice, "that wouldn't stop grown-up people. If Mummy married Mr. Goodrich, should we go to live in Wales?"

"He might not want to have us," Jeremy said.

"Oh yes, he would, he would want to have me, he said I was his sweetheart. Well, I could go with him, and you could stay here with Daddy, and sometimes we could meet and ask each other how we were getting on. You'd miss me, wouldn't you, Jeremy?"

"I dunno," said Jeremy. "Perhaps I should, but of course you are rather a handful."

"All the same you'd miss me," said Janice eyeing him. "You wouldn't have anyone to play with, and Daddy would be away all day, and Susan would say, 'It's my afternoon out.' And you would think of me in Wales, and I should be a little Welsh girl, with a red cloak and a black pointed hat like, well, like a——"

"Witch," put in Jeremy.

"No, no, no, no, not like that at all. And I should have a real nursemaid, not a general, like Susan is—only it doesn't mean an Army general—and lots and lots of presents, and I should send you a picture postcard sometimes, of—well, of—well, of—well, of—me, perhaps looking like a little Welsh girl. And you and Daddy would say: "There she is! That's her exactly!'"

"Who told you all this?" asked Jeremy.

"Well, nobody told me exactly, but Mr. Goodrich said about the Welsh clothes. Oh, but it would be fun! And you, Jeremy, I don't know what you would do *exactly*, but you could carry Daddy's clubs when he plays golf, and on half-holidays you could play tennis by yourself against the wall, and you would write me letters. You would still be my brother, in a way, and I should still be your sister, in a way but not exactly because of being a Welsh girl. And Daddy would be our father but not exactly, because part of that would be for Mr. Goodrich, and Mummy would be our mother, but not exactly, because you would be here in Marshport, and she could only love you from a distance. And of course we should be grander than you are, but Mummy says that doesn't matter, or shouldn't."

Jeremy bit his lip. He turned unseeing eyes towards the unseeing windows, at one of which his mother's face should have appeared, calling them in to lunch. He couldn't speak because of the lump in his throat, so he pretended to be interested in something that was happening a few yards away at the other end of the garden. "It's nothing," he said aloud to test his voice. Talking to oneself was a practice which each allowed the other: it provoked no comment. Then he said:

"Don't you want Mummy to come back?"

"Oh, I dunno," said Janice. Another gust of wind blew, and she danced to it. "Yes, in a way, but it would be so *exciting* if she didn't. Everyone would be so *sorry* for us.

They would say, 'Poor little girl, her mother's left her'—and they would be quite sorry for you, too, and perhaps for Daddy. But he would marry someone else, of course: men always do, because they have to be fathers. Then we should have two fathers and two mothers, and that would be a good thing in a way, because they would all have to give us presents, and love us very much."

"I bet you——" said Jeremy suddenly.

"Oh, but you mustn't bet."

"I bet you," repeated Jeremy, "that the day after to-morrow by this time—that is"—he looked at his watch—"at 12.58 hours 30 seconds—Mummy will be back."

"What will you bet?"

"I'll bet my bottom dollar."

"Oh, you haven't one."

"Yes, I have, it's in my money-box. If Mummy isn't here——"

There was a tap at the French window, and Susan's pretty face behind the glass. But when they reached it they found that it was fastened.

"She's forgot to open it. We can't get in!" whimpered Janice. "We're shut out!"

"We'll go round by the garage," Jeremy said. "The front door's sure to be open."

But for once it wasn't, and they had to ring the bell.

28

ISABEL was wondering whether she should ask Harold to divorce her.

The emotional side of her nature was new to her: it had developed only since her meeting with Alec. It had the overwhelming force of any new obsession. It was on top. Below it her other faculties went on working, and though at a disadvantage, for reason and affection are almost help-less against love, they still had idealism to back them up. To cut and run, to walk out, as Elspeth had, was quite un-thinkable to Isabel: it was not in the pattern of civilized behaviour. But her idealism was divided against itself: her first duty she felt was to Alec's art. Only she could save it from the warping, stultifying effect of Elspeth's domination. She would hardly have admitted to herself that she was in love with Alec, for to be in love has no relish of salvation in it. She mistook love for its signs—the urge to make the beloved happy, to help him, to do him good, to be all in all to him. Love is a form of self-immolation and so is duty: she confused the two.

And she had another duty, that fought for Alec, her duty to experience, her duty to herself. She had convinced herself that she was not naturally maternal, or even suited to mar-riage; she could go through the motions of family and domestic life, put up a show, but her heart wasn't in it—an eleven years' trial, which was surely long enough, had shown her that.

She wasn't altogether self-deceived in believing herself to be actuated by a sense of duty. Most people, she was aware, acted from impulse or inclination or the power of Grace (she thought that pure self-interest was a motive confined to business men); but from a child she had been acted upon by successive idealisms stronger than any personal desire of her own—those of her parents, her school, and the associates of her London days: and the last had been the strongest if not the most deeply-seated. Aspiration! She could not do without it and turned instinctively to whatever sun was occupying the heavens. Now it was Alec and his art: his art that had been blighted and debased by his *âme damnée,* Elspeth.

Harold she didn't so much worry about. Harold would re-marry, she was sure. He needed only companionship—he barely needed that: during the last few months it had been increasingly borne in on her how little she counted for him as a human being. He needed someone to complete his vision of himself as husband, father and succesful business man. Plenty of women would be glad to fill that rôle; Harold was still attractive—as the eyes of other women told her—and he had to offer, besides himself, a comfortable home and an assured social position.

She needn't worry about him. But about the children she did worry, rather: their problem didn't yield so readily to the solvents in her thoughts. Even her London friends had agreed that in cases of this kind the children were a complication. Better not have any! But she had them, and though their physical appearances remained so indistinct to her that she had to consult their photographs to remind herself what they were really like, she thought a lot about them.

She had done her best for them. She had studied mother-craft and the latest theories about child-welfare: she was nothing if not a theorist. But she had never been very close to them, she believed, and why? Because they meant so much to each other. Almost from the start they had had a private understanding, a private world from which she was excluded. If she took sides in their disputes, as she some-times did, she never knew if she was doing the right thing —it was like interfering between husband and wife, they both resented it. Difficult as it was for her to imagine them together it was impossible for her to imagine them apart. She saw Jeremy bowed over Janice like a question-mark, as if she was a problem he was trying to solve; while Janice fluttered round him, like the symbol X, challenging him to find the answer. Emotionally they were sufficient unto themselves; they didn't depend on her; they needed maternal care, no doubt, but not maternal love.

Maternal care another woman could give them at least as well as she could, and perhaps maternal love, too: most women had it. Another woman might be able to break down their reserve and give them what she felt sure they needed: the sense of an enfolding love, including and transcending their relationship with each other: a security beyond the accidents of their daily life, with its ups and downs of feeling and its too intense dependence on each other.

She couldn't, for she was constitutionally un-maternal, but another woman might, a stepmother.

By some such reasoning she half convinced herself that Jeremy and Janice would be better off without her. Whereas she and only she could heal the hurt in Alec's soul. His wife she might not be, she didn't care, as long as she could be the midwife of that masterpiece in the major key which had been conceived under her star and which, she helping him, would be delivered to the world.

But if Alec *wanted* her to marry him——!

She couldn't expect that Harold would let her divorce him; even if he consented to, his mother would prevent him. He would divorce her and be granted custody of the children; so, they would be taken off her hands, so, they would not be parted. And what a small affair they were compared with Alec's book.

She had said that she was going to her mother, and to her mother she went. In widowhood, Mrs. Knighton was not the woman she had been; losing her husband she had lost her *raison d'être*. Losing her position as his wife she could no longer sweep the parish before her in a great gale of high endeavour. She was diminished, but she was not extinguished; extinguished, for her daughter, she could never be. No sooner had Isabel set foot in the house than she felt her mother's influence seeping into her. It was not the old, roomy house, full of associations; it was a small cramped house, smaller than her own, almost a stranger's house, for her visits had been rare. It was not the mother of her girlhood, whose full-rigged majesty had towered above her; even physically Mrs. Knighton had shrunk. She stooped and age had scooped out hollows in her. At sight of her Isabel felt a rush of pity, but it was short-lived. She could not pity someone of whom she was still in awe, in whose presence, diminished as it was, she felt herself growing smaller, contracting to that core of being which was her last redoubt, her last defence against her mother's ascendancy. For weeks she hadn't had this sensation: it had vanished in the afflatus that possessed her spirit. Now she was a little girl again, asking leave to do the simplest things—have a bath, wear a day dress for dinner.

She longed to get away, as she had longed to get away before she married Harold. And she did get away, it wasn't difficult: on the pretext that she wanted to see her London friends, whom she had scarcely seen in all these years, and get clothes which she couldn't get in Marshport. Sometimes she stayed the night: once she had stayed two nights.

Alec was in London, too, he had come up to be with her. Films, theatres, concerts, everything she had once dreamed of doing she now did, and in a dream. The civilized life, at last! In this environment, anonymous and at large, she felt no guilt in her happiness, as she had at Marshport, as she had still more when she returned to her mother's roof. And between whiles—for Alec was writing hard and, so he said, successfully—she visited her old friends. She had scarcely kept up with them at all, so alien had been the mere thought of them to the life she led at Marshport. Some had gone away, some had changed their names, all who remained looked strangely older, the glamour had worn off them. From the eminence of her association with Alec, they seemed a little second-rate. But at heart they were the same, and they still embraced experience with both hands. They teased her for having become so staid—as they believed her to be—*"une vraie femme de province"*, but the teasing only gave her a secret thrill. If only she could tell them! She didn't, of course, but the fact that she was now as they were, and yet so far above them, gave her as much confidence with them as if she had told them. How their eyes would have bulged had they known the truth! For they still talked of Alexander Goodrich, not with the reverence of old days, for they too felt as the reviewers did (and some of them were reviewers) that Alec's art had reached a dead end, and that it might be better for his reputation if he ceased to write and rested on his laurels, as some other novelists had. They didn't think him promising, but they still took him into account and mentioned his name with those of younger writers as one who had made his niche, even if he was growing rather mouldy in it. "All that self-pity, my dear! He really ought to snap out of it! After the war it doesn't cut any ice. Our private feelings matter to us, of course, where should we be without them? To us they are as important as they ever were. But they're not a subject for fiction any longer. Those little wails that Goodrich used to send up when one or other of his girl-friends by-passed him (I'll never believe his novels aren't autobiographical) made quite a noise at the time; we wept for him. But not now, when we've heard such much louder noises, flying bombs, high-explosive bombs, V.2 bombs, atom bombs, and soon may hear the hydrogen bomb! What we want now, but what he can't or will not give us, is a different sort of report—a good report of humanity in general—not the individual's screech of pain, we aren't interested in that, but in another sort of noise, a cheerful communal murmur, the sort of noise the rooks make in the springtime. Don't think I'm advocating a return to Nature-worship—the London pigeons would do just as well—but a nice friendly caw or coo that we can all join in—something quite humble and collective —something about Ron and Don and Des and Les. We don't want moral indignation, we've had too much of that, it whips up war: it was all right in the Spanish War, but now the word 'ought' is a dead letter. And we don't want tragedy or catastrophe or any high-powered emotion, because the individual doesn't count any more. Good Lord, I'm not a Communist, but for good or ill, the great movements of the century—Freudian, Marxian, Trades Union, Welfare State—have all been movements that affected everyone, that was their point: and any truthful account of our day, such as serious novelists are supposed to give, must be founded on experience within the reach of all—be conditioned by that. It mustn't aim too high, because we are too tired to aim high, and it mustn't be about people wanting to get on, in any sense, because (a) there's nowhere to get to, and (b) we don't *want* to get ahead of other people now, we don't *want* to jump the queue! Quiet little sins, not ending in suicide or murder, quiet little virtues that no one takes too seriously, quiet little jokes that you don't see at once, quiet little episodes touched with fantasy that leave you where you started—that's what we want—and our greatest excitement the excitement of getting out the crossword puzzle. That's the safest outlet for seriousness, and you mustn't be too brilliant at it either, or you will make someone feel inferior. I mean, competitiveness must be canalized. The lowest common denominator, that's your aim, if aim you must have. In that way you can feel the common good of living, which has nothing to do with Communism. A sort of Auld Lang Syne, everyone holding hands and laughing with each other—the more pointlessly the better. There is in the mere act of living when it's shared at the lowest level something that can keep people going and make them feel their value, which, boring as it is, is what we want to feel—without stepping on the gas and running people down. A slow shuffle, that's what we need. But Goodrich is old-fashioned—he still thinks a novelist must give a yell loud enough to be heard above the general murmur—but it's bad manners, really. And, Knighton, I suspect you feel the same, after vegetating all this while in your bourgeois seclusion—which is a hot-bed of explosive feelings. Besides, you always wanted us to suffer, or to make others suffer, or to do good, or to be good, or be *something*—something that we weren't meant to be. But suffer chiefly, Knighton, suffer in the name of aspiration. Don't you remember, boys and girls, how shocked she was because in a novel—I forget its name—somebody, some naughty, naughty woman, broke up a happy home? Oh, what a long face she pulled! As if it mattered! All that mattered was everybody behaving as if it mattered. Relax, my dears, relax! They should have mucked in together, the whole crowd of them, and settled their disputes in bed."

To more than one tirade of this kind Isabel listened, and with a secret smile; they thought it mattered so tremendously, to prove that nothing mattered! They had changed, just as her mother had: they were diminished. Experience was no longer a duty, for duty had been abolished; but none the less, the liberty to explore it was all they asked of life. And just as her mother's presence, muted as it was, cramped the style of her thoughts, so theirs, though much less potent than it had been, freed and enlarged them, confirming her in her love and in the object of her love, now being accomplished—the renewal, the rebirth of Alec's gift under a happier star. "Let's all muck in together!" It was a form of aspiration, after all; and wasn't she fulfilling it?

At first Isabel had only meant to stay away for the inside of a week. So sensitive was she to her environment that she felt, when at her mother's, that she must take the next train back to Marshport, and when in London, that she could prolong her truancy for ever. Between these extreme moods lay a mean in which her attitude was fairly sane: enjoyment and responsibility seemed to inhabit the same world, and listen amicably to each other's counsels. Just three more days, enjoyment begged; and responsibility replied, Well, three more days. But just as an unanswered letter seems to need answering less, rather than more, as days go by, and finally not to need answering at all, so it was with her: insensibly her new life grew into a habit.

Nothing outside her urged her to go home. Her mother didn't, she was glad to have her daughter; and Harold didn't.

Isabel was surprised by this, but too much relieved to be offended, even in the inmost and tenderest regions of her vanity. She had had few letters from him in their married life, they were so seldom separated: his letter from St. Milo's had been the last. Now she had had several letters from him, all written in a style that wasn't quite like him. She didn't notice the discrepancy as she would have once, for her mood, too, was changed: a letter from Mars would not have seemed extraordinary. Harold's letter contained imaginative and rather daring phrases like "We're getting on like a house on fire." How peculiar, she thought, similes are: why should getting on like a house on fire mean that everything was going well? And again, "The children are getting on like one o'clock, especially Janice." Why should one o'clock, the zero-hour in The Kitchen, be used to denote a prosperous state of affairs? Thinking how unaccountable language was —for Alec had made her sensitive to its niceties—she didn't realize that these rapturous references to things at home implied a comment on her absence. Nor even when he wrote, as he did in every letter, "Don't hurry to come back—I'm sure the change is doing you good"—or some such phrase— did she think it strange.

"With Susan here we feel as safe as houses." Are houses safe? Not when they are on fire—and yet, in the other letter, he had used that as a metaphor of reassurance. "The children dote on her." "Dote" implied love bordering on idiocy, it wasn't one of Harold's words, still less one of his thoughts: what had come over his vocabulary? Still, it was reassuring that the children doted on Susan: let them dote, by all means. Isabel didn't feel one twinge of jealousy.

The letters were, in fact, not only a permit but a request to stay away, and Isabel eagerly responded to it.

Just one phrase was like a crumpled rose-leaf: "Have you seen Mother yet?"

Isabel hadn't and she knew she must; so that when Mrs. Knighton proposed that Mrs. Eastwood should be asked to tea, she agreed at once.

She knew it would be an ordeal, and it was.

The two ladies, though living in the same town, saw as little of each other as they could. Both were exceedingly strong characters; neither had any doubt that hers was the right attitude to life. Each had been born with it: Mrs. Eastwood's materialism was as natural to her as Mrs. Knighton's idealism was to her. But between them was the sense of social inferiority which Mrs. Knighton could not fail to induce in anyone who was at all subject to it—as Mrs. Eastwood was, despite her comfortable bank-balance, and despite the fact that she had gone up in the world whereas Mrs. Knighton had come down. She thought that Mrs. Knighton thought that Isabel had thrown herself away on Harold. And Mrs. Knighton did think so, though not in the way that Mrs. Eastwood meant. Too confident of her own social position to mind greatly about other people's, Mrs. Knighton didn't now object to Harold on that score, but she did mind what she thought of as his money-grubbing disposition, and the absence in him of any quality that could be called spiritual.

Not many days but too many had elapsed before they got in touch with Mrs. Eastwood. A slight reserve in Mrs. Eastwood's manner hinted at this. "I've been up to London a good deal," Isabel said. "It's ages since I've been there for more than a day."

"Have you seen any shows?" asked Mrs. Eastwood.

"Yes, one or two, and concerts."

"I like a matinée myself," said Mrs. Eastwood, "when I go up to Town. At least I used to, when Arthur was alive. It's not so much fun going alone. But you have friends in London, Isabel?"

"Oh yes, I lived there once, you remember, in the war."

"It's a pity Harold couldn't join you. But perhaps he did?"

"No, he is very busy. And now we have a maid——"

"Yes, they can be a godsend. Mine is quite a treasure." A pause, perhaps to remind Mrs. Knighton that she couldn't afford this luxury; but Mrs. Knighton answered, disappointingly:

"Servants, but what are servants? Surely we are better off without them? Personally I much prefer doing for myself. And they will put things cornerwise, you know, diagonally. I like things to be straight."

Mrs. Eastwood, who also liked things cornerwise, thought this must be a thrust, though it was not.

"Still, I think Isabel can count herself lucky," she said quietly, "to have an opportunity to get away, when so many young mothers are more or less house-bound."

"Oh yes, I am lucky," Isabel said guiltily.

"And Harold is lucky, too," said Mrs. Knighton, "to have a wife who can adapt herself as Isabel has. No, Isabel, don't blush, my dear. I'm sure that Mrs. Eastwood would agree that you've done very well. Harold has given you every material comfort; but you take after me and after your father, and in my young days girls had such big ideas of what they could do in the world outside the domestic circle."

"Well, she's having an opportunity now, aren't you,

244

Isabel?" said Mrs. Eastwood, giving Isabel her bright placid stare.

Between being talked to and talked about, Isabel hardly knew which way to look.

"Harold has been very good to me," she said with an effort, "and, of course, the children——"

She broke off, shocked and miserable at the falsity of what she was saying, or going to say. Oh, to be out of this! Oh, to be in London, where the feelings were recognized as the only guide! Oh, to be back in Alec's arms!

Again they were talking, half to her and half at her, about the children, this time.

"Oh, but they must spread their wings a little, you know, Mrs. Eastwood, they mustn't get a Marshport point of view. I'm sure Isabel wouldn't like that, even if Harold did. They must make friends in many places. Nothing widens one's horizon like having friends. Marshport must be so limited and limiting."

Mrs. Eastwood took her up.

"Harold saw a good deal of the world when he was in the Army," she said, "but when my husband and I bought Tilecotes for him, he was glad to settle there. I'm sure Isabel wouldn't want him to be a rolling stone, would you, Isabel?"

"No indeed, Mrs. Eastwood."

"There, you see. One's own home is the best place, Mrs. Knighton. Harold has got on as he has by sticking to it. Money, if you'll excuse me saying so, has to be earned; and it can't be earned if you're always gadding about looking for someone to do good to!"

"Oh, but it can," Mrs. Knighton said, surprisingly. "Think of all the philanthropists you have ever known." She paused for Mrs. Eastwood to think of them. "They were all rich men, and all most anxious to do good in the world."

"They didn't start being generous till they had made their pile," said Mrs. Eastwood, who had known no philanthropists.

"Excuse me, but I think you are mistaken," said Mrs. Knighton earnestly. "I think you'd find that all through their lives, and they began in a small way, some of them—

245

there's no harm in that—they gave to charity all they could afford."

Isabel marvelled at her mother's tactlessness: the Eastwoods were a by-word in the district for being close-fisted. But Mrs. Knighton never let personal considerations weigh with her, was even unaware of them, when she had an aim in view which, she felt, transcended individual claims. When Mrs. Eastwood made no comment she went on:

"Harold and Isabel will take care, I'm sure, that this advance in their material fortunes, for which I'm deeply grateful, will also advance their power of being of service— we must be of service to someone, Mrs. Eastwood, or why are we put here? Even in a place like Marshport, which personally I'd never heard of till they went there, there must be opportunities. Don't let yourself get too domesticated, Isabel, or too provincialized, and don't let Harold. We must always try to look beyond our immediate horizons. My lot has been to live here: it isn't the place I would have chosen: but I can truly say that when my husband was alive —my means are now restricted, unfortunately, in every sense—we did all we could to make this parish feel that it was part of a larger whole, in fact of the world—the world to which I myself belonged, though that is neither here nor there. The Rectory seemed a small house when I came, it seems a large house now, as you know, they've turned it into flats—but large or small, we used it not for ourselves, not for our family which was, alas, too small, not, thank God, as a sort of bank to hoard our pennies in—but for the general good. My daughter remembers that, don't you, Isabel? And you, too, will remember, Mrs. Eastwood, for you came there sometimes in the old days."

"Not very often," Mrs. Eastwood said, "I don't remember coming very often. Perhaps I wasn't asked."

But Mrs. Knighton swept on.

"We asked everyone we could, you know, we didn't discriminate. We had our personal friends, of course, one has to have them" (Mrs. Knighton spoke as if personal friends were a necessary evil). "I'm sure we asked you, Mrs. Eastwood: my memory is treacherous, but you must have

246

come to meetings—for, of course, my husband's saintly life reduced our purely social contacts to a minimum. Yes, I am sure you came, and Harold, too, that's how he first met Isabel—on our tennis-lawn. A dark, good-looking boy, small for his age—oh yes, I remember. I hope he didn't feel out of it! Well, those days are over, and I am now a lonely old woman, without a say in things. But I don't regret them, they left a precious memory—and they left Harold and Isabel, and Jeremy and Janice, such darling children. If anyone had told us, Mrs. Eastwood, that one day you and I would be their grandmothers, how surprised we should have been! It did seem so unlikely."

"Yes, I suppose it did," said Mrs. Eastwood drily.

"Oh well, it did. And now the children are how old, Isabel? Nine and seven?—and they have their lives before them, but I should be sorry if they grew up to think that money counted—oh, no, I don't mean that, of course it counts—but counted to the exclusion of other things— usefulness and service. When I was young, money——"

"Yes?" said Mrs. Eastwood.

"Well, we just had it. We didn't think about it much. But money-*making*——"

"You don't believe in money-making?" Mrs. Eastwood said.

Mrs. Knighton shrugged.

"Only as a means to an end."

"But Isabel has her servant."

"Yes, but, Isabel dear, you'd rather have no servant, wouldn't you, than feel you couldn't serve yourself—in a wider field than Marshport?" She paused, irritated at having expressed herself so lamely, irritated at having had to formulate her credo, to which her life had been a witness much more eloquent than her words, and which, in her younger days, she would never have had to explain or apologize for, least of all to such a person as Mrs. Eastwood.

"It is for Isabel to decide whether she thinks Marshport, close to her husband's business, a place worth living in," said Mrs. Eastwood, who thought the time had come for a showdown. "Let her speak for herself."

This Isabel couldn't do, nor could she stay longer in a

room so stifling with hostility. Making an excuse she rose and left abruptly, nor did she return until, a minute or two later, she heard the front door shut in no uncertain manner. She had fled exasperated and indignant; she returned, so potent was her mother's influence, contrite and dismayed.

"I'm sorry, Mother," she said, "but I didn't feel I could serve any useful purpose by staying."

If she was unaware of the irony of the words, so was her mother, a thin shadow of the galleon she had once been, but upright and breasting with proud front the angry waves.

"I never could like that woman," she said, "although she is Harold's mother. But I'm afraid you will have to call and apologize to her, Isabel."

"I will," said Isabel meekly.

Later, freed from the temporary embarrassment caused by the clash between her mother and mother-in-law, she felt that her mother had answered the question "Shall I ask Harold to divorce me?" and answered it in the affirmative.

Next day she went to London by an early train. She did not return that night or the next. Alec's time was his own: he did not have to be in any special place, though sometimes he gave reasons for having to be. With him Isabel felt she was all her mother wanted her to be: she was serving, she was useful, and in a wider sphere than Marshport. Yet the thought of her mother's tutelage was as distasteful to her as the thought of Marshport, and the daily round of duties which she must substitute for love. She could not see herself there; her vision of herself was one of standing at Alec's side on a London kerb-stone, outside some theatre, while the commissionaire called a taxi to take them back to his hotel.

Two days after her flight, she received an envelope forwarded by her mother. Whose was the childish handwriting which had been crossed out? Jeremy's, of course. She opened the letter with a sigh. To her surprise it contained, as well as a sheet of writing paper, a picture postcard. The postcard showed a general view of Marshport, which included, in the extreme right-hand corner, some indistinguishable feature marked with a cross, from which came a string to a balloon, neatly encircling the one word, Tilecotes.

"Dearest Mummy," [Jeremy had written]

"We do hope you are having a lovely time as we are here. Susan is super, Daddy says, a perfect brick, and she is giving us a lovely time, when Daddy isn't here, but I wish you were here and so I think does Janice though she hasn't said so yet. If you had been here by 12.59 p.m. on Friday I should still have my bottom dollar, the one Daddy gave me. Janice has it now because I bet her you would be back by then but you weren't. She is trying to spend it but the shops won't take it, I am glad to say, as it isn't real money except in America where it is called a greenback.

"It is now Tuesday, as you see. I won't bet any more it is extravagant but please come back all the same.

Your loving
Jeremy.

"P.S. I have marked our house with a cross.
"P.S.S. I haven't written on the postcard in case you should want to send it away."

Isabel's eyes filled as she read this letter. Were her tears for Jeremy, or were they the tears of generalized emotion that she shed so easily nowadays? She didn't know, but by the evening she had made all her farewells, including the most difficult of all, and two days later, having apologized to her mother-in-law, who was very gracious over it, she was back.

29

"I THOUGHT you would have stayed away longer," Harold said.

What comfort to her conscience, and what sadness to her heart, did those words bring! So she could have stayed, and Harold wouldn't have minded! *Au fond*, as Alec sometimes said, *au fond* Harold was a really nice man. He might so easily have reproached her, just for form's sake, just to give himself a grievance, with her extended absence.

"How long *have* I been away?" she asked.

"Well, you should know."

"It wasn't a fortnight, was it?"

"Ask Jeremy. He's got it all worked out to the last second."

"I haven't seen the children yet."

"They're still at school. You have forgotten their habits."

"But you are here. You . . . you met me at the station."

"Yes, Thursday's my day off. You've forgotten that, too."

This playfulness in Harold was quite new. No, not quite new, new since their courting days, when he used to tease her.

"Will they be pleased to see me?"

"Jeremy will be. I don't know so much about Janice. Do you know what Janice has been saying about you?"

Isabel opened her eyes wide.

"No, what?"

"She says you've fallen in love with Alec."

For once Isabel turned pale instead of red.

"She says I've fallen in love with Alec?" she repeated jerkily, the words dropping from her lips as if they burnt her. "What could have put that idea into her head?"

"I think she's fallen in love with him herself."

At last Isabel dared to steal a glance at Harold. His lips were smiling under his moustache. He looked younger and better than when she had last seen him.

"And what did you say?" she was emboldened to ask.

"I said it was high time you fell in love with someone."

"Oh, Harold, how could you? I don't believe you did."

She burst into hysterical laughter that was close on tears. This dress-rehearsal of the moment she was dreading, how unalarming it was! It didn't signify, of course; it didn't alter the true situation. And yet in a way it did; it was like the tiny inoculation that steals the thunder of the real disease. If the secret ever came out (but now it never would —Janice had somehow scotched it) she could remind Harold of this moment.

"I'm glad you didn't miss me too much," she murmured, hardly knowing what she said.

"Oh, I won't say I didn't miss you from time to time," said Harold.

Again that teasing tone. And it was so familiar to her, though not on Harold's lips. Irresistibly it brought back to her the mood of the past days. She had braced herself to meet the alien atmosphere of home, the sunlessness, the smilelessness, the necessity to feel, and think and act from the dry, dusty centre of her being, without the energizing power of love. Love was not here, how could this pleasant stranger be in love with her? And yet there was a simulacrum of it, to which her heart responded.

A clatter broke out in the hall, and after one or two furtive pushes the door of the lounge opened.

"Look who's here!" said Harold.

Janice came running into the room and flung herself on Isabel. Tumultuous embracements followed. Jeremy watched them at a distance, looking at his mother gravely, almost without a smile, as if he could not believe that it was she. "Aren't you going to kiss me, Jeremy?" she said, when Janice had at last released her. It was a question that she knew he hated, for he shrank from kissing and still more from being asked to kiss, but alone of the three he had made her feel guilty, as a woman should feel who had abandoned her family and her husband for another man, and she wanted him to say it was all right. Supposing he refused? He didn't, but slowly crossed the room towards her anxious, pleading eyes, and planted on the brow above her stiff, expectant face, a token kiss. When she pulled his face down to her and kissed it with something like maternal ardour he almost struggled, and stood up. He was always like that, but it wounded her, and she bit the lip that had just kissed him.

"It was sweet of you to send me——" she began, hoping to reach and mollify the stubborn part of him that still held out against her; but a look of terror came into his eyes, she realized that the postcard had been his own idea, a secret, and hastily added, "to send me your love so many times. You did," she added half accusingly; "you know you did, by Daddy."

"Yes, I know I did," he repeated, and if her voice had held an accusation, so did his.

Gradually he thawed, and whatever it was that had been checking the current of his love for her, melted or seemed to melt: she grasped at his forgiveness before she was certain that she had it.

The autumn-coloured days followed each other, and in spite of her separation from Alec they were the happiest days she remembered at Tilecotes since she and Harold were first installed there. She knew that they ought not to be, that she ought to be feeling guilty, guilty as well as soured and dry and sad and full of longing, but she was not. She didn't even feel guilty when Alec's letters came, type-written envelopes with a London postmark. He was still in London, he said, but if he wasn't the letters would still come from London: he had a trusted agent there. The letters were love-letters indeed; she dared not keep them, she had no safe place. It went to her heart to destroy them, they were such wonderful letters; but it was the reassurance of his love she treasured, not the paper and ink with which it was expressed. What need had she of material proofs? The deeds and documents were laid up in her heart. Almost it pleased her to think that another woman, favoured as she had been, would have kept the letters at all costs, as scalps and trophies for posterity. Such tuft-hunting was not for her.

Yet she could not help sometimes asking herself: How with all this deceit can I possibly be happy? For she wasn't naturally deceitful, and though she knew that love created its own climate, its own transforming atmosphere, that single minute when Jeremy had been shy with her was a warning that her flower would wither if a cold draught struck it. But there was none; no cold draught: nothing but soft, caressing airs.

So in a reverie of Alec she continued, a daydream which, far from disabling her for her daily tasks, made them much easier. She was beginning to take this for granted; but when she asked herself how it had come about, she had to admit that Harold was the cause, Harold whose changed demeanour made her Eden habitable. Instead of being the angel with the flaming sword, he was its guardian. Sometimes she caught herself identifying him with Alec; and once, to her horror, she addressed him as Alec, but he didn't seem to notice. She almost felt that she could go to him and say: "It's true what Janice said, that I love Alec: do you mind?"

Then why bother to ask Harold to divorce her? She was free to go to London when she liked. She was no longer pricked by guilt, her double life had become second nature to her. She felt she had grown up, and in growing up had shed such adolescent bogies as the fear of being found out. She had proved empirically that she could be both wife and mistress, wife only in name, perhaps, for Harold—it seemed part of his new delicacy of feeling—had not asked her to be so in fact—and mistress at a distance, but loving and loved as both. It was no sophism to say that she was now a better wife and mother than she had been before—and as for Alec, she knew what she meant to him, for he told her, almost every day. And she was not just his floosie, she was his Egeria. The novel, the happy novel, the novel in which (so he had hinted) his attitude towards her sex had been transformed, was nearly finished. Was she its heroine? So, without leaving Marshport and without leaving Harold, she had done what her mother wanted of her: exercised her influence in a wider sphere and one that nobody could call materialistic. "You are my radar," Alec had written. "Marshport is your station. From Marshport you give out the rays that steer this ship."

Harold, for his part, had been as happy as she was. His

253

needs were the opposite of hers: she wanted someone to look up to, he wanted someone to look down on, protectively and, if need be, patronizingly. He had never been able to look down on Isabel, and she had never been able to look up to him. Each wanted a higher concentration of being, for that is the essential experience of love. But whereas this meant for him a closing in of all his forces on the centre, with her it meant a fleeing from the centre, an enlargement of the spirit that would take her out of and above herself and make her feel even physically taller. What Harold craved, she dreaded.

In Irma's company he had what he wanted. Sometimes she laughed at him, but never in a way that hurt his masculine pride. If he hadn't liked it when she called him "sweet" it was because he was then uncertain of himself and thought she might be hinting at a weakness; if Isabel had ever called him "sweet" he would have been certain she was getting at him. But his growing confidence in himself gave him a sweet tooth for endearment—Irma could call him the silliest things—"treasure", "little sparrow", "sugar-mouth"—and he would lap them up. Being a foreigner she could be always laughed at—being a foreigner she was always in need of help: perhaps no Englishwoman could have given back to Harold the self-pride that Isabel had taken from him. Sometimes in Irma's presence a military mood came over him and he longed to order her about: " 'Shun! Stand at ease! Stand easy!" The thought of her jumping to it gave him a delicious thrill.

Love made the outside world unreal to Isabel; she went about in a dream. Harold, too, had his dream and like hers it acted as a dynamo; but he kept it apart, in a secret place, an engine-room. Love made him more aware of external reality, not less, and it was his power over external reality, in love as well as in business, that gave him added value to himself. He made the machinery of his affair with Irma a matter of routine: she mustn't take a step without consulting him. He enjoyed calculating the risks, he enjoyed the risks themselves. Some could be taken, some not, it was for him to decide. Decision was a mental process; but its effect was to increase his passion, for it wrapped Irma in a flawless circle of protectiveness, bristling on the outside but within as soft as an embrace. An indiscreet proposal on her part, though it was to bring them together, he wouldn't have entertained; even a chance meeting he would have felt jealous of, because luck had a hand in it as well as he. He was a born planner and had no use for the fortuitous, except in Irma's face. There, in that little structure of skin and bone, which had not been thought out carefully, rather dashed off in one of the Creator's careless moods, he worshipped it and dwelt on every unpredictable change; and if he planned, as he sometimes did, what he should say to her, it was to make her say the unexpected thing, and give him the unexpected look. Seeking these, he was more resourceful than either he or anyone could have believed.

But like most planners, he had a rigid mind. Its power lay in its capacity for exclusion. Outside the bright circle of reality which was his purview, darkness lay, and to that darkness he consigned all sorts of eventualities: what would happen if Isabel found him out was one. Like a general he did not envisage the possibility of defeat: he was there to win. Recognition of the fact that circumstances alter cases required more flexibility of mind than he possessed. His eye was fixed on the present. If he thought of the future, and Irma's place in it, he saw it as an extension of the present. He would not look for another house because his own had now too few rooms; he would build another storey on to it, and he didn't pause to consider whether the foundations would stand the strain.

One evening Isabel said, in an artificial tone which he couldn't help noticing:

"Our benefactor's coming down to see us."

"Our benefactor?" echoed Harold.

"Well, Alec. He is our benefactor, isn't he?"

"Oh yes, of course he is. Good old Alec."

Isabel, who had withdrawn her eyes from Harold's face to make the announcement, glanced at him again, and had the illusion that his face was further away from her than it had been.

"What's he coming about?" asked Harold.

"On business, he said. He said he was writing to you."

"I expect I shall get the letter in the morning. . . . Will he stay with us?"

"No, at the Royal, he said."

They talked of other things but for the first time since Isabel's return constraint appeared between them.

To each the news had been a shock. To Isabel a delicious shock, in spite of the nervous tremors that it started. She longed for the sight and sound and touch of Alec. His presence in her mind was much, but his real presence was more. She did not doubt his love for her, but in love faith is no substitute for certainty. She had known he might come back and trusted to luck to see her through. But to Harold it was a disagreeable shock; for Alec's return was one of the eventualities on which he had not counted. It lay in the darkness outside his scrutiny. What was Alec coming back for? To try to take Irma from him?

Remembering the way that Alec had received the news of his attachment to Irma, Harold didn't think so. Alec had taken the blow in the most generous fashion; had wished him luck, had apparently withdrawn from competition. He had never liked Alec as well as he did at that moment; it had coloured all his thoughts of him, and warmed his feelings. As a rival he had counted Alec out. Had he been premature?

During the evening, moodily chewing the cud of these reflections, automatically relegating Isabel to her old position of unnoticed, unaddressed companion-help, he gradually convinced himself of Alec's bona-fides. To do so he had to call to his aid the vision of Alec as a kind of comic, whose feelings might seem real in books, but would not seem real to a woman. He posed, he postured, he talked a lot of hot air. Besides, if he did try any funny business, had not Irma said she did not love him? By bedtime he had reduced the threat of Alec to a shadow, and was kind, almost loverlike, to Isabel again.

But that night, for the first time, he dreamed of Alec, and in his dream Alec assumed proportions very different from those his waking thoughts had whittled him down to. All his bulbous characteristics, and he had others besides his eyes, were grotesquely exaggerated. Like a djinn in an Eastern story, he swelled and swelled, and Harold had to crane his neck to see him. I am a giant-killer, he thought, I must kill Alec. But the thought faded, partly from the sheer impossibility of its execution, for Alec was obviously immortal, partly from the fact that Alec wasn't hostile to him. From the carriage in the train, which now he seemed to fill, Alec smiled down at him: he wanted him to be his partner. To this Harold agreed, and in succeeding scenes, which vaguely recalled their times together, he acted as Alec's only half-unwilling slave. And in those scenes, from the first seeming miracles—the retirement of the ticket-collector, routed and saluting, and the rape (it might be called) of Jacob Henry's house in Dymport—he was aware of Alec's complete immunity from mortal and material limitations. Now on some magic carpet they had crossed the sea and were approaching a high range of mountains. It was night, but from one of them stuck up a dazzling white cone, as luminous as if it had been floodlit; and on this cone hundreds of men like ants were wielding pickaxes and drills. Through the cold, clear air he could hear the reverberation and distinctly feel the mountain shuddering under the assault. And he felt a hundred times more strongly than he had before that this was an outrage, an outrage against Nature and an outrage against business. What right had Alec to be disembowelling the mountain? He didn't put the question to Alec, he didn't dare, but Alec answered it by producing from his pocket a dirty commercial-looking envelope, from which he took a flimsy sheet of paper. "This is my warrant," he exclaimed triumphantly, and Harold saw it was a dividend warrant, imperfectly perforated, and typewritten, not printed. The sum to be paid wasn't even typewritten, it was scribbled in ink. For a moment Harold couldn't see the figure: then, in the glare from the approaching mountain, which it now seemed they were going to hit, he read it easily: one million pounds.

"Aha!" said Alec, giving him a nudge and an ogre's full-grown, toothy smile: "And some of this is for you, my boy!"

Harold woke up and immediately, in self-protection, reminded himself that the only dividends he had seen from

Alec's South American investment were for £5 19s. 4d. and £3 16s. 2d. respectively. The figures were burnt into his brain. "Fluctuating" sounded well, and Alec had made great play with it: but so far the fluctuation hadn't been impressive.

In spite of this he couldn't rid himself of this vision of the super-Alec: it haunted his sleep, though without episodes to illustrate it, and was still troubling him when he woke up.

30

Two days later Isabel went to London, ostensibly to try on some clothes that she had ordered before she left. The possession of a maid had made her extravagant in other ways but it wasn't only that: being with Alec had altered her idea of what became her, she wanted to have her new outfit ready for his visit. He wasn't a judge of clothes himself, he made mistakes with his own, as Harold had pointed out: the women in his books were often dressed explicitly out of the fashion, to emphasize their apartness. But if she was to appear in this latest one she wanted to be dressed right for the part, and once or twice she had asked him, "Do you like me in this?"—hoping he would take the hint and so describe her. Soft reds were becoming to her, soft reds, russets, sulky yellows, browns, the tints she saw around her on the autumn trees.

She hoped that if he put her in he would endow her with a sense of humour. Living with Harold she had lost it, but with Alec she believed that she had got it back. Quite often she had made him laugh, though when she recalled the pleasantries afterwards she didn't think much of them. But she had told herself repeatedly that she mustn't be too much in awe of him, too conscious of the differences between them. How could she help him if she were? Pertness was better than subservience.

The leading women in his books never made jokes; they seldom smiled and if they laughed it was in cruelty and bitterness. They were fatal from the beginning, tense all the way through. You must be tense to have a tune played on you: but there were two tensions; one of vitality, the other of the nerves. She hoped the first was hers. The Nut-Brown Maid! That would be a good title for a book.

But besides the clothes there was another matter—a woman's symptom—which had troubled her—sometimes with dread, sometimes with hope, according to her mood. She would ask a doctor about it—a doctor Alec sometimes went to, who was also a woman's doctor. Was it wise to have chosen him? Perhaps not; but anything to do with Alec drew her: he had only to mention a shop to make her want to deal there. And on the telephone, making the appointment, the doctor's voice had sounded kind. She pretty well knew what he would say, that he could tell her nothing definite, and she wouldn't be going to see him—it was another needless extravagance, a sign of the *épanouissement* of her spirit—if Harold hadn't been so strange the night before. It needed only a slight jolt from him to turn her from a radiant mistress into a guilty wife.

Harold had been strange the next day, too, but not in the same way, with a subdued excitement. She caught him looking at her speculatively. Had he heard from Alec? she asked. Yes, he had heard, And was it a business matter? Well, it was really a matter for a solicitor. For a solicitor? asked Isabel, trembling. Yes, for a solicitor—though he, as an accountant, knew something about it. Could he tell her, or was it very private? Well, it was private in a way, though it concerned her as much as him. He couldn't tell her without Alec's permission. And hadn't Alec given it? Isabel asked. Oh no, said Harold, it was a business letter. "But perhaps he took it for granted you would tell me?" Isabel pleaded, getting more and more worked up. Harold stared at her in astonishment, as if such a suggestion was most improper, as if a business letter had the seal of the confessional on it. "If he chooses to tell you himself," he began. "You think he will?" Isabel broke in. "You'll have to know sometime," said Harold grudgingly, "since it concerns us both." "I wish you could tell me, Harold. Can't you?" "I'm afraid not, my dear." "Is it something pleasant, something I shall like to hear?" "Now, darling, you mustn't try to worm it out of me."

With this she had had to be content. But surely if it had been divorce proceedings, even Harold, unhuman as he was in certain moods, couldn't have introduced the subject quite like that? Even if Alec had told him everything, and Harold couldn't wait to get rid of her, surely he would have made something like a scene, not given this display of excited, tight-lipped secrecy?

The nearer London came the more did Alec's influence dispel her fears. On the thought of him her heart reposed. This expedition was for him: for him the pretty clothes, for him the expensive restaurant where they had often lunched together, for him, yes, for him, the visit to the doctor. And when the doctor told her, as she suspected he would, that he couldn't tell her, she must wait, her feelings swung right over. Divorce now seemed a heaven-sent word. Divorce would settle everything. Divorce, and a new married life with Alec, and their child.

But this sanguine mood didn't outlast her return. On the station platform it faltered at Harold's greeting, which had regained its recent warmth; on the threshold of Tilecotes, where it should have been strong, it stumbled; and in the children's bedroom, saying good night, it nearly disappeared. Not quite, however, for she was still two people, and could not tell which would be uppermost.

"Any more news from Alec?" Isabel asked. She couldn't keep away from the subject.

"Nope." Harold had lately taken to saying "Nope". For years he hadn't dared to, because Isabel had once told him she disliked it. To use it was a sign of emancipation: it showed he could impose himself. It showed he was in a good humour, too.

"Nope," he repeated. "The next step is to see a solicitor."

"Oh, Harold," she exclaimed, ignoring "Nope", "why all this mystification?"

"You'll find out in good time," he said, grinning at her as he might have grinned at Irma.

Irma was late for dinner. What could have happened to her? She had never been late before. Harold had given her careful instructions but perhaps she could not find her way to this new rendezvous. Each time they met he had changed the place of meeting: and she had always found it. Punctuality was one of her graces, an unexpected one: for she was of too gossamer a substance to be tethered to a time-table. Always when she arrived so dead on time it seemed like a coincidence. But it wasn't; so what could have kept her now?

There was another thought he could take out and play with, while he was waiting for her. It was a comfortable thought, a warm thought, and he could have basked in its glow. But he didn't invoke it or even formulate it. Let it hang like a peach on the wall to ripen. Alec would not make trouble: Alec had a good reason for coming down to Marshport, a very good reason indeed. He didn't have to think of Alec when he thought of Irma.

Why didn't she come?

He had something special to tell her. It would not be easy to tell her, and all the less easy because he himself didn't quite know what he meant to say. These clandestine dinners in Downhaven must stop, that was the first thing. They were too risky: sooner or later somebody would spot him. The office was quite safe, of course, as safe as houses: then why not meet at the office and cut out the dinner? But Harold wouldn't contemplate that idea: it offended him. It was too crude, too inconsiderate: it would be treating Irma like a prostitute. Before she entertained him, he must entertain her: that was the form, and Harold was a stickler for form. She must, in fact, be given the opportunity—a token opportunity, perhaps—to refuse to play. He must woo her afresh each time. This was implicit in his idea of their relationship. It wasn't due so much to delicacy of feeling, as to the fact that he preferred it that way: starved of romance, he found romance in these exciting interchanges across the table-cloth—the whispered words, the nonsense, the endearments. Besides, he suspected that she didn't eat enough, she was so thin: and one square meal——

Why didn't she come?

If he had money enough—and now, since Alec's latest proposal, he thought he might have—perhaps he could take a flat for her in Downhaven, and set her up there. That was what many rich men did. She could go on with her work at the Green Dragon, but she would have a place of her own to go to, which would be much nicer for her than her lodgings in Marshport, he felt sure, though he had never seen them. She could go in and out by bus. There he could drop in and see her, by day as well as by night: he had almost forgotten what she looked like by daylight. And their little dinners would be cooked by her, with the delicious, funny-sounding Viennese dishes she had told him about: but not too many of them.

He had given up watching the door, feeling that if he went on watching she would never come: and just as he withdrew his gaze, just as he was least expecting her to come, she was there, beside the table.

Through the golden mist of his delight and relief at seeing her, he saw at once that something had gone wrong: she was pale and trembling, and her eyes looked large and frightened.

I won't ask her yet what's the matter, he decided. Easy does it.

He plied her with drinks and little attentions, and was rewarded by seeing colour return to her cheeks and naturalness to her manner.

Presently he said:

"Well, tell me what's been happening. What made you so late, sugar-mouth?"

At that her agitation returned, and for a moment she couldn't speak.

"Oh, it was nothing," she said, pronouncing the "o" in "nothing" like the "o" in "not". "Nothing at all."

"Oh come," said Harold, "it couldn't have been nothing, it must have been something, or you wouldn't have arrived" (he searched for words that wouldn't alarm or wound her) "well . . . late and out of breath."

"Oh, it was nothing," Irma repeated, trying to smile. "He didn't really mean it."

"Who didn't mean it?" Harold asked, and his thoughts flew to Alec. "Who's he, Irma?"

"Yes, he," said Irma, as if Harold must know who "he" was. "He didn't mean it, but he threatened me."

"He threatened you?" said Harold. The word rolled across the horizon of his mind like thunder. "Who threatened you?"

"He threatened me," said Irma. "He said that if I didn't——" She stopped.

"But who threatened you?" insisted Harold.

With a rush, and clearly most unwilling to say the name, she answered:

"He did, Otto. He stopped me just as I was out starting. He had been waiting for me."

"The blackguard!" exclaimed Harold, snatching at the first insult he could think of. "The great lousy blackguard! How dare he?"

"Oh no, he isn't!" cried Irma. "Really he is good and kind, but he is so violent. And he had heard . . . he had heard" (she hesitated and her voice dropped), "I had been out with someone."

"What's that to him?" demanded Harold.

"Nothing, nothing. I tell him, I tell him over and over again, that I am not for him. A ring in pledge he gave me, but I have given it back to him. I say to him, 'You have no right to speak to me like this'."

"What did he say?" asked Harold.

"Oh, he say most wicked, stupid words, I can't remember, and please not ask me, Harrold."

Her English grew more and more faulty in her agitation.

"You see I can manage him," said Irma, "but it was in the dark and no one near, and he got hold of me."

"He got hold of you?" said Harold, shocked and horrified.

"Yes, he got hold of me——" She rubbed her wrist and Harold saw the bruise gathering there, like a cloud on a pale sky. "He get hold of me," Irma repeated, "and he say what he would do. He hurt me."

She put her lips to her wrist and began to cry.

"Did he know about me?" asked Harold, after a pause.

"Oh no, he said 'another man.' And I said 'Who? There is no other man.' Oh yes, I lied to him, I'm afraid," she said, a little proudly.

"We ought to tell the police," Harold began, and stopped, realizing what dangerous allies the police would be.

"Oh, no," said Irma. "Besides, in the end I pacify him. You see, he is good, really. It is working with the animals that makes him rough. I made him promise——"

"What did you make him promise?" Harold asked.

"Well, what you say in English to a child, 'be good,

264

be good.' He said he would be. He cried a little, too."

"He cried?" said Harold, incredulously.

"Oh yes, in Germany men do. He cried, and then he let me go."

"Great hulking brute," said Harold.

"Oh no, he isn't, and I know he love me very much, but I love you, Harrold."

"That's all very well," growled Harold, almost angry with Irma for taking Otto's part.

"He is uneducated, that is all," said Irma, simply. She now seemed less upset than Harold was. "Please, do not let us speak of him again," she said, drawing herself up with fragile dignity. "He is, well, he is——" She waved her hands to show that Otto had been dismissed.

Harold did not bring up the question of the love-nest; he thought that Irma had had enough to think about for one evening. He felt his masculinity had been challenged, and stuck his elbows out, and creased his face into stern horizontal lines. Here was a cavalier she could rely on; if only he had been present when Otto—— He said as much; and Irma, laughing, said: "Harrold, you are so sweet!" Then the cloud lifted somewhat; but it remained a curl of smoke in the air, a question-mark; this was not the same as other evenings had been, and would it, should it, end as they had ended? The question grew into a problem, as he watched her smoking her cigarette, and puffing at it, in the inexpert way some women have—as if she had scarcely enough breath in her body to keep it alight. Perhaps it was too much to ask of her, to stay on the way back; but he would not entertain this thought, because in it there sounded, though so faintly, a changed voice that was like farewell. More slowly than usual he drove towards his office, wondering not how soon, but how late, he could get there; they crawled along between the dark, bow-windowed houses. At last he pulled up.

"We're here, Irma," he said.

She didn't answer, and he saw that she had fallen asleep.

"We're here," he repeated, raising his voice a little.

She started. "Oh, where are we, Harrold?"

"Outside my office. Would you like to come up?"

The gruffness in his voice alarmed her.

"Were you asking me?" she said.

"I thought you might be tired," he answered with all possible gentleness, "and would rather go straight home."

"Are *you* tired?" she asked him.

"Me? I'm never tired." A steel thread in the voice: he, Harold, tired! "But, Irma, it isn't me you want to think of. Think of yourself, for a change. Try to think how *you* feel."

"Oh, you would like me selfish?"

"No, just be yourself. Try to think I'm not here, or try to think that I'm your chauffeur, and say, Drive on!—that is, if you want to. It's for you to say."

"Myself, you want me to be myself? But how can I be myself without you?" she said, trying to track down an elusive thought. "Myself what am I? Just a barmaid—a God-damned barmaid." She laughed for both of them, for Harold didn't join in. " 'Where's that bloody barmaid gone?' "—she mimicked the voice of an impatient customer. " 'Oh, I know, she's having her night out!' A barmaid having her night out, that's what I am, myself. And I have one or two bruises, what you say in English?—blue and black. And because of that I am not myself, not very gay to-night—not what you call good company."

"I think you'd rather go home, Irma," Harold said.

"Without you I should," she answered elliptically. "And if I go now, I go without you, isn't it so, even though you are sitting by my side? We should be just two people driving, driving into the dark. It is a long time I live here before you came, Harrold. It went very quickly. If I had known that you were coming, oh how slow the time would have seemed! Empty and slow, because we have yet to meet! And now if I call on the future, Harrold, it does not hear me, it does not answer, why is that? It used to answer, just one word, one day of all the days of the week. Do you know which day, Harrold? And just one name, one name of all the English names; do you know which name, Harrold? But now it only gives me back the sound of my own voice, as if it hadn't any more to tell me. Oh, take me in your arms, Harrold, and say you love me!"

He did so, babbling endearments to her, searching his mind for reassurances. "This is the future answering you," he said. "Can't you hear it? It's saying Thursday and Harold, Thursday and Harold, Thursday and Harold. And to me it's saying Thursday and Irma, Thursday and Irma, Thursday and Irma." Over and over again he chanted the words until they got muddled up, and then she laughed and began to stir beneath his caresses. As afraid of silence as if it had been the silence of the future, he went on pouring words into her ear, regardless of their sense; until one sentence haphazardly clothed itself in meaning, and Irma answered it, "Please, yes."

31

THE next morning, soon after ten o'clock, the telephone bell rang.

"Hullo, Isabel," said the voice, its natural warmth of tone subdued to the possibility of being overheard. "How are you? Are you up yet?"

"Good heavens, Alec, yes, you forget I'm a working woman."

"Well, all I can say is, you don't look like one. . . . Hullo?"

Delighted confusion had momentarily taken away Isabel's power of speech. She made a noise to indicate she was there.

"Well, I've got to go out now, but could you stagger round here about twelve o'clock and have a drink with me?"

"Just let me think." The instincts of a lady must be shown, not the headlong impatience of a mistress. "Yes, I could."

"*A bientôt,* then."

Alec rang off.

A few minutes later the telephone rang again. This time it was Harold. He wouldn't be coming back to lunch, he told her; he had an unexpected engagement which would last most of the morning, and he would lunch in Downhaven off a sandwich. And he wouldn't be back to tea either—he had a very full day before him.

"But you will be back for supper?" Isabel asked, half hoping that Alec would ask her to dine with him.

"Supper, yes. I won't desert you two nights running."

He rang off before she could tell him, as she fully meant to, that Alec had arrived.

Nearly two hours of blissful thinking awaited her, and then an hour of bliss. Some of it she spent reading a book of his she hadn't read, so that she could talk about it to him. But his image kept blotting out the pages; it was strange how visual her feeling for him was, she couldn't think of him without seeing him. He wasn't good-looking, she knew that, but her dearest occupation was to evoke his face. That face wasn't like the face in the book, which was a tortured face. The first moment of seeing him was in a way the sweetest of all, like the first puff of a cigarette: the pure fulfilment of desire, which could only be achieved by the imagination, the rest was experience; and experience, even with Alec, had sometimes disappointed her—disappointed her not with him but with herself. Other raptures might go deeper, but for pure bliss the eyes had it. "The Ayes have it." Yes, indeed they have! It was odd how since she had been with Alec words and even puns had come to mean a great deal to her.

She wanted to be worthy of this meeting, the first she would have had in Marshport since the early times, not many weeks ago, when she was still a stranger to his inmost heart, and he to hers, without the right of entry, an alien without a passport. Treading among the uncertainties, terrified of putting a foot wrong, she could only guess at what he wanted her to be; she could not be herself: it seemed too presumptuous to suppose that he would be satisfied with Isabel Eastwood, after eleven years of married life. Then, by trial and error, she had discovered the personality that he liked—or so she thought: but was she really his creation? Did she exist in her own right, apart from him? Yes, because she had influenced his work, she had changed the colour of his mind, made him accessible to new emotional experiences: no mere projection of himself, in woman's form, could have done that. To that she clung; she had broken Elspeth's spell and exorcized him.

In spite of the reverence and awe in which she still held him, and which was essential to her feeling for him, she could still humbly regard herself as his benefactress.

She was also his accredited mistress—his *maîtresse-en-titre*: she had a place and a status in his life, she occupied the position once so unworthily held by Elspeth, Elspeth Elworthy—"those two unaspirated Hells" as Alec had once said. How Isabel had laughed! She must not abuse her power, as Elspeth had; but she must not be afraid to exercise it, for Alec needed a lot of looking after, as well as a great deal of support. New responsibilities would be thrust on her, new adaptabilities required. She rejoiced in the idea of this. She was no longer a coiled spring, but full of softness and resilience. Walking down through the town she held herself carefully, as if she were a dedicated vessel that might spill its precious liquid.

Her first sight of him was all that she had hoped for. He was sitting in the lounge of the hotel with his back to her; his tawny hair, a little thin on top (this touched her), shone in the sunlight. As she approached he got up from the leather chair to fetch an ashtray from a neighbouring table: unaware of being watched, he belonged to himself, and this was how, in spite of her possessiveness, she liked to think of him, a perfectly free creature. A moment later he saw her, his eyes lit up, and they decorously shook hands.

The things she had prepared to say fled from her, and instead words came out which had no origin in her conscious mind: she forgot them as soon as they were uttered. Presently she realized she was chattering to fill a vacancy: his mind wasn't really on what she was saying, or on what he said. He seldom looked her squarely in the eyes—this wasn't easy for him since his had a cast—but he had other ways of looking at her: sometimes he played her with a half-smile which intoxicated her. To-day his eyes swept the floor at her feet in restless pendulum movement. To Isabel this was a deprivation; she missed the look that says more than words can, and hoping to evoke it she suddenly remembered something that would surely fix his ocular attention on her.

"What mischief have you and Harold been hatching between you?" she asked, as lightly as she could. "He's so cagey, he won't tell me."

"Oh, hasn't he told you?" Alec said.

"No, he said he must have your permission. Alec, it isn't——?"

"Isn't what?" he said.

She couldn't finish her question. In the face of his, she wondered how she dared to think of putting it.

"I do wish you would tell me," she begged. "Is it something very important?"

"Oh no," he said, "it isn't. It's just something that I

270

wanted to do. I think I'd rather not tell you myself, you might think you ought to thank me, and that would embarrass me."

"I could thank you now," said Isabel, "and so shorten your embarrassment."

He smiled.

"No, get Harold to tell you. Tell him I said he was to. He's a good fellow, Harold, don't forget it."

On most occasions, and from most people, Isabel was pleased to hear Harold praised; but for this once she wasn't.

"Oh, I know he is as good as gold," she said. "You needn't tell me. But I am so curious. Couldn't you give me just the least idea?"

"It's to do with my new book," he said reluctantly.

"Oh, have you dedicated it to——" At once she stopped. This was a worse indiscretion than the other. "To anyone I know?" she lamely finished.

He shot a glance at her—not quite the glance she had been hoping for—and shook his head.

"I feel I ought to spare you. No one has the *dédicace* so far, but you can have the first refusal, if you like."

She laughed. "The first refusal! Well, I'll take it now."

"You mustn't buy a pig in a poke," he said, more seriously than she expected. "You mightn't like it. And another drawback is, I've lost it."

"Lost it?"

"Well, not lost it, but can't find it. I shall find it, of course."

But she could see that he looked worried.

"When did you last have it?"

"At St. Milo's, just before I left. I was going to bring it with me to make some alterations——"

"Oh, so it's finished!" Isabel broke in.

"Yes, but I haven't got it."

"It must be somewhere," Isabel said, trying to sound helpful.

"Yes, it's damn' well got to be, because it's my only copy."

"Oh, Alec, you need someone to look after you!"

"Well, I have, haven't I?"

271

At this they should have kissed, but couldn't, and the moment slipping by left a slight sense of anti-climax and frustration.

"Have you found a title for the book?" asked Isabel.

"No, not yet."

"When will it come out?" asked Isabel.

"Not for six months or more."

Isabel clicked her tongue with disappointment, but Alec seemed relieved. "I shall probably be abroad then," he said.

"Abroad?" repeated Isabel. If he had said he was starting the next day, she couldn't have felt more bereft.

"Yes, I generally go abroad when one of my books comes out. I feel it's safer."

"Safer for whom?"

"For me."

"Who are you afraid of? The reviewers?"

"Well, they haven't been very kind to me lately."

"They'll like this book, though."

"They may say it's diabetic—too much sugar. You put it there, you know."

He sounded half reproachful.

"May I see it, when you've found it?" Isabel asked.

"The typescript? Better not, I think. It's not quite hatched. I don't like my eggs being looked at while I'm sitting—it makes me want to desert."

"Has anyone read it?" Isabel couldn't help asking.

"No, no one. It's a secret process with me, writing. It's like a love-affair."

"But you don't sound as if you were in love with this book," Isabel said.

"Well, perhaps I'm not. It's the reaction, you know. I always have it when I've finished a novel. '*Omne animal post coitum triste*', and all that."

Isabel discarded several unsuitable replies. It cramped her style, having to talk to Alec in this local public place, where they couldn't even use their natural voices, much less an endearment. Not being able to say what she wanted to say, she couldn't feel what she wanted to feel. If she had been on the platform of a railway station, saying good-bye, she could at any rate have shed some tears.

"Darling," she said, defying the whole room to hear her—and after all the word was common coin—"I hoped that you were feeling as happy about the book as I do. At any rate, let's drink to its success."

"Good Lord!" said Alec, starting up. "And I never even offered you a drink!"

He looked the picture of compunction, and Isabel felt more than half ashamed, for she had never asked him or anyone for a drink before. When they were served, Alec raised his glass.

"Here's looking at you!" he said, but he didn't look at her, or rather only one of his eyes did.

"To the author, and his book!" said Isabel, charging the toast with all the feeling she possessed. Her eyes shone. "All the luck in the world to them!" she added.

"Amen, amen," he responded, rather moodily. "And to you, too, my dear."

At the words "my dear," which seemed to restore her sense of their relationship, her eyes filled with tears. She felt that she could leave him now—and it was more than time she left him—on something like the note of their old intimacy. Picking her bag up from the floor beside her, she began to make departure movements, hoping in her heart he would detain her: but he didn't.

Now she was on her feet.

"You'll be staying for a day or two?" she said. She couldn't help it, though she knew he hated being asked his plans.

"Oh yes, if you don't mind."

"Mind? I was hoping you would have supper with us to-night."

"With pleasure," he said.

"By then," she said, still seeking some excuse to linger, "I shall have learned your secret."

"What secret?" he asked.

"Have you so many? I meant the one you share with Harold!"

"Oh yes," he said, with a sigh that was half-way to a yawn, as he led the way to the entrance. "A novelist is a wasting asset," he told her suddenly. "The more of himself he puts into his books the less of him there is."

Puzzled, she left him.

It was past one o'clock when she got home. Vaguely she looked about for Harold, but of course he wasn't coming. If only she could be alone with her thoughts of Alec! But she couldn't, because of the voices, children's voices, her children's voices, coming from the garden.

"Janice, go back!"

"Oh, Jeremy, I never moved."

"You did. I saw you."

"I never."

"Oh, Janice, I wish you wouldn't cheat."

"Lunch, children!" Isabel cried, opening the French window.

The summons broke the gathering knot of tension, and they came towards her, Janice in front. She made some dancing steps.

"We thought you were never, never, *never* coming!" she chanted.

"I had to go into the town."

"And so you missed the lady—didn't she, Jeremy?"

Jeremy assented without enthusiasm, but added, brightening, "She came in a Jaguar."

"What lady?" Isabel asked.

"Oh, she was such a strange lady, wasn't she, Jeremy?"

"Oh, I dunno," said Jeremy, as if all ladies were alike to him.

"Oh, but she *was*. She had such a funny hat."

"What was it like?"

Janice screwed her face up into an expression of the utmost seriousness.

"Oh, it was white," she said, trying to draw it in the air with her finger, "and very, very, *very* small. And she had quite a *large* face."

"What was her name?"

"She didn't tell us, did she, Jeremy?"

"We didn't ask her," Jeremy said.

"Well, Susan will know," said Isabel, "I'll ask her, here she is."

Susan was bringing in the lunch.

"No, Madam," she said, "I never saw the lady. She didn't knock or ring or anything. It wasn't very nice, was it? She must have come in soft-footed, or I should have heard her, because naturally I was in the kitchen."

"Oh yes, she did," said Janice. "She walked like this." On tiptoe Janice executed a sort of tiger-prowl across the room, putting her finger on her lips to assist the illusion of silence. "And she said in such a *funny* voice, 'I found the door open so I walked straight in'."

"Do you think the children imagined it all?" said Isabel to Susan, mystified.

"I couldn't say, I'm sure, Madam. But if anything is missing I couldn't be held responsible."

"Of course not," Isabel said.

"There isn't anything missing," Jeremy said, "but there's something that wasn't here before—a book, she left a book."

"A book?"

"Well, it isn't really a book," said Janice. "Because, you see, it's larger than a book for one thing and the edges are all crumply."

"She said it was a book," said Jeremy.

"Where is it?" Isabel asked.

"She put it on a chair, no, not that one, this one."

Isabel eyed the volume with its ragged edges under a blue cardboard cover. But she did not move towards it—rather, she backed away.

"Did she tell you what book it was?" she asked the children.

"Oh no," said Janice, as if one couldn't have expected that. "She said, 'Give it to your mother when she comes in. Good-bye, my dears, good-bye, good-bye.'" Janice, in an actressy voice, imitated a still more actressy voice. "She was rather silly, wasn't she, Jeremy?"

"I didn't notice specially," said Jeremy.

Isabel took a step towards the volume and again recoiled.

"Let's have lunch first," she said.

But she could hardly eat any: all her appetite had transferred itself to what she knew was Alec's novel.

32

ISABEL was a quick reader and before the light had faded from the October sky she had finished Alec's book. She read the last part upstairs in her bedroom; she didn't want to be interrupted by the children, she didn't want them to watch her reading it, she didn't want them to see the book again.

Then arose the question what to do with it: where to hide it. She knew of no safe place.

She could return it to him, of course, and perhaps she ought to. She could make a parcel of it and Harold would take it to the Royal. But she couldn't endure the thought of even this much communication with him. Besides, there are limits, prescribed mathematical limits, to turning the other cheek.

His letters she had burnt. With infinite sorrow she had burnt his letters; with infinite pleasure she would burn his book. Revenge! Revenge! She had never understood how anyone could find pleasure in it, but now she did, for at the heart of all her disillusion and anguish there was a nerve that throbbed with hatred. How dare he treat her so, how dare he?

Just as when she was with him her mind flew to literary allusions, to keep his company, as she believed, so now she thought of Hedda Gabler—how wantonly, with how much less reason than she had, burning Lövborg's life work: "I am burning his child!" Well, people had blamed Hedda; no one would blame her.

She stole downstairs, carrying the book under her arm. Its touch contaminated her as if it had been something dirty, as indeed it was, it was, it was, it was. Alec had been very, very naughty.

In the lounge the children were playing, very quietly, for Isabel had told them she wasn't feeling well: which was true enough, and anyhow it was best to be prepared for all emergencies. "Oh, Mummy, you've got the book!" cried Janice. "Is it a *nice* book?" "No, not very nice," said Isabel, in an uneven voice, and on an impulse she sought out Susan and asked her to take the children for a walk. With unexpected willingness, Susan complied; the children were delighted at this new departure. Happy and excited, the trio got under way, Janice taking Susan's hand. Isabel was left alone.

The fire—the fire that she had kept for Alec's letters—was burning low. She stoked it up, but not so much as to obscure the red part. Then on another impulse, for she could not keep in one mind, she thrust the manuscript under the sofa, behind the valances. It had become a fetish to her; it was numinous; the sight and touch of it could do her harm. Away with it!

She stared into the fire, and, her mind reverting to literary allusion—partly to escape the pain of her own thoughts—she remembered an essay of Max Beerbohm's in which, with characteristic urbanity, he had enlarged on the difficulty of burning a book. It simply wouldn't burn. It would put the fire out first! But if she tore it leaf by leaf and fed them singly to the flames, then it would burn all right. She imagined herself doing so.

Like a murderer, forgetful of what made him do the crime, for that was in another life, she had but one idea—how to dispose of the body. She saw the charred pages cluttering the fireplace—"What on earth have you been doing, Isabel?" Wouldn't it be better to take it under cover of darkness to the canal—and drown it, deeper than ever plummet sounded?

She was considering this alternative when the door-bell rang. Who could it be? A woman stood on the threshold: "My name is Mrs. Elworthy," she said. "You don't know me; but may I come in?"

"Come in," said Isabel.

At last she was face to face with Elspeth, the woman she had hated, but now did not hate—oh no, for they were fellow-victims, victims of Alec's treachery.

"Come in," she repeated, and Elspeth followed her into the lounge.

And yet she could not like her, there was something about this florid woman, with her air of conscious Edwardian gentility, that repelled her.

"Please sit down," she said.

With a deliberate spreading of her skirts Elspeth sat down. She looked around her.

"So this is where you live," she said.

The words spoke volumes.

"Yes," said Isabel briefly. "But I don't think you came to talk about my house."

"Only because he describes it," Elspeth said. "You must have recognized it. Or didn't you read the book?"

"Yes, I have read it."

"And have you burnt it?"

"No, not yet," said Isabel.

"You ought to have your brains tested. I brought it for you to burn—when you had read it. Do you know it's the only copy?"

Isabel said she did know. "But," she added, stung by some impulse of perversity, "he could rewrite it."

Elspeth held her hands up, the palms outwards, like traffic signals barring the way to any comment Isabel might make.

"Oh no, he couldn't. He can't rewrite. How often have I heard him say, 'The prairie fire can't burn the same patch twice.' Is that news to you?"

Isabel admitted that he hadn't told her.

"He didn't tell you everything, you see. But he told you about me, I suppose?"

"Yes, something," Isabel said.

"I can imagine what. But do you think I had an easy time with him, the eighteen years we were together—well, we are still together—the best years of a woman's life?"

"He said you made him suffer. He said you said so."

"If I did, his nature asked for it, and his work throve on it. And didn't he make *me* suffer? All those years, tied to a man who couldn't see a woman, except through the distorting lens of his imagination? But I have put up with it, I took from him things that no other woman would have. And now it's your turn. Where's the book?"

"I have it somewhere," Isabel said, "not here."

"Did you enjoy his picture of you," Elspeth asked, "as the stepping-stone, the half-way house to his real love? You, the barrister's wife, so captivated by him that you never saw, when he made love to you, that his eye was fixed on someone far beyond you—and oh, so much above you!—your own Italian maid who waited on you at table. 'The Constant Nymphomaniac' he called you. By the way, I didn't know you had a maid—he didn't tell me."

"We have one now," said Isabel.

"But not, I expect, an Italian. No, in a novelist's mind, such details get mixed up. You, for instance, are not quite like the Mrs. Blandford of his book. But—he was your lover, wasn't he? And you thought he loved you, didn't you? You didn't realize that all the time his purpose was to be near the object of his real affections, with whom he ultimately goes off?"

Isabel said nothing.

"It was very touching," Elspeth went on, "the way you thought you were being a comfort to him, because you spoke his language and had read Flaubert! You were putting him at his ease, his ease in life! You were his guardian angel, reconciling him to our sex. And all the while he was deceiving you with his Italian servant, lying in her arms (I don't know where) on her days off, and sucking out of her, not you, those vital juices, so necessary to men, that Latin women have, but that you and I, Mrs. Eastwood, don't have. It was she, first the idea of her, and then, well, the reality of her, the flesh and blood, that gave him the emotional consolation that the barrister's wife thought she was giving him. 'The Constant Nymphomaniac'! If you have the book, I should like to show you a passage in it."

"I haven't got it here," said Isabel.

"Well, never mind, you've read it, I've no doubt—the scene in which he finally deserts the barrister's wife, with all her tiresome intellectual pretensions, and flies off with his Angiolina—such an angel!—to lead the simple life in Ischia—a perpetual honeymoon. A bit banal, isn't it?"

"Look, Mrs. Elworthy," said Isabel, "don't let us talk any more about Alec's book. I'd much rather we didn't."

"I've nearly done," said Elspeth. "But you and I, Mrs.

Eastwood, we know who this Angiolina is; she's an Austrian girl called Irma, the barmaid at a local public house. You tried to procure her for Alec, didn't you, because you loved him, and when she didn't seem to want him (clever girl!) he seemed to turn to you."

"How did you know all this?" asked Isabel.

"He told me. Oh, we were nothing like so estranged from each other all this time as he made out to you, and we are still together, in a way. But what I want to know is——"

"I'm afraid I haven't much more time," said Isabel, glancing wildly at the clock. "My children, and my husband——"

"Your children and your husband? Well, I've nearly done. But I wanted to ask you something about this Irma. Has she a young man? I mean a *young* man, not an old man twice her age? A girl like that must have a young man—when I say young I mean young."

"I believe there is somebody," Isabel said. "But I don't think she sees him any more. He doesn't live in Marshport: he lives in Blastwick, about twelve miles away."

"What sort of a fellow is he, Mrs. Eastwood? Does he write novels, is he literary? He doesn't come into the book, you see, and nor do I."

"He's German, a farm labourer, I think," said Isabel, relieved to be able to talk about someone who wasn't in the story. "A very simple sort of man—almost a simpleton, I gathered. She spoke to me about him once. His name is Otto Killian."

"Did she say what he looked like?"

"Only that he was blond and very tall, almost a giant."

"You don't know where he lives in Blastwick?"

"No."

"He would know where she lives, of course, and Alec's here, he's at the Royal?"

Isabel said he was.

"That's all I wanted to know. Well, Mrs. Eastwood, I was jealous of you once, but I'm not jealous now." She rose and began her panther prowl about the room, examining each piece of furniture as if she was pricing it. Stopping in front of a bureau, she said:

"I should like to see the book again. It was silly of me to have parted with it. It's mine in a way—all his books are mine, though I don't come into this one. You say it isn't here, but can I trust you? There are several drawers in this bureau"—she tapped it—"might it be in this one, for instance, or in this one?"

Isabel also rose.

"No, Mrs. Elworthy, it isn't."

Her visitor took a step towards her.

"You would do well to give it me, I think."

Isabel stood her ground before the powerfully-built woman, whose sunken eyes still gleamed. "Did you do well to leave it here?" she asked.

Mrs. Elworthy shrugged and turned away. "Perhaps not. I thought you had more spirit. I must go now, but my advice to you is: Burn it, burn Alec's book. Do you want to live your whole life in it?"

She moved towards the door, as if her entrances and exits depended on her own volition and concerned no one but herself. Her hostess didn't count. Isabel followed her and on an impulse said:

"Where are you staying?"

Elspeth shrugged again.

"The world is wide," she said, pointing to the night. She was disappearing into it when Isabel said:

"You've forgotten something."

"What?" asked her visitor, turning back.

"Your broomstick."

Without waiting for an answer, Isabel shut the door on her, and for the first time in her life slipped up the safety-catch.

Trembling she went back. The threat of violence had both stimulated and unnerved her. It seemed so incongruous in the safe atmosphere of Tilecotes: "an outpost of civilization", as Alec had called it, "in darkest Marshport."

Janice was right: Elspeth was rather silly. She must have been an actress, Isabel thought: an actress who acted better off the stage than on it. She had put on an act: but stripped of histrionics, what did it amount to? Only the spiteful gesture of a jealous woman, who had hoped to kill two birds with one stone: Isabel's happiness and Alec's book. Well, she had killed the first—the Bluebird of Isabel's life; and as for the second—what had she told Isabel that Isabel didn't know? One thing, that Alec couldn't rewrite his book.

There was a stab for her in that, and quite a deep stab, for Isabel believed that Alec had told her everything about his writing. But did it matter much? And did it matter much that he had discussed her, and perhaps laughed about her with Elspeth, who, so he said, had walked out on him? Elspeth had perhaps not told the truth about that: she had said that she was always with Alec "in a way", but if she was, why did she mind his straying?

What really mattered was that it was not she, Isabel, but Irma who was the presiding deity of his new book. Irma, not she, had made him happy; Irma, not she, had sweetened his imagination; and all the time she thought she had him to herself she was really sharing him with Irma—no, not sharing, for so far as love went, Irma had had the lion's share, the whole. His vision of her had persisted through his other visions—if he had them.

At last he had "got hold" of Irma. And who had willed it? Who had helped him to it? She had. Suddenly she realized she was sitting on or over the book, like little Aggie in *The Awkward Age*, a novel that Alec had recommended to her. With a cry between hysteria and laughter she dived for it and, overcoming her unwillingness to touch it, took it upstairs and buried it, in a shroud of tissue-paper, in an old-fashioned square hat-box of her mother's.

"Mummy! Mummy!"

The children were back, full of their walk with Susan, at least Janice was: for Janice it was Susan, Susan all the way. "Why don't you take us for a walk, Mummy? You never do." "You talk too much, Janice," Susan reprimanded her. "You don't let Jeremy get a word in." "Oh, what an untruth!" protested Janice, outraged. "When me and Jeremy are by ourselves he talks, he talks, he talks"—playing for time, she swivelled her bright eyes from Isabel's face to Susan's—"he talks my head off!"

"I haven't noticed it, have you, Susan?" Isabel said.

"No," said Janice, reasonably, "because you're not there to see. You're never, never, *never* there—is she, Jeremy?"

For some reason the words hurt Isabel unbearably. They seemed to annihilate her, to deny her very being. She was a wraith to her own children; she existed only in a book; and how!

"Tea," she cried. "Come along, it's late!"

All these voices! Now someone else was calling for her: Harold, and in no uncertain tones. "Isabel! Isabel!" It was a command, and down she came.

"Well, how's tricks?" he asked, and there was so much animation in his eyes that she thought he was going to make love to her.

"Not so good," she answered, trying to meet him on the plane of banter. "I've somehow spent a silly day."

"Oh, I don't suppose you have," said Harold, and she clutched at this straw of reassurance, which it was so unlike him to have held out. "You've seen Alec, anyhow."

"How did you know?" she said.

"My secret service. Well, it wasn't very secret. He told me he was going to see you."

"Did he tell you about the book?"

Isabel shook her head. Then she remembered he had said something about the book, but she shook her head again.

"Funny, he told me he was going to tell you, but I expect he was too bashful. Poor old Alec! It's the first time I've ever known him be. He's not usually backward in coming forward, is he?"

Isabel made a suitable noise in answer.

Harold was in high good humour: Isabel had seldom seen him so pleased with himself, the world, and her. For the first time there was no reservation in his tone when he spoke of Alec. A touch of condescension still but some affection and even more approval.

"He wanted to spare your blushes, I expect, as well as his. Well, it's all settled now, and since he wouldn't tell you, I suppose that I must."

"What is it?" Isabel asked.

"You don't sound very enthusiastic, but you will be, when you hear. Briefly, Alec has made a settlement."

"A settlement?"

"Yes. It's a bit complicated, but I'll make it as simple as I can. He's settled the proceeds of this new book of his on Jeremy and Janice and on . . . on any other children we may have."

The pause grew longer. What can I say? thought Isabel. No other thoughts would come, to help her tongue. Harold's voice broke the spell.

"I don't wonder you're surprised," he said.

"Could you explain a little more?" asked Isabel.

"Yes, of course I will." How strange it was, this new expansiveness in Harold, and about business matters. "By this arrangement, he'll save a lot of income tax. What I mean is, the Government won't get it. It will be a sacrifice for him, of course, because he won't profit from the book himself; but as he pays tax at the rate of—well, no matter— the total saving will be considerable. Jeremy and Janice won't pay income tax, you see, or hardly any. It's like an endowment. Our children will be provided for, that's what it means."

"I think I see," said Isabel. "But how does Alec know the book will be a success? They haven't all been."

"No, but some have. There was one he told me of—I've forgotten its name—but what with sales, and film rights, and broadcasting rights, and dramatic rights, and translation rights, and all the other rights—it made well over seven thousand pounds."

The word "rights" sang in Isabel's ears but they sounded wrong to her.

"What makes him think that this book's going to be a success?" she asked again.

"Darling," said Harold gently—and again the word struck her like a blow, for he so seldom used it—"I don't think we ought to ask that question. Isn't there something about not looking a gift-horse in the mouth? But, as a matter of fact, Alec thinks it *will* be a winner, because he's given it a happy ending, which he never has before, and the public like that —I don't blame them. He says his publisher tells him there's a lot of advance interest in this book—more than with any of his other books—and it's practically sure of a good sale.

A film company is interested in it already. He's working on the publicity side himself, making the right contacts, and so on. Oh, he's cute, Alec is. He doesn't let the grass grow under his feet. I didn't call him smart-alec for nothing."

Isabel wiped her hand across her face so hard that some of her make-up came off on the palm. Wretched though she was, the feeling of nakedness increased her wretchedness. When she had repaired the damage, she said, as steadily as she could:

"Harold, I'm afraid we can't accept Alec's offer."

"Can't accept it?" Harold repeated, thunderstruck. "Why not?"

"Why, for a thousand reasons. For one, it puts us under too great an obligation."

"I don't know about that. He owes me something, too. I've saved him quite a packet."

"Yes, but you've been paid for doing it. And then, what would people say?"

"You mean they might say that you'd vamped him?" Harold's smile of infinite indulgence broadened; he laughed and laughed. "Well, it's quite true, you did set your cap at him, I never thought of that. But, apart from any question of undue influence, who's to know he's made the money over to the children? No one but ourselves and a few business men and civil servants. Why should they make a fuss? Alec won't tell anyone. He wouldn't even tell you."

"I know, I know," said Isabel. "But I still don't like the idea of it. I beg you not to accept it, Harold."

"Why, what's come over you?" he said, looking at her for the first time curiously. "What's wrong with you? You must be mad, my darling; you ought to have your brains tested."

He said it far more kindly than Elspeth had, but it was too much, and Isabel began to cry.

"Oh, please don't take it, Harold," she sobbed. "Let's go on as we were before we ever knew Alec. We were so happy then."

"Now look here, look here," he said, his voice rough with unaccustomed tenderness that he had learned from Irma. "It's no good your taking on, you see, because the matter's settled. It's settled, signed and sealed. You can't renounce the children's rights, on their behalf, how can you? The whole thing's out of your hands now. The trust deed's been drawn up. You should have spoken before."

"But I wasn't t-told!" moaned Isabel.

"I know, but we took it for granted you would agree. Agree! That you would jump at it! It's the chance of a lifetime!" He came and sat beside her on the sofa and put his arm round her. "You can't guess the difference it will make to us—but you can! One thing you've always wanted!" and he drew her closer and whispered in her ear.

At that moment the telephone bell rang. Harold gently disengaged himself, and giving Isabel a loving look, he took up the receiver.

"It's Alec," he said, closing the mouthpiece with his hand. "He wants to know what time dinner is. I didn't know you'd asked him."

"I did," said Isabel, "but I'd forgotten"—which was the truth. "I haven't got anything ready and I don't feel well. Oh, Harold, I have such a headache! Please, Harold, tell him not to come. Make any excuse you can."

"Shall I say to-morrow, then?"

"Oh no, no, no, no, no."

She didn't hear what Harold said to Alec, but when he came back he sat a long time with her, utterly bewildered by her grief, but holding her hands and trying to console her.

33

ISABEL didn't sleep at all that night: it was a *nuit blanche*, the first she had ever had. All through the dreary hours a resolution kept forming and unforming in her mind. Two resolutions, indeed, went whirling round in her like coloured balls, but one was a satellite of the other. She couldn't take the second step till she had taken the first.

What should she do about the typescript that now lay in her mother's hat-box, lined with blue moiré silk: that was the second step. Should she in some quite quiet unostentatious way (not burning) destroy it—or give it to the dustman to destroy? That would be one way out, the tidiest way, the way of least resistance. It would also be the way of revenge. Revenge was out of fashion and Isabel was not vindictive, but Alec had hurt her and if she did not want to hurt him in return she wouldn't mind hurting him.

Besides, the book once out of the way, all the problems connected with it would be solved, it couldn't be published, nor could blood-money ooze from it. By destroying the book she would wipe the slate as clean as it ever could be wiped.

Constitutionally she was unable to take a realistic view. She had to impose some kind of idealism, some relish of salvation on events: otherwise they were merely things that happened, predetermined, dead. Nor did she flinch from being idealistic on other people's behalf, or at their expense. If Jeremy and Janice had to forgo the advantages of Alec's benefaction, let them. She had enough faith in spiritual values to feel that they would be the better for it. The wages of sin did no one any good.

The wages of sin! She realized that this strange *démarche* had been a move of Alec's conscience. He had one, and it had pricked him into making, in advance, dishonourable amends for what she was to suffer. He had given their love-affair six months to live—six months before the bomb went off, when he would be abroad. Perhaps not so long; perhaps he would have cooled off before that date, so far as passion went, the bomb would only have blown up a ruin, or at most an empty house.

But if he had no feeling for her feelings, did he also disregard her reputation, which would be living and vulnerable after they were dead? Didn't he mind what people thought of her, what her husband and her family and her friends thought of her?

Perhaps—and this was the first consoling thought she had had for many hours—they wouldn't recognize her in the story. The circumstances were sufficiently unlike. Harold, if he ever read the book, might not put two and two together. Outside his profession, he seldom made that small addition sum. Probably he thought, if he ever thought about it, that a novelist's work had no relation to his own experience—it came out of a pigeon-hole labelled PLOTS. In the book he played the part of a wronged husband who, when he found out that his wife was deceiving him, behaved extremely well.

All this was on the negative side, the stricken area of calamity: it was salvaging among the ruins. Only in the small hours, oddly enough, did Isabel begin to take a different view.

Then it occurred to her—a thing that neither she nor Elspeth had admitted when they pressed their parallel but never confluent attacks on Alec—that this book was his best book, the book that Isabel had always wanted him to write: his masterpiece, in fact. Sordid as it was, and graceless as was the rôle she played in it, it had in it that feeling for human goodness that his other books had lacked.

So why destroy it? Why rob the world of something that might be of lasting value? She was part-creator of it, and if in creating it she had destroyed herself, well, that was just too bad: but many better women than she had suffered the same fate.

And how disappointed Elspeth would be, if it ever appeared in the shop windows!

Later still, when the morning light was whitening the ceiling above her window-curtains, she thought of the legal aspect. Legally she had no right to keep the book: legally she was a receiver of stolen goods, a fence, as it was called.

288

Legally her first action should be to return the book to Alec, who must be worrying about it.

The idea that he still had rights and feelings to be considered, that he was still a person, and alive, though dead to her, struggled for recognition in her mind.

But these were surface thoughts—hardly more real to her than counting sheep, and sometimes deliberately induced to encourage sleep—with which she beguiled the weary hours. Beneath them was the throb and smart of the infected wound, that drained away her life and poisoned it: all the ecstasy she had felt, that great river, with its thousand tributaries in her heart and mind, belonged to another woman, every drop of it belonged to Irma.

She had some stiffening in her nature, derived from her forebears: but she did not feel she could survive this knowledge. Was it to be a choice between the book and her? She tried to feel the force of the alternative, the validity, as a guide to action, of the either . . . or. But it was a literary device, a meaningless antithesis, a parlour game her feelings wouldn't play at. How would it really help her, if the book were to be destroyed and she lived on?

There was only one thing to do, but she took the whole morning making up her mind to do it. Twice Alec rang up to ask how she was and whether he could come to see her; twice she told Susan, with apologies for making her the vehicle of a lie (they were wasted, for Susan was almost offended at the idea she couldn't tell one), to say that she was out. After a pretence lunch with the children, at which she couldn't eat a mouthful, she started out for Irma's lodgings.

Only by knowing how she really felt about Alec could she decide what to do with the manuscript; and only by seeing Irma could she discover what she really felt about him. To see Irma or not to see her: that was the chief question which had occupied her night-thoughts.

On the same afternoon, Elspeth, too, set out, but in the opposite direction, towards Blastwick. She was always over-dressed for any occasion; her clothes had a garden-party or a tea-gown air, suggesting elegancies that were dated. For this occasion, whatever it should turn out to be, she wore a party frock that ill accorded with the bus-stop from which her mission started. And with the weather, too; it was a cold, blustery day in late October, the shabbiest, untidiest season of the year. Long gloves she wore, whenever she could wear them; with golden bracelets bulging under them, and if one looked at her, as one couldn't help looking, it was the hollows above her elbows that caught one's eye, where the gloves wrinkled on their way to her upper arms. To-day she wore a woollen coat and yet those gloves seemed visible through the sleeves.

She had the visibility of a lighthouse, when she was there, and the same static, monumental quality: yet how she came to be there was another matter, for one didn't seem to see her coming or going.

It was a forty-minute drive to Blastwick. Elspeth sat on the top deck of the bus, her short blue furled umbrella held truncheon-like across her lap, too much absorbed in her own thoughts to notice the landscape, with its subtle variations on a monotonous theme—the wall of shingle on the left, crowned at intervals by Martello towers, and on the right, where the hills that guarded Marshport had sunk into the plain, the illimitable marsh. Her indifference to the view was something positive, as though nothing it could do or be would make her take an interest in it; and this indifference she extended to her fellow-passengers in the bus: by the way she sat and looked she created round her a prohibited area. The conductor coming to collect her fare felt he was trespassing on highly-scented private ground.

At last they passed under the shadow of the tall church tower that had long, unseen by her, dominated the flat, watery land. The bus stopped. "Is this Blastwick?" she asked, in tragic tones, of a woman across the gangway who was so surprised at being addressed that she answered, "Yes, I think it is," although it was her own home and destination.

Almost everyone got out: they made what seemed like a procession in the mean streets of the little town, which, but for them, were empty. They all went one way, and she followed them; but she must ask a question.

"Where is the police-station?" she demanded.

Two or three homely faces, men's and women's, turned to her, their carefree, holiday look suddenly transformed into a gaping stare. "The police-station? It's there," a man volunteered, pointing along the street. "The last house on the right."

"I wanted to ask for an address," boomed Elspeth in a tragic voice.

"I doubt if you'll find anyone in," the man said. "You see, to-day's the Blastwick Carnival. They'll all be on the Slype."

"The Slype?" said Elspeth coldly.

"Yes, that's where we're all going. Perhaps I could help you."

"The name is Otto Killian," said Elspeth. "He is a German farmworker."

When she spoke she gave full value to each syllable, making the voices round her seem to mumble.

"Oh, I know him," the man said, "we all know him here. We shall be passing his place in a moment, but he'll be on the Slype the same as the others."

Leaving her on the doorstep the little party hastened on, relieved. Some drops of rain were falling. Elspeth knocked.

The door opened on a tiny living-room, where four people, two men and two girls, sat playing ludo. They looked up in surprise. A fire was burning in the Queen Anne grate, and though it was only three in the afternoon they had the electric light on—an unshaded bulb which beat down on the tow-headed men and their brown-haired companions.

"Does Otto Killian live here?" Elspeth asked.

"He lives here," said one of the men with a strong German accent, "and we are expecting him to come back."

"May I wait till he comes?" Elspeth asked.

Immediately they made her welcome: the one easy chair was drawn up by the fire for her: the chocolates—in a large gay box that flanked the ludo board—were handed to her. Cigarettes were offered. Elspeth took her ease.

But the game languished in her presence. The veiled glances, the shy flirtation, the exchange of remarks that stopped half-way before they reached a sentence, the fortunes of the game, which no one took seriously except as an accompaniment to a tune played on the heart-strings: a blight crept over them. Another onlooker, according to his mood, might have found the scene touching, or sad, or ironical, or hopeful: the peaceful meeting of once enemy nations; the voices murmuring with different accents, but all shot with laughter; the whispered advice and explanation; the softness on the faces, where they could be seen, the quartet of bowed heads almost touching each other. And presiding over all, the huge chocolate box, piled with chocolates wrapped in silver foil and gold foil, gleaming richly, succulently: the expensive contribution that the men had made to give their celebration a party air, an air of recklessness and extravagance, to do honour to the two English girls, to make them feel how desirable and desired they were, to put them in a melting mood, as melting as the chocolates.

To some all this would have been moving, but not to Elspeth, for her mind was fixed on one thing, and closed to other impressions.

"And why are you not on the Slype?" she intoned at length.

To this they didn't reply, but smiled and exchanged glances as if there could only be one answer.

Then she saw how it was: the explanation flashed on her, and the reason why Otto Killian was not there. His companions had each found a girl, but he had not. That was why he was staying away, out in the rain, on the Slype, whatever it was; that was why he preferred exposure to the elements to this warm, comfortable interior. He didn't want to butt in, still less to parade his hungry girl-less state in their girl-fed presence. It would be a reproach to him. Realizing this, Elspeth rose at once and said:

"I must be getting on my way. Thank you for letting me sit here."

One of the men went with her to the door and bowed her out: he told her where and what the Slype was.

It was still raining gently. Elspeth put up her umbrella, passed the open mouths of one or two long empty streets, and then the great expanse of turf burst into view.

Blastwick was small but the Slype was so large that the whole town could have gone into it. And the whole town had gone into it, or rather round it, for a dipping rope made a vast elliptical enclosure, round which the spectators, seated on chairs or standing two and three deep, watched the proceedings in the middle.

A motor-bicycle race was going on. The competitors, facing backwards to their course, each drew a perambulator in which a man was hunched up, knees to chin. At every bump in the ground the perambulators threatened to fall over, and often did fall, spilling their human freight, who then put their vehicles in going order and climbed in again. Much laughter greeted their mishaps, and cheers announced the winner; but to Elspeth it all seemed unbearably childish and irrelevant. Her eyes on the spectators, not the spectacle, she began to circumambulate the immense area.

Here there were sideshows mounted on lorries and drawn up by the rope-side, waiting their turn to parade before the judges—how should one describe them? Some came obviously from the neighbouring camps, and showed the soldiers' sense of humour. One truck was styled The Devil's Cook-house. Men with blackened faces and blackened bodies, wearing white cooks' hats but dressed as devils where they were not naked, with pitchforks stoked a smoking tar-boiler. At intervals they scooped out of its depths and ladled into dixies the nauseous liquid, which they then offered to their hungry customers—only to have it waved away with airs of well-bred scorn. Their glistening, rain-streaked bodies shivered in the blast. Sometimes a customer would stick out his foot and neatly send a diabolic cook's-mate sprawling, whereupon the victim jumped up nimbly, flourishing his pitchfork and holding his long tail in a manner at once delicate and provocative. Further on came a more sophisticated exhibit: "The Studio of Dior" it was called, and Elspeth, much as she despised all this, did vaguely wonder who in Blastwick had ever heard of Dior. Here, too, the mannequins were men: dressed in every kind of plume and flounce, jingling with barbaric necklaces, and painted red, they posed and minced and strutted up and down their platform, swaying their hips and sticking out their bottoms; nor did the rain, which bedraggled their finery, in the least damp their ardour.

Disgusted, Elspeth twitched her gloves under the loose grey woollen sleeves, and turned her gaze from the spectacle to the spectators, who were quite thick at this point, though only mildly amused by what was being shown them.

Ten minutes had gone by, and she had almost completed the circuit, without a glimpse of him she was in search of, when a new event began: this was men on horseback, variously attired. Red Indians, generals, bareback riders, clergymen and clowns trotted or galloped past her field of vision. Last of all came a figure riding a white horse. Who could this be? Almost nude save for an exaggerated pink brassière, the figure was unquestionably a man's; from his head hung a great mane of straw-coloured hair, which sometimes wrapped him round, and sometimes streamed behind. Alone of the competitors, he couldn't control his steed; every moment he looked like falling off. Alone and left behind, out of the procession, out of the competition, almost out of the picture, his horse, going crabwise, passed so near to Elspeth that she could see the label on its crupper: Lady Godiva, it said.

Something startled the horse: it reared and plunged. Down came its rider in a flat dive which must have knocked the breath out of his body, for the pneumatic squelch could be heard yards away. He lay without moving, while roars of laughter, the most spontaneous signs of enjoyment that the crowd had shown, burst out all round him. Indifferently Elspeth wondered if he was dead, or hurt, or shamming; and then the man picked himself up and looked round him with the desperate, hunted eyes of an animal hemmed in by a ring of fire. In the fall his headdress had come off; it lay beside him, a sort of coconut, to which were attached long streamers of coarse tow, twisted and matted by the rain. His own hair was of much the same colour, but cropped to convict shortness. Standing, he revealed himself as a man of giant stature. His horse had ambled off to another part of the field: someone came out and led it away.

Elspeth had never seen a face which looked as if life held less in store for it. He had ceased to look about him, he had an inward-turning gaze with which he sought to neutralize

294

the stare of the spectators. Then he raised his eyes to heaven as though in supplication, and began to fumble with the brassière, the ridiculous, indecent brassière, trying to take it off; but couldn't reach the fastening between his shoulder-blades. At this the crowd roared again and he desisted, perhaps for fear of making more of a fool of himself than he had already, or of appearing more naked than he was already, for his only other garment was a bathing-suit. His hands dropped to his sides, and he looked as bereft of dignity as any human being could.

He was only a few feet away from Elspeth. It would be too much to say that she felt sorry for him, but she took in his plight and saw in it her opportunity. "Is your name Otto Killian?" she asked.

He seemed to have difficulty in focusing her, and in understanding what she said, but he nodded.

"I thought so," she said. "Come over here, will you?"

Command was as natural to her as obedience was to him; and she had mercifully broken the ring of isolation that surrounded him. Grateful, he stepped over the low rope and stood beside her, looking shyly down at her, seeming more at his ease. It made a poignant contrast, his nakedness and her dressiness, and many eyes were turned their way, but Elspeth did not heed them: the next item was beginning, and would soon distract them. The rain hadn't left off: it was running down his body, making the sodden brassière stick to his chest muscles. She felt she must be quick.

"I have something to tell you," she said. "There is a girl called Irma——"

It didn't take her long to say what she had to say. She laid it on, she did not spare him, and if in the recital he lost his flicker of self-assurance, and looked, if possible, more woe-begone and desperate than before, she welcomed it, for it was the reaction she had hoped for. She had put a spoke in that wheel, anyway. Leaving him, for the carnival had lost what little interest it had ever had for her, she looked back, and saw him jerk his elbow upwards in a sudden convulsive gesture, which brought the back of his hand across his eyes, as if he had been blinded: and a picture floated into her mind—Polyphemus being taunted by Ulysses.

34

IT was a long time since Isabel had thought seriously about Irma, indeed, since she had thought about her at all. From the moment when Alec made it plain, to Isabel at any rate, that it was her he wanted, Irma had passed out of her mind. Now she and Alec were its chief occupants.

Isabel's thoughts were just to Irma. She realized that she, more than anyone else, was to blame for what had happened. She had done her best to bring Alec and Irma together: it was what she had wished for both of them, rationally, as she believed, for Irma, emotionally, as she now saw, for Alec. If Alec had taken up with Irma from the start, she would, she thought, have given it her blessing. Giving him Irma, she would have given him herself. Irma was her substitute.

Or so it had seemed then. In the light of her present feelings she believed that she would have minded it as much then as she did now.

For her feelings were not fair to Irma. Her feelings regarded Irma as an interloper who, like Jacob, had stolen the blessing from her. To Irma belonged the credit for Alec's masterpiece, if masterpiece it was, and to Isabel the shabby rôle of *entrepreneuse*. This was how he had seen it, in his book: not as an act of self-abnegation on her part, but as something done with an eye to the main chance. The beauty in the book was all for the Italian maid, who, by her long resistance to what Isabel had snatched at, convinced the roving sensualist (not a novelist) who was the hero of the story, that in woman, or in some women, could be found a quality of intelligent self-sacrifice which nourishes life, as opposed to the sheer will of the male, which devastates it. But this discovery he had made in spite of Isabel, not because of her: she was "the Constant Nymphomaniac."

Harold had got off lightly. A rising barrister (the social position of the Eastwoods had been much stepped up, another sop to Cerberus), he had welcomed the explorer (for as such Alec had portrayed himself) to his home, all the more gladly, it is true, because the explorer had put some business in his way; but he didn't realize what the man was up to, or what his wife was up to, until the end, when he behaved far better than anyone would have expected of him.

Harold was in the clear; his wife and the explorer were the villains of the piece, and of the two Isabel came out worse; there was very little to be said of her.

She began to confuse herself with the character in the story whose prototype she was, and half to believe that the thoughts and actions attributed to her there were really hers. Who was she then, this composite human being who was slowly—oh, so slowly—making her way to Irma's lodgings? She had lost track of herself. The image of herself that she had grown up with was flawed and seamed beyond all recognition. Who was she? She could no longer accept her own estimate of herself, and she wouldn't accept Alec's. But all this was like something someone else was telling her: it wasn't really related to the pain in her mind, which wasn't analysable.

Her steps came still more slowly. Should she retrace them? That would mean returning to the fetish in the hat-box, and the insoluble problem of what to do with it. Some sort of action was imperative, and this one seemed to be the outcome of all the forces working on her. Choice it was not: it was some kind of compulsion.

Her ring was answered by the landlady. Yes, Miss Irma was at home. Irma was sitting by the window reading. The room was so small that it looked like a cell, not a bed-sitting-room: the narrow iron bed, with its white counterpane, was like a property, not like a real bed. All the prettiness was concentrated round the window—curtains and flowers and a checked table-cloth.

Irma jumped up.

"Oh, Mrs. Eastwood!"

She laid the book down, face upwards. It was one of Alec's novels.

"Oh," said Isabel, when they had shaken hands, "I see you are reading that!"

Irma made her sit down in the easy chair and drew up the other.

"Yes," she said. "You were kind enough to lend it to me, do you remember, and I'm enjoying it. But——" She spread out her hands.

"What were you going to say?" asked Isabel.

"Only that his way of looking at us seems so sad."

"At us?" said Isabel.

"Well, pardon if I do not quite explain myself, but we are both women, although you are a lady."

"I see," said Isabel. "Yes, we are both women, but we don't come into the book, do we?"

Irma laughed.

"Oh no, we don't come into it, Mrs. Eastwood, I am glad to say. If you and I came into it, the things that happen wouldn't have happened, if you understand me. His women are so false and hurtful and we——" She stopped.

"He has just written another book," said Isabel slowly, "and we do come into it, Irma, both of us."

She heard herself speaking, but without being conscious of herself uttering the words: they were like sounds projected on the air.

"Pardon, but I do not quite understand," said Irma. "What is this book, if I may ask?"

"It is a book," began Isabel, "it is a book . . . a novel. . . . He wrote it a little while ago, after he had been here, and got to know us. We all come into it, you, and I, and he, and Harold, my husband. It is about us, you see."

"About us?" Irma turned pale and began to interlace her fingers. "But surely, Mrs. Eastwood. . . . How can he have done such a cruel thing? We never did him any harm, did we? But do not believe what he says, Mrs. Eastwood, it is all false, I'm sure it is!"

"I wish I could think so," Isabel said, "but I'm afraid it's true."

She gave Irma a long, deep, sad look, it was not accusing, but a simple recognition of the facts.

"Oh, but it is not possible," said Irma wildly, "that he say such things about me! Why, he hardly knows me! Do not believe him, Mrs. Eastwood, please do not believe him!"

"I'm afraid it is true," Isabel repeated. "Not true to circumstances, of course, but true essentially. I haven't come to reproach you, Irma——"

"Oh," cried Irma, rising from the chair, and standing behind it, clasping it for support. "But you wouldn't have come to see me, if you thought——"

"That's why I did come," Isabel said, "to hear it from your own lips."

There was a long pause, then Irma said, "I have been wrong, so wrong. . . . But, Mrs. Eastwood, I did not mean to hurt you, I really did not! It was because he seemed . . . but how can I say this to you? He seemed so lonely, and then he was so sweet! He is sweet, Mrs. Eastwood. I did not really want to. I cried——" She was crying now. "I said, oh, many things. I said no, many times. I did not think I could so often say no. Oh, I would not have hurt you! But I was lonely, too, here in this place. I do not seek to excuse myself. Men, they are not like us, they want something. . . . And so it happened, because we were lonely. . . . But how could he be lonely, you may say, when he had you? But, Mrs. Eastwood, there is always somewhere, some corner of the heart that isn't filled, and it was there I crept in, but I didn't mean to, and I know it is you he really loves."

Looking at Irma's face, and listening to her voice, which was more eloquent than her words, Isabel began to entertain another feeling, and a softer one, than the harsh facts seemed to warrant, and Irma noticed this.

"Oh, but he is so good," she went on. "You know that better than I. And yet, please forgive me for saying it, there may be something I understand of him more than you do, though you are his wife——"

"His wife?" said Isabel, and it might have been "knife," by the way the word cut the air. "His wife? Whom are we talking of?" She began to laugh hysterically. "I am not Alec's wife."

"Alec? Alec?" repeated Irma, utterly bewildered. "Oh, Mr. Goodrich." She spoke as if it was a faraway name, taken at random from the telephone book. "No, it was Harrold I was speaking of, your husband, Harrold. Mr. Goodrich, he is just a writer. It is of Harrold I speak, and I was going to say, for I could never say it again, not any other time, but only now, because I must never see him again, no, I must not, nor you, Mrs. Eastwood, that he is very sweet, a dear, dear man."

She ended almost defiantly, and as if challenging Isabel to contradict her: it was the one flash of her own feeling for Harrold that she allowed herself, the one note of possessiveness.

She swayed and Isabel jumped up and helped her into the easy chair, where she sat sobbing uncontrollably. She is too frail for so much emotion, Isabel thought, and it was the first thought she had had since she read Alec's book that was not about herself. I shouldn't have put this strain on her, she thought. What relief, what healing there was in self-reproach. Released and at a little distance from herself she murmured, "Please don't cry." It hurt her that Irma would not look at her, but covered her eyes with her hand: ought I to go? she thought. A moment before it hadn't seemed to matter where she was. Why had the load shifted from her heart? She couldn't take in this new situation or size up what Irma's revelation meant to her; how could it have improved things? Yet somehow it had—the book, the book no longer seemed as though it was her death-warrant: she had found a way out of its cruel pages: she had her own existence now, even if that existence was bound up with an unfaithful husband, who was also a dear, dear man.

At last Irma took her hand away from her eyes and looked at Isabel.

"And so he said all this?" she said. "Mr. Goodrich said it, in his book?"

"No, no, he didn't," Isabel said. How much could she tell Irma of what he *had* said? After Irma's confession she found the position of a virtuous wife rebuking sin impossible to hold. Two mistresses, two ex-mistresses, consoling each other, that was what they were. "I was in love with him," she said, and seeing no surprise on Irma's face she added, "Well, perhaps you guessed that. And I thought he was in love with me, but he wasn't . . . not . . . not in the book. We were lovers, but it was all on my side. It was you he really loved."

"Me?" said Irma.

"Yes. He looked through me, over me, past me, to you—and, well, loving you did for him what I thought I had done: you gave him what he wanted—just the thought of you gave it him."

"But I was not his mistress?" asked Irma anxiously. "Not his mistress, in the book? Because I never, never, never could have been."

Idly Isabel asked, "Why not?"

"Oh, because I am not like that. Oh, please believe me, Mrs. Eastwood. There is a hollowness inside him, there is something missing. Where he should love there is an empti-ness—just thoughts and words. And what he wish to happen, in his book he make it happen—to feel sad or happy, while he is writing it. That is his art, where he lives: he does not live in his life. Why, Mrs. Eastwood, that lady told us so, when she made that talk to the Institute of Women. She said, but I don't remember the words as she said them, that a novelist translates and trans . . . trans . . . trans. . . ."

"Transposes, perhaps," said Isabel.

"Transposes his feelings from one person to another, from you to me, it might be, Mrs. Eastwood, because he cannot love a nice good woman with a home and children, because that would be too ordinary, too dull, anyone might do it, but he must love a common barmaid and pretend that she is nice. But how can she be, for she is only a barmaid, not a lady, not good, not clever, not even English, nothing—it is all pretence, all put on, as you say. And that is what he has done, Mrs. Eastwood; he's put me in your place, I know he has, to make it all come right in his mind. If he had known me, he couldn't have written about me as you say he did. Oh no! He would have grown sick of me in fifteen minutes. Pouf! Pouf!" And Irma blew herself out like a candle. "He would have laughed at me!" She laughed at herself, through tears. "We must not be too angry with him, we must not hate him, because, you see, he is not made like us. He think to himself, 'Let us have some goodness for a change, a good woman, instead of those dreadful women,' oh dear, oh dear" (Irma shook her head sadly for the dreadful women), "he have had in his books: all nails and claws they are, scratch, scratch. And then he finds her in you, this good woman, but he thinks 'Oh, no, I cannot copy what I see, no artist copies' (the lady said that to the Institute of Women, Mrs. Eastwood) 'so I will trans . . . trans. . . .'"

"Transpose," said Isabel.

"'Transpose her into this . . . this bloody barmaid' (excuse me, Mrs. Eastwood, but that is what they say when I am out of the room: 'Where is that bloody barmaid?'), 'so I shall not be copying, I shall be inventing and creating, I shall be mixing myself with what I write, because you would not look to find such goodness in a barmaid.' And if he had looked, Mrs. Eastwood, what would he have found? What I have just told you, nothing good at all, just very bad, which was to be expected."

Irma's tears started afresh. She looked at Isabel despairingly and said:

"Yes, very bad, too bad to speak of, and how shall I say?— a fault of taste as well, that I did speak of it to you. I don't count now. I'm out of it. But something I hand on, saying good-bye"—she searched for words—"it is for Harrold's sake, not mine, that you should see——"

"Yes, what?" said Isabel, when Irma paused.

"Oh, nothing—but something that I saw and you didn't see."

"Something he showed to you, perhaps, some side of himself that he didn't show to me," said Isabel.

"Well, but it's there, you'll find it, yes, I promise. I have . . . I have *fixed* it for you," Irma said.

They rose to shake hands.

"But it isn't good-bye," said Isabel.

"Oh yes, I think it must be. Because, you see, now I shall get married."

"Get married?" Isabel echoed.

"Yes, get married, and stop being a barmaid, and go to live in another place, in Blastwick." She laughed and for a moment all her gaiety returned. "You think no one will marry me? But he will, he has asked me many times. It is Otto Killian, a farm-worker, I told you of him. He is a great strong man, and very rough, and terribly, terribly jealous.

Ooh!" said Irma, closing her eyes in rapture at the thought of Otto's jealousy. "But I shall tame him, for he is really very good and very sweet, and next time he asks me, I shall say, Please, yes!"

The smile that was like a blessing was still on Irma's face when the two women parted at the door.

35

ITS glow remained with Isabel, too, as she walked home-wards. What had happened, she asked herself, that had so altered and restored her mind? A sordid revelation, sur-prised almost by a trick, though an unconscious trick, out of an ignorant girl?—a revelation that, as a married woman, she should have minded more than any: it should have been the last dregs of her humiliation. But somehow it wasn't; and far from never wanting to see Harold again, she found herself wanting to see him, wanting to see him very much—at this moment, now—she quickened her pace, but of course he wouldn't be home yet.

It was a wet, blustery day: the rain was falling: she put up her umbrella. How snug she felt, under its shelter! And how snug Marshport looked, with the great church tower standing sentinel. Yes, and more than snug — it was romantic, picturesque, unique, with its enfolded contrasts of civilian and soldier, hill and plain, slow waveless canal and, outside, the hungry, howling sea. How could she have ever thought it tame and townish when so much history clung to it, when round the corner, only just out of sight, was the castle from which the four knights rode away?

For the first time her thoughts turned to Alec, and behold, the pain was gone, or nearly gone. Not Alec the traitor but Alec the transposer, the transposer of experience and emotion, the master of transposition. Isabel hadn't really believed that bit; what had won her, softened her, was Irma's wanting her to believe it. Alec had been very, very naughty. "Being in love with someone is the only excuse for behaving badly to them," he had once said. With her, he hadn't even that excuse. But hadn't they all been naughty, even Harold, even Irma naughty, and did not their naughtinesses cancel each other out? There was much comfort in that thought.

She began to climb the hill to Tilecotes, between the

hedged-in gardens, so trim in spring and summer, now all unkempt with autumn's disarray. Even their tidiness had had to give way before a power greater than their owners wielded—those owners in their shirt-sleeves with their shears and clippers, so active and intent on summer evenings! Now all their efforts seemed of no avail, but in the spring!——

The first thing was to take the fetish from the hat-box: only it was no longer a fetish, it had been decontaminated: it was a work of the imagination, composed of very interesting transpositions, a fine work, perhaps the author's best, and it must at once go back to him, for he would be worrying about it. No note, no note should be enclosed: it was not yet time for that: that should go later. No explanation should accompany it, and the address should be in printed characters—as if a poison-pen had written them. Later, Susan should take the precious parcel to the Royal and leave it without a word. How he would wonder where it came from!

No secrecy, no tiptoeing, no furtive glancing at the glass to see if she was tall enough to-day. Isabel fetched paper and string and arranged the sealing-wax and matches and scissors on the dining-room table, as though to wrap up an ordinary parcel.

Now it was done; the die was cast: she hadn't realized that a doubt still lingered, but there must have been one, to judge by her relief.

When the telephone bell rang, she would answer it.

The minutes passed and Isabel sat, her gaze travelling to and fro between the parcel and the telephone, impatient at having to wait for time to confirm what her mind had already settled. Susan came in to lay the tea-table.

"Has anyone rung up?" Isabel asked.

"No, Madam. I hope you are feeling better?"

"Oh yes, quite well, thank you."

Isabel had forgotten she was supposed to be feeling ill.

She would give Alec until six o'clock, and if he hadn't rung up by then she would ring him up.

A fever, a fury, a demon of forgiveness possessed her. Everyone must be forgiven, everyone, starting and finishing with herself. In ecstasy she murmured to herself the lines:

> Throughout all eternity
> I forgive you, you forgive me.

She wanted to hand out bouquets to everyone. How beautifully we have all behaved!

To whom should the first bunch go? To Harold, undoubtedly. She did not blame him for his affair with Irma: she was almost grateful to him for it, for had it not taken away her own reproach? And made him much more interesting, besides? She could never again take for granted, still less despise in her secret heart, someone who had been a dear, dear man to another woman. What did he need? What did he want? What present should she give him? She realized she didn't know his needs and wants; for years she hadn't studied them. She gave him presents at Christmas, of course: gloves, handkerchiefs, a scarf, even a tie—that dangerous present to a man. What matter if he didn't like it? It was still a present. Now she thought of him minutely, inch by inch. What colour represented him, what time of day? If she thought of enough analogies for him, one of them might yield the present, one might even *be* the present. It was delicious thinking up analogies for Harold. Small, spare, tight, tidy—something that was the essence of itself, that didn't overflow, or sprawl, or superabound—a malacca cane, for instance, or a shooting-stick?

And Irma, what should she have? To Irma she owed everything, she felt. Her time with Irma had been a cure; Irma had wrought a miracle upon her, Irma had freed her from the bondage of the book, had given her back a life outside it. But for Irma, she might now be floating in the canal, Ophelia-like among the autumn leaves. For Irma it must be something that she, Isabel, liked herself, a present she would not want to give away; it must have the element of sacrifice. Fusing herself with Irma, she tried to find their highest common factor: how difficult to express it in concrete terms: how easy in terms of love! Her love, Irma already had: but it was too cheap a present. A bed, perhaps, to replace that iron one? Poor wounded name, my bosom

as a bed shall lodge thee. It would be nice to think of Irma
sleeping warmly, soundly, comfortably; and it would be a
sort of sacrifice, for she had long wanted to change the bed
she shared with Harold: she had wanted (but how believe
that now?) to change it for two beds. Irma's would be a
single bed, but very, very lovely. . . .

And Alec? Did she really want to give him a present?
Was he still within the circle of her love? Experimentally
she flashed the spotlight on him. Did it quite reach him?
Yes, it did, with a warm, generalized ray, the ray of friendship, not the ray of passion. What present could she give
him, when he had everything, including (she smiled to think
of it) the fluctuating dividend from Ecuador that irritated
Harold? But there was one present, one, that only she could
give him, and it lay on the table, ready to be taken to him.

To whom else could she show gratitude for this great
deliverance?

Suddenly Jeremy and Janice were upon her, no, not upon
her, for they came in with exaggerated quietness, and kept
away from her as if she was a leper. In Jeremy this was not
unusual, but for Janice to be so subdued was quite portentous. Tiptoeing towards her, Janice said:

"Are you better, Mummy?"

"Why, who said I was ill?"

"Well, Susan did. She said: 'Your Mummy's not herself.
She isn't well enough to have Mr. Goodrich in the house'."

At this intrusion of the outer world, the cynical,
unregenerate outer world, an enormous lassitude spread
through Isabel. After living with emotions, how could she
face facts, facts from the past, that were like a hangover on
the morning of a new day, with no relation to her present
feelings? A sensation of emptiness succeeded, a horrible
vacuity that would not let in anything from outside; and
then again impatience, impatience with Time for not
conspiring with her, for going in slow motion, keeping her
on tenterhooks.

"Tea! tea!" she cried, and sat down behind the teapot.

"But isn't Mr. Goodrich coming?" Janice asked. "You've
always wanted him to come, you know you have! And he'll
have brought us presents—don't you want us to have them?"

"Sh, Janice, Mummy's thinking!" Jeremy said.

Oh yes, she was thinking, but thinking to no purpose; and here was Harold, and he said:

"Well, old girl, how have you been keeping? Headache any better?"

Keeping—as if she was something in a larder!

That they could all be oblivious to her spiritual crisis! But of course they were; no inkling could they have of what had happened to her. She glanced towards the parcel, now lying on the sideboard.

"Alec has not shown up, has he?" Harold asked. When she didn't answer, he repeated the question: "Has old Alec given any sign of life?"

"Well, no, he hasn't," Isabel said.

"What about stirring him up? We could give him some dinner, couldn't we?"

"I'm afraid it's too late to do anything now."

"Well, shall I phone him, and ask him to feed with us to-morrow? We really must do something for the poor old bird."

"What time is it?" asked Isabel.

"Just half-past five."

"Let's wait an hour," said Isabel. "I . . . rather think he's working and won't want to be disturbed."

"Oh well, in *that* case! Mustn't interrupt the genius-work."

He smiled at Isabel, a warm, knowing smile.

Why did she still shrink from making peace with Alec? Had the wound not healed? Was she becoming once again the prisoner of the book, a thin ghost crushed between its pages?

"When you've spoken to him," she said, "call me, and I'll come and speak to him."

"Why, won't you be here?"

"I may be doing something upstairs."

The minutes went by on leaden feet. At twenty-five-past six Isabel, as casually as she could, withdrew. She crept up to her bedroom, fell on her knees, and prayed for strength to speak to Alec. The forgiveness had not been as complete as she imagined.

308

But as she prayed it seemed to come, come in a fuller measure than before, and with more sense of reality. Praying, she felt her father's influence on her, to whom forgiveness had not been just a mood, a transient mood, such as a drink might conjure up, but a reality based on experience. She sought for help from Irma, too, and thought she had it, so vivid was her vision of the girl, with downcast glowing eyes, and face alight, waving good-bye.

Still on her knees, but ready now, she waited for Harold's call. Her prayer had seemed timeless, but now Time nudged her elbow, literally almost: for her elbow, pressing on the bed, had gone to sleep. What a long talk they must be having! Harold didn't like long telephone conversations, but Alec did. How should she begin? "Hullo, Alec, it's Isabel!" Or should she take a deep breath and say, "Hullo, Alec, it's Monica!"—the name he had given her in the book?

Then all the cards would be on the table.

Still Harold hadn't called her, and it was nearly seven. She stole downstairs. Harold was sitting in the lounge, not near the telephone. It didn't look like him, but it must be he, for who else could it be?

"You didn't call me?" said Isabel, to this stranger.

Looking up at her, he tried to speak, but couldn't, and shook his head.

She came up to him and said, "Why, darling, what's the matter? Didn't you telephone?"

"Yes, I did," said Harold at last. "And there's bad news, Isabel. An accident . . . two accidents. . . ."

"To whom?"

"Well, one was to Alec . . . and the other"—his voice choked—"to the girl at the bar—you knew her, Irma."

"What sort of accident, Harold? A motor accident?"

"No, worse than that: shooting. He shot them both."

"Who shot them?"

"A German fellow did. He's given himself up."

"Were they together, then?"

"No, no, not together."

In the room all sounds seemed to cease, and all sights faded out but one: the brown paper parcel on the sideboard.

36

WHEN Alec's novel came out, seven months later, Isabel and
Harold had removed from Marshport to a large town west
of London. Harold had business interests there: it wasn't
only that they found the thought of living on in Marshport
unendurable. This brought them within easy reach of their
respective mothers, which had not seemed a desirable
arrangement once, but now seemed to be so, for they both
felt the need of other than social ties. The trial had done
what seemed impossible, brought Mrs. Knighton and Mrs.
Eastwood senior together: in making a common family
front they sank their differences.

Alec had not given the book a title, but his literary
executors had decided to call it *The Italian Maid*. To-day
was Sunday: during the week reviews of Alec's book had
appeared in two newspapers. Isabel had kept them, but she
could not bring herself to read what the critics said; she sat
musing, and wishing Harold would come. He had mysterious
Sunday morning occupations, masculine rites connected
with the garden or the car, often involving the use of a
tool-box. This did not mean he would have to change for
church: he could do the dirtiest job without making himself
dirty. When he comes, she thought, I'll ask him to read the
reviews aloud to me. Once she would not have asked him
to do this, and he would not have wanted to.

She was ashamed of her faint-heartedness. It was the last
relic of the stand her weaker nature had put up against
remembering the trial and all that had led up to it. After
the dark days when Isabel held herself to blame for everything came days of panic: remorse was swamped by fear.
All would come out, she thought: her life and Harold's
would be ruined. This didn't happen; nor did she feel again,
except at times, the pangs of extreme guilt and the gnawing
sense of sorrow: she built up a defence-mechanism to make
her memories more bearable. She knew she ought to face

those memories and acquire an attitude towards them, based on a synthesis of all the issues: too often she took refuge in imagining what might have happened if—and following the line of thought to a conclusion happier than the real one. If only she hadn't told Elspeth about Otto Killian! At the time it hadn't seemed like mischief-making; how could she have known what Elspeth had in mind?

Scenes from the court came back to her, snatches without sequence. Elspeth had borne herself magnificently. She had not come forward at first, which went against her, and the police had almost as much difficulty in tracing her as other people had. She was not to be found at St. Milo's: and the servants there did not know her address. But for once her gift of invisibility had failed her; failed her with the police, failed her at Blastwick, for the four ludo-players identified her, the spectators who had seen her talking to Killian identified her, and Killian identified her himself.

Why did you, counsel asked, tell him this cruel story? What good could it do? To this she answered frankly and with dignity that for eighteen years she had lived on intimate terms with Alexander Goodrich, and when she knew that he was carrying on with another woman she took the most obvious steps she knew to stop it. She told the man whose girl he had seduced what the position was. How could she guess the man would do what he did do?

Here she broke down. Dressed in deepest black, possessing more personal force than anyone else in the court, the judge included, and more ability to get it over, she made a great impression. The fact that she had been Alec's mistress did not go against her, as it might have done once: it invested her with romance and won the sympathy of almost everyone. Elspeth was extremely photogenic: the pictures of her leaving the court would have moved a heart of stone. The counsel for the defence heckled her: "I put it to you that you acted out of spite?" "I acted as my heart told me to act," she answered; "and as any woman who loved as I loved would have acted." Thus she established her common humanity with the erring: the safest position that anyone can take up. "I suggest to you that you worked upon his feelings," counsel went on, "that you deliberately inflamed the passions of this simple, faithful man, and made him what is called 'see red'?" "I only told him," she replied, "what any man who is a man would want to know: that the girl he trusted was deceiving him." "Deceiving him with the man whose mistress you were," counsel said, allowing himself a sneer. "It wasn't very pretty, was it?" "With the man whose mistress I had been for eighteen years," she answered, "and whose wife I should have been if I hadn't known too well his tendency to stray." Eighteen years faithful to an unfaithful man: there was a proof of staunchness, if you like! This grey-haired woman lost nothing by advertising her age. But counsel had another shot in his locker. "Is it true," he asked, "that those eighteen years passed more happily for you than for the very distinguished man of letters to whom you had, if I may put it so, attached yourself? Is it not true that you did, as someone has said, persecute this long-suffering man with your malignant fidelity? And that, at the very moment when this tragedy occurred, he was doing his utmost to terminate those eighteen years?"

Many felt that this was an unfair as well as an ungentlemanly question. "He may have been," she said. "It wouldn't surprise me. He had left me many times, only to come crawling back." But counsel's discomfiture was only momentary. "And how did you discover," he asked, "this last instance of his infidelity? Did you employ a private detective, or did you do your own snooping?" The counsel for the prosecution protested against this question, but it was allowed. "I used my wits," she answered, "as I had had to use them often before. A friend of Alexander Goodrich's, a Mrs. Eastwood, gave me some information."

This was how Isabel came into it. In the end she got off lightly because she held a trump card: the fact that Elspeth had stolen Alec's manuscript. This Isabel had returned to Alec's executors, saying it had come into her possession, but not saying how. Others besides Isabel knew of Alec's loss: the servants at St. Milo's knew. If Elspeth had wanted to involve her further in the business she wouldn't have dared to, with this threat of exposure hanging over her. But Isabel went through much agony of mind wondering if the secret of her relationship to Alec would come out, and Harold was no less alarmed on his own account. Asked if she knew Irma, Isabel said yes, she knew her well. Asked if she knew Alec, she also said yes. Asked if she thought Irma had been Alec's mistress, she said she did not know.

This was a lie, of course, more, it was perjury, and she hated saying it—not least on Irma's account, who had so passionately denied that she was or could have been Alec's mistress. All the information she had given Mrs. Elworthy, she said, was the name and whereabouts of Otto Killian.

"Why did you give her them?"

"Because she asked me."

"You had no wish to injure the dead woman?"

"None."

That at least was true, but Isabel owed her escape from further questioning to a lie. And out of court, in daily life, when the case was discussed, suppression of the truth became a habit with her: she had to keep a watch upon her tongue lest she should give herself away.

She tried not to worry about this, but it blurred her image of herself as someone who didn't do that kind of thing. She felt she had invalidated her own judgment. Apart from moral questions, she hesitated to give her opinion on any problem: what right had she to speak? She felt that anything she said came from a tainted source—as if, to borrow a simile from Harold's world, with which she was now so much more familiar, she had been a fraudulent financier asked to give his opinion on the value of an invest-ment. Her parents had, according to their lights, maintained their respective standards of value. She had let hers down.

Well, well, perhaps it was a useful lesson in humility. At least some people would have said it was, though she herself distrusted such reasoning, and thought it amounted to acquiescence in an ever-falling standard, with a special clause to exculpate herself.

Sometimes she half wished she hadn't got off so lightly, and thought that a good dose of punishment might have put her on better terms with herself. Sometimes she wished that the symptom she had taken to the doctor hadn't turned out to be a false alarm, for an incarnation of her experience with Alec, its expression in flesh and blood, with the prime necessity to love it, rather than analyse and brood over it, would have banished the abstractions, the warring abstractions that beset her mind. She was all too prone to see herself as a case, a moral instance, neatly divided into pros and cons. After all, she was a living entity, not the sum of what she thought about herself, or what other people might think about her.

So her life was muted and subdued. She enjoyed herself quite often: but she didn't often enjoy being herself—that simple pleasure we are all entitled to. Considering herself, using the word "I", she started with a handicap, something to catch up, something to get over. One's nature demands fulfilment in the present: she couldn't fulfil hers. She suffered from a form of self-dislike, and felt that if people knew more about her they would dislike her too. She would be outside the pale of normal human sympathy, and tolerated only by the understanding and the well-disposed. She was under sufferance, on probation, and anyone could catch her out. Light-weight her words, light-weight her thoughts, light-weight her feelings; who was she to speak, or think, or feel?

She had an uneasy feeling that though they had forgiven each other, she and Harold, much still remained to forgive. If together they gave the impression that a good time was being had by all, it was a false impression, so far as Isabel was concerned. The sunlessness, the haze over her spirits affected everything she did; her spiritual account, she felt, was overdrawn, and she would never get back into the clear.

But there was one thing: thanks to Irma she had been delivered from the tyranny of the book. However dimly she lived, she lived outside its pages, she was not book-bound.

And there was another thing, much more important. The episode had brought her very close to Harold: theirs was now a real relationship of heart and mind. They had no secrets from each other. She did not always want to confide in him, or he in her, but when they wanted to, they could. Each was conscious of the other as a person in his or her own right, a person who for a short time had meant to someone else as much as any human being can do—a sovereign with one adoring subject—no, that wasn't true, for Harold had meant more to Irma than she, apparently, had ever meant to Alec. Still it was nearly the same thing. Each brought to their relationship, and pooled, this gift of personal sovereignty which neither had possessed before, or recognized in the other.

Harold had been luckier in a way than she had; his grief for Irma had been a natural manifestation of feeling, without guilt or after-thoughts: it had run its course and purged itself, leaving no complications. Harold was an extrovert, thank goodness.

She herself did not grieve over-much for Irma, for her last impression of the girl lived on in her mind as one of such singular beauty that death had crowned, not killed. It was only when she thought of Otto Killian, detained during the Queen's pleasure, that her thoughts sometimes became unbearable. Without a word to his housemates he had ridden over to Marshport on his motor-bicycle, his shot-gun slung behind him. Irma's landlady was out: the girl herself was getting ready to go to the Green Dragon, and he must have shot her almost at sight, for the scarf she wore was half tied round her head. Then he went to the Royal, and asked for Mr. Goodrich. He didn't wait inside the hotel, but went back to his motor-bicycle. Alec, to whom his name meant nothing, but who was always pleased to talk to strangers, went down the steps to meet him and the porter thought they did speak for a moment before the gun went off.

Isabel reconstructed these scenes in many ways, and they always brought an urgent need for Harold's presence—as they did now.

"Harold!"

"I'm just coming, old girl, wait a minute, I'll be with you."

After about five minutes he appeared, wearing the refreshed and youthful look he always had after his encounters with the tool-box.

"There are some reviews of Alec's book. It's coming out to-morrow. I wish you'd read them to me: I don't feel up to reading them myself."

"Which one shall I read?"

"I don't think it matters."

"I hope they will be favourable."

"Why?" asked Isabel.

"Well, you know, because of El Dorado."

"El Dorado" was one of several facetious, allusive euphemisms they had invented for Alec's settlement on the children. Isabel still tried not to think of it, and speaking of it was sure to bring on one of her most far-reaching blushes.

Struggling with this, as with a hydra, she inquired:

"What did you last hear from the publishers?"

"That advance interest was most encouraging," Harold replied. He meant to sound lugubrious, but cheerfulness broke in. "And by the way," he added, "Alec's dividend from South America turned up yesterday, you know, the fluctuating one."

"Was it a big one?" Isabel asked.

"Oh yes," said Harold cautiously, "quite big."

"How big?"

"Well, four figures."

"Harold," commanded Isabel, "I insist on knowing the exact sum."

"One thousand three hundred and forty-nine pounds six shillings, if you want to know," said Harold, with the air of a stone giving up its blood. "Poor old Alec. . . . Now"— he cleared his throat—"shall I begin?"

"You may as well."

"Have you the brandy ready?"

At that moment there was a shuffling and scratching outside the door, the door itself swayed to and fro, and in came the children, Janice as usual leading.

"We were playing in the garden," Janice said.

"What were you playing?"

"Oh, some old game. I don't quite remember. Oh yes, I do, the 'ladder game' it was."

"I didn't think you played that now," said Isabel.

"Well, not so much, because Jeremy says it's stale. But this morning we did play it because, you see, it's still my favourite, favourite, *favourite* game."

"But I didn't hear Jeremy call out 'Janice, go back'," said Isabel.

"Oh no," put in Jeremy, bending over Janice with his grave, considering look. "Because now she does go back."

"You mean without being told to?"

"Yes, sometimes."

A look of extreme cunning spread over Janice's face, and her gleaming eyes sought first her father's, then her mother's.

"You see he likes it better that way," she explained.

"I do see. . . . And now, children, you must run away because Daddy's going to read me something."

"Oh, but we want to hear!"

"It wouldn't interest you a bit."

"Oh, but it would, it's my favourite, favourite, *favourite*—— What's it about?"

Isabel drew a long breath. Children shouldn't be deceived or put off with excuses. "It's a review in the newspaper, a sort of criticism—of Mr. Goodrich's last book."

"Oh, but we must hear it," Janice cried, "because, you see, we loved him so and now he's dead. The wicked German shot him—don't you remember?"

"Yes, of course we do. Now sit down very quietly."

Isabel couldn't take in everything that Harold was reading. Words and phrases stuck out, like rocks in the swish of surge. She seemed half to hear, and half to see them.

" 'Lacking the author's final revision. . . . The tragedy of his death. . . . Possibly the writer's most impressive, certainly (it seems ironical to say so) his most promising book. . . . Marks a new departure in his attitude to life, especially to women. . . . Sense of having come to terms with life. . . . Self-pity, sourness of outlook much less noticeable. . . . Compassion. . . . Compassion extended to all the characters, except perhaps the exemplary husband, who behaves almost too well and therefore doesn't need it, besides has resources in himself, business interests, old-fashioned sense of chivalry, idea of himself as someone who should tolerate his wife's behaviour. . . .' "

"Hmm," said Harold. "There's quite a good deal more."

"Please go on," said Isabel.

"Yes, *please* go on," said Janice.

"Where was I?" said Harold. "Oh, compassion. He seems to have 'a thing' about compassion. 'Compassion particularly for Monica the wife, who having tried to procure'——"

"What does procure mean?" Jeremy asked.

"Well, in this context," Harold said, trying to read forward, "it means get, get hold of. 'Procure the Italian maid for the explorer'—— Do we want to hear all this?"

"Oh yes, *yes*," cried Janice, "it is *so* exciting."

". . . 'The Italian maid for the explorer, out of her love for him, a love of which she herself is then unconscious, and having failed in this, herself becomes his mistress——'"

"What's mistress mean, Daddy?" Jeremy asked.

"Well, you know what a schoolmistress is, and Mummy's the mistress of this house."

"I don't quite see——" said Jeremy.

"Well, you will see. 'Becomes his mistress, little realizing that the attention he shows her is not meant for her, but for the seemingly unobtainable Italian maid, and that the reason for his frequent visits is not to lie in her arms. . . .'"

"Lie in her arms?"

"Oh, shut up, Jeremy. 'But to be near the object of his real affection, whom ultimately he seduces——'"

"Seduces?" Jeremy's thirst for knowledge was insatiable: no wonder he got on so well at school.

"'Turns from the proper path. Gets hold of, if you like. Seduces and . . . but perhaps I should not give away too much of the plot.' ("No, I should think not," interpolated Harold vindictively.) 'The ending is decidedly sentimental; for Goodrich, almost incredibly sentimental. The absconding lovers have, of course, our compassion; but the portrait that remains and pulls our heartstrings is that of the doubly-deceived Monica, surely one of the most touching and beautiful creations in modern fiction, a pelican who feeds her loved one with her own blood. Monica is someone with whom we can all sympathize. The selflessness, the delicate imaginative insight with which she realizes the explorer's need and sets about to satisfy it, regardless of the cost to herself, brings tears to the eyes. While her subsequent disillusionment . . . a perfect woman, nobly planned . . . unflinchingly modern in her outlook. . . . Perhaps Mr. Goodrich should have let her commit suicide; it seems almost too cruel to condemn her to live on with her husband, so tiresomely correct, so unnaturally willing to take her back and let bygones be bygones. But if this be cruel, as I think it is, it is the one instance of cruelty in a work which throbs with sympathy for our human condition . . . an adult and challenging book, and perhaps his best.' "

Harold looked up. "Well, what do you think of that? Or shall I read the other?"

"Thank you very much, darling, but perhaps not now."

"Oh yes, oh yes," cried Janice. "I want to hear some more about that lovely lady."

"Which lovely lady?" Harold asked.

"Well, the mistress. The one who fed her loved one with her own blood."

"Oh, that one," her father said.

"Yes, do you know who's she like? Do you know who she reminds me of?"

Janice's teasing, mischievous eyes swept their three faces. No one could answer.

"Someone not very far from here."

Still they couldn't guess.

"Somebody in this room!"

They stared at each other, Isabel hardest of all.

"Why, Mummy, of course!"

An absolute silence followed.

"Oh, nonsense, Janice," Isabel said. "I'm not in the least like her. Now run away and get ready for church."

The parents were left alone together. They bit their lips; they exchanged glances; they each essayed a smile.

"I must get ready, too," said Isabel suddenly, and rose. She wanted to be alone with her thoughts, even Harold must not share them, for they were too disgraceful. She disapproved—disapproved violently—of what the reviewer had said: it was pernicious rubbish, she knew, and could carry no weight with any thinking person. And yet one part of her delighted in it. "Monica is someone with whom we can all sympathize. A perfect woman, nobly planned."

Was that how Alec had really thought of her? Would she now *want* to live in the pages of his book?

Damp it down as she would, her exultation mounted.

A few minutes later they assembled in the hall, a pious quartet, with stiffened Sunday faces.

As they set out——

"I was just thinking of Elspeth," Isabel said. "She doesn't come into the book."

"No, I should hope not, the b——." Harold, whose reactions to the review had been less favourable than Isabel's, bit off the unsabbatical word.

"I don't like to think of her still at large and roaming about, do you? Shut the front door, my darling."

"I have shut it."

Made and printed in Great Britain
for The Companion Book Club (Odhams Press Ltd.)
by Odhams (Watford) Limited
Watford, Herts
S.1056.ZT